Anita

HEISS

Tiddas

London · New York · Sydney · Toronto · New Delhi

TIDDAS
First published in Australia in 2014 by
Simon & Schuster (Australia) Pty Limited
Suite 19A, Level 1, Building C, 450 Miller Street, Cammeray, NSW 2062
This edition published in 2022

10 9 8 7 6 5 4 3 2 1

Sydney New York London Toronto New Delhi
Visit our website at www.simonandschuster.com.au

A catalogue record for this book is available from the National Library of Australia

ISBN: 9781761104909

Cover design: Luke Causby
Cover Photography: Claudine Thornton Creative
Cover image: huythoai / Adobe Stock
Typeset by Midland Typesetters, Australia
Printed and bound in Australia by Griffin Press

The paper this book is printed on is certified against the Forest Stewardship Council® Standards. Griffin Press holds chain of custody certification SGSHK-COC-005088. FSC® promotes environmentally responsible, socially beneficial and economically viable management of the world's forests

Praise for *Tiddas*

'Brisbane through jacaranda-tinted glasses, the river and a group of loud-mouthed, big-hearted girlfriends flowing through it. Generous, witty, a paean to BrizVegas, friendship and sophisticated urban Aboriginal life: only Anita Heiss is writing this new contemporary women's story.'
Susan Johnson

'This enjoyable and human story is impressively interwoven with historical and contemporary Aboriginal issues.'
The Sun Herald

Praise for *Bila Yarrudhanggalangdhuray*

'A powerful story of family, place and belonging.'
Kate Grenville, author of *A Room Made of Leaves*

'There are books you encounter as an adult that you wish you could press into the hands of your younger self. *Bila Yarrudhanggalangdhuray* is one of those books – a novel that turns Australia's long-mythologised settler history into a raw and resilient heartsong.'
The Guardian

'A remarkable story of courage and a love of country . . . Anita Heiss writes with heart and energy on every page of this novel.'
Tony Birch, author of *The White Girl*

Praise for *Barbed Wire and Cherry Blossoms*

'The history has been meticulously researched, and the result is Heiss's great achievement: the reader is transported in place and time.'
The Australian

'Heiss's tact and intelligence are sustained to the end of this bold novel of the wartime home front.'
Sydney Morning Herald

Also by Anita Heiss

Fiction

Not Meeting Mr Right (2007)
Avoiding Mr Right (2008)
Manhattan Dreaming (2010)
Paris Dreaming (2011)
The Tightening Grip,
written with the students of St Laurence's College, Brisbane (2012)
Barbed Wire and Cherry Blossoms (2016)
Bila Yarrudhanggalangdhuray (2021)

Nonfiction

Sacred Cows (1996)
Dhuluu-Yala: Publishing Indigenous Literature (2003)
I'm Not Racist, But – (2007)
Am I Black Enough For You? (2012)

Young adult and kids

Who Am I? The Diary of Mary Talence (2001)
Yirra and Her Deadly Dog, Demon,
written with the students of La Perouse Public School (2007)
Demon Guards the School Yard,
written with the students of La Perouse Public School (2011)

Poetry

Token Koori (1998)

Anthology (ed)

Life in Gadigal Country (2002)
Macquarie PEN Anthology of Aboriginal Literature,
edited with Peter Minter (2008)
Growing Up Aboriginal in Australia (2018)

To my tiddas,
for lifting me from life's moments of darkness
into the light again

Author Note

I am incredibly excited about this edition of *Tiddas*, which coincides with the premiere of the stage adaption of the novel.

In early 2020, I began the journey of writing my first play, taking my thoughts and experiences on friendship and sisterhood, coupled with my love of Brisbane, from the page to the stage. Thanks to La Boite Theatre and QPAC, I was very patiently guided by Nadine McDonald-Dowd, Sanja Simic and Jane Harrison, and over the course of two years, *Tiddas* was transformed into a physical story to be premiered at the 2022 Brisbane Festival.

What a challenging but enriching journey it's been, learning a new craft, playwriting, where the dramaturg, producer, actors and others have input into the script. It is at the opposite end of the spectrum to writing solo, to be edited by one. And while it was sometimes difficult to take on endless feedback, every day there was laughter, collegiality, warmth and support: all the 'feels' the women in *Tiddas* experience in their relationships with each other.

The cover of the original edition of *Tiddas* was a stunning jacaranda, a much-loved symbol of Brisbane life. This new cover reflects the women I wrote about in the novel, and the love that we as tiddas share every day. I was so thrilled my dear Murri sisters here in Brisbane – Louisa, Lauren, Kirrily and Kiana – agreed to be part of it, and the day we did our photoshoot will always remain a fond 'tidda memory' for all of us.

I hope this story of contemporary sistahood speaks to you and your tiddas too, wherever you are and whatever your journey is.

Anita x

‘Some people go to priests; others to poetry; I to my friends.’

Virginia Woolf

1

Vixens

'I'm pregnant,' Izzy said nervously, squeezing her eyes tight with fear of the expected response from down the phone line.

'Oh, you're hilarious. Save the humour for TV,' Tracey said with a laugh, not believing her pseudo-celebrity client. 'Have you had a chance to read the contract I sent through? It'd be good to turn it around before the end of the week.'

Izzy looked at the still unopened yellow envelope on her desk sitting next to three empty pregnancy test boxes.

'I'm *really* pregnant,' Izzy said seriously but softly, hoping she wouldn't have to say it again. The words only reminded her of what was now an unfathomable situation.

'Honey, it's not funny a second time.'

Izzy could hear a tinge of fright in Tracey's voice and could picture her sitting upright at her desk in Sydney. It was the first time she was glad her agent was in another state and they weren't having the conversation face to face.

'I'm not trying to be funny,' Izzy said cautiously, still waiting for the fallout from the best contract negotiator in the business.

Tracey was tiny and friendly, but like a pit bull terrier when it came to cutting deals for Izzy. And while they had never argued, Izzy had seen how angry her passionate and determined agent could get with people who stuffed her around. Tracey had already spent eighteen months negotiating a deal with a new digital station about her client hosting a chat show on their network. Izzy *knew* she'd be pissed off if it all fell through now because of an unexpected 'situation'.

'You *can't* be pregnant, you don't even *like* kids,' Tracey said, affirming a decade of what Izzy had professed at every opportunity. 'Careers before kids. Moët over breast milk. Stretch limos not stretch marks!' These had been Izzy's mottos since deciding upon a career on camera at thirty. 'And you don't even have a boyfriend,' Tracey added. 'Or do you?'

Izzy stood shaking her head. She *was* pregnant, she *didn't* like kids and she *didn't* have a boyfriend – just Asher, her friend with benefits.

'Izzy?'

There was silence.

'Izzy?' Tracey pressed. 'Tell me this isn't true. It'll be the end of your yet-to-even-begin mainstream television career, the one I've been busting my bony arse to help you build for the last decade.' Her voice got louder and more aggressive.

'The career *we've* been strategising over, waiting for the big break. The break that is in that contract I sent you.'

Izzy put the phone on speaker, picked up the envelope and pulled out the pages with yellow tags where she was meant to sign. It was the contract she'd wanted and worked for all her professional life: her own show; her own brand; her own audience; the first Blackfella to host a mainstream talk show on free-to-air television. She *was* going to be Australia's Oprah. She held her dream carefully in her hands, and her nightmare unwillingingly in her belly.

She slid slowly into the red leather bucket chair she'd bought herself when she landed the Brisbane-based contract to host the news channel for Queensland Arts and Culture. Her stories specifically focused on Brisbane's cultural precinct and events, and artists associated with the Queensland Performing Arts Centre, the State Library, the Queensland Museum and the nearby art galleries. The show was broadcast on Arts Queensland's own online station. It was a valuable stepping stone for Izzy and she loved it. So proud of her achievement in simply landing the job, she ordered the chair and had it shipped from the US as a gift to herself. It was where she sat to read scripts, her research notes, the newspaper and books for her book club. She'd been known to nap in the chair too.

'Izzy,' Tracey said gently, 'are you sure?'

Izzy looked with nausea at the half-eaten Mars Bar and sultana sandwich over on the breakfast bar, something she assumed came from what were known in the pregnancy world as cravings. She'd also been drinking more water and was wanting to eat oranges and pickles at odd times of the day.

'Three pregnancy tests and some . . . symptoms,' she said matter-of-factly. 'So, yes, I am sure.'

'Who have you told?'

Izzy could hear Tracey's mind ticking over, going into damage control, as was her job when things didn't go to plan.

'Just you.' Izzy's voice quivered. She could feel her tear ducts beginning to fill.

'What about your mother? Because if you've told her then we may as well say goodbye now.' In her mind's eye Izzy could see Tracey pacing the mezzanine floor of her office and running a hand through her thick black hair. 'You know the Koori grapevine will be spreading the news like there's no tomorrow, and there'll certainly be no tomorrow for your career if this gets out.'

Tracey was the only Black agent in the country and she knew the value of confidentiality on every level. Izzy knew she had to appease her though, aware her anxiety levels would be rising.

'I haven't told Mum.'

Izzy couldn't fathom telling her mother. It was a call to Mudgee she wasn't willing to make just yet, and maybe never would. Trish wanted to start knitting booties whenever Izzy told her she was simply going on a date; she'd buy up the whole of Baby World if she thought there was actually another grandchild on the way. More importantly, Izzy's mum had never forgiven her only daughter for breaking off her long-term engagement to Jack – the perfect son-in-law-to-be – because she wanted to have a career on the screen and not in the school canteen. Izzy knew that her mum'd completely disown her now if she chose a job over a child. And Trish would never approve of an abortion, or of Izzy being an unmarried mother – not as a Catholic, not as a woman wanting more grannies and not as a Wiradjuri Elder conscious of the role women had in growing the mob. Izzy and Tracey were both avoiding the subject of a termination in the conversation, and it was one that Izzy was trying not to think about at all.

'What about the father? Have you told him? Do you know who it is?' Tracey's questions came bullet-fast and hit Izzy just as painfully.

'Oh for God's sake, of course I know who it is.'

Izzy thought back to the last time she'd seen Asher. It had been four weeks ago and they'd loved each other more than usual because he was going to Townsville for six weeks to train young Murri wanna-be chefs. She smiled, remembering the glow that had lasted the entire next day, but then remembered the condom that had somehow disappeared, needing to be retrieved with some skill and a lot of giggles. The penny dropped and so did her chin.

'Izzy?' Tracey pressed down the line. 'Well?'

'No, I haven't told him.' She was suddenly consumed by nausea and wasn't sure if it was morning sickness or fear causing it.

'Good! Don't tell *anyone* else. Keep it to yourself for now,' Tracey demanded, taking control of the situation. 'I have to go to a meeting, I'll call you later.' She sounded businesslike but she was worried about her client, who was also a friend. Izzy's career was important, but so too was her emotional and mental wellbeing. As if reading Izzy's mind, Tracey added warmly, 'And don't beat yourself up, that won't help the situation.'

The phone went dead and Izzy put her head back against the cold leather of the chair. She closed her eyes and took a deep breath in through her nose, sighing outwardly through her mouth. Her iPhone alert went off. It was a text from Xanthe –

See you at book club tonight 7pm.

The last thing Izzy wanted to do was see Xanthe. How could she sit there and listen to her tidda discuss the desperate lengths she and her perfect husband – the English humanitarian lawyer they called 'Mr Darcy' – were going to in order to fall pregnant? They'd been married for five years already and for at least the past twelve months Xanthe had been trying to conceive. They *wanted* to be parents. Xanthe actually *wanted* morning sickness and a bulging belly and someone to knit her baby booties. How could Izzy possibly face her pregnant with a baby she didn't plan, couldn't really look after and didn't actually want?

Her phone went again. This time it was her sister-in-law Nadine.

Looking forward to a decent drink and a yarn about a book that's not mine. XX

Bugger! Izzy thought. She loved her tiddas; they were her closest friends, they were her sistas in an Aboriginal sense, even though Nadine and Veronica were white. She had supported them, and vice versa, since school, and theirs was a bond stronger than words could define. And yet, today Izzy wanted to move the sisterhood boundary a little because she knew Nadine would be urging her to drink so she wasn't the only lush, Xanthe would unknowingly be making her feel guilty about having the 'luck' she didn't, Ellen would be complaining about the lack of eligible men in Brisbane and Veronica would be talking about her three perfect sons. Izzy didn't want to talk about children or men *at all*. And she was fairly sure she wasn't supposed to drink either. She just wanted to be alone. She wasn't ready to talk to the girls about 'it' yet. That would only make 'it' more *real*.

Her mobile beeped again. She'd have to go.

Izzy took a few deep breaths as she drove to her brother Richard and Nadine's mansion in Upper Brookfield. Her sleek, fast, no-good-for-passengers silver convertible wasn't designed for a baby seat in the back. The convertible that she'd convinced herself she could have because she would *never* have to pay school fees. The convertible that had caused one or two Blackfellas to accuse her of selling out, becoming white, turning too flash for her own good. Her convertible: the most comfortable place after her bed and her red chair.

She parked the car and checked her lipstick in the rear-view mirror. She needed an eyebrow wax and her chin lasered.

She wondered if the hormone changes during pregnancy would mean more facial hair. She hoped not. For the time being she was grateful that being in the public eye meant that all her beauty needs were tax deductible.

She looked down the length of Richard and Nadine's driveway and at their perfectly manicured front garden – full of roses, gardenias and camellias – and realised how different her brother's life was to hers in West End, and indeed, to her own personal life. Izzy could never imagine living on an acreage, but Nadine wanted the semi-rural life, and with the inheritance from her father's winery when he passed on, she and Richard had built an amazing, architect-designed house. It was on the top of a small mountain with 360-degree views, a lift, a chef's kitchen, five bedrooms all with built-ins and ensuites, and a beautiful outdoor spa perched on top of an adjacent ridge. It was extravagant by any measure, and especially by Black standards, but Izzy was pleased her older brother had married for love, a love that just coincidentally came with money. The property was worth around six million so none of the girls ever argued when Nadine offered to pay for dinner. If anyone could afford to shout them, it was her.

Although wealthy, Nadine was still thrifty; she always had been. She was completely unaffected by how much money she and Richard had in the bank. To her, money was a means to an end. She knew she was lucky, very lucky compared to most, and that her tiddas would pull her into line if she ever forgot it. Apart from living in the massive mansion with top-of-the-range everything, buying outrageously generous gifts for her tiddas come birthdays and Christmas, and having a private

Pilates instructor, she shipped an endless supply of wines and gourmet treats from Mudgee to her pantry – to support her home-town community, she'd tell Richard, because she didn't want to be one of those people who took money out of the region and never gave back. She might be a lush but she was a loyal one. Her generosity was only kept in check by her sometimes penny-pinching ways; she made Richard shop for the basics at Aldi in Ashgrove because Veronica swore they were the cheapest.

Upper Brookfield – or UB, as the girls called it – worked for Nadine, who saw herself an 'eccentric writer' of sorts; she was often broody and people mistook that for creative genius at work. Life in UB worked for her family too. Her stay-at-home husband did all the maintenance around the house, grew all their vegetables and was the main caregiver for their two overindulged children – Brittany and Cameron – who went to the local independent school. Richard was a landscape architect by trade, and only needed to work on a few properties in the local area to make him feel he was doing something professional and at least making some coin. Hired by the wealthy to make their properties look even better, it was a job he loved and did with ease – and he didn't have to do much of it to feel useful. It was obvious to all who knew him that Richard continued to work when he didn't need to because he'd feel completely emasculated otherwise. What he and Nadine had never told a soul, not even Izzy because neither were 'big-noters', as they joked to themselves, was that all his income was sent to his and Izzy's mother back in Mudgee, which meant that in her own circle she bought the

RSL lunches and threw the best morning teas. Richard paid it forward to his mum and then Trish paid it forward to her friends. It was the Wiradjuri way.

When they'd first looked at the property, Richard had met with the local native title body to find out who the traditional owners were and how he and Nadine might negotiate something that acknowledged and respected them as custodians. While Nadine had no problem with some formal recognition of land of the local Blackfellas, she was reluctant to do much more. She did, however, agree to pay a generous donation to the representative body as a form of 'paying the rent' and they in turn set up a trust fund for educating their local mob. A local Elder smoked the house and site before they moved in. Together they named the property *Bumbar* – which was Turrbul for tree blossom or flower.

Brookfield didn't have the cafés, bars and groovy shops that Boundary Street in West End was famous for, so when Nadine needed a decent caffeine fix or just something more than grass to look at, Richard would drive his unlicensed wife to the Brookfield General Store, where she would drink the surprisingly good coffee and write for hours. With her laptop or pages from her latest manuscript in front of her, she would sit editing, re-drafting, thinking up new plots and characters, and trying not to get drawn into conversations with any of the locals.

Nadine had celebrity status but she loathed it. She hated how strangers sometimes thought they knew her simply because they'd bought her books, or heard her on the radio, or seen her on the telly. She hated that she had to be nice all the time, even when she was feeling down or, as she was most days, hungover. If the General Store served alcohol Nadine would have spent even more time there. Instead, she had to wait for Richard to pick her up after he dropped the kids home from school and then have her own happy hour at *Bumbar.* On Fridays, while Richard did the grocery shopping, she'd sit in the Kenmore Tavern for a couple of hours. Then they'd both have the '12 at 12' luncheon special – Nadine at her thrifty best.

As Izzy walked up the drive she saw Xanthe's and Veronica's cars already lined up perfectly as if they'd been valeted. Nadine had so much money Izzy hadn't been surprised when she'd hired valets to park cars at a New Year's Eve party they'd hosted. Izzy was proud of her sister-in-law and her success as a novelist, and glad Nadine had married her brother, who'd never read a book cover to cover until his wife made the bestseller list. Now at least he read his wife's books, and occasionally the books the women read for book club. Izzy wasn't a crime fanatic but she had read all of Nadine's works, secretly searching for a character based on her. There never was one. She hadn't seen any trace of the other tiddas in them either. In fact, there were no Blackfellas in any of Nadine's books, which hadn't gone unnoticed by the media worker and self-appointed lit critic.

'I'd either have to make you the murdered or the murderer,' Nadine had once said to Izzy, explaining why she never wrote about any of her friends or family in her crime novels. 'And I don't want to think of any of you that way.'

Izzy rang the doorbell as she walked in the front door. It always amazed her that the house was often left completely unlocked, unlike her own chained and deadlocked West End door – a true sign of living in the city. As her phone rang for the third time that day with Tracey's name flashing, she sent it to voicemail again.

'Darling,' Nadine said, approaching her half-sloshed and yet looking far healthier than Izzy had felt all week.

'Hi there, lovey,' Izzy said, kissing her sister-in-law on the cheek and handing over a bottle of sauv blanc, knowing that any gift of alcohol would be appreciated. She wanted to drown her sorrows but was determined not to drink a drop. Just in case.

'Ooh, you know I love this, thanks. The girls are on the veranda, books in hands, bottles at the ready. What can I get you?' Nadine was the perfect hostess, and at least usually *appeared* to be happy and upbeat, depending on how many drinks she'd had.

'Nothing just yet,' Izzy said. At least tomorrow she wouldn't have a hangover.

'Don't be silly, we *always* have a bevy on book club night.'

Nadine raised a wine glass the size of a small ice bucket in the air. They did always have a bevy on book club night because it was the one guaranteed night a month they all got together – using a book as an excuse – to catch up on each other's lives. Izzy knew of other book clubs that functioned in the same way. She also knew women who used their book club as an excuse to get away from their husband or partner or kids for a few hours each month, to drink, goss and have a laugh. She didn't want to become one of those women, though; she *had* a life, and didn't need any excuse to get away from people she was supposed to love. A pang of panic struck her, but with Nadine busy opening another bottle, the flash of horror on her face went unnoticed.

'Hello!' Izzy said with some effort, attempting to be cheery as she walked outside onto the veranda.

The sun was setting; citronella coils were burning to ward off the mozzies. It was still steaming hot weather for March and with no breeze Izzy desperately wanted to be inside under a blast of air-conditioning.

'Hey,' the women all chorused, and hugs and kisses followed.

Izzy pulled up a wooden chair and put this month's novel on the table, hoping no-one would notice anything different about her. She was convinced she *looked* pregnant, but wasn't quite sure how that could be; by her calculations she was only about a month. She thought back to the moment she realised she was late; going to the toilet in the middle of the night for the third day running was something out of the ordinary and kept her awake long after she'd finished peeing. On the third night she decided to do some work, cracked open her diary and while flicking pages realised her bleed was overdue. The tenderness in her breasts she thought was related to her period was in fact not. She was frightened that night, and she was frightened now that Veronica and Xanthe, who were obsessed with children and having children, would notice something, and she wasn't ready to dissect it.

'Where's Richard and the kids?' Ellen asked Nadine, as she carried a platter of food to the table.

The mere thought of eating dolmades or blue vein cheese turned Izzy's stomach, let alone the smell of them.

'There's something on at the school tonight, they're all there,' Nadine said matter-of-factly.

'Shouldn't *you* be there?' Xanthe sounded mortified. 'We could've changed our night.'

'Shouldn't *I* be there too?' Izzy exclaimed, embarrassed that she hadn't enquired first about her own family.

'God no, Richard always does the school thing, not me. I hate that school; they let the kids run amok, do whatever they want. Cam wants to paint, they let him paint. These fancy independent schools shit me. It's nothing like when we went to Mudgee Public where all the families were working class, parents pitched in and did working bees, and we were all disciplined. No, at this school everyone's uppity. We just get a bill for whatever needs doing at the school and the kids pretty much run their own race. A "worldy" approach – ' Nadine made quote signs in the air with her fingers – 'to getting the kids to be grown up, apparently.' Her tone was noticeably sarcastic. 'I get in an argument every time I go there, so it's best I don't go.'

Nadine set about making small plates for each of the girls, loving her role as hostess. Book club was the only real social life she had outside of book tours and talks, which she increasingly resented.

'Why do you send them to that school then, if you don't like going there?' Veronica asked. 'I was *always* at the school where my boys went. I did tuckshop, P & C, was a voluntary reader in the classroom. Not for my boys, though; they were brilliant readers, of course. Did I tell you that John was writing publishable short stories in 6th class?'

'Yes,' the others answered in unison.

Veronica – mostly referred to by her tiddas as 'Vee' – was so proud of her boys they could never do wrong. And even though they'd all finished school and only one still lived at home, Veronica's sole identity remained that of being mother to Jonathan, Neil and Marcus. Her conversation nearly always focused on her sons.

'Anyway,' Nadine said, 'the suburb was *my* choice and the school was Richard's. He's quite happy running the house day to day and looking after the kids.'

Izzy wasn't convinced her brother was completely happy keeping the household on an even keel while his wife was earning most of the money, but they seemed to be content so she never said anything; it wasn't her place to anyway. The other tiddas thought Nadine was the luckiest woman on the planet having her man do the domestics, chase after the kids and, as Ellen had always put it, look drop dead gorgeous to boot.

'I trust his judgement completely on the schooling front,' Nadine said seriously. 'It's not like it was when we were kids where you had no choice but to go to Mudgee Public if you lived west, north or east of the train line, and to Cudgegong Valley if you lived south. And it was just lucky that we all went to Mudgee High, and school and home were almost the same. Remember? We were hardly ever separated and *never* inside on weekends.' Nadine smiled at the women she'd had sleepovers with as a teenager, recalling weekends together down by the river learning to smoke, school dances where they'd snuck some moselle behind the hall and how in summer they could be at the local pool from daylight until dark. 'I worry teen life won't be the same for Cam and Brit. Everything is about technology these days.' They all thought back to how it had been in Mudgee, with boundaries always dictating who went where. 'As for me and school, let's face it, I'm not the best person to be advising on education, not having finished school myself.'

The least academic of the group, Nadine had dropped out of Mudgee High in Year 10 before she got expelled for wagging for the tenth time by May that year. She was creative, though, good with her hands and had an eye for fashion and grooming, or so she thought after successfully braiding all her tiddas' hair during a winter slumber party. She quickly found a traineeship as a hairdresser but she soon dropped out of that too. Back then and for years after, the girls all sang the *Grease* hit 'Beauty School Dropout' to her, laughing in hindsight at the dreadful dye jobs they had each allowed her to perform on them at the age of sixteen. Even though they were now all heading towards their fortieth birthdays, stories of Nadine's hairdressing past could still make them laugh.

'But you've done so well,' Izzy said, proud that Nadine was the most famous Mudgee woman anyone knew, and that she married Izzy's brother who only cracked it with the gardening business after they'd moved to Brookfield. In many ways they were the perfect match professionally once they both found their niche. Nadine was good at writing novels, she liked it, and didn't even think about 'dropping out'; while Richard not only had a green thumb, he had *two*, so he was also able to maintain interest and output without any effort or real challenge.

'I agree,' Ellen said. 'Thirteen novels, some made into their own TV series and one a feature film. Hell, you're an advertisement for *not* going to school. Maybe if I'd followed your lead I'd have a much more interesting love life instead of finding blokes at barbecues,' Ellen joked.

They all cracked up at Ellen's way of describing her job as a funeral celebrant. She often came to the book club with bizarre cremation stories and others of dates she'd had with family members of those she'd helped laid to rest. Ellen was happily single, but getting tired of the lack of dating potential in Bris-Vegas. She'd said at the last meeting she was ready to do something drastic, but her tiddas didn't really know what that meant. Neither did she.

'As I was saying . . .' Nadine, although the reluctant celebrity, was often the most outgoing, the loudest of the group, especially when juiced up, and therefore remained desperate to stay in the limelight and determined to keep her friends out of it. 'I let Richard guide their schooling, and he loves hanging out with the mothers. They all think he's hot, which he is, and he gets a little ego boost there.'

Nadine was sizzling herself: with a lean build, she stood six feet tall and although she drank like a fish, almost everything she ate was organically grown at home or locally produced. Her personal Pilates instructor visited three times a week and her body was as taut and toned as any woman could hope for. Unlike the women at the school with their Botox parties, Nadine had vowed never to let the bacteria that causes botulism go anywhere near her head.

She ran her manicured nails through her blonde hair and continued. 'Quite frankly, when I tried to be part of the parenting community there, all they wanted to do was sit around all day, eat sticky date pudding, discuss the latest cosmetic surgery or talk about the next school fair. I realised pretty quickly that if I spent too much time with them I'd write a book with characters based on them and have them all killed off and then we'd have to leave Brookfield altogether. And I don't want to leave here, it reminds me so much of Mudgee.' She swept her arms through the air towards the trees and rolling hills beyond. 'This is where I want to stay.'

Nadine took a seat at the table and the five women watched the sun finally disappearing behind some jacaranda trees. While the signature purple flowers had disappeared, the fine green foliage was still something to appreciate.

'Who'd have thought we'd all end up in Bris-Vegas, eh? Mudgee is a world away from here,' Izzy said, contemplative and momentarily forgetting about her situation, recalling how she had arrived in the northern city at twenty-three years of age, straight out of uni in Bathurst, inspired by Veronica and grateful that she had already settled there with her family three years prior. Richard and Nadine had followed Izzy within the year because Trish was worried about her daughter, and they'd had enough of Mudgee. They weren't sure where they wanted to be but having at least one family member in Brisbane helped them decide. It was another four years before Xanthe arrived, via Sydney University, to work with a local Aboriginal community organisation, sharing a flat with Izzy for the first couple of years and partying hard. When Ellen showed up three years later ready to take over Murri funerals in Brisbane, it was like old times.

'No, it's not a world away at all,' Nadine said, passing a white ceramic bowl around. 'These are Mudgee olives,' she smiled.

'And the wine?' Ellen raised an eyebrow.

'Well, someone's got to keep the wineries afloat,' Nadine laughed, raising her glass.

Even without the book sales and TV deals she'd always had money. Always had the best, and always had whatever she wanted, including Richard, who for a long time as a teenager had loved her, but never thought he was up to her standards. Nadine could easily have been a snob with her wealth, but she'd grown up knocking around with all the other working-class kids, and money had never changed her.

'Oh!' Xanthe exclaimed. 'I just remembered, my cousin asked if she could join our book group, but I said I'd have to ask.' She smiled, hoping for a positive response.

'No,' Nadine said adamantly.

'That's not very kind,' Xanthe said, wounded, as she was quite easily prone to be.

'Well, this group is really the Mudgee group. Did your cousin go to Mudgee High with us?'

Nadine sounded a little nasty and a tad crazy but Izzy tended to agree with her. She didn't like the thought of someone else coming into their little tidda gathering and changing the dynamics. It could be complex enough at times with the diversity of personalities already within the group without adding another one to the mix.

'No, she grew up in Wagga,' Xanthe said, 'but she's my family.'

'Well?' Nadine looked around the table for comment from the others.

'Wagga Wagga is Wiradjuri country too, so there's another link,' Veronica said, always the peacemaker and hating conflict. She didn't care who else joined the group, given the monthly meetings were her only chance at conversation with other women, and she wanted and needed as much intellectual stimulation as possible.

Everyone nodded in agreement.

'I know she's family, and she's Wiradjuri and Wagga also has a great boutique winery at the Charles Sturt Uni in case you didn't know, *and* they have a fabulous writers' centre, right opposite the winery, which of course makes it the perfect setting for any writer . . .' Nadine sounded like she might be coming round. 'But – '

'But what?' Xanthe cut in. 'What's the problem then?'

'It's just that I had an idea about the name of our group.' Nadine grabbed a small gold gift bag from the chair next to her as she spoke, and pulled out professionally produced name tags. 'I think we should call ourselves the "Vixens"! She made air quotes and looked rather proud of herself.

'The what?' Ellen asked.

'Why do we need a name, especially one like *that*?' questioned Xanthe, the most conservative of the group.

'Hear me out,' Nadine said. She took another long sip from her wine glass. 'Vixen is the acronym our names spell.'

She pointed to each woman as she spoke: 'Veronica, Izzy, Xanthe, Ellen and Nadine.' She poked herself in the chest to make the point.

'Right,' Izzy said. 'Makes sense.'

'So, unless your cousin's name begins with an "S", dear Xanthe, then the answer is no, she cannot join because she will ruin my acronym, and *I* am the writer and *I* get to choose the words around here.' Nadine was only half kidding. Although she rarely talked about her work, she did pull authorly rank when it suited her.

'I don't like it though; it's kind of like cougars,' Veronica said. 'And *I* am *not* a cougar. I certainly don't prey on – or want – young men.'

'None of us are cougars,' Nadine laughed.

'Speak for yourself,' Ellen chimed in. 'I'll take what I can get at this stage!'

'Look, aside from Ellen, who is joking, I'm sure,' Xanthe said, sounding somewhat unsure of herself, 'some of the group are actually happily married.' She held up her ring finger with its stunning, princess-cut stone surrounded by tiny pink Argyle diamonds.

'I think I'd rather be a cougar than a vixen,' Ellen said. 'Let's face it, who wants to be known as a malicious woman with a bad temper?'

'I thought we'd simply make the word a positive. You know, use artistic licence.' Nadine was walking up and down the veranda, a firm grasp on her glass, as if she were pacing out a storyline for one of her novels. 'Let's see,' she was thinking out loud. 'Vixens can also spell out . . . Very . . . intelligent . . . xenophilian . . .'

'Xeno what?' Ellen asked.

'Xenophilia is the opposite of xenophobia, so we *love* foreigners,' Izzy chimed in, having learned the word recently while interviewing a former Democrats senator about the latest disaster in refugee intakes and offshore processing on Manus Island.

'And you're proof of that, aren't you, Xanthe, married to Mr Darcy and all?' Nadine smiled at Xanthe who blushed like a new bride.

'As I was saying, very intelligent xenophilian . . .' Nadine closed her eyes and they all waited for the final words. '. . . easy-going natives.'

'No,' they cried out simultaneously, laughing.

'For one, you're not a "native", as you put it!' Ellen said. 'And sorry, sleeping with a Blackfella doesn't mean Aboriginality has been sexually transmitted either.'

'Let's brainstorm it then,' Nadine said. 'I can wheel my whiteboard out here.' She had one leg inside the house but Izzy grabbed the back of her cotton dress before she could get her other leg in.

'We'll go with "Vixens", okay? Can we just get into the book?' Veronica looked to the others for agreement mainly to avoid a potential disagreement, which was the norm between Nadine and Ellen.

The tiddas smiled and nodded simply to move the discussion along. Nadine sat down feeling like she'd won, Ellen poured them all some water and Izzy began the discussion.

'Well, the novel is the fictionalised story of the relationship between the author and her father.' She stopped abruptly, realising that the issue of parenthood was going to be a large part of the discussion and she wasn't prepared for it. But to her great relief Veronica jumped in and started listing the political issues covered in the book.

'Aside from the personal relationships portrayed in *Legacy,*' Veronica took her role in the discussions far more seriously than any of the others, 'there's the cleverly woven history of the tent embassy, as well as a layman's guide to native title and sovereignty . . .' She smiled, proud of her immediate contribution.

The other women looked at the post-it notes throughout her copy of the book and her debating-style cards with a handwritten scrawl across them. Veronica was the only one who took the meetings that seriously, but each in their own head was grateful for it. Veronica read every book twice before each meeting, simply because she had the time. Since her doctor husband of twenty-two years had left her for his oh-so-stereotypical receptionist, she had not only got the house at The Gap and a nice Lexus, but with the ongoing 'guilt payments' he made without being asked, she'd never have to work. Not that she'd ever had a long-term or full-time job anyway. Marrying the local doctor in Mudgee because she was pregnant when she was only eighteen was the talk of the town at the time, but she loved him, and that meant something, *everything* to her. The problem now was this tidda had no real sense of herself; she'd gone from being known as 'the doctor's wife' to being 'the boys' mother' with nothing else in between. They were all working on helping Veronica find a new path, a career, and an interest in something other than her never-can-do-wrong sons. Izzy was always glad to see Veronica; for one thing, she reminded her of why a career was important, and that while a marriage certificate might give you financial security, it didn't necessarily guarantee relationship longevity.

2

Addictions, Obsessions and Delayed Confessions

Xanthe's dark green eyes popped thanks to her smoky eye make-up and blood-red lips. It was 7 p.m. on a Tuesday and she sat in a hip-hugging black Thai silk frock waiting for her husband to arrive. Although they'd both promised to keep the date free to celebrate, she was still grateful that neither had cancelled due to work, as often happened, which was why they were celebrating four months late. They were both workaholics, but still very much in love, and they remained committed to adding to the other's happiness in life.

'Can I get you something to drink, Xanthe?'

The waiter knew her by name. She was a regular at the popular La Trobe Terrace venue as it was within walking distance of home and had the best desserts around.

'Just some water for now, thanks, Matt,' she answered with a warm smile. 'But when Spencer arrives could you bring us a bottle of your finest sparkling?'

Her perfect white teeth looked bright against her dark skin. The eyes she got from her Greek father, the skin from her Wiradjuri mother. As a child she was her dad's 'Delphorigine Princess' (he came from the island of Delphi), and he still wrote the endearment in her birthday card each year. She was reminded of the anniversary card her parents had sent from Mudgee. She opened it and sighed, missing her parents who seemed so far away.

Having already decided what she was going to eat, Xanthe flicked through the brochures she'd picked up from the IVF Clinic in Wickham Terrace on the way home from work. All she could see in the dim restaurant light were key words and phrases: blood tests, egg collection, injections, laboratories, procedures and fertility treatments. Xanthe was physically strong for her petite frame; she lived an almost athletic lifestyle, but she didn't know if she could physically or emotionally cope with going through the process of IVF. The problem was she and Spencer were growing increasingly desperate as they both headed towards their fortieth birthdays and there was still no sign of fertilisation. As she waited for Spencer to arrive, Xanthe scanned her diary, not only for when she was next due to ovulate, but also looking at the enormous workload ahead of her in the coming months. Then the restaurant door opened and she saw the love of her life. He was wearing a dark blue suit and a pale blue shirt, minus the tie he'd left home in that morning.

'Hello, Princess,' he said, planting a kiss on her full lips, holding it for five seconds. Xanthe felt dizzy with desire and grateful that she still got horny even though they were counting days and taking temperatures and having sex when essential in the hope of conceiving. There was still enough lust between them to ensure the lovemaking was about something more than just getting pregnant.

'You look as handsome as you did the day I met you in Musgrave Park,' she said. 'And I still prefer you in jeans and a t-shirt.' She thought back to the day of the rally against the Northern Territory Intervention in June 2007 when she first saw Spencer holding a 'STOP THE INTERVENTION' banner while he bellowed loud and strong about human rights for all.

'I've got a few more greys now though,' he smiled, running his hands through his mostly sandy-coloured hair. With his white skin and broad shoulders, Spencer was the complete opposite of his wife. He was outgoing, self-assured, with a confidence that always made Xanthe feel safe and secure.

The waiter poured some champagne in two stemmed flutes and the couple raised their glasses in a toast to each other.

'To us,' Spencer said.

'And they said it wouldn't last.' Xanthe smiled.

'I don't know who *they* are, but someone upstairs has decided we'll be together, and I've got my money on them!' They both sipped, not taking their eyes off each other. 'You look beautiful,' Spencer whispered, taking his wife's hand.

'I look tired,' she responded, meaning it, feeling it.

'Babe, you haven't stopped running since you left Spark HR.' Spencer was still cranky that she had played a significant role building a client base and developing a niche in Indigenous cultural awareness training, but never got credited for any of it. 'Don't get me wrong, I'm glad you left them.'

So was Xanthe; she hadn't looked back. Within two years she'd set up her own consultancy and had secured her place as one of the most respected trainers in the country. Her package, directed at upper management and designed to simplify the complexities around history, the diversity of Aboriginal culture, and basic ways of incorporating Indigenous protocols and content in the workplace, was being used by a range of organisations and government bodies nationally. Xanthe was also hoping to move into the education sector to help teachers embed Indigenous Studies into their content, as the national curriculum was soon to kick in.

'Can you believe we've been married for five years?' Xanthe asked.

'Can you remember how bloody hot and humid it was that day?'

'It was a couple of weeks off Christmas, we must have been crazy. You didn't want to wait to marry me.' Xanthe smiled coquettishly.

'I know.'

Outside of the stress of her work, Xanthe retreated to her two-person bubble with Spencer. It had been love at first sight for both of them, and five months later, in the middle of a steamy December, they married in the Botanical Gardens. But it was the day they met that they cherished most, both believing that even with extreme cultural differences, 'someone upstairs' – as Spencer often said – meant for them to be together.

The couple were happy and content in their own orbit, needing nothing more than each other, the local cafés and the hills. Everything they wanted was right on their doorstep, including an exercise regime. The rollercoaster hills were famous in Brisbane and Xanthe and Spencer would walk, run and stroll the suburb every chance they got to unwind together. As they both travelled so much for work, often spending days and weeks in the sky and on the road, when they were in Brisbane they just wanted their feet on the ground in Paddington. So they had their Sunday morning organic shopping and breakfast at Fundies and afternoon iced coffee at Anouk, and if they were feeling naughty might indulge in some banoffee or peanut butter pie.

Their home suburb was all they needed, aside from a baby.

'I'm exhausted,' Xanthe said to Spencer down the phone, three days later. 'Thank God it's Friday.'

'Big day, Princess?'

'The usual ignorant questions and comments: why organisations have to have Reconciliation Action Plans, what right do Indigenous staff have to get NAIDOC Day off work? Blah blah blah.'

'You'll have fun with the girls tonight though, right? You can relax, I'll be home by midnight.'

Xanthe sighed deeply, gladly anticipating her tiddas – the Vixens, she moaned to herself, still not comfortable with the name the others seemed to easily adopt – visiting for the April book club meeting, and not thinking about work for a while.

She prepared her home as if nesting was her only role in life; she cleaned like a professional, catered like royalty was visiting, and made sure every cushion and ornament was in its correct spot. Xanthe took great pleasure in playing interior decorator at home, matching the curtains with table runners, rugs with coffee tables, cushions with candles. Her attention to detail in her home was as much a mark of self-pride as her commitment to her own personal style. While she wore business suits and basic black pumps to work, she loved the structured looks of locally designed fashions from Maiocchi and the vintage clothes from Retro Metro, both only a stone's throw or so from home. And she loved a colourful slingback. For tonight's book club she wore a fitted red dress that showed off her tiny waist, and black pointy patent shoes she'd picked up while working in Geraldton, on the west coast.

Xanthe gently placed her copy of the novel they'd be discussing on the mahogany coffee table, next to a pile of books about getting pregnant: *Female Fertility and the Body Fat Connection, Getting Pregnant: What You Need to Know Right Now,* and her latest purchase, *Taking Charge of Your Fertility: The Definitive Guide to Natural Birth Control, Pregnancy Achievement and Reproductive Health.* She hadn't started reading it yet but had skimmed it enough to know it could help her maximise her chances of conception or expedite fertility treatment by identifying the obstacles to becoming pregnant. This one book could apparently also increase the likelihood of being able to choose the gender of her baby. Xanthe's head began to spin.

Her desperation about getting pregnant was like a cloud hanging over her constantly; the only time she wasn't reading about having a baby, or thinking about having a baby, or actually having sex to make a baby, Xanthe was completely focused at work or catching up with her tiddas at book club.

When she wasn't on the Internet reading conception and fertility blogs, or searching Amazon for the best books on getting pregnant, she was looking at websites and following Twitter accounts in the hope that the miracle answer would appear in 140 characters. When she was exercising she was thinking about it, when she was on the bus or driving or flying and not reading her work papers, she was thinking about it. She was thinking about it in her sleep.

Ever since she and Spencer had decided to have a family, everywhere Xanthe looked she saw women in various stages of pregnancy, babies in strollers, kids' clothes in catalogues, baby formula on the shelf in the supermarket. At any given time she had at least one pregnancy test in her bag and one in the bathroom drawer. She'd been known to take a test if she was a day late. To her credit, Xanthe was aware of her obsession, though she wasn't concerned; she imagined it was normal for any woman who was maternal to be like she was. But tonight, after trying to consume all the IVF literature she'd amassed recently, she was just grateful for something other than work and conceiving to think about, even for a few hours. She was also looking forward to drinking something other than the Chinese herbs one of her clients had recommended.

The doorbell rang, shocking Xanthe out of her pregnancy headspace. As she slipped the books into a drawer in the sideboard in the entry hall, she could hear her friends' cackles even before she reached the front door.

'Hey!' She smiled as her four tiddas stood with books and bottles and gifts of flowers and chocolates in their hands.

Richard had dropped the designated-drinker Nadine to Veronica's in The Gap and they arrived together. Izzy had picked Ellen up from a memorial service at the Greek Club in West End and like clockwork all the tiddas had pulled up in the leafy street at the same time.

'Welcome to my humble abode,' Xanthe said proudly as she ushered the ladies through to the living room.

'You've done wonders with this place, Xanthe,' said Izzy admiringly. 'It looks amazing, and *tidy*.'

It had been five months since Izzy had last been there and she was mentally comparing the spotless space to the mess her own flat was. She had lost all interest in keeping house in the last two months or so as she was trying to work, having to deal with morning sickness *and* still deciding what to do about her pregnancy. Izzy was clear about her career; it was the most important thing in her life. A child would only destroy her plans – and her waistline, she reminded herself. And between her work and training she'd not even made the time for a consultation with her local GP about a procedure.

But she was thinking about herself, number one, and what made her happy each day was still her main concern. Her obsession about *not* wanting a baby was only matched by Xanthe's about *having* one.

'Oh, it's home,' Xanthe smiled with pride as she put the sunshine yellow gerberas and liliums Nadine had given her in a vase while the girls settled themselves on couches. 'We like it, but it does get hot here sometimes without a breeze. Other than that, it's great.'

'Sis, you've got a good set up here in Paddo,' Ellen said. She'd been semi-homeless since the floods forced her to evacuate her riverside apartment at Kangaroo Point. 'You can't really complain about life here, eh?'

'Is this upper or lower Paddington?' Nadine asked, not meaning to sound as bourgeois as she did.

'Very funny,' Xanthe said, pouring Pimms and vodka cocktails from a glass jug into highballs for everyone, only pausing when Izzy put a hand over the top of her glass to decline.

'I'm good,' she mouthed silently.

'I'm never going to be upper anything, and as I'm at the bottom of a hill, I doubt it could be classified as upper anyway.' Xanthe had never heard of 'upper Paddington'.

'Love, if nothing else, at least you live at the top of the food chain,' Izzy said, always one for a good meal, before she was nauseous all the time, that is.

Xanthe looked confused. 'What do you mean?'

'Paddo is the top of the restaurant hierarchy, after New Farm which is for foodies, and my own West End, which is far less pretentious than here.'

Xanthe was offended. 'I'm not pretentious!'

'Of course you're not, Xanthe – everyone drinks Pimms, daaaahling!' Ellen said cheekily, waving her already half-drunk cocktail in the air.

'What I meant,' Izzy glared at Ellen who was always trying to be funny and sometimes missed the mark, 'is that Paddington is a great suburb for food. *And* in some places it *is* pretentious, but you shouldn't be so surprised, or offended.'

Veronica sat quietly listening, loving her own suburb of The Gap and not really interested in the conversation. She was preoccupied with her own home-life woes and didn't feel like sharing them.

Izzy took a sip of the mineral water she'd poured for herself and continued. 'I'd live here but I love the river too much. Just own where you live, tidda, and be proud.'

Xanthe hadn't thought much about status before, and certainly not in recent times with her work and ongoing obsession with getting pregnant. But the truth was she had a mortgage worth more than many would see in a lifetime. She only bought organic produce, and she and Spencer ate regularly at the fancy restaurants along La Trobe Terrace. She wasn't embarrassed about her lifestyle, but she didn't like being labelled as 'upper'. Just as she hadn't liked being labelled 'boong' and 'abo' back in Mudgee as she walked to and from school and the kids from the rival public school hurled abuse at her from across the road. It was bad enough she was Koori, they'd say, but she was part-wog too. Xanthe sighed deeply, recalling the pain of a young child who did not understand the racism that was rife in the late 1970s, or the senseless labels that came with it. Labels she now worked hard to explain to her clients were archaic and socially unhelpful. Labels of any kind rarely served a purpose, and she rejected them all.

The little-town-girl-done-good was proud of what she had achieved as an adult in the big smoke – Brisbane being big smoke compared to country New South Wales, even if still 'little smoke' compared to London, as Spencer had pointed out. And they'd agreed that Brisbane was warmer than both their hometowns, and aside from each other, that's what kept them there. They'd worked hard to buy their house and had done most of the interior renovations themselves to make it *their* home. Xanthe had studied diligently at uni, and worked even harder now that she was running her own business. She *did* own her lot in life and wasn't apologising to anyone. It was a mantra that she often repeated to herself, especially when working with people who brought their stereotypes into the room and suggested she had to be poor, welfare dependent and uneducated to be Aboriginal. She was never going to fulfil someone else's stereotype of being Black in Australia in the twenty-first century. It was why she was so good at what she did as a career: she walked the talk.

'Actually, we're saving for a Queenslander,' Xanthe said proudly. 'Spencer is already looking around here for one.'

'That'd be right, the coloniser wants the manager's quarters; the worker's cottage isn't good enough, is it?' Ellen was only half-joking. She couldn't imagine ever hooking up with an Englishman, let alone having the means to fund a Queenslander in Paddington.

'Don't be so ridiculous. *Or* mean!' Xanthe said seriously, pulling Ellen back into line. 'The Queenslanders are on top of the hill, they get all the breeze!'

Xanthe shook her head; she knew that Ellen didn't approve of Spencer with his posh, plummy English voice, but she didn't imagine her friend could be jealous of her success, could she? They were tiddas, and tiddas were happy for each other's achievements. They may have lost touch for some years when studying, moving and having families, but once they re-connected in Brisbane in their twenties, they had been as tight as they were in their teens. And they knew each other's flaws – and fabulousness – inside out. Keeping that in mind, Xanthe knew that whatever the issue was, it was Ellen's problem, not hers.

And while her tiddas joked about Spencer being 'the coloniser' she never took it seriously. She could laugh about it most of the time. Besides, Spencer liked Xanthe's tiddas, and they liked him because he adored Xanthe. But at the end of the day it didn't matter what they thought; all that mattered in her world was that she loved him; he was gentle and kind, they had the same world views, and they wanted to share views across Brisbane from the wrap-around veranda of a house on a hill.

'Why wouldn't I want to live in a Queenslander? I want to be able to look across town at the gorgeous jacarandas and the silky oaks and the azaleas in bloom.' Xanthe looked out the front window towards the house across the street. 'Right now, I have to go to Eurovida and sit at the window at the back of the restaurant to get a good view.'

'Oh, I love that back window, I haven't been there for ages. We should do breakfast one day,' Veronica finally spoke, although sounding flat. The girls all nodded. 'Easter perhaps?' She reached for her iPhone to log the date in her calendar. It was an outing to look forward to, and time away from her now mostly empty family home.

Izzy, Nadine and Ellen all looked at Veronica, each registering her unusually sullen mood, but Xanthe continued with where she'd left off. It wasn't unusual for the hostess of the monthly book club to have the most to say when they met in their own home. Izzy liked that it took the pressure off to be, as she called it, 'on duty'. Her job meant she was constantly either talking or listening or smiling for the camera. At least with her tiddas she could just chill. Or so she thought, until Xanthe started talking pregnancy.

'When we get pregnant, we'll need a bigger place than this anyway, of course. And I don't want to be moving while I've got a bellyful, or worse, already have a baby. I just want to focus on being a mum.' Xanthe was completely unaware that she'd fallen into talking about babies without even intending to do so. Every topic somehow became a natural progression to discussing them.

'Won't you miss Armstrong Terrace?' Nadine asked. 'You love this place. You've spent years doing it up. Richard is so proud of how he helped Spencer with the back garden.'

'I'll miss it, of course, and we love the garden too. Hopefully Richard can help with the new place as well.' Xanthe passed a bowl of pistachios to Nadine. 'But you know we originally moved here not just because I loved the layout but because it was where the Blackfellas used to camp in the old days when it was Armstrong's Paddock.

'Not living on my own country, the history mattered to me. I mean, it still does. And if I was going to be in the apparently "gentrified" part of town,' Xanthe grinned at Ellen, 'then I wanted to at least have some connection to the Turrbul mob.'

Izzy nodded. Being close to the local community and the stories of a place mattered to her too. It was the reason she loved West End so much – for its history, the ongoing political presence of the mob in Musgrave Park, the local organisations and simply seeing Blackfellas on Boundary Street any time of day or night.

'Oh God, these are delicious,' Ellen swooned, biting into a rice ball.

'They're from a new place not far from here. We do a lot of our shopping there, all their products are organic.' Xanthe handed a bowl of Mexicana corn chips and a bowl of dip to Izzy, who, not being able to handle the smell, passed it straight on to Veronica.

'We're trying to be as healthy as we can, now we're trying to have a baby.'

'You are the healthiest person I know!' Nadine declared. 'Look at Xanthe's calves,' she said to the others, as she stood and headed to the kitchen. 'And while you do that I'll just pop into the kitchen and make another batch of this fabulous aperitif!' She looked to Xanthe for approval, but wasn't going to stop even if she didn't get it.

'Well, *you* climb these hills every day and you'll have them too,' the hostess called after Nadine. 'Seriously, it doesn't matter what direction I go in, there's a hill. It means I can eat just about anything I want.' She grabbed a handful of corn chips and pretended to be a glutton.

'You've always been tiny,' Veronica reminded her, a look of envy on her face. 'I remember how little you were at school. Your dad could put his hands around your waist when you were ten, remember, you were so small.'

'And I was the giant.' Nadine strolled back into the room with a full jug, recalling how she used to slouch because she was always a head taller than her friends. 'All legs, no boobs. I was like a bloke! Can't believe Richard ever looked at me.'

'But when your boobs *did* come in, they *really* came in, didn't they?' Izzy grabbed a handful of her own ample breasts, and laughed, recalling the rapid growth spurt Nadine had at fifteen and how her brother started taking notice of her best friend.

'Speaking of good bodies, Miss Aboriginal Athlete, are you still doing that hot yoga thing?' Izzy asked Xanthe.

'Yes! Do you want to come with me?' Xanthe seemed excited at the prospect of one of her tiddas going with her; she was always looking for an exercising buddy. 'I notice you're not drinking, are you on a health kick now or what?'

'Oh God, you're not detoxing again? How boring!' Nadine was onto her third drink.

'I'm not detoxing,' Izzy said, thinking that Nadine was the one who needed to get off the grog.

'Because Bikram is great for detoxing, you sweat all that crap out.' Xanthe was still trying to solicit at least one tidda.

'I couldn't think of anything worse than sweating like that around strangers,' Veronica said quietly.

'Nor I, Vee,' Izzy admitted. 'And I really don't like the heat *that* much.'

Izzy wondered if she should just take a sip of something so she didn't appear to be out of sorts, but she didn't feel like a drink. She was seven weeks' pregnant, and while she had buried herself in work as usual, she had also allowed a sense of denial to replace the urgency of having to 'do something' about the situation. She wasn't so much undecided as she was inactive. Izzy didn't want the baby, but she didn't want to have to do the unmentionable about it either. As she sat there in Paddington, she knew that with Xanthe dominating the night's yarn with her talk about babies, there was no way she could confide in her tiddas. Not right now, anyway.

'What about you, Nadine? Do you want to sweat out some unnecessary fluids?' Xanthe was being diplomatic, but the other girls knew what she was getting at. Except for Nadine, who let the real intent of the question fly right over her head.

'I love your sense of humour, Xanthe, it's so endearing.' Aside from having her personal Pilates trainer come to her house, the only exercise Nadine did was lifting her glass.

Xanthe was a little hurt by Nadine's comment, as if she'd been spoken to like she was a cute child.

'I was serious, I thought you might get something out of it.' Xanthe wished she'd been more blatant about Nadine's toxic waste needing to go.

'Oh relax, I was kidding. You know me well enough to know I couldn't cope with all those people in a room and no bar in sight. That's my idea of torture, really. Really!' She shook her head, crossed her legs and sipped her drink. Izzy and Ellen shook their heads as well, but for a different reason.

Hating any form of conflict, Veronica spoke up. It was time to change the subject. 'April really is a lovely time here in Brisbane, isn't it? The humidity drops, it's easier to sleep and I love walking around The Gap at dusk. Everything is just more comfortable.'

'Oh yes! Definitely! Thank God!' came the chorus of agreement after the steamiest summer on record.

'Spring is gorgeous here too. I have this great bloom of dark and light mauve outside the back window come late September,' Xanthe shared her passion for the calmer weather.

'The yesterday, today and tomorrow flower,' Nadine stated knowingly.

'That's it,' Xanthe said, remembering hearing its name from a neighbour not so long ago.

The women had settled in comfortably for the night with their usual banter regarding what was going on in each other's lives. The book could wait, as it often did.

'Well, I have some news,' Ellen chimed in enthusiastically.

'You've met someone?' Xanthe asked.

'Why do you all think any news I have is always man related?'

'Because it usually is!' Izzy said with a chuckle.

'Which reminds me,' Ellen continued. 'Why hasn't Spencer set me up with one of his friends? It's a recession; I don't care if he's a coloniser. I told you last month I was about to do something drastic. I might just take on a reconciliation project with a pom!'

'I think suggesting you'll date someone as a last resort based on where they come from is racist, so why don't you just get on with your news?' Nadine who was, like Xanthe, in an inter-racial relationship, had a very short fuse when it came to people who joked about mixed marriages. And as she got more sloshed, Nadine's fuse got shorter.

'Fine,' Ellen said, rolling her eyes like a chastised teenager. 'My news is that after a year of post-flood sleeping on other people's couches, including yours, Nadine – thank you very much – I am finally moving into my *own* place. I've settled on a property!' She clapped her hands as if applauding her own achievement.

'Yay! That's great! Finally!' the tiddas responded in a chorus, most of them out of the property-buying loop that Ellen was in. Her sex life *was* usually her main topic at book club get-togethers.

Ellen burst into song, crooning the chorus from one of her favourite Stevie Wonder songs, 'Signed, Sealed, Delivered, I'm Yours'.

'Not that ugly place in Kangaroo Point?' Nadine slurred, remembering when she went house hunting with Ellen and they found an old building that they imagined had previously been nurses' quarters for St Vincent's Hospital.

'Yes, the ugly place on Main Street. But it's not going to be ugly for long, just on the outside. I'm going to go full steam ahead with some serious renos and turn it into my own little paradise. Just like Xanthe and the col– I mean *Spencer* did here.'

'Cheers, it's great to hear good news.' Veronica raised her glass in a genuine toast to Ellen, although inside she was crying. Her divorce papers had been delivered that day and she hoped she wasn't weighing the entire room down with her mood. She didn't want to ruin the moment with her own misery. 'You're a first home buyer, congratulations.'

'I can't believe it's been more than a year since you were evacuated,' Izzy said. 'Or me, for that matter. At least it was only the garage that got flooded.'

'Personally, I can't believe how the clean-up was done so quickly.' Xanthe passed around roasted eggplant, garlic bruschetta and some grilled vegetables with tarragon vinaigrette as the women all thought back to their own flood stories.

'Well *I* can't believe that someone said to me that they'd hoped we'd beat the 1974 flood,' Ellen said. 'I think their words were, "If we're going to flood, we may as well break the record."'

'What? Who said that? That's just fucked!' the women responded over the top of each other, having resumed their normal way of sharing.

'Some dickhead cab driver I had, yet another reason why I ride a bike or get the City Cat most places!' Ellen didn't own a car, preferring to lessen her carbon footprint when she could.

'And you're staying in Kangaroo Point, so that's good.' Izzy knew how much her tidda liked living close to the river, and the Story Bridge Hotel.

'Yeah, it's my home. I love the river; it reminds me of the Cudgegong back home, only it's five million times the size, of course. But I used to find so much peace there under the gum trees when I was young. I feel at peace being near the Brisbane River somehow too, if that makes sense at all.'

Ellen regularly took the ferry from Thornton Street to Eagle Street Pier and then the City Cat down to Bretts Wharf and back. If she was in the mood she'd get off at New Farm Park, walk the three minutes to the Powerhouse, and have a beer and listen to music. Sunday was 'Ellen time'. She didn't need company to be entertained. She liked being alone. She needed time alone. She couldn't imagine ever living with anyone. A legacy of having too many siblings, some she never heard from, even on birthdays. She wondered if removing herself from Mudgee had pissed them all off. She didn't care at this point. If they didn't need her, she didn't need them either.

The river was the most important thing in Ellen's day; in her life. She ran and walked beside it. She lost herself looking into it. She rode it to work, to Izzy's, to the city. The only thing she was grateful to Campbell Newman for was introducing the public bike system when he was Brisbane City Mayor. She'd often grab a bike from CT White Park and leave it at any number of designated spots around town, depending on what was on her schedule. On days when she had to visit a bereaved family or do a service that was too far to get a cab she'd book a share car. It was still cheaper and better for the environment than buying her own car.

But it was the City Cat rides Ellen liked most. She shamelessly enjoyed perving on the ferrymen in their Hard Yakka shorts minus the bum crack made famous by tradies. She'd give each guy a score out of ten for their 'arse shape', and then check to see whether they wore a wedding ring or not.

That flirting option was not open to her, men who had wives or partners.

'I completely understand. Walking along the river at West End totally centres me,' Izzy nodded, knowing exactly the power of water and the calming way it affected her. It was why she got the City Cat to work each day too, because the physical motion – prior to morning sickness – and the breeze on her face made her feel alive and rejuvenated.

'And now that I'm turning forty I feel better having a place that's all mine. In some ways the flood kicked me into gear on that front. And I'd been meaning to clear out my place for a while; the flood just did it for me.' Ellen smiled a painful smile, because in reality she'd lost a lot of things she loved, including a box of thank-you cards from families she'd helped farewell their loved ones. She tried not to get too personal or connected to the families she worked with, but that was near impossible, meeting people at the most traumatic times of their lives.

Nadine started laughing hysterically, slamming her glass on the table.

'What's so funny?' Veronica asked. Her lack of self-esteem meant she was often paranoid that the joke might be on her.

'I remember driving with Richard to pick Ellen up when her place was flooded, and she was walking towards us holding her crocodile boots in the air. Funniest fucken thing I'd ever seen.' Nadine slapped her linen-covered legs in hysterics.

They all laughed at the memory of the photo Nadine took on her iPhone and sent them all immediately. Of course it wasn't funny at the time.

'Hey, those boots are important to me, and they were the only things that I could carry, given my backpack was full of photos.'

'Oh the boots, the boots,' Nadine kept laughing.

Ellen smiled, but the truth was she was depressed for a long time after the floods, having lost most of her books as well, and she had always been an avid reader.

'The only reason I come to book club is so I can build up my library again. You know that, right?' She refilled her glass and her plate almost simultaneously. 'It's not so I can be trashed by the comedic lush!'

'I'd have to say, Vee, this was a great choice for us to read,' Nadine said, pushing her copy of *The Old School* towards the middle of the table. 'I loved it. Inter-racial relationships, female lead detective, and do you know I hadn't even tried pho before reading this book?'

'Were you living under a rock?' Izzy joked.

'Obviously!' Ellen put a humus-covered cracker in her mouth.

'I thought incorporating the Aboriginal Legal Service was brave myself, but it needed to be done. I was impressed with the whole storyline. It'd be great as a telemovie,' Xanthe said, having also discussed the novel with Spencer.

'Who'd play the character called Mabo? Wayne Blair?' Veronica asked, knowing there was a strong pool of Indigenous actors ready and capable of taking on such a role.

Izzy, Ellen and Xanthe all thought back to when they'd got together to watch *Redfern Now* on TV. They had talked about it for weeks afterwards.

'I think Jack Charles would be perfect!'

Veronica was spot on. She knew a lot about the arts sector and attended many Murri cultural events around Brisbane. She was the perfect example of reconciliation at work: the appreciation of and respect for Indigenous Australian cultures.

Izzy had read this month's book as an escape from thinking about her own situation, and she too liked the storyline. 'This Newton woman has done a deadly job incorporating Aboriginal characters and issues into the story, I reckon. I've never read an Aussie novel like that.'

Nadine felt a pang of guilt and wondered if her sister-in-law was having a dig at her for never including Kooris – or Murris, as Blackfellas called themselves in Brisbane – in her own novels, but she never really knew how to, and Richard wasn't big on talking about books. But even in her drunken haze she felt compelled to say something. 'I really like Pam's work too, we've done a few festivals together. She makes me want to lift my game.'

'I thought it was interesting she was a detective before becoming an author. All those details, I knew she had to have inside information somehow,' Veronica added.

'Turns out she was her own insider.' Nadine slugged back another cocktail. She needed an insider to help her write the next book, even though she didn't know what it was going to be. *This Newton woman might tip me off the bestseller list,* she thought to herself.

'We need some Black crime novelists too,' Izzy added.

'Actually,' Ellen said, pulling a book out of her bag like a magician, 'I know we're doing crime right now, but can we do this one in the next few months?' She held up *The Boundary*; there was a blood-red feather on the cover. 'It's set in West End.' She raised her eyebrows and threw a nod of *interesting, eh* to Izzy.

'Then we should do it when we have book club at *my* place, that'd make sense,' said Izzy.

The tiddas all nodded in agreement.

'But what should we read for May?'

Everyone looked at Veronica; she usually made the recommendations based on her being the one with time to suss out the bookshops.

'Leave it with me,' she said, glassy-eyed and not really listening.

At midnight the tiddas walked outside into the cool night air and said their goodbyes. Richard waited in the car for Nadine; both Cam and Brit were having sleepovers with school friends. Ellen and Izzy climbed into Izzy's convertible, while Veronica slipped into the comfort of her Lexus and burst into tears. She felt a pang of guilt that she'd hated hearing Xanthe talk about her future with Spencer, planning a family and buying their house together. She could see the love they shared, a love she now accepted she had never experienced with Alex. And it was the same with Nadine and Richard. As tears blurred her vision, she tried hard to remember a time when Alex had waited for her *anywhere*. It was always she who had waited, doted, sacrificed. Alex was emotionally absent even when he was physically there, taking only minor interest when the boys played football on weekends in winter. It was she who went to meetings with teachers and to kids' birthday parties, often making excuses for a father who appeared to be disinterested, a husband who had a take-it-or-leave-it attitude to his wife.

'Oh God,' Veronica cried out, recalling the last time they'd even made love in a way that wasn't simply about coming, with feeling, with any sense of desire. It had been years. And then it hit her that it had also been years since she'd felt wanted or even appreciated by the man she had devoted her life and her heart to. As rain began to fall, Veronica sobbed uncontrollably in the darkness. 'Why, why, why?' she moaned, blaming herself, as women often do, for loving an emotionally inept man who couldn't love her back.

Richard being there for Nadine on a daily basis was another painful reminder of the life she *didn't* have with her ex; hers had only ever been a life of washing and cleaning and cooking and being mother and wife. It was a life she'd always been content with because she felt needed, loved, even wanted, by at least one of her sons at any given time. It never bothered her until she wasn't needed or wanted anymore, by anyone. Since Alex and her eldest two sons had left the family home, all that she felt she had was low self-esteem and no sense of identity.

Veronica hadn't signed the divorce papers when the courier delivered them earlier in the day. Instead, she'd just collapsed against the wall and wept, feeling a sense of complete personal and matrimonial failure. She had convinced herself long ago the divorce would be her penance for getting pregnant to the first man she met and slept with and then had to marry. And although she loved him, and the children she and Alex had together, she still filled her head with a silent conversation that could only cause more harm to her already brutalised heart. As far as Veronica could tell, the other tiddas appeared to have anguish-free lives. They were happy and content; she was the loser of the group. She didn't want to add to her own sense of helplessness by exposing herself in all her woe-is-me misery, but she didn't know how much more sadness she could lug around with her either. Something had to give.

Inside, Xanthe in her organised way tidied up the living room and crawled into bed, aiming to stay awake until Spencer got home from visiting his brother down at Helensvale. She tried to meditate, to stop thinking about anything at all: next week's schedule, Ellen and Izzy's comments about her being 'upper', how Nadine had managed to spill a drink on her favourite cushion. Admittedly, she'd offered to pay to get it dry-cleaned, but Xanthe just wished her tidda wouldn't get pissed every time they got together. As she tried to block everything from her mind, she ran her hand over her belly and started getting maudlin.

She was thirty-nine; even with IVF she only stood a fifty-five per cent chance of a live birth, not just a pregnancy. Was it even worth the effort? What would Spencer think? Could they afford it? They'd only broached the subject briefly, but this week she'd started researching for the first time. Why couldn't she just fall pregnant like other women did?

3

Damning Disclosures

It was an overcast but warm Easter Saturday. The city was peaceful but the tiddas were all in different states of emotional chaos. Izzy was feeling nauseous; she wasn't sure if it was from being pregnant, or because she'd decided she was finally going to tell her closest friends she was 'expecting'. She needed support, help and advice, and she needed to be reassured that whatever decision she made would be supported by her friends. She needed wisdom from the women she trusted most, and women who had already had children, or at least thought positively about having children. She hoped she could count on her tiddas, because she would need the courage to tell her mother and advice on whether or not to tell Asher at all. In the meantime, Tracey had left so many messages on her phone, Izzy's voicemail was full.

Veronica was cleaning the house, trying to pass time and not think about the meaningless life she felt she now led.

She had taken her anti-depressants, which helped to a degree, but she often fell back into her negative way of thinking. She hated taking the pills. Being married to a doctor, she'd seen and heard about enough women over the years who got sucked into what they thought was helping them, and in some instances was nothing more than a placebo. She was walking every day to clear her head as much as possible, but she just couldn't stop crying.

Xanthe and Spencer were post-coital, bodies entwined, physically united, but their thoughts couldn't be any further apart. Xanthe wondered why they weren't talking about IVF when she'd broached it a number of times, but knew Spencer was probably more concerned about the next month's State of Origin match. Spencer stroked Xanthe's hair and dozed back to sleep.

Meanwhile Ellen woke up in her new flat with a six-pack lying next to her in bed. His hairless butt faced upwards, the word 'Rockstar' tattooed in red ink stretched across the biggest bicep she'd ever seen. The electrician, known only to her as 'The Sparky', had come over on Thursday afternoon to do some wiring in the bathroom, and hadn't left since. *I'm reno-dating,* she thought to herself.

Nadine sat on her back veranda watching the kids and Richard work in the vegie patch – there were now a dozen pumpkins she had no idea what they'd do with. Pumpkin scones, pumpkin bread, roasted pumpkin, dip, soup, curry, what else? Was there a pumpkin cocktail she didn't know about or should invent? She observed the action through dark glasses, with blurry vision and a pounding head – a normal Saturday morning for her. Although only a passenger, Nadine wasn't really looking forward to the long drive into Paddington, and hoped they made a good Bloody Mary at Eurovida.

'I just don't understand why he doesn't want to talk about IVF as an option.' Xanthe was on the verge of tears as the girls listened again to her conception problems.

'Isn't it too early to be thinking about it though? Have you actually been trying naturally for that long?' Veronica asked.

'We're both thirty-nine,' Xanthe took a deep breath, 'and they say a woman's fertility drops at thirty-six, and we've been trying for a year. In reality, we probably should've started talking about this six months ago, two years ago even.' Xanthe was agitated, angry with herself for being so career-focused she'd almost forgotten about having the family they'd both talked about before even getting married.

'For what it's worth, I don't buy all that test-tube crap,' Nadine added coldly, as if they were talking about choosing a brand of toothpaste, not a method of conceiving. 'Just relax and let it happen naturally,' she added unsympathetically, still wearing her sunglasses and twirling the celery in her Bloody Mary.

Veronica glared at Nadine for being so insensitive, and Xanthe struck back with anger and sarcasm in her shaky voice. 'That's easy for you to say, when without any effort you had two children who you don't even seem to like half the time.'

There was silence all round as Xanthe's words hit everyone with the same degree of 'Ouch!'

Xanthe retracted her statement immediately. 'I'm sorry, really. I shouldn't have said that. This whole situation is making me nuts. But that's no excuse, I really am sorry, Nadine.' Xanthe reached across the table, and put her hand on top of Nadine's in a warm display of apology and friendship.

'Like water off a duck's back,' Nadine said generously. 'No offence taken, darling, you're right. I don't like them half the time, you can borrow them whenever you like. And then you'll prefer contraception over conception, believe me.' Although she loved her kids, Nadine knew she was a crappy mother a lot of the time. She was trying to lighten the mood, but it didn't help Xanthe.

Two waitresses brought a round of coffees and breakfasts and the atmosphere immediately became less tense. The table was alive with colour and aromas: Middle Eastern fruit loaf, grilled chorizo, eggs, macadamia and cranberry granola, and another Bloody Mary for Nadine. The girls started on what looked to be the perfect Easter feast and while the conversation slowed, it hadn't ended.

Spreading the pineapple honey quark on her toast, Xanthe continued, 'What about you, Vee? What do you think I should do?' Xanthe was determined to walk away with some clarity on the issue, at least for herself. She needed to put her mind at rest. If her husband wasn't interested in IVF, and her dearest friends thought it was a bad idea, then maybe she should just let it go. 'I value your point of view, Vee.' Xanthe also assumed that having been married to a GP for so long Veronica might have some added insight.

'Medically, I think IVF is an important option for couples who might otherwise never be able to have children. I know how distressing it was for Alex when he had to tell couples they were infertile and couldn't conceive.' Veronica momentarily thought back to the years when she and her husband still talked about his working day, and he off-loaded the stress, without breaking confidentiality; he appreciated his wife's sympathetic ear. That had been many years ago, but she'd never forgotten those times. 'To tell someone they've run out of options when it came to having their own child was one of the hardest things about his job, I think.'

'Oh Vee, I want to have a baby so badly, and IVF means there's one more option for me doing that.' With that, it seemed as if Xanthe had made up her mind that it would be the next step in trying. The only step. The last step. But she couldn't take the step without Spencer.

'Then I think you should investigate how to go about it, and if it's right for you, then go for it.' Veronica appeared fully supportive as she dug deep into her granola.

Xanthe felt happy, positive, supported and mostly grateful to Veronica, and expressed her gratitude with what she thought was a compliment: 'I want to have a healthy family like yours.'

To everyone's surprise Veronica burst into tears.

'Oh God, what's wrong?' Izzy asked, quickly grabbing a tissue from her tote and handing it to Veronica.

'What did I say?' Xanthe felt guilty – and perplexed – at inadvertently upsetting her dear tidda.

'Everyone's healthy, but there's no family anymore. I'm so sad all the time. I have no life. I have no purpose. I have nothing.' Veronica cried harder and put her head in her hands; her wedding, engagement and eternity rings still on her left hand looked like they'd just been cleaned.

'I signed the divorce papers recently,' she sniffed, 'and it was as if the marriage meant nothing.' She blew her nose hard and reached into her handbag to search for a hanky. 'I'm sorry, Xanthe,' Veronica took a breath, 'I didn't mean to interfere with your conversation this morning.'

'Don't be silly,' Xanthe said, touching her tidda's forearm. 'I'm worried about you. We're all worried about you.' Xanthe looked to the other women for support, which they returned with smiles, nods and words of agreement. 'It's just that you seem so much wiser than me, having kids so young and raising them and making a home life while we were all still at uni or working. It just feels like you're the big sister I never had.' Xanthe was sincere, and for the first time articulated what the other tiddas had also always felt about Vee. The role of the 'wise one' was not something Veronica had ever considered, but it was a mantle that gave her some strength now. Not one to hog attention, however, she wanted to turn the spotlight back on Xanthe.

'Please, let's talk about you, about you having a baby,' Veronica managed to get out in one breath. 'At least you're doing it the right way around, Xanthe,' Veronica added, sounding more like her mother – or the big sister, as it were. 'Not like me, getting married because I was pregnant.' She burst into tears again.

'You loved each other when you got married, Vee. You know that, *he* knows that. You had two decades of marriage which many people today don't have.' That was what Xanthe was thinking about when she said she wanted a family like Veronica's. The foundation was there, even if Alex had decided to walk away from it later on.

'And the kids turned out great, they're perfect,' Izzy said.

'Perfect!' the other women echoed seriously.

Even though they all got bored over the years hearing about how 'perfect' Vee's kids were, they knew that her success as a mother was the most important thing in her world. She measured her own self-esteem by how her boys were doing; and her tiddas all acknowledged Veronica's sons were well-mannered, wonderful young men because of their mother. Apart from leading sporting and debating teams at school, as Veronica's sons matured into young men, they would do anything around the house she asked them to without effort or argument. They always offered a seat and a cuppa to the tiddas when they visited, and would often take the time to yarn with their mother after their father abandoned her. By most standards of Australian males, Vee's boys *were* perfect, and all the tiddas knew it.

'Yes, but there's no family left now,' Veronica sniffed some more. 'He's gone, they've gone and all I have are divorce papers, and a mostly empty house.' She felt gutted, her heart ripped out, no spirit left in her. 'I'm just so sad all the time,' she sobbed again.

'Ah, but you've got the Lexus!' Ellen grinned at her friend in an attempt to lighten the moment.

'And the boys adore you, and John will probably never move out of home,' Izzy said.

Veronica smiled at the thought of the baby of the family living in the huge house with her. 'John is a good boy. I don't want him to move out. I probably wouldn't eat much if I didn't have to cook for him and his mates.' Veronica finally smiled, realising the joy being a mum brought her, and it spurred her to get back to the topic of Xanthe's IVF commitment.

'Enough of my misery,' she said, wiping her nose, 'let's talk about beautiful things like babies, because they can turn out to be like John. And my kids are my greatest achievement in life.' She smiled again, feeling that she had done at least one useful thing to date.

Ellen moved some of the plates and empty coffee cups to the table next to them, looking as if her mind was miles away.

'You've been very quiet this morning, Isobel,' Nadine said to her sister-in-law in a somewhat serious voice.

Only Izzy's mother called her Isobel and that was reserved for when she was in trouble as a child and teenager. Izzy started tearing a serviette into tiny pieces.

'What is it?' Nadine asked, concern in her voice. 'Don't make me go home and get Richard to call his little sister for a chat.'

Oh God, that was the last thing that Izzy wanted. She hadn't even thought about how her brother might react.

His little sister pregnant to someone he'd never even met. He'd never liked any bloke she'd introduced him to in the past and that was usually a nothing situation. Telling him about the baby would almost be worse than telling her mother. She didn't want to tell either of them, and was only telling the girls because she was desperate. Keeping it to herself as she experienced a whole range of body changes was sending her quietly insane.

'Izzy,' Ellen said firmly, knowing her friend well enough to see something was wrong.

Izzy dropped the serviette on the table as a wave of nausea swept across her. It was the sickest she'd felt since watching the distinct pink stripe appear on the pregnancy test stick. She closed her eyes and thought back to the warm Wednesday morning when she'd sat with the bathroom door open in her flat, waiting, waiting, waiting. Squatting over the toilet trying to pee on the stick had been awkward, but it was nothing compared to how awkward she felt when she'd been bluntly told three times, by three different sticks, that she was pregnant. Tears of shock had fallen that morning, but she hadn't cried since. She blew air out her mouth again as she noticed her tiddas glaring at her with anticipation.

'What's wrong?' Xanthe asked.

Izzy took a deep breath and struggled to look Xanthe in the eye; she knew what she was about to say was going to hit her tidda like a ton of pregnancy tests, none of them with pink stripes. 'I didn't know we were going to be talking about all this stuff today, important stuff, I mean your IVF plans, Xanthe.' She turned to Veronica. 'Or your sense of loss, Vee.'

Veronica felt tears well again as Izzy looked at her with sympathy in her eyes.

'I'm sorry, really I'm sorry it's me and not you,' she said directly to Xanthe.

'Sorry for what? What's you and not me?' Xanthe asked, articulating everyone's confusion.

'It's just . . .' Izzy was stalling. The inevitable announcement would upset one of the people she loved most in the world.

'What?' Xanthe's mind was racing. What could her tidda possibly have done to make her seem so angst-ridden?

'I don't know how to say this, and I really wish I didn't have to.' Izzy got that pre-vomit saliva build-up in her mouth and thought she should bolt from the table, but she swallowed hard and hoped it would stay down.

'For fuck's sake Izzy, just say it, we're all worried now,' Ellen said, echoing what the others were thinking.

Izzy took a deep breath. 'I'm pregnant,' she said matter-of-factly. She sighed with relief and looked straight into her coffee cup, which was firmly gripped in both hands. She was grateful for the release, but still she felt like she'd just confessed to a serious crime.

Silence fell as heavily on the tiddas as the humidity that usually blanketed the city in summer. The women looked anywhere else than at Xanthe. Izzy was pregnant. Xanthe wasn't. Izzy never talked about wanting kids; her career, her media projects were her babies. It seemed like forever before someone said something.

'Congratulations,' Veronica offered half-heartedly, as if it was the only thing that could be said, or should be said, even though she felt Xanthe's pain.

'Oh yes, congratulations, Izzy. It's a surprise, but . . .' Xanthe choked up. 'I'm happy for you,' she said, swiftly pushing her chair from the table and fleeing to the ladies' room.

'How long?' Nadine asked softly.

'Going on ten weeks now.'

'The father?' Nadine asked again.

'I haven't told him, I haven't told anyone except you girls, and Tracey.'

'You told your agent before the father? That's pretty fucked.' Nadine's softness disappeared as quickly as Xanthe had. 'Not even I would do that, and I know you all think *I've* got problems.'

The waitress appeared at the table and took another round of coffee orders. Everyone ordered cake as well. It was comfort food time; when conversation was difficult, food was always easy.

Xanthe returned with a freshly washed face. 'So, when are you due?' she asked.

Izzy couldn't tell if there was a tone to the question or not. 'November.' She paused. 'I think.'

'You think? How can you not know?' Xanthe was angry at how vague her friend was about bringing a new life into the world.

'Because, Xanthe,' Izzy's voice was strained, as she tried to remain calm, 'I didn't plan this, obviously, and I don't even know if I'm going to keep it.'

'WHAT?' Xanthe yelled. She banged her fists on the table in a display that in the twenty-plus years of their friendship no-one had seen before. The entire café of patrons and staff threw stares at their table.

'Shhh, love, calm down.' Veronica was playing the wise one again, placing her hand on Xanthe's and hoping the moment didn't turn into a full public spectacle. Veronica believed if you had to be loud and argue, you should at least do it at home.

Xanthe took a breath and lowered her voice. 'You can't have an abortion,' she said as if in a position to control Izzy's life and any other that may come along.

'I don't think you can really tell Izzy what she can or can't do, Xanthe.' Nadine stepped in to show support for her sister-in-law.

'People like me are desperate to have kids and can't. I think I'm allowed to comment, don't you?' Xanthe replied. She looked back to Izzy. 'Especially when *you*,' Xanthe almost spat the words out, 'just act like it's a choice about having milk in your coffee or not.'

'Xanthe!' Nadine snapped. 'Stop it, you're being unfair.'

'Unfair? I'll tell you what's un-fucking-fair . . .' Xanthe sat on the edge of her seat and unleashed a tirade, the sort of which she wished she could use with her racist clients. Her thoughts were completely focused on Izzy though, and how betrayed by the universe she felt at that moment. All the anger she had built up in disappointment, in frustration, in confusion about Spencer's actions lately in relation to IVF had all brewed in an emotional pot that was going to be dumped right on Izzy's shoulders in an unassuming café in Paddington.

Xanthe put her hands palms down on the table as if to support her stance and give more air to her lungs. She leant over to Izzy's side of the table. 'Unfair is a woman, not just *any* woman, but a sistagirl – one of my best friends – who sits down casually in front of me on a Saturday morning and acts all blasé about something as significant and life-changing as being pregnant, when she knows full well *I'm* going insane because I can't conceive!' Xanthe's temper was at boiling point; her heart was racing, her body was hot and her hands were shaking.

Veronica put her arm around Xanthe's shoulder in an attempt to calm the petite woman. Ellen looked on with concern while Nadine was deeply in Izzy's corner.

'Jesus, Xanthe, this isn't easy for me at all. Of course it's life-changing, it's *my* fucking life that's changing.' Izzy thought about the morning sickness, the cravings, the changes in her breasts. The fact that she couldn't believe that she'd actually missed a period; since she was thirteen they had arrived like clockwork every twenty-eight days. 'I'm not blasé at all. I'm distressed. I didn't even want to tell you and now I wish I hadn't.'

'I wish you hadn't either,' Xanthe said, now quietly crying. 'Haven't you heard a thing I've said this morning, or the last few months?' Xanthe wiped the tears that spilled down her cheeks, and Veronica's eyes began to well again.

'Christ, Xanthe, not everything is about *you!*' Nadine's third Bloody Mary was now talking; she even took her sunglasses off in an attempt to give Xanthe a red eyeballing. 'This is about Izzy right now. Is she supposed to calculate her sex life like you do? For fuck's sake, leave her alone.' Nadine and Izzy may not have seen eye to eye on everything but she was fiercely loyal when it came to family, and she wasn't going to let Izzy get pummelled, especially when she was obviously in a fragile state.

'It's fine,' Izzy said softly, touching Nadine's arm in thanks for the show of back up. She looked over at Xanthe. 'I've heard everything you've said,' she said gently, 'every detail about how often you have to have sex, the dates you're ovulating, all the herbal remedies you've been advised to take, the names you're already thinking about, how you want to buy a bigger house and may have to try IVF.' Izzy couldn't believe how much she'd actually mentally recorded about Xanthe's pregnancy woes. 'Yes, I've heard everything. I know you want to have a baby, and I'm truly sorry that you can't, and I'm sorry that I am pregnant and you aren't.' Izzy started crying. 'Mostly I am sorry that I am pregnant and that I am feeling completely overwhelmed.'

Silence fell heavily again. Xanthe was weeping, Veronica was wiping away tears. Izzy was distraught and coughing to camouflage her own crying. Nadine was angry with Xanthe. It was up to Ellen to do her best to change the mood, again.

'It's Easter Saturday, you all need to stop fucking crying. Jesus is rising tomorrow, it's supposed to be a joyful and happy occasion and the Lord won't have time for you sooks!' None of them was overly religious or celebrated Easter in its traditional sense, so Ellen's words fell like a lead balloon. 'And I probably shouldn't have said fucking and Jesus in the one mouthful either,' she added, desperate for something to change.

'Can you just be serious for one fucking minute?' Nadine said through gritted teeth. 'You've said nothing helpful at all this morning for anyone.'

'You've only noticed because you're only half fucking pissed today and not *completely* fucking pissed,' Ellen retorted. 'But wait on, it's only 11 a.m. so there's plenty of time for that.'

It looked like a true bitch fight was brewing and as Nadine leant into the table and glared at Ellen, Veronica went into mediator mode straightaway. Raising three boys who fought like any normal teenagers living under the same roof, Veronica had mastered the art of finding common ground. It had been years since she'd had to separate Ellen and Nadine, and the last aggressive words they'd exchanged had seen Nadine fall off her chair. At a New Year's Eve party Nadine had accused Ellen of flirting with Richard. It was the most insane accusation, and everyone knew it. Richard was like a brother to Ellen, just as he was to his blood sister Izzy. But the booze had made Nadine volatile, just like it had this morning. Veronica had feared getting a punch that night when she'd stepped in to help Nadine up off the ground, but the last thing she wanted was one of them falling off a chair this morning, accident or otherwise.

'Can you two potty mouths please stop swearing? People are watching. And don't be so unkind to each other. We're all friends, remember?'

Nadine and Ellen looked around in turn and smiled apologetically to the other café patrons. They may have stepped back into their corners but Xanthe wasn't finished with her dissection of Izzy's situation.

'Ellen, what do you think about Izzy's declaration of impending motherhood?' she asked, the bitter pill still in her mouth.

'Oh don't ask *me*.' Ellen sipped her coffee, looking straight into the white porcelain cup.

'But I *am* asking you. Everyone else is having a say, what's yours?' Xanthe waited, like a teacher who had instructed a student to answer a question. 'Don't worry, it's not like I can get any more upset, or more offended than I already am.' There was a hint of sarcasm in her voice.

Nadine groaned with the drama of it all. Veronica put her finger to her lips and mimed 'shhhh'.

Nadine mouthed back. 'Fine!'

Ellen really didn't want to have a say. She'd woken up happy, with a hot man in her bed and now she was surrounded by her tiddas in tears and was wanting to slap Nadine the first chance she got.

'Ellen?' Xanthe pressed. 'Is it me? Am I wrong?'

'I'm not picking sides, Xanthe, and you shouldn't expect any of us to.' Ellen wanted to be Switzerland in this war.

'But you must have an opinion one way or another, surely. You understand the value of life, you're around death so much.'

Xanthe was getting out of control in her need to be right about something that had no right or wrong answers. Her tidda was on shaky ground if she was going to move into values and morals, Izzy thought. She was not prepared to sit there and be judged by *anyone*, not even Xanthe.

'Well, if you must know, I support you about the IVF,' Ellen said at last, 'and I'll support Izzy with whatever she decides too. But it's not my body so I don't really have an opinion on what either of you do with yours.'

'That's a cop-out, Ellen. Of course you have an opinion, one way or another.'

'No, Xanthe, I don't. These are very personal decisions you're both making, that only *you* can make for yourselves. It's not my place to throw my take on it all at you.'

'That's funny, you always seem to have a fuck– ' Nadine stopped herself from cussing, and continued, '. . . freaking opinion on everything else.'

Ellen bit her tongue, not wanting to inflame the situation any further, but slyly she gave Nadine the finger.

'I'd really like to know what you think, Ellen, please,' Xanthe begged. 'Let's all just be honest today. There's already no turning back for some.'

Izzy knew the comment was meant for her by the bitter look Xanthe threw in her direction.

Ellen felt uncomfortable and, unexpectedly, under extreme pressure. 'I don't see the need for all this confessing about our most intimate selves, celebrating Easter with tears instead of chocolate eggs,' she said, still trying to avoid any real input into the conversation.

'It's not confessing, Ellen, it's sharing, that's what we're doing.' Xanthe was starting to sound calmer and more rational but she was still driving the agenda.

'Sharing eh? Is that what we're doing?' Ellen looked around the table at the watery red eyes of each woman, including

Nadine. They all looked back, waiting. 'Fine, well then I'm going to share in the same vein and I know this is going to freak some of you out . . .' She looked at Xanthe and Izzy.

'Oh, for fuck's sake just spill it,' Nadine said, exasperated.

'I had my tubes tied when I was twenty-six,' Ellen blurted, as if she was in a confessional.

The women all looked shocked, except Veronica who had helped, through Alex, get the referral so Ellen could have the procedure.

'Bullshit!' Izzy said in total disbelief. 'You would've told us before now.' She looked at the others. 'Wouldn't she?'

'She told me,' Veronica said, divulging the secret she'd carried for over a decade.

'You told Vee, and not us?' There was a hint of ugliness in Izzy's tone.

They all thought it but said nothing: Ellen had told a white woman about her tubal ligation but not breathed a word about it to her Black sisters. Why?

Ellen frowned. 'Why would I tell you? It's not like Black women often get their tubes tied. How many do you know?' There was silence. 'That's right, it's worse than – ' she stopped herself.

'Worse than what?' Izzy asked with one eyebrow arched. 'An abortion? Is that what you were going to say?' Izzy knew they were as bad as each other in some women's eyes, and she was prepared for the guilt trips she was going to get if she made the decision to terminate. She didn't plan this baby, she didn't want children, but she still didn't see the need to act – just yet. *And* she had now managed to drag her friends into her drama, and upset those she loved at the same time. In the meantime she felt herself being judged.

Ellen felt it too. 'Look, we all grew up together, so you know how much the old ladies want grannies, and the pressure is always on us to procreate, maintain the race, be the matriarch.' Izzy just nodded. 'I told Vee because she was neutral in terms of what goes on with our mob, and Alex organised the connections for me in Sydney. So I had some moral and practical support, which I needed. It was a big deal for me at the time, and I didn't want to make it any bigger.' Ellen was thinking that she didn't want to be like Xanthe and have everyone know her business.

'Of course I understand,' Izzy said. 'It's why I'm struggling with my lot now. I know how the old women think. It's probably why Xanthe is so desperate to have a baby too. Partly? Maybe?'

Izzy was desperate to soften the hard air between her and Xanthe by including her tidda in her answer – and in the shared responsibility they all knew they had as Aboriginal women. Izzy, Ellen and Xanthe were strong role models in each of their families, and some of the only women in their clans who had gone to university and built careers that gave back to the mobs. Their own role models were their mothers, their grandmothers and their aunties. When white women talked about feminism and the male networks they were left out of, the three tiddas laughed, knowing that the Wiradjuri sistahood they shared could be broken by no man, Black or white. These tiddas had listened to and learned from their elders, and knew that even in their modern, city-based lives they were still expected – even with the degrees and careers – to keep breeding; it was simply the done thing. This was something that Nadine and Veronica might never understand, only ever accountable to themselves, and coincidentally, both already mothers.

'Why, Ellen?' Xanthe was gobsmacked, unable to understand her tidda's unusual confession, or why any woman would make herself permanently unable to have children before she'd even had one, at *least* one.

'The truth is, after having been co-parent to five younger brothers and sisters when I was just twelve, it felt like I'd already raised a family just by helping out Mum. I hardly had a childhood after that arsehole who some still refer to as "my father" left.'

Ellen wasn't one to get emotional but she felt a lump in her throat at the thought of her mother and the hard life they shared when she was growing up, thanks to the good-for-nothing sperm donor who had left them all for a better life, but no-one knew where.

'Any maternal instinct I may have had was completely crushed by having to cook, clean and care for the kids because my poor mother was working seven days a week either cleaning at the school or at the hospital and sometimes both in the one day, just to keep a roof over our head and food in our bellies.' Ellen shook her head with disappointment in the man who had fathered her.

The other women felt guilty for not realising the pressure Ellen had been under as a teenager. Izzy thought of Ellen mainly by the river in a purple cozzie and long plaits, always cheerful. Xanthe remembered Ellen as the best sprinter at the sports carnival. Veronica recalled how Ellen was a dynamo at elastics on the playground. And later in life Nadine had always compared Ellen and herself to the girls from *Puberty Blues*, only in the country and not at the beach. It was clear to the tiddas now that Ellen had managed to hide the challenges she faced at home, making the most of being with her friends when she could.

'Let's face it, in high school we were so busy talking about boys and INXS and George Michael. And you two,' Ellen nodded to Veronica and Xanthe, 'had crushes on Whitney Houston and Rick Astley. No-one was talking about what was going on at home. You just never noticed the shit I had to put up with.' She smiled calmly. 'So, in all honesty I can say that I support you, Izzy, in whatever you decide because it's *your* life to lead, just as yours is yours, Xanthe.'

'Well, isn't this just the perfect circle then. One will never have a baby, one's pregnant and doesn't want it, and one can't get pregnant,' Nadine summarised.

'Thanks for the analysis,' Ellen said sarcastically. 'Talk about not offering anything of use. Why don't you have another drink?'

Nadine just smiled back, having already found comfort in the cosy drunken place where she could just bliss out.

'I should be getting home,' Xanthe said, looking at her watch before pulling cash from her purse and putting a couple of notes in the middle of the table.

'I've got it,' Nadine said. 'In lieu of buying anyone chocolates for Easter.'

No-one had the emotional energy to even try to argue with her.

Xanthe walked around the table and pecked everyone on the cheek in a false display that she was okay, and that everything between them was all right. But nobody really believed that it was. As she walked out of the café, Xanthe knew the women would still be talking.

Back at the table, Veronica turned to Izzy. 'Why haven't you told the father?' she asked seriously.

'I don't know if I should.'

'Of course you should,' Veronica answered, as if it were a no-brainer.

'But . . . if I'm not going to have the baby, does he even need to know?' Izzy didn't know the answer; all she knew was that she was glad that Xanthe had left. 'What should I do?' She looked at Nadine.

'You should talk to your mother; she's the wisest woman you know. She mightn't like me, but I respect her and know she'll have whatever answers you need.'

'Mum likes you,' Izzy said, only half convincingly, unwilling to offer 'love' as the emotion Trish might feel for her daughter-in-law. Izzy also wanted to shift the subject away from calling her mother, which she was sure would not end well.

Nadine brushed off Izzy's reply. Whether or not her mother-in-law liked her didn't matter that much when she lived so far away. 'The thing is, mothers are good to talk to about these things. And yours will be the same. I know, and don't shout me down, I would be devastated if Brit thought she couldn't come to me with something this big.'

'And it *is* big, Izzy, it's not something you should be dealing with by yourself,' Veronica said.

'Yes, it's *your* decision, but either way, we'll be here to support you,' Ellen reassured her. 'And Xanthe will come around, it's just really hard for her right now.'

Izzy contemplated what it would be like to have the baby by herself, even though she didn't believe she was emotionally, let alone mentally, equipped to do so. If she raised the baby alone would the child end up hating Asher, like Ellen hated her dad?

'Do you ever hear about your fath– I mean the arsehole anymore?' she asked Ellen.

'No. And Mum never mentions him. He could be dead for all I know. And for all I care. I'm not scarred by not having a father. I was surrounded, am *still* surrounded, by people I love and who love me.'

Nadine smiled at Ellen.

'You know you love me,' Ellen grinned widely, wanting to reconcile for the sake of all the tiddas, but also because she loved Nadine too. '*And* I will be a wonderful aunty if and when the need arises.'

4

Mummy's Wish

The following week Xanthe was feeling lonely. Between Spencer's humanitarian legal work and Xanthe being an active member of the local Aboriginal community – volunteering in a tutoring program and at Murri Radio – the pair were at an endless stream of charity events and fund-raisers, sometimes together, but mostly flying solo. They both agreed that they would do as much as they could in terms of their paid work and 'love jobs' – volunteering – until they had a family of their own, because they knew that then their priorities would naturally shift.

Xanthe usually asked her tiddas if they wanted to join her at events, and when they could they would. Living almost thirty minutes from the city and not driving herself, Nadine rarely went but she always donated a box of autographed books for the raffles and, if pushed, would offer a manuscript assessment for auction as well. Given her celebrity status in Brisbane, such a prize became an increasingly lucrative money spinner for several lucky not-for-profit organisations.

Xanthe hadn't mentioned one fundraiser to her friends when she'd heard about it a few days earlier. She was still stewing over the news of Izzy's pregnancy and Ellen's tubal ligation, which had left her the only Black woman in the group wanting to be a mother. Her head was still spinning about how different she had turned out compared to her long-time friends. Significant differences she'd never seen or even thought about before had arisen at the Easter breakfast. Differences she wasn't sure they would overcome. She wondered if their shared history growing up in Mudgee, their commitment to community, their political views and their love of books would be enough to keep them as tight-knit as they were before the dreaded confessions of last weekend.

Xanthe had always imagined all their kids growing up together – except for Veronica's, but she'd be having grandkids soon enough anyway – reliving the circle of friendship they'd had as young girls. Tonight, she was heading into the city, having not spoken to any of her tiddas since Saturday, and hoping that at least someone would get around to organising Nadine's birthday which was fast approaching. It was abnormal to go so long without even a yarn on the phone; she knew it, they knew it too.

Xanthe had an ulterior motive for attending the Mummy's Wish Glam It for Charity event at the Vintage Hotel in George Street. Of course she wanted to help raise money and would buy raffle tickets on top of her ticket to the fundraiser. She and Spencer didn't skimp on charities. But the truth was she was hoping she might meet other women like her, women wanting children and still desperately waiting to conceive. She didn't think of herself as selfish at all; she'd lost all notion of what was logical and fair in her obsession with getting pregnant. But she now felt there was no way she could ask Izzy or Ellen to go to anything like this with her. Nadine was just too high maintenance with her drinking and Veronica seemed to get upset at the slightest thing these days. Xanthe was quite happy to attend this one solo.

Being in the business of talking to people from all walks of life every day, Xanthe had no trouble mixing with strangers; she didn't find it difficult in the least to strike up a conversation with someone she had no prior knowledge of. From a distance she spotted a woman who also ran the hills around Paddington and on recognising each other they started talking easily.

'Great dress,' the other woman said.

Xanthe smiled. 'Sacha Drake, thanks.' It was something she'd tried on one Sunday and Spencer had surprised her with it the next day. 'Just because,' he'd said.

'And I picked these shoes up at DFO, a sale on the sale on top of another sale,' the other woman said, impressing Xanthe; the one thing she loved more than anything was a good bargain.

'That mauve is really your colour . . .' Xanthe extended her hand.

'Kylie, thanks.'

'I'm Xanthe, this is my first Mummy's Wish event. What a great turnout.'

'Mine too. A good friend was recently helped enormously by this organisation so I wanted to come along and support them.' She waved a handful of raffle tickets in the air.

'I need to get some of those,' Xanthe said, looking around for a seller.

Just as Xanthe turned around a staff member suggested the women take their seats downstairs.

'I'm on table four,' Xanthe said.

'So am I. We probably could've shared a cab here,' Kylie laughed.

'Well, I'm happy to share one home.' They hadn't had more than a few minutes together but Xanthe was pleased to have relaxed into conversation with this woman so quickly, given her social life, as with the other tiddas, revolved around each other. Four close friends were better than dozens of acquaintances, she'd always thought, but now and then it was good to mix it up a bit.

At table four the white tablecloth was littered with little pink foil-covered chocolate hearts and handmade red cardboard hearts. There were brochures and business cards of supporters, and a list of raffle prizes. When Xanthe managed to finally buy her tickets she declared, 'I don't care if I don't win anything.' But in her head she was hoping her number would be called out for the remedial massage or the Princess Chic shoes.

'It's all about the cause, really,' she assured herself and the other women at the table. They all nodded in agreement, while also scanning the prize list for what they secretly wanted to win.

A glamorous burlesque show with petite, elegant dancers was entertaining but slightly wasted on the all-female crowd. 'They should've got Manpower!' Kylie said, as the voluptuous women took over the restaurant for fifteen minutes.

When the dancing stopped, Kylie went to the bar. Xanthe discreetly listened to other conversations at the table, mostly about kids. She felt sad and started wishing she hadn't come at all. She could easily have made a donation or bought $200 worth of tickets and increased her chance of winning something at the same time. Maybe she would've won the pearl earrings.

'Ladies and gentlemen, thank you for coming along tonight . . .' The speeches started and the coordinator, in a long emerald green dress, not only ran through the generous things the organisation did by providing domestic help, fuel vouchers, parking vouchers and even laptops to women in hospital so they could Skype their kids, but she also talked about women battling cancer while pregnant. Xanthe hated herself a little at that moment for not recognising how incredibly lucky she was; she might not be pregnant, but nor did she have cancer. She mentally smacked herself in the head, knowing she needed to look at the life she had and be grateful. As she slumped into her chair, she wallowed in her own guilt, but quickly became conscious of another woman at the table wearing a royal blue kaftan who was complaining about not winning in the raffle. Xanthe wanted to smack her as well.

Someone's birthday is approaching. I hope we're doing something fun!

The text message had been sent by Veronica. She couldn't stand the silence that had shrouded the group since Easter. Someone had to break the ice and she had no qualms about being that person. It'd been ten days and communication between the tiddas had all but stopped, and every one of the women had felt the gap in their day. Even though they mainly saw each other at book club and for events that often took weeks to organise, most days there was a flurry of texts flying around with goss, jokes and anything else that kept them connected. Since their group confession, the days had been long, tense, awkward, silent and anxious.

The other four women were relieved and grateful.

'Yes. When? Definitely. Please!' came the responses from Izzy, Ellen, Xanthe and Nadine.

Each was conscious of her own role on that fateful Saturday. Each was missing her tiddas and wanting things to be back to normal, or as normal as they could be with each of the five struggling in a key area of her life. The tiddas loved each other; they just didn't love themselves sometimes. A birthday celebration was as good a reason as any to try to move on as if nothing had happened. At least they were all willing to forgive each other.

They sat in Piaf on Grey Street, looking at the menu. Nadine put a $50 note in the middle of the table. 'Dare someone to order the spatchCOCK!' She rounded her mouth perfectly when she said 'cock' without even a hint of a smile. It was a game they had played before, laughing like teenage girls at something so stupid. But it worked a treat and the women were in tears of laughter again. 'Thank God,' Nadine said, 'I was frightened we'd all lost our sense of humour.'

When a young waiter came to the table the tiddas were still catching their breath, giggling, wiping tears from cheeks.

'I can see it's going to be a long but fun night,' he said cheekily. 'Is that my tip already?' He looked hopefully at Nadine's cash.

'Actually no, that's mine,' Ellen said, putting the note seductively in her bra. 'I'll have the spatch*COCK*!' she said, eyeballing the lad who would've been in his mid-twenties.

'Oh, that's original. Haven't had anyone do that before,' he fired back.

They all laughed some more. It was like old times, but after recent events, they knew the mood could change soon enough.

Their orders taken and drinks poured, the women relaxed, with no real agenda other than to celebrate Nadine's birthday and hopefully get back to feeling comfortable with each other's current emotional circumstances and life choices.

'Are you going to the Brookfield Show?' Izzy asked Nadine. 'Thought I'd go with you and hang with d'niece and d'nephew.'

Nadine almost spat her wine out with laugher. 'You must be kidding?'

'No?' Izzy was a bit confused. 'Why would I be kidding?'

'You know me well enough to know that I'm not remotely interested in cooking, drawing or needlework.'

'Fair call,' Izzy said, reminded of how undomesticated her sister-in-law was.

But she was shocked to hear Nadine continue, 'I'm more likely to stick a needle in a voodoo doll of one of the women who live in Brookfield.'

Izzy couldn't believe what came out of her sister-in-law's mouth sometimes, but the one good thing about Nadine was you knew where you stood. She was brutally honest, but at least she was honest.

'I'll take the kids then, will I? And go with Richard.'

'They'd love that. You are an excellent aunty,' Nadine said, raising her wine glass in appreciation of Izzy's efforts with her kids. No-one commented that she'd also make an excellent mum.

'The kids do love buying butterfly cakes there, and Richard always wants to sit and eat scones. Me? I prefer the Happy Hour Bar, so I may just see you there.'

It was like nothing had happened two weeks before; conversation was easy, there was no bitching and the mood was gentle. They were all on their best behaviour. Xanthe was conscious of the effort she was making not to bring up her conception dramas, Ellen wasn't talking about being single and shaggable, Izzy was twelve weeks and had started counting the days. Time was running out for a termination.

As the night got late, the spatchcock, the pork belly, the seared scallops, the almond-butter-glazed seasonal greens, and the roasted baby beetroots had disappeared. And Nadine was not-so-slowly getting pissed on what Izzy realised was the third bottle of Beaujolais to arrive at the table.

'Must be time for presents, is it?' Xanthe was conscious of getting home to Spencer, given he'd been away for three days and she was ovulating. She kept that information to herself though. 'I hope you like this.' She handed Nadine a white gift bag with canary yellow tissue paper sticking out the top.

'I'm sure I will,' Nadine said, peeking into the bag.

'If they don't fit, let me know; they're easily exchanged.'

Nadine pulled out a pair of yoga pants and three tops.

'I know you do Pilates at home but you still need the right gear to train in,' Xanthe said.

'These are perfect. You know I hate shopping and I do need some new clothes.' Nadine leaned over and kissed Xanthe on the cheek, losing her balance just enough to be noticed before she saved herself from falling onto the table.

'This is my funny gift for you.' Ellen handed Nadine what was obviously a book.

'Oh, let me guess, it's a fit ball,' Nadine shook it around, pretending to wonder what it was.

'Just open it,' Ellen said.

'*Fifty Shades of Grey,* hmmm, yes, well, I think you need this more than I do. I've got all the sex I want, and I've got plenty of better books than this to read.'

'Oh, I know, I just thought it was funny. I'm going to write my own book and call it *Fifty Shades of Black*, but it's about identity.' Ellen had it all sorted.

'I like that,' Izzy said, taking her notebook out and scribbling quickly. 'I might pinch that title for a segment on contemporary visual art.'

'And here's my serious gift for you.' Ellen slid a small box down the length of the table.

Nadine opened the gift as if it were a delicate egg, easily broken. 'They're gorgeous, El, thank you.' She took out the hoop earrings she was wearing and with some help from Izzy, who was sitting next to her, put in the small sapphire studs.

'I thought they were understated but nice, like you.' Ellen rolled her eyes at her attempt to be generous and sincere without sounding too corny.

'I am seriously lucky. You girls know I don't really expect gifts, don't you?' Nadine meant it; even though she was incredibly generous herself, she really didn't require her friendships to come with tangible evidence of caring. But the tiddas always celebrated birthdays in style.

'Well, I'll just keep this for myself then,' Izzy said, waving a silver envelope in the air.

'Oh, give it here. If you've written on a card, then at least let me read it.'

It was a gift voucher to a day spa in Brisbane.

'I thought we could go together, you know, spend some sisterly time together or something,' Izzy said, trying to play down the effort she was making, but acknowledging that Nadine and Richard and their children were her only blood family this side of the Queensland border.

'It's a great idea, thank you, Izzy. I'm really, really chuffed.

Really, I am.' Nadine was beginning to not only slur her words but also repeat them. 'I'm really chuffed,' she said again.

Veronica looked over towards the waiter and winked. The tiddas' energy levels had lowered and the mood was peaceful.

'I didn't know what to buy you, Nadine, you seem to have everything, so I just made you something.' Veronica smiled as, on cue, a pale pink cake made in the shape of a gift box with a white ribbon bow of icing appeared at the table. Four candles, one for each decade, had been lit and the cheeky waiter started the table singing a speedy version of 'Happy Birthday'. The women cheered, hip hip hoorayed and Nadine made a wish.

'This is absolutely beautiful, Vee,' Nadine said, smiling through glassy eyes. 'Thank you so much, you are very clever and generous. I can't remember if I've ever baked a cake.' Nadine started cutting slices and putting them on plates. 'You are very clever and generous,' she repeated.

'I like to bake, it makes me happy. Well, happier,' Veronica said sullenly. 'I almost wish the boys were still at school so I could bake cakes for their fetes and fundraisers. It's good to be busy.'

Veronica appeared a little scatty but she hadn't been drinking. Xanthe wondered what was going on with her, and realised that she'd looked at her watch so many times during the evening, that she hadn't noticed how sad Veronica appeared.

'Are you all right, Vee?' she finally asked.

'Yes, I'm fine. I've been drawing, and baking, and I joined a gym. I don't really like doing weights, but it's good because there are other women there, and sometimes we have coffee.' She was rambling.

'What's going on, Vee? There's something you're not telling us,' Ellen said.

Veronica felt embarrassed, ashamed even, but she didn't know why. Perhaps it was because she'd seen how each of the tiddas had reacted to the various confessions of recent weeks.

'I'm seeing a therapist,' Veronica said softly, looking around to make sure no-one else in the restaurant could hear. 'A Jungian therapist.'

'Why?' Nadine asked. 'You are more together than any of us.' It was meant to be a compliment to Veronica, but came out as a slap in the face to the others.

'Speak for yourself,' Ellen said.

Veronica ignored Ellen and for the first time kept the focus on herself. 'I can't remember the last time I was happy. I just want to be happy again. I think I've done a good job keeping my depression at bay by exercising and being healthy. I don't want to take medication. And I've given up caffeine; it seems to exacerbate every emotion, in a negative way.

'You *will* be happy, Vee, it's just going to take some time.'

'But how long? How much time does it take? I can't keep going on like this.' Veronica started weeping. 'Bloody hell. I'm paying this woman and I sit there and cry, and then I go home and cry, and now I'm here crying.'

'What does the therapist say, Vee?' Izzy hoped Veronica was getting some decent advice.

'She thinks I might be bipolar . . .' Veronica broke down in tears again.

'Oh for fuck's sake, you're not bipolar, or ADHADBDFEFG or whatever the fuck they call it these days,' Ellen said, exasperated.

'That's not the politically correct term, Ellen,' Xanthe said. 'And what do you know about being bipolar, or having ADHD?'

'The point I am trying to make to our dear friend,' Ellen looked directly at Veronica, 'is that you're just sad and emotional. Crying isn't a bad thing. It's a way of releasing what you feel.'

'Tears are the cleanest water you can wash your face with,' Nadine added. 'That's what your mother always tells the kids anyway,' she said to Izzy.

Ellen glared at Nadine. She was trying to have a serious, sensible conversation with someone who was clearly sad, perhaps suffering from depression, but who should not be diagnosed by someone not qualified to do it. 'I'm so over people labelling everyone with a medical condition when sometimes it's just about heartache or pain or sadness. I see sad people every day. They are overcome with grief. Sometimes it takes years for them to recover. But they are not sick, they do not have a mental illness, they are just fucking sad.'

'It's like adults are bipolar, kids have ADHD and every second person is allergic to something,' Nadine agreed, surprising the others. 'None of us had anaphylactic fits at school. My kids can't even take peanut butter sandwiches for their lunch anymore, did you know that?' Nadine was over the limit in her usual fashion but the other women did their best to ignore her and focus on Veronica.

'I'm fine, I'm going to be fine,' Veronica said. 'I just need to keep busy, I need a new focus.' She blew her nose. 'The boys are all doing their own thing, they don't want to be hanging out with their mother. You are the only other people in my life, my only real friends and I'm feeling really socially isolated now. That's what happens when you focus all your energy on your family and have no outside interests. I really need to change that.'

'You know what they say, Vee, the quickest way to get over a man is to get under another one.' Ellen's words were outrageous.

Nadine wanted to slap Ellen. 'For fuck's sake, she doesn't need another bloke.'

'I don't *need* or want another man, I just want a life, a meaningful life, for *me!*' Veronica put her hand on her chest, acknowledging that her commitment over a solid two decades had been about creating meaningful lives for her children and husband. He'd walked out on her two years ago for another woman and she'd been grieving ever since. But it was time to stop. It was *her* turn to live, her turn to be supported, and her turn to be loved.

'Anyway, I've never been with another man. I don't even think I could trust another one.'

'Amen to that!' Ellen said. 'We don't need men to be happy, Vee, and some of us don't need children either.' Ellen could feel Xanthe's look but said nothing more. She knew only too well that happiness came from within. No man or kid could be expected to make a woman happy if she wasn't already mostly there.

'You're right, Ellen, and even just talking about this with you is making me feel better. Thank you,' Veronica said gratefully.

'Do you need to go to the therapist though, Vee?' Izzy asked. 'I mean *we* can listen if you just want to talk.'

'And we can cry with you too,' Xanthe offered.

'Honestly, I *am* feeling a bit better, but I will go back to her because I promised myself at least six sessions. I'm committed to giving it a good go. She did come highly recommended.'

As if on cue the waiter returned to clear the plates from the table.

'I'll be back in a second,' Veronica said. 'Just going to the ladies.'

'You want me to come with you?' Ellen asked, half raising herself from her seat.

'No, sit down. I'm fine. I just need to pee.' Veronica glanced at the waiter and smiled. He had heard her.

As soon as she had left the table, the other tiddas expressed their concern – and their guilt – at not supporting Veronica in her time of need.

'She's always been there for me when I need to debrief after a really draining service. I usually call her on the way home and just off-load,' Ellen said.

'She lets me talk about pregnancy like she's never even heard me mention it before,' Xanthe admitted.

'As the other white woman in this group, sometimes she's the only one who knows what it's like,' Nadine said to the surprise of the three Koori women who each wondered whether it was the booze talking now or if Nadine actually did feel there was some kind of separatist action going on.

Izzy put her hand on her belly. 'I really just love her. I feel awful that Vee doesn't feel supported enough.'

'I think we should organise a fortieth for her,' Ellen said.

'I'm in,' Nadine said. 'I can do some research on it.'

'I'll be there too, of course,' Xanthe said, with slight hesitation, always thinking about her baby plans, whether or not she'd be doing IVF when Veronica's birthday rolled around.

5

Reno-dating

As the weather turned cooler during May, Ellen found it a little harder to get up and go running in the mornings. But as she made her way to the river she still found an unexpected appreciation for urban life. It had hit her in the face like a refreshing wind on a hot day when she first moved to Brisbane, and the feeling didn't wane with the falling temperatures. Looking across the river to the towers that peppered the city streets, Ellen was surprised that such a landscape could nourish her spirit at all after growing up on lush Wiradjuri country. Even during the floods she chose to focus on the magic and strength of the river rather than the devastation.

Every morning she ran from one end of Kangaroo Point under the Story Bridge to the Friendship Bridge at South Bank and back. She passed groups of joggers, boot campers, mothers with prams, strolling retirees and cyclists talking to each other about subjects she sometimes didn't want to hear about.

Of an evening she would walk in the other direction out of the heat of the westerly sun. There was a different crowd at night and it was less hectic. Ellen was one of those who walked to soak up the moment, smell the roses, or the mangroves, as it were.

Today, Ellen picked up her pace along the boardwalk at Kangaroo Point. She'd followed the same routine every morning for years, and even when she was crashing on other people's couches in other suburbs, she always found her way to a place on the river, somewhere, anywhere that gave her a sense of peace. As sweat trickled down the back of her dark red singlet and onto the waistband of her black running shorts, she pounded the pavement in time with the sounds of Michael Bublé blaring through her iPhone. She knew it was loud because those who ran past her smiled in acknowledgement of each song. *This can't possibly be good for my ears,* she thought to herself.

Although it was autumn, it was still warmer in Brisbane than it was in Mudgee at this time of year, and she didn't miss the frosty mornings one bit. It was the year-round warmer weather and the buzz of activity along the river that had allowed her to fall in love with Brisbane within weeks of arriving. And it was the river, her tiddas and the fact there were more men in the city than the country, that had kept her content ever since.

Ellen paused to stretch her calves and for the umpteenth time to admire the public artwork. As far as she was concerned, Brisbane was way ahead of some other cities with its integration of local art into the environment. Athletic as a teenager, Ellen had remained the fittest of her tiddas, getting outdoors and exercising whenever she could. On weekends she'd cycle as far as the Eleanor Schonell Bridge in St Lucia, always stopping to consider the words of Murri poet Samuel Wagan Watson inscribed beneath, glad to see some local Indigenous art getting a start as well.

'If only they'd thought about commissioning a local Blackfella to do something, they might not have ended up with this,' she'd said to Izzy when they checked out the elephant sculpture outside GOMA together. They both wondered how the Maori mob would feel if a Murri artist had won such a commission in Aotearoa. Ellen doubted that would ever happen.

As she reached the steps at the base of the Kangaroo Point Cliffs, boot camp clients were doing their routines up and down the stairs. Ellen took note of the mostly fit, mostly pale people. As both her parents were Wiradjuri, Ellen and her siblings were all much darker skinned than the other tiddas, including Xanthe, whose father was Greek. Hanging out in Kangaroo Point, Ellen had realised she was also darker than many of the locals she passed in nearby streets. Although it was complicated when it came to native title, it was largely accepted among Murris that north of the river was home to the Turrbul mob before the British colonisers arrived. These days, Kangaroo Point had the highest population of Brisbanites living in flats, with a slightly higher percentage of males than females, according to the last census, at least. This statistic alone was enough to keep Ellen loyal to the area.

Ellen felt that Brisbane was still a very white city in many ways. She often thought about her own ancestry as one of the Wiradjuri mob, the largest in New South Wales. 'And with the best looking people,' Izzy would always joke. She thought about how living on country growing up, knowing her family lines and still working with the mob, had instilled in her a strong sense of Aboriginal identity. And while she never thought about her father, she knew he was a good-looking bloke when he was young; her mother had said so. In fact her mother never spoke harshly of the man she had six children to, not wanting her kids to hate their father. If they chose to do so, it wouldn't be because they'd been brainwashed. Ellen didn't need brainwashing though; she simply believed that any man who would leave a woman with six kids was a prick and an arsehole, someone worth hating.

Mudgee was full of beautiful Wiradjuri women, and Ellen's mother was gorgeous. 'We breed them good out this way,' her mum would often say.

But when Ellen was old enough to date, it was different. The boys didn't seem as good looking as the women, or maybe it was that they just didn't appeal to her. Apart from that, she was related to every second Koori in Mudgee. It was simply too small a town for the life she wanted. She missed out on so much in her teens helping to raise her siblings, but she knew enough to know she had to get to the city to not miss out on anything in her twenties.

In some ways, Ellen's unusual career was a blessing. She never imagined she'd end up as a funeral celebrant: 'the accidental celebrant' was how she often defined herself at parties.

Truth was, it wasn't a hard gig to get for a Blackfella. There was plenty of experience to be had attending Aboriginal funerals of family and friends. For her mob, deaths happened too regularly to ever make plans very far ahead.

After delivering a few eulogies for cousins who died young, and uncles and aunties she adored, Ellen became known as the 'eulogy giver' in Mudgee. Soon she was being asked by extended family across Wiradjuri country to help pull together services that were inclusive of cultural elements, while fitting into whatever denomination the deceased had been. It didn't take long for Ellen to learn that Blackfellas were 'practising' everything. Many were Christians: Catholic, Methodist and Baptist. And while she knew few Kooris or Murris who went to church on a regular basis, most of them wanted a religious service as a send-off. Many also wanted to get married in a church, regardless of having no faith, as if it was simply a venue for hire. Ellen didn't judge though, that wasn't her role. Hers was to help the family give the best send off and find as much peace for themselves on the day as they could.

Ellen's days were full of the pain that loss, tragedy, death and mourning carry. But she had a gift for making those suffering feel better about their own lot, and about the future of those they were farewelling. It was at the sixth funeral in a week that Ellen decided she wanted to dedicate herself to making the experience of saying goodbye better for her people. With some urging from the local florist in Mudgee, who had connections in the 'funeral circuit', Ellen enrolled in and completed the Australian funeral celebrant training by distance.

Once certified, she could conduct services herself, legally and professionally. She set up her own business and when she was twenty-three became the first Aboriginal funeral celebrant in the country. It was big news in town at the time, even making the *Mudgee Guardian*. She became a popular choice for many, not only because she was Black, but also because she was one of the few women offering such a service.

Ellen loved working for the mob; she carried out her duties with care, with consideration, with cultural sensitivity. But constantly being at the centre of other people's grief and burying community members every other day soon took its toll, and there was little reprieve in Mudgee. Surrounded by wineries and living in a place where little else provided 'fun', Ellen was a little like Nadine had become in recent years. The only way to unwind was with a glass of red each night; a glass that often turned into a bottle.

Fancy gyms, health centres and zumba classes were not part of Ellen's life back then. And bikram yoga, like Xanthe did, hadn't even been thought of in Australia. As for dating, it was difficult to get a discreet lay in Mudgee; the place was too small, country New South Wales was too small. And even though she met some deadly fellas when she was doing community funerals, she rarely hooked up with anyone. The Koori grapevine would punish her and her business if word got out that she helped lay people to rest and then got laid herself.

Ellen struggled to charge family and friends, most of them known to if not related to her. Unsurprisingly, she didn't easily make ends meet. Only when she started doing services for whitefellas did she understand that she needed to treat her role as a business. When she started to realise how good she was at her work, she appreciated herself even more.

Even though Mudgee was her country, her home with its rolling hills, peaceful countryside and historic buildings, she needed a change of scenery and a different personal challenge. There was more to her life than other people's deaths. She needed a bloke to play with, and she needed to pay her bills, if nothing else. She really wanted a Koori boyfriend, thinking he'd understand better what she did and the issues within the community, but therein lay the problem for her, for all Blackfellas: to hook up with someone in Mudgee who wasn't your own mob was hard enough, but to find someone who wasn't related *and* you found attractive was near impossible.

So, at twenty-six Ellen left Mudgee for the big smoke of Brisbane, and with her other tiddas already living there by the time she arrived, it was an easy transition. She'd been happy ever since. She went home a few times a year, mainly to see her family for Christmas and birthdays, and when she could afford to get there to perform funerals. It was those visits and her memories that left her feeling still connected to her true home, even as she climbed the stairs at Kangaroo Cliffs.

Ellen took two steps at a time, her quads taking all the weight, her arms swinging to give her lift, all the while smiling to herself, knowing she was building buns of steel. It was the café and coffee at the top that really inspired the final burst of energy following her three-kilometre run.

On reaching street level, she adjusted the baseball cap that sheltered her latest haircut and colour – almost a short back and sides with red highlights. 'People think you're a lesbian because you change your hair colour every other week and you look like a boy,' Nadine had once said, to Ellen's horror. Not to be mistaken for a lesbian, but a male. She always fancied herself as a pretty girl; it was just too hot in Brisbane for her to manage a long mane.

Having short hair hadn't affected her dating though. Ellen had had a string of flings in recent years, nothing lasting more than two months. A hazard of the job, she told herself. Anyway, she didn't want to be committed to spending Sundays with someone else and that's when most couples, apparently, saw each other. And while many a man had smiled at her at the Cliffs Café, she never indulged any of them either. That was her private thinking place – private in public, that is. Unlike in Mudgee, where she had a no-dating policy in relation to her work, Ellen had been kept entertained in the bedroom largely by the family members of those she'd buried in Brisbane; the 'sympathy shag' was a real plus in the job. As an undiagnosed commitaphobe who thought the concept of love was overrated, Ellen was never looking for something serious, just something – or someone – to do. But outside of her 'industry-related lovemaking', dating in Brisbane was difficult.

Her coffee finished, Ellen walked back down Main Street to the 'ugliest building on the planet', the apartment block she now called home. She thought about the service she was going to perform that day: a young Murri woman had died in a car accident. The family were devastated, in shock, grief-stricken on too many levels to make all the decisions for the service. Ellen had helped with some suggestions for prayers and poetry, sitting with the older brothers and father while the mother was sedated.

Much of the work she acquired now was through word of mouth, and her unique inclusion of words of Aboriginal wisdom set her aside from the standard, albeit dignified, memorial services offered by her peers in flash offices in the city. Ellen went to great lengths to ensure each service was unique, just as every person buried or cremated was. Before meeting with a family she would take time out at the Cliffs Café overlooking the city skyline and the river. Sometimes she'd sit in this 'office' for hours, thinking and going through collections of poetry, breaking only to examine the slow movement of cranes poised atop the building sites to her left near South Bank. She wondered who owned the sailing boats moored in the river, and how many had actually ended up in Moreton Bay during the floods.

On Friday night Ellen was excited about the housewarming cum book club meeting she was hosting. It was the first time her tiddas had seen her place with everything unpacked. They'd all offered to help her move but Ellen was as independent as ever and managed most of it on her own, although she had accepted Veronica's offer of devoting one entire Tuesday to help her sort. It was a small place so getting organised hadn't taken long, and Ellen had been busy renovating since.

She lit tea-light candles along the windowsill and turned on some salsa music, loud enough to drown out the traffic pulsing across Story Bridge. She hoped she'd eventually get used to the sounds of trucks at all hours of the night. When she first moved in, it felt as if they were racing right through her apartment. But it didn't stop her loving the place, her place, and a space she could now call home.

The flat was full of swatches and brochures, business cards and quotes, which she bundled up and put in a corner. It was cosy, compact, and she needed as much room as possible to host her guests. Five women would be a full house in her flat.

The walls were painted White Swan – a colour she chose as much for the name as the shade – but they were still bare, and she needed a red rug and a gold lampshade. Other than that she was happy with the transition she'd made from homeless and sleeping on other people's couches to being a first homebuyer. *I'm an adult now,* she thought to herself, aware too that her fortieth was fast approaching. *And I've got a good eye for decorating,* she applauded herself as she looked around at what she had already achieved since moving in.

She heard laughter on the landing and knew the lift with her friends had made it to the sixth floor.

'Welcome to my humble, once ugly abode,' she greeted the tiddas, bowing and waving them into the tiled entry.

'This looks amazing, really amazing,' Veronica said, knowing how much the purchase had meant to Ellen, who gave her a hug of gratitude.

'Yes, who'd know from the ugly outside it was quite, let's say, funky in here,' Nadine added, looking snobbishly around the space. 'I think we need a toast to your achievement in fixing this place up.' She handed Ellen a gift basket of goodies from Mudgee: wine, honey, nuts, pickles and some handmade chocolates. She pulled the wine out as Ellen took the basket from her.

'You love me,' Ellen cuddled Nadine.

'I love wine and nibblies,' Nadine said, gently pushing Ellen away.

'Don't fight it, you love me,' Ellen laughed, unpacking the goodies.

'Look, I'm not big on giving – or receiving – dust collectors. I like consumables,' Nadine said, as if it would kill her to agree with Ellen. She looked around for some glasses with a sense of urgency.

'Well, that would be *my* cue, I guess,' said Izzy, looking at Nadine. 'I thought you'd like some nice wine glasses for when you entertain.' She rinsed them quickly in the sink, much to the agitation of Nadine, who was desperate for a drink and annoyed with the delay in getting one, and took them into the lounge.

Meanwhile, Veronica handed Ellen a housewarming gift, wrapped carefully in brown paper and string. Ellen unwrapped it slowly.

'Wow, Vee, this is amazing.' She was overwhelmed with the batik print, but more so Vee's extreme generosity. 'I'm a little lost for words.'

'That'd be a first,' Nadine mumbled as she poured wine.

'That is stunning!' Xanthe desperately wanted to run her hands over it. Veronica smiled at the tiddas' appreciation of her gift.

'Is that an Angela Gardner? I've got something a little similar at home,' Nadine asked, not meaning to big-note herself. They all knew her mansion was full of deadly artwork from around the world. 'It's actually my prized possession.'

'Why do you say *an* and not *by*?' Izzy asked, a little annoyed as she sometimes could be by her bourgeois sister-in-law, who bought whatever she wanted and never had to think about the price. Izzy herself had a work by the same artist but didn't mention it; it would only sound like she was competing, and that was one tiff she didn't want to have tonight.

Nadine ignored Izzy. 'Gardner's a local Brisbane artist, you're lucky to get her now, Ellen, she's going to be huge.' She spoke as if she were an art critic, and moved her hands apart to demonstrate enormity.

'Wow, is it an Angela Gardner, Vee? I mean, is it *by* her?' Ellen had a spark in her eye. She'd never owned anything so posh.

'It's actually mine,' Veronica shyly admitted.

'What?' the four other women asked simultaneously.

'It's mine. I did it. It's *mine*,' Veronica said, as if laying her claim on something more than the artwork.

'That's seriously impressive, Vee,' said Xanthe, still gushing. 'I'd love to give one to Spencer for his birthday. Are you going to do any more?' she asked hopefully, but trying not to stretch the friendship.

Veronica was shocked. She had not imagined any of them thinking it was that good. 'If you're serious, I'd love to make something for Spencer.'

'How long have you been doing this?' Izzy asked. 'You

were always good at art at school.' Izzy recalled Vee being asked to work on the sets of the drama productions at Mudgee High because she could translate detailed sketches into stage-sized backdrops.

'I've always sketched, or painted. It was something I could do when the kids were asleep. And when Alex left me, it helped keep me sane, almost.' Veronica's smiled dropped with the final word.

'But where did you learn to do batik, Vee?' Nadine asked, equally impressed with her friend's talent. 'It's not your typical stay-at-home kind of work one does while the kids are napping. Or is it?' She'd suddenly realised she wasn't the typical stay-at-home mother either.

'Our last family holiday to Bali was long, too long in fact, given that Alex and I were already living virtually separate lives and constantly arguing. He took the boys out a lot, and while they were doing parasailing and windsurfing, I did workshops.' Veronica was happy that she had the chance to talk about something other than her children. Her artwork brought her a real sense of achievement; it was something that other people could celebrate as well. 'I've been practising since we got back and this is my first completed work. I wanted you to have it, Ellen. Buying your first home is a big deal.'

Ellen got teary then and shook her head, unable to speak. She hid her emotion by getting up and propping the piece against the back of the sofa, then leant it against the bare wall.

'Looks perfect already,' she said, still choked up.

'John helped me turn the guest room into a studio,' Veronica continued. 'I spend a lot of time in there now.'

She had planned on working a few hours every day painting, drawing and sketching but in fact she mostly just cried. The girls were watching her closely now, knowing how fragile she still was and how difficult life had been for their tidda during the past few months.

Izzy jumped up. 'I've got it. Vee, you should enrol in a fine arts degree at QUT. Imagine studying art. And you're so good at it you might even be able to make a living out of it at the end.'

'What a great idea, Izzy.' Ellen was excited about the potential for Veronica's further education as well and offered her endorsement. 'Vee, I totally think you should do that. I can come with you to Kelvin Grove and you could suss it out if you want.'

Veronica felt more pressured than flattered.

'Oh, that's all a bit much, don't you think? I've only done *one* piece.'

'Just think about it, Vee.' Nadine put her hand on her tidda's arm. 'You've got the talent, and you've got the time. Why not?'

All of a sudden, Veronica realised what support she had in her tiddas. She couldn't remember the last time she'd felt such happiness.

'Well, dear Vee,' said Ellen, 'this is going to look incredibly special on my wall, when I finally get it hung. But for now I think it looks deadly just there.'

'Oh yes. Perfect. Stunning. Sets off the whole room.' The women might have sounded generous in their responses, but they were being completely honest.

Xanthe was impressed at Ellen's renos too, knowing how much work was involved in turning an older place into something fresh and homey.

'Looks like you've done a lot around here already, Ellen. You said it was brown and blokey when you bought it, so this is a massive transformation in a few weeks.'

'I've had a bit of help,' Ellen said nonchalantly.

'Was there a working bee I didn't know about? Sorry.' Xanthe assumed the tiddas must have been helping Ellen while she was in Rocky doing cross-cultural awareness training.

'No working bees.' Ellen smiled with a devilish sparkle in her eye.

'Spill it!' Izzy knew she'd been up to something.

'I've been reno-dating.' Ellen smiled so broadly her face ached.

'Reno-what?'

'Reno-dating. Dating renovators. Well, not technically renovators, tradies really, and not really *dating*, just shagging.' Ellen grinned some more. 'But hell, they've all got amazing bodies.'

'I really think tradies are underrated, generally,' Veronica said.

'All the tradies we used were great; they do sometimes get a bad rap though,' Xanthe added.

'Mine got a good rap all right, wrapped up in my sheets.' Ellen giggled loudly.

Her tiddas squealed with shock and titillation.

'Details,' Nadine demanded, 'for the old married women here.' She glanced across at Veronica and apologised.

'I'm not old, just not married,' Veronica said darkly.

'None of us are old,' Xanthe said, looking sympathetically at Veronica, but then reminding herself that forty might be too old to conceive.

'You want details?' Ellen was bursting to share. 'Really?'

'Oh, go on,' Izzy said, feigning disinterest.

'The carpenter who came to put in the new skirting boards, well, did he have the best-packed tool belt I've ever seen? Ummm, yes he did.' Ellen panned the room as if looking for something. 'I need to find some more woodwork that needs doing.'

'You're terrible, Ellen,' Xanthe said, looking a bit shocked.

'And the plumber – well, he fitted the new shower hose, and then he fitted his hose too,' Ellen laughed at her own joke, and Izzy and Nadine couldn't resist giggling as well.

'And two days ago, with the sparky, well did the sparks fly with him! There was enough electricity between us to light up the entire Brisbane grid.'

Xanthe was totally shocked now, Veronica was jealous, Nadine was slowly getting pissed and Izzy didn't really think or feel anything other than being pleased to see her tidda so happy.

'Aren't you worried about AIDS?' Xanthe asked.

'What?' Ellen thought the question odd.

'Aren't you afraid of catching something, with all these different blokes?' Xanthe sounded judgemental without meaning too.

'I practise safe sex, I'm not an idiot!' Ellen wasn't sure if she was annoyed because Xanthe thought she was stupid and didn't know about safe sex, or because Xanthe was stupid and didn't know about safe sex. Either way, she didn't like where the conversation was going, especially as it was meant to be a positive one.

'Don't you feel, you know, a bit weird in the morning, with strangers in your home?' Veronica asked innocently, having only ever woken up with her husband for twenty years. 'I know I sound naive, but how does it work?'

Ellen felt uncomfortable. What was she supposed to say? *Well, usually you wake up, make love, have a shower, and they leave.* All of a sudden her reno-dating seemed to be less about fun and more about her morals.

'Gorgeous skirt, Ellen,' Izzy said, sensing the need for a quick change of topic.

Ellen was relieved. 'Ten bucks at the South Bank markets, can you believe it?' She stood up and did a twirl; the multi-coloured cotton flared out. 'The guy should sell cars he was so persistent.'

'Did you sleep with him too?' Nadine asked jokingly.

Ellen ignored her.

'You should've bought two, it looks fab on you,' Izzy continued, doing her best to steer the conversation away from what was increasingly looking like another dig at her tidda.

'It's perfect for this heat too.' Ellen wiped a bead of sweat from her brow, shut the sliding glass door and cranked up the air-conditioning. 'I think we should eat, no?'

Ellen stepped around Veronica and into the kitchen. She passed out breadsticks and a platter of oysters, prawns, lemon wedges and avocado. Everything was placed on a sleek, white coffee table in the middle of the room and the women rested plates in their laps. The flat was too small for a dining room table, and it was pointless squeezing five of them around the small table she had pushed up against the wall.

Hours later, the women were still chatting.

'I met this author at the Brisbane Writers' Festival,' said Nadine. 'You all know I hardly ever do big events anymore, not my scene, to be honest they never were.' She was getting pissed and starting to ramble in her attempt to get the discussion going on the book they were doing for May.

'But I did this one, this festival, and I was *sooo* glad,' she slurred. Her tiddas were used to her ways and let her go, this time because they had all enjoyed the novel she'd chosen.

'I was totally blown away by her. And so was Richard. I think he was trying to see if they were related, even though she's originally from the Torres Strait. Or should I say he was using it as an excuse to talk to her.' Nadine rolled her eyes, remembering back to her husband's borderline flirting.

'What?' Izzy shook her head.

'Oh, she's hot, I mean sexy and funny and can sing. Your brother was drooling. I had to pick his chin up off the floor.' Nadine laughed; she had never felt threatened by any other women.

'As if, he'd *never* look at another woman, not in front of you anyway,' Izzy said, dismissing any suggestion that her brother would be unfaithful.

'Don't kid yourself. Your *brother*,' Nadine pointed her finger at Izzy, 'is still a man. He still looks at women.' Nadine crossed and re-crossed her legs, took a sip from her glass.

'He just knows that no matter where he gets his appetite he has to eat at home.'

Veronica was dying inside. She couldn't remember the last time her ex-husband had looked at her with wanting in his eyes. She couldn't remember if he'd *ever* drooled over her. All she remembered was that he'd stopped eating at home many, many years ago. She felt a huge flush of sadness and hoped that she wouldn't start to cry. She hadn't taken her medication because she knew she'd want to have a drink and didn't want to mix the two.

'Anyway, I bought her book and loved it. Richard even read it, and you know he only ever reads *mine* because he wants to see if he's in there.' The girls were all guilty of doing the same thing but said nothing. 'And finally, because it's time I let someone else speak – '

Ellen cut her off. 'Why? Don't let go of the microphone on account of four other people with opinions, Nadine,' she mocked.

Nadine ignored the comment, and finished her spiel. 'I really wanted to know what you tiddas thought.' She looked especially at the Koori women in the room.

Xanthe leant forward on the couch. 'I loved *Butterfly Song*. The main character had career aspirations, lived in the city, had a love life *and* had commitment to community.' She nodded, as if to herself. 'Actually, Tarena Shaw reminded me a little of me.'

'Me too,' Izzy said excitedly. 'It was like when I went to uni, although there were far fewer Blackfellas doing degrees back then. She's an inspiring character and could act as a role model in literature to heaps of young women. I hope they teach this in schools.' Izzy got out her Moleskine, always writing down notes for potential ideas related to her program. She'd check on Monday if there was a chance of an interview with the author at some stage, and make sure there were multiple copies of the novel in the library. She was already thinking about hooks for a story.

'Actually,' Veronica finally found a place she could contribute, not always knowing when it was okay for her to comment on 'Black' issues when she was a whajin, or migloo, as they said in Queensland. 'The new national curriculum has a focus on Indigenous studies so hopefully there'll be more novels like this in schools.'

'That's good, because I reckon this is the closest thing to the great Australian novel that I've ever read,' Izzy added. 'It just encompasses so much of this country's spirit.'

'I agree,' Ellen added. 'It's a love story, a legal lesson, and a comment on modern Blackfellas just like us.' The conversation had suddenly become the most analytical they'd seen at book club for a long time.

'For me, as an author,' Nadine said, cementing her authority, 'I loved that it was a treasure trove of eloquent writing. I wish I could write like that.' She sipped her drink, wondering if prose could be so elegant in a novel about murder, crime, blood and gore.

Xanthe, ever the hopeless romantic, appreciated something different all together. 'I loved the story of the grandparents, guitarman Kit and Francesca his frangipani princess.' She smiled, thinking back to the scenes she liked most.

'I liked how their eternal love was symbolised in the butterfly brooch Kit carved for his lady.' Xanthe sighed deeply, recalling Spencer's romantic gestures: breakfast in bed, holding her hand while watching television, bringing home flowers just for the sake of it. He was her Kit, even if he wouldn't talk about IVF.

'That's interesting, Xanthe, because I actually read it as a form of crime novel,' Nadine said, not arguing but clearly having a different reading of the book.

'Really?' Xanthe frowned. *How could we both read it so differently*, she thought to herself.

'Well, the brooch *was* stolen at one point, which led Tarena to research and defend her first case, without yet receiving her uni marks. She plays detective *and* lawyer.'

'Fair enough,' Xanthe said, accepting that Nadine's reading was as valid as her own.

With her reconciliation mind ticking over, Veronica added, 'I really appreciated getting a simple understanding of native title and the Mabo decision. I want to be able to articulate it better when I meet people who are racist.'

'It's an important book for Murris in Queensland too, especially given the size of the Torres Strait Islander population, even just here in Brisbane,' Xanthe said, offering the last couple of oysters to the girls.

Izzy nearly gagged, and hoped that no-one noticed. No-one had asked about the pregnancy, and she didn't want to talk about it.

'Speaking of Islanders, that reminds me we should go to this.' Xanthe handed a flyer to Ellen.

She scanned it and handed it to Veronica. 'I'm not going, take Veronica and Nadine with you.'

'Why?' Xanthe asked, disappointed.

'Cos I can assure you the audience will be all whitefellas, and you'll probably be the youngest ones there too.'

Xanthe was offended by Ellen's response. 'What's wrong with you? Aren't you interested in learning about your fellow Indigenous Australians?'

'Hey, this is Aboriginal land. I am interested in learning about Aboriginal people. I don't say I'm Indigenous, do you?' Ellen looked sternly at Xanthe and then glanced across at Izzy.

'I prefer Wiradjuri, Koori or Aboriginal if need be,' Izzy said, knowing the conversation inside out. 'I rarely say Indigenous because we're different to Torres Strait Islanders.'

'What are you talking about? Aren't you all Indigenous to Australia?' Veronica couldn't understand what the girls were arguing about.

'Actually, my tidda,' Xanthe responded in training mode, calmly and diplomatically, 'We are the first peoples of Australia. The Torres Strait Islands were annexed to Queensland in 1879 by an act of Parliament. The truth is, they could easily have been annexed to Papua New Guinea instead.'

Xanthe looked to Izzy for some follow-up.

'Yes, Vee, we are different peoples, different cultures, different identities. I'm a bit sick of being clumped in with another group all the time simply because of some bit of old legislation.'

'Wow, that's full-on,' Nadine said. 'Richard never talks about things like this.'

'Richard is disconnected from a lot, living up there with you and the kids. He never comes to events, never marches. He should be taking his kids to experience what goes on down here in the cultural precinct and in Musgrave Park on NAIDOC Day, even if it's just for the stalls and music.' Izzy was getting agitated; her brother's apathy towards local Aboriginal politics pissed her off sometimes. 'I'm always emailing him information about what we've got on – events, storytelling, kids' days, weekend activities. He doesn't even bother responding.' Izzy was really annoyed. 'And he doesn't *talk* about it because he's never in a space *to* talk about it. And if our get-togethers didn't come with booze, then *you* wouldn't be here to talk about it either.'

Izzy was immediately sorry she had descended to that level, but it was true. Richard was so busy looking after his wife and kids that he didn't get involved in anything outside of their immediate lives. And he rarely went back to Mudgee. Izzy felt he wasn't setting a good example for his son in the way he related to his own mother or their culture. Not that Richard had a bad relationship with Trish; he just didn't make an effort. And when Richard did call or do anything else, Trish was so grateful she gushed for weeks.

'I'm the aunty, I can take Brit and Cam to community things, but they've got parents, and a lot of stuff is *your* job.'

Nadine felt a massive pang of guilt and the room went quiet.

'On that note, I think it's time for some tiramsu,' Ellen said. Food always got the group back on track.

Two of the tiddas were in sky blue and the other three wore maroon. They used the State of Origin as an excuse to catch up. Since Veronica had announced her depression, each of the others had become conscious of the need to support her, and pretending to give a shit about football was a good disguise for giving that support.

'You are both traitors!' Nadine said to Ellen and Izzy, who were backing the cane toads.

'Listen, I want to barrack for the Blues, but ever since Andrew Johns called Greg Inglis a "Black C" I can't support them,' Izzy said, remembering how disgusted she was when she first saw the news reports in 2010.

'But Laurie Daley is the coach. Richard said we have to support him because he copped an unfair mouthful from Mundine just like Geale did,' Nadine said.

'Oh yes, that's true, but Queensland has the most Blackfellas playing, which means they've got more good-looking players *and* the best chance to win.' Ellen had her own reasons for crossing borders.

Veronica wasn't sold on Ellen's argument. 'I might be wrong, Ellen, but I think it could be racist to go for a team because of the colour of their players.'

'Oh for fuck's sake, I was joking, Vee. We can be Black *and* have a sense of humour, you know? It's okay, we even laugh at ourselves a lot.'

Veronica felt chastised. Ellen felt immediately guilty; of all the people she didn't want to upset it was Vee. Ellen moved closer and put her arm around her tidda's shoulder. 'Oh don't be offended, you know me well enough. Truth is, I'm glad you keep us on our toes, Vee, but don't go telling any tales at your reconciliation meeting, okay? What we say here is sacred, just for us.'

'Of course,' Veronica said, feeling the love from Ellen. 'Tidda time is *our* time.'

The end of May came quickly, the temperature dropped back to average – twenty-three degrees during the day and at its lowest it was still thirteen degrees of a night. Everyone was grateful for a reprieve from the humidity and there'd even been some rain in the past week.

Izzy was trying to ignore that she'd pretty much reached the legal cut-off for terminating. There was no need to call her mother for advice now. Ellen and Nadine quietly asked her every other day how she was going, when she was going to 'visit the clinic', why she hadn't told Asher yet, but Izzy would just shrug them off. Without saying it out loud, she knew the decision had already been made. She was glad, though, that Xanthe didn't have the emotional capacity to pretend Izzy's pregnancy was okay with her and therefore didn't ask, and Veronica was still embroiled in her own emotional state of mind.

Izzy was as busy as ever producing cultural programs for the arts channel. It was the end of Reconciliation Week and there was a whole schedule of events being held in the cultural precinct celebrating every art form. She was flat out; hip hop sensation The Last Kinection had performed, the talking circle at kuril dhagun – the Indigenous Knowledge Centre – had held community open mic sessions, and the Australian Indigenous Youth Academy had run a successful forum for young local Murris. Izzy had been on the go from daylight to dark with interviews, vox pops and editing, and while she was thrilled with the extent of the activity she got to cover, she was tired and grateful for a decent lunch break with Ellen who had what she called a 'death-free day'.

Ellen and Izzy headed along Grey Street after a talk by Vernon Ah Kee at the Gallery of Modern Art. As they strolled towards the restaurants at South Bank, a white ute with ladders and paint supplies slowed down as it passed them. Ellen pulled out her phone and started dialling the number on the side of the van.

'What *are* you doing?' Izzy asked, her curiosity laced with anger.

'Getting a quote and maybe a poke,' Ellen said seriously.

'Are you crazy?' Izzy grabbed the phone from Ellen's hand and ended the call.

Ellen wasn't impressed. 'Do you know what my life is like? I can't keep relying on finding bedroom happiness in other people's funeral sadness.'

6

West End Dreaming

Izzy rose, still dreamy from the sleep she had needed so badly, and fumbled for her running gear in the dark. She liked to exercise when she could and early morning along the river at West End was the best place to clear her head. She needed to walk or run today but her legs felt like lead. She was desperate for fresh air though and kept moving. Only the promise of the energy that the river and its tree-lined bank could give her forced her to put one foot in front of the other. It was going to be a long day, she already knew that. She felt a slight dizzy spell, something that had become quite frequent of late. She wasn't sure if it was her blood sugar levels but when she finally went to see her GP, she told Izzy to start eating more small meals throughout the day, to get more rest and to stand up slowly. *So much to remember,* she thought to herself.

As she turned into Hoogley Street she listened to a voicemail message from Tracey, who said she was just checking in and letting her know she was buying some time with the broadcaster. 'Trust me, it'll work out,' she'd signed off.

Izzy was relieved that her agent took her client's whole life into consideration, and had her best interests – professional and personal – at heart. The role on mainstream telly wasn't going to wait forever though, and Izzy knew it. But she was going to let Tracey worry about it; that was her job.

As she got closer to the ferry terminal, Izzy saw James, the *Big Issue* seller, and waved on approach.

'Sorry, mate, don't have my wallet.' She turned her palms up as she spoke, wishing she'd shoved a $5 note into her bra.

'No worries,' he said sincerely.

'I'll catch you later on my way to work.' She smiled and headed along the path past an idling bus due to depart for the city then on to Teneriffe.

Izzy always bought the community newspaper from James, and not simply because he complimented her on her clothes, 'a nice pink top' or a 'pretty dress'. James wasn't trying to make a sale, his kind words were genuine. He was, Izzy thought, a decent, charming guy, and she appreciated him for that. And the articles were interesting. Without ruining the pages, she'd skim the paper sold by homeless people as a means of having employment, and then hand it back to James the next morning so he could resell it, or she'd pass it onto another seller. The best form of recycling there was, she believed.

The morning serenity, the trees, the lush grass, James, the joggers, the dog walkers, the tai chi crew – all were part of

Izzy's daily routine, and why she felt at peace in West End. It wasn't until she had finally settled into her flat in Ryan Street that she got her first good night's sleep in Brisbane. When she had first arrived in the big smoke at twenty-three – anything after Mudgee and Bathurst seemed 'big' – she wanted to be in the heart of the city, within walking distance of the mall and all the excitement it could offer. But it was noisy and chaotic during the day and duller than she expected after dark. She never slept properly in her apartment on Leichardt Street in Spring Hill; the lift in the building banged and clattered non-stop, and sometimes the racket drove her to tears.

Izzy liked her flat near the river though. She had turned it into a cosy home. She was distraught when the floods of 2011 took over the car park and everyone had to evacuate the building. She only had to move things out of the storage area and put them upstairs though, and she was grateful that her second floor unit was safe from the raging waters that rose rapidly over two days at the peak of the disaster. However, when she was forced to evacuate the building along with all her neighbours, she took with her some of her most prized possessions, including the camp dog artwork *Jamu,* made with pandanus and ochre pigments by Yolanda Rostron who hailed from South Central Arnhem Land. Izzy much preferred her silent dog to the annoying local scrub turkeys any day, and there was no way she was going to risk losing it, even if the water rising another five metres was highly improbable.

Unlike her four tiddas, who all owned or were paying off their homes, Izzy wasn't obsessed with owning her walls, but she did own what hung on them and what lined them – paintings, prints and books. Izzy had invested in works by a couple of Aboriginal artists she'd interviewed for her program. It meant something to her to have met the creators of the pieces she so admired. However, since she'd fallen pregnant and found herself less focused on her job than usual, she would stare for hours at the Angela Gardner print *Brightfield Symbols* and imagine the swirls as embryos growing inside her. One moment she thought it a beautiful idea, the next she was thrown into panic about her life, the embryo's life and both their futures.

The truth was Izzy had a great life, a comfortable life and, most notably, a self-centred life. There was no mortgage to worry her, she bought what she wanted, and she had manicures and pedicures and spa days. She read the newspaper cover to cover every Saturday, took a nap on Sunday afternoons, ran every morning, and could have a bag of Twisties for dinner if it took her fancy. The thought of having to look after herself *and* someone else, while also reaching her career goals, still didn't feel right to her, didn't in fact seem possible to her. Being pregnant was completely at odds with what she had planned for her life. She didn't want her life to change, at least not so dramatically. But it was going to.

Since entering the workforce after finishing uni in her early twenties, Izzy had put in many years and lots of effort into building the lifestyle she enjoyed in West End. Over time, she'd fallen in love with a number of local shops, eateries and bars in her hood. She became attached and loyal to those, and only on the odd occasion did she share her love with other venues.

It was at one of Nadine's book launches that Izzy first developed a crush on the Boundary Street icon, Avid Reader. It had the best of what West End had to offer and everything she liked: books, a café, a sense of community. Izzy found herself browsing and buying there most weekends. She was a big reader, way beyond what the monthly book club prescribed for her, and there was always a pile of books next to her bed. In her flat, bookcases lined two walls in the living room and both bedrooms. Her shelves included acclaimed Australian writers like Alex Miller, Kate Grenville and Thea Astley alongside the complete works of William Blake, John Keats and Oscar Wilde. Izzy had a worldview of storytelling, even if she often came back to those who wrote about her own country, like Oodgeroo Noonuccal, Alexis Wright and Jack Davis.

After her walk – the run just didn't come easily enough today – Izzy sat on her balcony facing the grey wall of the flash new building next door. Her shoulder-length, wavy, caramel-coloured hair needed a cut, and she wondered if she might get it permanently straightened; she was sick of having to spend so much time doing it herself every day. The cowlicks in her fringe that constantly required pulling her mini-GHD from her handbag were shitting her more than usual, and pregnancy seemed to make Izzy more impatient with each passing day.

The morning was quiet and Izzy appreciated hearing birds chirping to each other, but admitted through a smile and a sigh that she missed the shirtless construction workers who for months gave her even more reason to check emails and read on her balcony. The men had disappeared now, and the rich people had moved in. Their air-conditioning units in summer drove her to despair, but who could blame them? The humidity from October to March in Brisbane was brutal; Izzy often just wanted to lie down on the tiles in the bathroom for relief. She didn't have air-con, only a ceiling fan, but at least it kept the mozzies at bay. It was a different heat to Mudgee; at home the air was dry, but at least in June she could be comfortable.

As she pushed an unwanted fringe-curl out of her eye, Izzy glanced at the plants on her balcony. Even the succulents were thirsty and screaming for attention. Unlike Richard, Izzy had never had a green thumb; she'd been known to kill cactus. She'd have to get her brother over to the plant casualty ward; hopefully he could coax them back to good health. She'd read an article in the local paper about a landscape architect who designed environmentally friendly rooftops and balcony gardens; it would be great to have one. Izzy frowned, trying to recall the woman's name. 'Sidonie Carpenter' appeared in her mind's eye. Izzy liked the name a lot; she could call her own child Sidonie. And there it was, another reminder of the accident that was now a stark reality in her belly.

Not one to ever take sickies, because she rarely got sick *and* loved her job, Izzy had decided the night before that she needed a mental health day to deal with a pregnancy that was now beginning to crowd her mind – and her body. She started to panic, which was unlike her usual calm state. Panic didn't work in media. Always controlled, passionate but controlled. Izzy hadn't spent any time imagining what it might be like being a mother. She hadn't felt there was any point until recently. But when Ellen and Nadine had asked why she hadn't gone to a clinic for the procedure, she'd had no answers. She just physically couldn't get herself there, let alone go through with it. Something had been stopping her, something she hadn't understood.

Izzy walked back inside and headed for the kitchen. She ran her hand over the art deco espresso maker Nadine and Richard had given her for Christmas. They knew how much she loved coffee and were impressed with themselves at having chosen the perfect gift. But they ignored the fact that Izzy lived in West End, which had some of the grooviest cafés in Brisbane. They didn't realise that her morning coffee from the Gunshop Café was a part of her daily ritual; that to give it up would put her momentum out of whack, her world off its axis. In short, completely fuck up her day. Izzy liked routine, she liked goals, and she liked a plan to follow. And just like the pregnancy, the coffee maker shifted her daily plan. Coffee from her favourite café was as necessary as wearing a bra, cleaning her teeth, or charging her mobile phone every night. There were things one simply did every day, without thinking.

Izzy used the coffee machine on the odd occasion of course; when the girls came over, when the three neighbours she spoke to came in, and of course, when Richard and Nadine visited. Today though, she couldn't be bothered with the coughing and spluttering of the machine. She didn't have the patience or the interest. She boiled the kettle and reached for a tea bag. As it sank into the water she opened the screen door and looked down the two flights of concrete stairs towards the back garden overlooking the river. The grass had been freshly mown and the smell reminded her of summer back in Mudgee; she loved being carried home to Wiradjuri country by nothing more than her sense of smell and a strong breeze. Today though, she couldn't imagine living anywhere else but West End.

She placed her mug on the table and collapsed into a chair, surprising even herself at how listless she was feeling. Maybe she should've had a strong coffee. Was coffee bad for you when you were pregnant? She didn't know, but she was going to have to find out. Unlike Xanthe, she hadn't raced out and bought books and magazines; nor had she searched Internet sites for blogs and chat rooms.

The lingering scent of freshly cut grass made her smile. A City Cat sped by with people heading downstream to any number of stops along the brown river. It was the same City Cat she should've been travelling on to work. But she felt sick, and it wasn't morning sickness. Those symptoms – nausea and vomiting – had subsided, thankfully. Rather, she felt like she had a hangover without the headache. And it didn't go away with a hamburger and chips. It didn't help if she put her fingers down her throat either. Nothing was going to help until she'd told Asher – and her mother.

But how would she even tell Asher? Her tiddas hadn't helped her in finding clarity at all, but that was her own fault. Ellen and Nadine wanted to help, were willing to talk to her about it, but she clammed up whenever they broached the subject. And exactly *what* would she tell him? She'd avoided him for weeks, and knew by his texts asking 'Is everything

OK?' that he was feeling neglected and confused. But he wasn't her boyfriend, wasn't likely to be her boyfriend. And even though he was the father, he didn't seem to be the fatherly type; he'd never talked about kids at all. Perhaps that's why they got on so well. They were both driven by their careers and desire for professional success, much more than anything else, including their love life. While she and Asher weren't in a relationship, they were good friends, and they had deep respect for each other. Would all that be lost with the news of an unplanned baby?

Izzy had never thought ill of Asher, but neither had she thought of him in any other way than as a friend, a wonderful lover and a great cook. She respected him for his achievements; he was chef at a groovy restaurant and bar in West End and the only deadly Black chef in Brisbane, or so he used to say.

'Flasher' was the pet name Izzy had given him because he had the best set of teeth she'd ever seen on anyone, Black or white. 'All the better to eat you with,' he would joke when they were alone, back at her flat after a night of cocktails at his work.

There was a mutual admiration between the two as well. Asher liked that Izzy had big dreams because he did too. He wanted to be the next Black Olive with his own catering company, cookbooks and a sous-chef trained by him. Izzy wanted to be Australia's Oprah. Between them they had enough belief in themselves and each other to make their dreams become realities.

Late at night, after lovemaking, they didn't whisper sweet nothings to each other. They talked about their goals, spoke with passion about how good life was when their hard work paid off every day. For Asher it might be a customer saying it was the best polenta they'd ever had, or the most divine chocolate mousse to ever slide down their throat. For Izzy it was receiving an email from someone who'd watched her program and learnt something about Aboriginal art and culture. Their careers defined their relationship; it wasn't about love and babies and happily ever afters.

Izzy noticed some movement in one of the many yellow brick apartments on the other side of the river. She wondered what the local mob thought about life on the river now, and how many Blackfellas living in Brisbane were Jagera or Turrbul. As a crane moved slowly over the top of a building she thought back to her communications degree at Charles Sturt Uni in Bathurst and the joy of studying Oodgeroo Noonuccal's poetry. It was when she first read 'Aboriginal Charter of Rights' that Izzy's political consciousness was awakened. Years later in Brisbane she'd read Samuel Wagan Watson's poem 'Recipe for Metropolis Brisbane' and thought it genius the way he had succinctly recorded the change in the landscape to this country.

Izzy's phone beeped. A text message from Asher. It was as if he had eyes watching her somewhere, or could read her mind from miles away. A connection that could not be explained, that she had never tried to explain in case any over-analysis ruined what they shared.

Can I cook for you soon? It's been a while ☺

It was Asher's way of inviting Izzy to the restaurant and then taking her home. He was horny, and so was she.

Of course ☺

She smiled, but then another wave of nausea came over her. *FUCK!* she thought. *I hate feeling like this. I didn't want this – and I'm sure he doesn't either.*

She put her head on the table, closed her eyes and wept. How on earth would she tell her mother? She already knew what Trish would say after giving Izzy a guilt-laden lecture about not being married. 'Why would you get pregnant to someone you're not married to? Why wouldn't you want a baby that God has gifted you?' And then she knew her mum would add something like, 'Your father would turn in his grave.' At least Asher was Black, she knew that would be regarded as a positive; in her mother's eyes it would lessen the blow. Richard, she knew, would be less than impressed. An unmarried Izzy being pregnant to a bloke he hadn't even met was not what anyone wanted for their little sister, was it?

A rower paddled along the river. This was what Izzy loved most about living in West End, watching the sunrise and early morning health fanatics on the waterfront. All year round it gave her the chance to get her exercise, soak up the changing landscape, have some contact with the general public, smiling to other regular walkers and runners. Most importantly, it gave her time to think. Forty minutes every day as the sun found its way into the sky was all she needed.

Most locals ran, walked and cycled with iPods but not Izzy. She didn't need the fast beat of songs to keep her pace. She didn't want any doof-doof clouding her thoughts. The morning was her time; she cleared her head, plotted her day, scripted any unpleasant things that needed saying at work, and drafted her weekly letter home to her mother, which always included some reference to a wayward scrub turkey that had frightened her.

Something startled Izzy out of her thoughts and she jumped. In West End scrub turkeys roaming free were normal, but no-one else flinched except for her. She blamed her neighbours for feeding the birds like they were domestic pets, even though everyone knew you weren't supposed to. When the males had destroyed their communal garden, Izzy suggested a turkey dinner but she was shouted down. The protected Queensland bird was treated like family.

Izzy stretched and glanced at her phone. It felt strange not to be getting ready for work. She loved everything about her job in the Cultural Precinct and her office at the State Library. Every day was a blessing, starting with her catamaran ride to work each morning. She got the 7.48, always sat out the back – she didn't mind riding backwards until she fell pregnant – and enjoyed the perfect view of the river. Spring was her favourite time of year with jacarandas lining both banks. And she loved all the vessels with Aboriginal places names: Gootcha meant Toowong, Tunamun was Petrie Bight and so on. 'Too deadly,' she'd said out loud when she first realised this.

'The ferry is like the tram but just on water,' she heard a woman tell her child the other morning. Izzy wasn't sure that made much sense. The child seemed happy with the explanation, but Izzy wondered whether she too would become a mother who said stupid things just to shut up an enquiring child.

Her routine each day included a private game where she counted the workers, tourists, business people, those reading newspapers and young girls playing with their hair. Useless statistics she could pull out at a dinner party if she ever needed to.

Occasionally, as the City Cat pulled into Regatta Point, she felt a memory force its way to the front of her mind, recollections of a lover who had once broken her heart. She should've known that a man wanting a first date in a pub was never going to be worth much. Her mother had always told her, 'You don't meet nice men in bars.'

The famous Regatta Hotel took longer to rebuild after the floods than her heart took to mend though. And the floating restaurant on the river where they had fallen in love had drifted away that fateful January and ended up in Moreton Bay. The man had floated away too, but it was for the best. When he chose a simple-minded woman who didn't challenge his intellect – and also happened to be white and so didn't question his politics – Izzy, a strong, intelligent Black woman, decided he wasn't worth caring for at all. She'd seen a few supposedly intelligent Black men opt for a less complex white woman; somehow, she reckoned, it made them feel smarter. She'd never wanted another serious relationship after that, and yet Asher was her intellectual equal. He was different to other men, she believed, but somewhere deep inside she felt that he too wasn't relationship material, and that every man had the capacity to be a bastard. In the end he'd leave her for someone without a career. It was fine for she and Asher to fuck, but their determination to succeed outside the bedroom could eventually present a problem.

She had first met Asher during an interview for the library. He was doing the catering for an event at kuril dhagun, and was demonstrating a bush twist on the lamington, which had been created in his hometown. As he spoke into the camera answering her questions, they both felt a chemistry that needed exploring.

'I'd love to learn how to bake,' Izzy had said off camera.

'I'd love to teach you,' Asher said with his signature grin.

That night the two spent time in his kitchen covering each other in cooking chocolate and coconut.

Izzy loved talking to authors, actors, directors and visual artists. She asked the questions that helped make their work more accessible to mobs all around the country. Interviews, news stories, profiles of successful Blackfellas – all helped to break down the negative stereotypes that the mainstream media had continued to perpetuate. Izzy loved working in tandem with the Murris in the library too, a team of solid women, with innovative programs aimed at educating and entertaining. Inspired by them, Izzy would disembark the City Cat each morning and head straight to the tropical rainforest walk. It was a soothing way to start the day, breathing in the lush foliage, greeting her favourite honeyeater.

On the way home after her usual nine-hour day, she'd stop at the Nepalese Peace Pagoda and feel the stress drain from her. If she felt strung out for any reason during the day she'd walk the length of the Grand Arbour and lose herself in the hundreds of bougainvilleas. It was too beautiful a place to remain angry or stressed.

The Friday night markets in Stanley Plaza were a relaxing way to end the week and Izzy would drop by on her way home from work. As soon as the sweet floury smell of churros hit her nostrils she knew her weekend had truly started. She resisted though; being on-camera, even for Blackfellas, meant you shouldn't get too fat or have too many pimples. She was often tempted by the homemade lemonade but usually passed on that too. Unless it was a special occasion when she lashed out on both. Sitting on the edge of the man-made swimming area she would imagine she was in Europe.

Exploring the markets at her own pace was what she liked to do most. Weaving through the stalls of locally designed jewellery, knick-knacks (or 'dust-gatherers', as Nadine called them) and cheap cotton dresses. She occasionally clicked her fingers to the beat of an artist belting out a tune at the nearby pub.

She collected printing blocks, and used one in particular as part of her signature when writing a birthday or Christmas card. She stopped at the same stall every week to see if there was something new to add to her collection. At last count, her collection of suns was at fifteen. As soon as she learned that Veronica was serious about her artwork, she started collecting some for her birthday.

At work the next day, Izzy walked around dazed. She felt her stomach often, wondering about the life she and Asher had created. She forced herself *not* to think about actually living with a child; she didn't believe she had the capacity to give a child the kind of life it needed or deserved. She simply wasn't maternal, and she accepted that without guilt. But time had run out. She was going to have to be all the things she needed to be.

She threw herself into her work – a welcome distraction – focussing on filming the latest library news and events round-up. There was story time in the Talking Circle of kuril dhagun so she interviewed a couple of aunties as a lead-up promo of what visitors to the library could expect. She also did a short piece in the library bookshop looking at all the latest releases and vox popping patrons in the library café. A full day, a complete day, a day that reminded Izzy of how much she loved her role, her cultural and community contributions . . . and her life just the way it was. Tracey had stopped asking her to return the contract, saying she'd stall the broadcaster as long as she could with 'negotiations', but even Izzy knew her options would become more limited.

On her way home, Izzy gazed up at the Wheel of Brisbane, known locally as the Lazy Eye. She watched the gondolas going around and around, the same thing over and over again. Is this what her life would become with a baby? If she had to turn down the TV role she had so desperately wanted, dreamed about, worked hard for? Perhaps the ride represented what her life had already become, her unvarying routine going to and from work each day: the same river walk, the same river ride, the same faces, the same, the same, the same. Perhaps a baby would give her a new focus. But she didn't want to end up like Veronica with no identity other than mother. Or worse still, like Nadine, who was largely detached from her children.

Izzy walked to the counter, bought a ticket and climbed aboard. She had a gondola all to herself; alone, but for the unborn child within her. She'd have to tell Asher when they got together for dinner, soon. She could hear an excited child in the next gondola: 'Wow, wow, wow.' What could the child see that she couldn't? There was no 'wow' for her, but then again she had seen the river, by day and by night, many times from the deck of the State Library. She had also seen some stunning views from the top of the Gallery of Modern Art when she attended Queensland University of Technology events. She'd had her fair share of 'wows' before today.

In the gondola she gave herself over to the running commentary about the history of Brisbane and its landmarks – the Gabba, the Goodwill Bridge, the Treasury Building. The didge music woven throughout sounded odd, but tourism companies knew that the haunting sounds of the wind instrument from the Top End was an expected part of the generic 'Aboriginal experience'.

As she disembarked Izzy started planning the upcoming book club gathering at her place on Friday night. She had mixed feelings about it, and butterflies just at the thought of seeing Asher, which she would have to do eventually.

The solid oak coffee table was littered with finger food – the easiest way to manage the catering. Pistachio nuts, cheeses, olives, vine leaves, falafels, and there were samosas and marinated chicken wings in the oven. Izzy wasn't drinking but she'd stocked the fridge with wine and mixers and had made a passionfruit mocktail. She rushed to change the towels in the bathroom, ran a broom over the balcony, which was constantly littered with falling leaves, and put on some George Benson. It had been six months since she'd had the girls all over together, even though Nadine and Richard had visited since, and Ellen had occasionally dropped by for a river run.

A more-obvious-than-normal-cleavage stared Izzy in the face via the bathroom mirror. Her t-shirt was tight but it still worked. Her jeans weren't comfortable though, so she opted for a linen wrap skirt she'd picked up on sale on Boundary Street. She broke out a new pair of shoes from Wittner with tiny blue tiles across the toe and wondered how long she would be able to walk in them. For the first time in years she let her hair dry naturally, the curls taking on their own new, free life. She couldn't resist running the GHD through her fringe though.

As she was lighting some candles in the bathroom, Izzy heard the sound of heels on the cement stairs. Her tiddas had arrived, all chatter and laughter. Within minutes they had said their hellos, had plates of food on their laps and the book discussion had begun. Izzy couldn't remember the last time a Vixen meeting had been so efficient.

'This was amazing!' Ellen said with gusto. 'It was the first novel I've read that talked about native title, social and emotional wellbeing, Black bureaucrats, police thuggery *and* Black deaths in custody.' She took a breath.

'And infidelity, stolen wages, Black on Black and white on Black racism,' Xanthe added.

Veronica couldn't be left out. 'All wrapped up in a skilful multi-murder mystery.'

Nadine shook her head, the shame clear on her face. 'I'm embarrassed I didn't know about the imaginary line called "the boundary" or the curfew in Brisbane last century.'

Izzy tried not to bite, but it was hard. It shat her that her sister-in-law knew so little about history, but doubted if she were sober more often that would make a difference. She gritted her teeth and was saved by Veronica.

'I liked how she tried to hide Musgrave Park as Meston and called it the land of the Corrowa people.'

'What about the characters?' Ellen said, wide-eyed. 'Because I'm sure I saw a few people I know in there!'

The women laughed; they all knew who at least one character represented in real life, but none of them was game to say it out loud.

Xanthe swallowed quickly, slapped her own chest as if anxious to get something out desperately. 'And,' she swallowed again, 'the racist, thuggish old-school cop Higgins, and his unsure-of-his-identity partner, Detective Jason Matthews, didn't do much to help us like the Queensland cops. God!' She shook her head.

'So true,' they all agreed.

'All I know is that reading it made me realise people need to choose a side,' Ellen said with authority. 'You either support traditional owners begging for their rightful claims to land ownership or you support the developers that governments feel they have the right to sell land to.'

Ellen's mobile rang on her last word. While the women kept talking she jumped up. She saw 'Mum' flashing on the screen and was tempted not to answer because she knew any conversation, regardless of the purpose of the call, would never be short. She looked at the name again and felt a pang of guilt.

'Mum,' she said enthusiastically.

'Ellen Jane,' her mother always addressed her by her Christian and middle name, 'you've got to come home.'

Ellen could tell by the sound of her mother's shaky voice that something was wrong. 'What's happened?'

The women noticed Ellen's worried frown; they stopped talking and watched her with concern.

'Aunty Molly passed away today. Just dropped dead at the bowlo. I can't go through this without you,' she sobbed.

Ellen managed to get as many details about her aunty's passing as she could and promised she'd be there as soon as possible. Then she ended the call and looked around at her tiddas.

'I'll help with the service, obviously,' she said, wiping her eyes and then blowing her nose.

'Of course.'

'Naturally.'

'That'd be beautiful.'

'When shall we leave?' Xanthe asked, grabbing hold of Ellen's hand.

'Yes, when?' Izzy would be heading home for Aunty Molly's funeral too.

'I'll probably go the day after tomorrow. I have a service in the morning, have to meet another family in the afternoon, and then I can get packed and leave fresh the next day.'

'I'd like to go with you, if you think that's okay?' Veronica was looking for endorsement but she just wanted to offer any support she could.

'It'd be lovely to be back there together,' Xanthe said.

'I guess you and Richard will take the kids down too, eh?' Izzy looked at Nadine.

'Yes, I'm just texting him now to come and get me so we can start planning.'

The women said their goodbyes solemnly, each with mixed emotions about heading back home to Mudgee to farewell a woman who had been part of all their lives. Aunty Molly was Ellen's biological aunty, but she was everyone's aunty otherwise. Although Xanthe, Ellen and Izzy had been away from country for a long time, they hadn't lost their sense of responsibility and commitment to community, often returning for funerals as a mark of respect. Nadine had always gone back with Richard; and Veronica, long a close tidda, was never far away. She had grown up understanding how significant funerals were to the local mob.

7

Back to Country

Mudgee airport was tiny, like a Lego building compared to the forever developing Brisbane airport they'd all arrived from via Sydney not long before. They knew they were home when their Aeropelican Jetstream aircraft was coming into land and they could see the township only five kilometres from the runway.

On the flight Veronica was quiet; her own parents long deceased, she reminisced about the good times and then thought about the only family she had left in Mudgee, her in-laws. She felt her usual insecure self, concerned about seeing Alex's parents for the first time since she and Alex had officially separated. Before then, she had always been close to his mother, receiving regular Sunday night phone calls, even when Alex was away on business. They had long shared recipes and a love of a good pot of Earl Grey. But the warmth had all but disappeared since the split, now that Alex was living with a new woman.

A mother's loyalty was always going to be to her son, and that was something even Veronica knew she couldn't argue with. However, she vowed to remain a dignified daughter-in-law and role-model mother, urging her own sons to write and call their grandparents on special occasions. She would maintain the tradition of getting them to sign their own names on Christmas and birthday cards. And she made sure they *always* returned a note of thanks for any gifts sent to them.

Across the aisle Izzy's symptoms of nausea, tender breasts, and fatigue were lessening, but now she felt a plague of butterflies running amok in her belly. She was dreading telling her mother about her 'condition', and still hadn't had the courage to tell Asher. On top of that she knew that Tracey's patience, however professional, was wearing thinner by the day. She hadn't scripted how she would tell her mother, or what responses she'd have to the questions that were likely to be thrown at her. All she knew was that she needed her mother's love and strength right now, and while she might not leave Mudgee with an endorsement, she knew she would leave with some level of emotional support. The real problem was that her mum was a God-fearing Catholic and there was no way their chat was going to be easy. She hadn't even mentioned Asher's name to her mother before. On top of Aunty Molly's funeral, which all the tiddas were upset about, the next few days were going to be challenging.

Ellen had spent the entire flight reading her notes, making comments on pages she had edited and re-edited over and over again in the previous twenty-four hours. Sick with nerves, she was grateful the family had decided on a church funeral rather than a crematorium or graveside service; it relieved her of the need to keep it together completely, as a priest would do the service. But she'd still assumed the role of coordinating everything in lieu of anyone else in the family being emotionally equipped to do so. Aunty Molly's sudden death had left the family and her friends not only grief-stricken, but in shock, dazed that a vibrant woman in her early sixties had just collapsed and died, her heart giving way long before her mind or her passion for life.

Before leaving Brisbane, Ellen had spoken to the priest, organised the funeral director, the flowers, the wake, the music *and* written a few words just in case she was asked or felt like she wanted to say something. It was often the case at Koori services that people were given the opportunity to speak, and she'd seen a lot of families disappointed when a Church – regardless of denomination – stuck to a timeframe which limited the mob participating. Negotiating a sense of community in church services was something Ellen prided herself on being able to achieve, but she wasn't always successful. At least in Mudgee, the town was tight and her aunt would be given the due respect and send-off she well deserved.

Staring out the window as the plane made its descent, Xanthe was looking forward to seeing her grandmother the most. In her nineties, Noonie was the matriarch of their large family and Xanthe trusted her judgement on almost any subject. She was determined to get some pearls of wisdom about her inability to fall pregnant. She quietly hoped the respected Elder might have some old ways of doing things that would help her and Spencer conceive. If not, she'd have to pressure her reluctant husband once more about IVF, and that wasn't something she felt excited about doing.

Nadine and Richard had taken the kids out of school and driven the 900 kilometres. They both wanted their children to see the countryside outside of Queensland; the changing landscape and the various flora and fauna along the Oxley Highway. The autumn leaves were breathtaking as they drove through Kamilaroi country and the township of Gunnedah. They stopped and took photos of the Namoi River and a memorial in Abbott Street to Cumbo Gunnerah, the Aboriginal warrior and leader of the Gunn-e-dar people.

The family of four, silent from the long, tiring drive and desperate to stretch their legs again, all noticed the stark change in temperature when they reached Mudgee. As they pulled into the central New South Wales town, they noticed the sign welcoming visitors to Wiradjuri country had been removed, stolen again. Richard didn't care though, or mind that the Aboriginal flag was upside down at the Town Hall. All he was looking forward to was seeing his mother and brothers again, and Brittany and Cameron spending time with their cousins. Nadine was anxious about doing a book signing in town, but when she was asked to do something as a teaser for the Mudgee Readers' Festival, she didn't feel she could say no. As soon as word got out the star author would be in town for the funeral, the invitation was extended. Her nerves made her want to drink though. At least she was in the right place for it; Mudgee was wine country.

The day of the funeral was sunny, the sky a blanket of baby blue with tufts of white clouds scattered across it. Hundreds of mourners gathered outside St. Mary of the Presentation Catholic Church on Market Street, many admiring the newly restored copper spires that could be seen from across town. The manicured lawns, covered with mourners now, would two days later be transformed into the farmers' market with locally produced wine, fruit and vegies, baked goods, nuts, cheese, eggs and meat. Many visitors to town would hang around a few days just to stock up on what the region had to offer.

The crowd included local Kooris as well as family who had travelled from towns across the state including Bathurst, Dubbo, Orange and Cowra. It was obvious many had popped into Rockmans or Rivers to update their red, black and yellow wardrobe, to be worn at funerals and other community events in the future.

Lifelong friends, local parishioners, members of the CWA, the mayor and three councillors were there – even local Mudgee girl Natarsha Belling, who was covering it for the news. Aunty Molly wasn't just anyone, she was known as one of the Matriarchs of Mudgee; an activist and feminist, just like the Mudgee heroine of the past, Louisa Lawson.

With crowds spilling onto Market Street, traffic was almost at a standstill on Church Street but there was no road rage. Everyone knew the score. Aunty Molly, known to many as 'the volunteer from Vinnies', was being laid to rest.

The service was scheduled to start at ten, but by nine thirty the church was full, with young men lining the walls and back of the church, kids already running around out of control and a constant low hum of people reuniting in wooden pews. Outside, smokers huddled in groups, happy to brave the chilly winter air for one last puff on their cancer sticks.

Six women carrying stems of orange gerberas lined one pew at the front of the church; they represented the volunteers from St Vincent de Paul across the road. They had all worked on a roster with Aunty Molly for years. Her death meant a hole not only in their roster but also in their hearts. About forty men and women in bowling whites took the last six rows on the left-hand side of the church. Many were present the day she collapsed during a social tournament and were still in shock that one of their favourite players would no longer be around to share her cheeky jokes. The 'bowlo' had been Aunty Molly's home every Tuesday and Thursday for nearly twenty-five years. Things wouldn't be the same without her.

As the clock rapidly approached ten, Ellen focused on the task at hand, liaising with the funeral director, the priest, her cousins, the organist, and the readers the family had chosen. Having to coordinate most aspects of the service had taken her mind off the sorrow that was burrowing deep in her heart, but every time she looked over to the casket draped in the Aboriginal flag and with a mountain of red, yellow, and dyed-black gerberas on top, she had to swallow hard.

Having left her mother in the care of her two younger sisters, Ellen briefed her three brothers and the three cousins who would be pallbearers. They were sitting behind their Uncle Ron, a once jovial man, now a distraught widower; apparently he'd not eaten since his wife had passed over.

It was during the eulogy, which Uncle Ron insisted on giving himself, that Ellen really came to understand the meaning of true love, of unconditional love, of the reason why couples actually got married and committed to each other for life. It was a love between man and woman she had never witnessed to such a depth before, and certainly never between her own parents. It was a love that she had never even thought about experiencing herself, nor had ever come close to feeling before. She wondered what her mother was thinking, listening to her brother-in-law talk about his love for her sister. Did she feel jealousy for the sister who chose the *right* man?

Uncle Ron told those gathered about his nearly fifty years of companionship with the love of his life, where a daily cup of tea on the veranda and morning walks along the Cudgegong River at Lawson Park was all they needed. These moments meant more to Uncle Ron than the 'trips to the big city young people had to do these days to experience romance'. Listening to his choked-up words, Ellen considered the meaning of the word 'love': affection, passion, adoration, respect, commitment.

As the funeral drew to a close, Ellen felt a pang of guilt for missing so much of what was going on in her family since moving to Brisbane. She knew her family loved her; even if she had never allowed herself to love or receive love from a man, love in its truest form had always been there for her. For the first time ever, she wondered if she might actually fall in love one day, if there was the possibility of someone loving her like Uncle Ron had loved – *still* loved – Aunty Molly.

As the casket was carried down the length of the aisle to the familiar sounds of the King of Country Roger Knox singing 'Koori Rose', Ellen walked behind it with her mother, who stumbled slightly on her frail legs. As rows and rows of cousins followed, Izzy fell in behind with Trish, Xanthe with her mother, then Richard, Nadine and the kids, and finally Veronica joined with the rest of the congregation.

Mudgee Bowling Club had a different heartbeat that afternoon. Ellen noticed little had changed since the last service she'd done there some years before. Women still queued for the three toilets and gossiped while they were surrounded by apricot and lolly-pink walls. The main bar area was full to capacity and spilled into the Lochiel Restaurant and out onto the sizeable shaded veranda. Every wooden-backed, cerise-coloured chair was taken. Large flat-screen TVs above the bar showed golf, club information and an American chat show. But most eyes were on the Keno screen.

Some locals and visitors stood close to the Internet betting wall which was busy with screens; everyone hoped for the 'big win'. 'The Aboriginal Bank', one uncle explained to a young lad, as he pointed to the TAB onsite. They both laughed.

Ceiling fans inside helped to circulate air while the distinctive poker machine 'music' was drowned out only by the sounds of laughter, cheers of reunions and the juke box playing the latest tunes from the back of the room. The blue felt pool table was getting a working over with coins lined up along one side. The mustard-coloured vinyl bar stools each had a cowboy half-seated on them, waiting for his turn to shoot. The Condo versus Cowra showdown took only a few minutes with the Erambie mob holding the table for three games.

For many Blackfellas funerals were the only time they got to see their mob, the extensive family network that sprawled across the state, and it was a reminder to Ellen of what she missed by moving to Brisbane. She read the blackboard menu near the pool table. *Someone has a sense of humour,* she smiled to herself.

Muppet Stew
Kangaroo Martinis
Grapefruit Sandwiches

Outside, the three bowling greens were busy; one had kicked off the Aunty Molly Memorial Cup; another had a social game in progress for out-of-towners; the third was a carefully planned kids' comp, complete with paid-for coordinator. Ellen knew there'd be lots of kids needing reining in, and she didn't want to be the one to do it, so she'd called in the best.

Club staff were working overtime and non-stop – not for the tips, but because they all knew Aunty Molly. Later that night the emerald green carpet would be wet with beer but also with the laughter and stories that had been walked into it that day.

In the auditorium, three of Aunty Molly's friends from her craft group were set up at easels, each painting a portrait of their late friend. Some locals had made casseroles for Ron, but these women wanted to make something more lasting to honour their beloved friend. None would make it to the Archibald, but all would undoubtedly be hung in a prominent setting in the family home or an organisation in town. Everyone who walked by stopped and admired the efforts; even the city folk understood this was a very country thing to do.

Xanthe sat in a corner holding her grandmother's wrinkled hand. She thought of all the work her Noonie had done while in service under the Protection Act, forced to cook and clean and cater to the needs of the family she worked for until her twenties.

'When are you going to start a family, Mima?'

The word was Wiradjuri for star, and it was the only name her grandmother called her by. Hearing it made Xanthe smile. However the question was one she had tired of long ago and she tried hard not to cry; it pierced her heart every time.

'I'm trying to get pregnant, Noon, but it's not happening,' she said, as a tear trickled down her cheek.

'Maybe that gubbah has bad swimmers,' her gran replied.

'Noon! Don't call him that, and his swimmers are fine.' Xanthe giggled but didn't really want her grandmother making insinuations about her husband's sperm.

'Ah, I'm just kidding my girl, I meant gubbah affectionately, but about his swimmers, you know there's nothing wrong with *our* side of the family,' she said, waving her hands around the room to signify the number of grannies she had. Xanthe had lost count of how many cousins she had, and every time she went home there were more. There certainly *wasn't* anything wrong with fertility on her side.

'I know, and we're doing all the right things, but it's not working,' Xanthe took a deep breath before she started crying. 'I want to try IVF. Do you know what that is, Gran?'

Her grandmother shook her head. 'Of course I know. I'm old, not *stupid!*'

'I'm sorry,' Xanthe said, feeling aptly scolded and wishing Spencer was there with her and not in court with one of his clients. But it was his dedication to social justice that she loved about him most.

'It means Indigenous Victorian Football.' The old lady laughed at her own joke, a Swannies supporter since the days when they were South Melbourne.

Xanthe smiled grimly.

'Look my girl,' her grandmother took a tone of authority to the nearly forty-year-old looking distressed in front of her. 'Babies in test-tubes and using other people's sperm and not your own man's . . . well, that is not what we are supposed to do.'

'But . . .' Xanthe wanted to say it was her last hope.

'Listen to me,' Noonie held her granddaughter's hand tightly. 'You must have faith in Biami to make you a mother, and you need to relax. Those lines on your forehead, they don't come from the Wiradjuri side of the family.' The old woman ran her hand across her own forehead. 'None of that blotox for me,' she laughed again, thinking she was funny, but Xanthe wasn't in the mood for humour. 'I've only ever used Oil of Olay, and look, no lines, no lines.' It was true that Wiradjuri women had exceptional skin, good genes as it were. High cheekbones, straight teeth and very few wrinkles. 'Sunlight soap growing up and no stress about making babies with other people's *stuff*!' The old lady screwed up her face and shook her head.

Xanthe smiled at the Wiradjuri wisdom. Only her grandmother could and would say out loud what she needed to hear. It was *her* wisdom but she offered it with such a sense of confidence it was as if it were truth from the Bible itself.

Across the room Izzy spotted her mother. She had decided to tell her about the baby at the wake, knowing she would be too concerned with what other people thought to get angry in public. Trish would never cause a scene at the bowlo, let alone after a funeral and by the time they got home, she would've calmed down at least slightly.

Izzy's brother Rory sidled up.

'You look chubby, Iz,' he said, poking her in the side.

'The big smoke might be good for your career, but it ain't good for your belly,' her younger brother Dave added, having arrived just as the conversation started. He laughed at his own joke. 'Whitefellas don't like seeing chubsters on their screens, don't you know that? You better not eat that dim sim or you might never become that big flash TV star.'

Izzy looked at the plate of fried food in front of her, desperately wishing someone would bring her one of the huge pepper steak pies they sold at the bar. It would be just as bad for her health, but she was starving and it was all that was on offer. Dave heard his name called and headed off across the room. Rory sat down, pinched one of the dim sims off his sister's plate.

'I need to tell you something,' Izzy said, and before being able to stop herself blurted out, 'I'm pregnant.' The minute she said it she wished she could suck the words straight back into her mouth, back into the baby brain she'd developed in recent months.

'Who the fuck is he?' Her brother stood up, immediately angry and protective of his older sister. 'Is he here?' He looked around the room.

'Sit down, you idiot!' Izzy grabbed her brother by his checked shirt and tugged hard enough to get him back on his chair. 'He's not here, *and* he's an amazing man.'

She shocked herself at the declaration she made out loud about Asher. She'd never had to define or describe him to anyone before. The sudden realisation that she thought he was amazing was an epiphany. It felt good.

'Is he a Blackfella at least? Might be good to know before I beat the crap out of him.'

It was hard to tell whether Rory was joking or not, but Izzy didn't want to risk it and maintained a level of seriousness.

'He's a Murri, from Toowoomba way, Gaibul Jarrowair mob,' she said proudly.

'At least he won't be a shit-skin kid then,' Rory said aggressively, taking a sip from his schooner.

'What the fuck?' Izzy said, loud enough for someone at a nearby table to look around. 'Sorry,' she mouthed and turned to her brother, feeling confused and angry. 'What are you talking about?'

'You know, Black mixed with white.' Rory was matter of fact. 'At least the kid'll be dark, that's what I'm trying to say.'

Izzy was disgusted by her brother at that moment. She didn't want to cause a scene, but she hated how her own blood talked stupid about skin colour. She swallowed her anger as Rory skolled his schooner.

'I'll love the kid, you know that. Blood is blood, sis, but don't let him get all lost in the big city, eh? Ya better bring 'im 'ome to country to hang out with my kids too.'

They looked at Rory's kids rolling around on the dance floor with their cousins – first, second and third – completely lacking any discipline at that moment and having a whale of a time. Izzy just nodded, smiled and unknowingly put her hand on her belly, imagining for the first time a future where her own child *would* be one of the cousins, one of the kids cleaning a dance floor with their clothes. A child would connect her even more to her nieces and nephews, and to her brothers, and it would give her mum her eighth grandchild.

'Have you told Mum yet?' Rory asked, a smirk of knowing on his face.

'No,' Izzy said cautiously, hoping her brother didn't do it before she had a chance to.

'Good luck with that. You know she's going to freak cos you ain't married. Me, I don't care, I only got married cos Caz said she'd marry that Jones loser if I didn't put a ring on her finger.'

'But you love Caz,' Izzy said, as much to convince herself as her brother.

'Yeah, she grew on me. No goin' back now anyway.'

Rory looked across the room to the mother of his children and smiled. *Such is the love in my family,* Izzy thought to herself as her brother walked off.

Her mother was sitting nearby with a crowd around her, telling yarns to eager listeners. Izzy waited impatiently for the moment when there was no-one else around. But before she had a chance there was a shouting match, drawing everyone's attention to a woman near the vending machine.

As the conversation in the auditorium lulled, people moved towards the main bar. The fear of a fight entered everyone's minds. Two distinctive voices were coming from the vending machine behind the pool table, and the racket carried across the crowded space. Nadine and Richard. Izzy moved as fast as she could to get them out of the club and away from everyone's eyes.

'I just want some fucking Cheezels, what's the big deal?' Nadine slurred loudly.

Richard responded in a hushed tone, embarrassed, aware everyone was listening. 'It's time to go, darling, come on.' He gently took his wife's arm and looked for his children.

Izzy had already gathered them and was motioning towards the door.

'Cheezels, that's all I ask for, nothing more. I came back to this fucking pit with you and you can't even buy me some fucking Cheezels. Do you need some money? I've got plenty of money.'

Richard let go of his wife's arm and walked towards the entrance, not far behind his sister and kids. Yelled at for no reason in front of his family and mob and with no recourse, he had no other alternative. He felt shamed, angry, emasculated.

Izzy turned around and saw her mother heading towards her sister-in-law. *This is not going to end well.*

By the time they got to the car both Brittany and Cameron were crying.

'We can't leave Mum there,' Brittany said, sobbing heavily.

'Why did she want Cheezels?' Cameron asked. 'And why didn't you just give them to her, Dad?'

Richard was now the bad guy in front of his children. 'Izzy, can you take the kids to the motel? I'll go back and get her if she'll come,' he said through clenched teeth. 'We'll grab a cab.'

This was the angriest Izzy could recall seeing Richard in a long time.

'Of course I can take them. We can watch a movie, eh kids?'

There was no response as the children quietly got in the car.

Richard was sweating as he re-entered the club. He was nervous; his wife was out of control and he didn't know what she might do next. The first thing he saw was his seventy-five-year-old mother with fire in her eyes talking sternly to Nadine, who by now was swaying. As he got closer he could hear the words that would ring in his ears for months.

'Don't come back here again. You make me shame. You give our family name shame.' Nadine just stood glassy-eyed, not saying anything. She was afraid of Trish and that was enough to keep her quiet.

Without being noticed, Veronica had left the wake early. She may have been surrounded by hundreds of people, including her closest friends, but she was lonely. She walked down Market Street to her boutique hotel across from Robertson Park. She needed time to think, some space to mourn her own losses: her parents, her husband, her once happy life. As she eased herself into the deep bath her tears spilled immediately. By the time she opened her eyes again, the water had cooled and she was pruney. Still, she didn't get out immediately. Instead she reminded herself it was the first time she'd been alone in a hotel room; no husband, no kids. *Would it be like this forever,* she wondered, fresh tears trickling down her cheek.

'Wake up to yourself,' she said out loud, dressing quickly. She put a fresh face of make-up on and took herself off to the hotel restaurant. As she picked through a Caesar salad, she noticed a table of men sitting nearby and assumed they were talking farming. Two wore pink shirts. Was there a large gay community in Mudgee, or had men in town become more fashionable over the years? *What else has changed in town,* she wondered, and, after finishing her meal she strolled to the local tourism centre only metres away.

Across town, Richard arrived back at the motel with Nadine gloomily in tow. He rushed out of the cab and back to the room, passing other Blackfellas who were standing around talking. Nadine went straight into the bathroom and ran the shower. Richard said little, just thanked his sister, and suggested she take their car overnight. He curled up with the kids on the queen-sized bed as they watched *Glee* on TV.

Izzy felt relieved to go. Nadine had stressed them all out. The sun had set by now and the temperature had dropped dramatically; she was cold and tired and the last thing she wanted was a houseful of people to deal with when she got to her mother's. As she turned right at the West End General Store, she still couldn't believe the family had always lived on tree-lined Cox Street. All the local Blackfellas knew about the road builder William Cox and what he thought about the local Wiradjuri. Most could recite his famous quote off the cuff and Izzy played it in her head as she pulled into the street:

> *The best thing that can be done is to shoot all blacks and manure the ground with their carcasses. That is all they are fit for! It is also recommended that all the women and children be shot. That is the most certain way of getting rid of this pestilent race.*

She wondered if her mother thought about the Cox family much; it was *their* history that was taught in the schools and talked about locally, even though most residents knew of the area's brutal past. The thought saddened her. But at least she'd moved from one West End to another.

She pulled into the driveway of the family home glad that there wasn't already a car under the carport. Across the road were three silver utes and Izzy hoped their owners weren't inside. She checked the letterbox that sat loose on the cream-coloured picket fence – not the clichéd white picket fence many aspired to – and smiled. The garden was tidy, not a weed in sight, the lattice archway over the front gate covered in green vine.

The screen and front door were both locked so she went around back. Her mother was alone on the glassed-in veranda, sitting in the dark, rosary beads in hand.

Izzy was hungry, desperate for peanut butter and jam on toast and a cup of peppermint tea. 'Helloooo,' she sang softly from the door. 'Are you okay?'

'Ah, come sit, daught. Give your old mum some good news.'

'I'll put the kettle on first, shall I? And make some toast. Have you eaten?'

'I'm not hungry,' her mother said. 'But I should eat something. Vegemite for me.'

As Izzy watched the steam come out of the kettle spout her mobile rang. Asher's named flashed big and bright.

'Hey,' she said, attempting enthusiasm but filled with fear.

'How are you? I've been thinking about you all day,' Asher said warmly down the line. 'I wish I could just give you a cuddle.'

Izzy felt uncomfortable, they'd never talked about cuddles before. They never really had calls when they were apart either, that wasn't normal. But she had told him about the funeral because he was pressing her about why they weren't catching up. At least she didn't have to lie.

'Izzy, are you okay?' Asher asked after a few moments of silence.

'It's fine, I'm fine. You know what these things are like. One big reunion, a few family blues and a lot of hangovers next day.' She tried to keep it light, upbeat.

'How's Ellen going?' Asher asked, genuinely interested, having heard Izzy talk about her friends and their book club a number of times.

'She's coping, it's been hard on all of us in different ways.' Izzy bit her lip and wished she hadn't set it up for more questions. Luckily, Asher was like most blokes and only needed the bare minimum of information.

'Okay, well I better get back into the kitchen. Call me when you get back and I'll cook for you.'

The phone went dead. Izzy stood still, forgetting what she was doing in the kitchen till she heard her mother sing out, 'Everything okay out there?'

'Sorry,' Izzy said as she carried out a metal tray with hot toast and a pot of tea. She laid it out on a laminate table alongside her mother's olive-green velvet Jason recliner.

'Your sister-in-law, she needs help,' her mother said quietly.

'I know. I'll talk to Richard about it, we'll sort her out when we get home.'

'Good,' is all her mother said, sipping her weak tea.

'There's something I need to tell you,' Izzy said, having already devoured one piece of toast and feeling immediately better for it.

'I already know.'

How could she know? She must be talking about something else. Maybe Rory said something.

'When are you due?' Trish asked.

'But, how did you know?' Izzy was shocked, confused.

'A mother knows these things, daught.' She took another sip of her tea. 'You can't hide being pregnant from your own mother.'

Izzy started to cry. Not because her mother was angry, she wasn't, but because she was closer to her mum than she realised.

'I can see that glow only pregnant women get. You're actually a bit shiny.'

Izzy had noticed the change in her skin in recent weeks also and bought some oil-free cleanser just a few days before.

'I'm due . . .' Izzy couldn't bring herself to tell her mother she was struggling with the prospect of motherhood.

'What's wrong, daught? What's wrong with you?'

Izzy shook her head and blew her nose into a ratty tissue she dragged from the bottom of her handbag.

'Izzy, you're nearly forty. I'm not going to tell you what to think, but you can do anything you choose to set your mind to. Trust me, though, when I say that you will *never* regret having children. You can do without a husband, men are nothing but trouble anyway, except for Richard who is perfect and too good for her, but that's another story.'

'What about my career?' Izzy sniffled.

'You've already *had* a career, you can still have a career in the future. But we are the women, daught, we are the matriarchs, we need to keep the family growing.'

'I can't do it by myself,' Izzy blew hard again.

'What's the father say?'

Izzy thought it odd her mother didn't ask who the father was.

'I haven't told him yet.'

'You *must* tell him, Isobel, and soon. This is part of *his* story too, his life, his future.'

This was a directive, not a suggestion, and Izzy knew it.

Izzy hadn't thought about it that way before. It had only ever been about her, *her* life, *her* future and the impact the baby would have on *her* own career plans. It was already impacting on her body, as her clothes were tighter and her breasts fuller.

'Is this fella going to run away?'

Izzy could tell her mother was being restrained. A Christian she may be, but that didn't mean she wasn't capable of bitching with the best of them, especially where her children were concerned.

'I don't know.'

And it was the truth. Izzy had no idea how Asher would react, but if his reaction was anything like hers, then he'd be confused and think immediately about himself and his future career.

Trish put her hand on top of her daughter's. 'I love you, you are my blood. We are strong Wiradjuri women and no matter what happens, I will support you all the way.' She reached down beside her chair and lifted up her knitting basket. 'Your cousin Tarsha is pregnant too. She asked me to make some booties for her. It's a girl,' she said, without taking her eyes off the needles. 'He's a nice fella, brickie, honest as the day is long. Kind of like that Jack you should've married.'

'Mum! Please don't.'

Izzy didn't want to go into the history of not marrying the 'perfect man' in her twenties. But she remembered how happy her mum was when they got engaged. Izzy had been happy too, or so she thought. It was the longest engagement in Mudgee's history and everyone joked about it, but Izzy just couldn't go through with marrying someone who had no ambition. Jack was a good man, hardworking, caring and gentle. He loved his job at the abattoir and she was glad her man was cheery of a night. But he never wanted to leave Mudgee; he didn't want to travel, not even to Sydney. All he talked about was settling down, having children and growing old in rocking chairs together. The abattoir had closed, but Jack still stayed put. If he made her feel old when she was only twenty-two, how would she feel at thirty with three kids? She just couldn't do it.

She poured another cup of tea. The crocheted tea cosy on the pot was one that Aunty Molly – one of Trish's best friends – had given her mum last Christmas.

'Well, what's this fella up in Brisbane like then? At least tell me he's Black!'

It was ladies night at Sajo's but none of the girls were interested in the $10 cocktails. Ellen felt completely drained,

Izzy was dizzy from the conversation with her mother, Xanthe was trying to take on board the words of her Noon, and Veronica was frightened that if she had anything to drink she would sink back into sadness again. No-one had heard from Nadine.

'Where did you end up today?' Xanthe asked Veronica. 'I looked for you but couldn't see you anywhere.'

Veronica was not going to tell them about her bath of tears. Instead, she popped a paper bag on the table with a heap of local produce to distribute. 'Oh, I got overwhelmed with all the noise and people so went for a stroll and stopped at the tourism office.' She started unpacking the items: wild lime marmalade, lilli pilli jam, dreaming green tea and wild rosella tea. 'There's a new Indigenous business in town called IndigiEarth, so grab what you like.'

With the relief of having at last talked to her mum, Izzy had found a new, heartier appetite and even though she'd eaten toast only an hour before, she had her eye on the chocolate fondant dessert even as she devoured the seared kangaroo on the menu. 'I guess this is what the old women would've been eating when they were pregnant way back when, eh?' she said, taking another bite. 'But perhaps without the snow peas,' she joked, realising she'd mentioned the pregnancy without being questioned. Her tiddas looked at each other but didn't say a word, waiting to see if Izzy followed through. She didn't.

'How did it end up with Nadine?' Veronica ventured, concerned but cautious not to gossip about their tidda.

'She's not in a good way. I left them all at the hotel. Mum was furious, but calm by the time I got home.'

'And?' Ellen asked impatiently, knowing that her tidda was going to talk to her mum about the pregnancy.

'I told her,' Izzy sighed. 'And she was fine, surprisingly. Reckoned she knew the minute she saw me. She thinks I'll be fine as a mum, but I'm not so sure.'

Ellen, Veronica and Xanthe exchanged looks, smiling.

'Of course you'll be fine. Mums know that stuff,' said Ellen.

'But Rory was an arse about whether or not Asher was a Blackfella,' Izzy said. 'I've got no time for mob calling people shit-skin or coconut. Really, haven't we moved past that yet?'

'It's the power of Western language once used against us, now used *by* us,' Xanthe said. 'I've had it all my life, what with Dad being Greek. I'm bicultural – I do roo souvlaki. Dad calls it roovlaki.' She was joking, and smiling, which came as a welcome change to the others. 'But I'm a Blackfella. How could I not be, born here on country, only knowing the stories from this place? Maybe if I were born in Greece it would be different, maybe I'd feel more Greek. As far as I'm concerned, the only person who has the right to question me is Dad. And you know what? He never does.'

8

Signs in the Sites

Mudgee was blessed with another blue-skied winter day, with some frost on the grass in the early morning. All the tiddas were doing their own thing. Ellen woke at dawn after a solid sleep, but she needed a good stretch. She had missed two days of running, so took herself down to the Cudgegong River at Lawson Park. It was a picture of peacefulness, other than the noise of the crows flying low above her. She imagined her late Aunty and her Uncle Ron on their morning walks there. How he would miss them now.

As she ran the path through the lush, manicured landscape, she saw only three other people: a woman on a yoga mat, a man jogging and a woman with a beagle on a leash. Since the last time she'd visited, flash exercise equipment had been installed along the path so she was able to do some leg lifts, lateral raises and chin ups between sprints. She warmed up quickly, peeling off the pink fleece top she'd packed for the cold. There was a tidy kids' playground but no kids. She smiled when she saw the hollowed trees she used to play hide and seek in as a child.

She stopped and photographed the memorial to William Lawson. The plate read:

To commemorate the achievements of Lieut William Lawson who was the first to traverse the site of Mudgee . . .

'Really?' Ellen said out loud to no-one. She planned on mentioning it to the girls, aiming to find out what memorials there were around town to mark the history of the local mob.

Veronica was awake at the same time, but went in search of coffee and breakfast rather than exercise. At 7 a.m. there were few bodies on the streets but lots of cars; she imagined they were shift workers, many from the local coalmines. She saw a dog tied to the back tray of a ute outside the newsagency, and couldn't remember ever seeing that at home at The Gap. The dog's owner returned wearing a bright fluorescent vest. She'd noticed a number of high-visibility vests in fluoro yellow and orange the day before but didn't know where those men worked. It was common knowledge that the mining companies wanted to fly below the radar and not attract any more attention than they already did. Thus, it was policy that staff had to change into civvies before going into town.

Veronica had been feeling nauseous about seeing her in-laws later that morning and as she entered the Butcher Shop Café she was contemplating cancelling. It was still her favourite place for breakfast. The red painted cement floor, the huge red letters reading BUTCHERY across the glossy white tiled wall and the French-inspired posters somehow comforted her. A cheeky barista and coffee delivered at record speed reminded her of what she loved about country hospitality. She chose a table in the corner and considered the eclectic mix of furniture: two mint-green laminate tables, one sky blue, the rest different variations of wood, except for hers, which had a tropical-looking top; it reminded her of the last family trip they'd taken to the Gold Coast, and her heart sank again.

As her poached eggs and second cappuccino arrived, Veronica decided she didn't want to see her in-laws; she contemplated texting them, but couldn't think of a lie that would sound like truth. She half-hoped, half-expected them not to show anyway. Life would be easier for her if they didn't and yet she didn't feel she would emotionally cope with another rejection. When Rita and Bob walked in smiling, she felt some sense of relief; maybe it would be okay. But that moment was short-lived, the exchanges were awkward, like those between strangers, air-kisses instead of full-blown hugs. They asked about their grandsons' wellbeing but didn't enquire about her own. There was no warmth, and no interest in what their former daughter-in-law was feeling or doing now. Veronica mentally beat herself up for even calling them and making the effort to see them in the first place. Why did she bother, when this is what it had come to? Loyalty to blood always won out over anything else. Veronica hoped she would not behave the same with her own boys' girlfriends or wives in the future. Rita and Bob each sipped a coffee while Veronica continued to eat. She needed the sustenance to get through the next few hours, which were to be spent being driven to a new winery the pair had just invested in. It was something they could leave to their grandsons.

At Uncle Ron's mid-morning there were dozens of family members from across the state still paying their respects. The aunties were drinking tea in the kitchen and the men were outside in the garden. Ellen saw her mother and her siblings in a different light. She had missed them and she finally had the chance to grieve for her aunt.

'You were your Aunt's favourite niece,' Uncle Ron had whispered to her as she washed what seemed to be an endless stream of teacups. 'But you're not supposed to have favourites so don't say that to anyone, bub, okay?' Uncle Ron rolled a cigarette.

'Okay.' Ellen was lost for words, grateful just for a few minutes alone with her Uncle before he was gone again, sitting outside with the other men, smoking, yarning, laughing about old times.

Xanthe woke early and called Spencer. The conversation was warm and loving, both having missed each other on many levels in recent weeks. Neither mentioned anything about babies or pregnancy. They talked about the funeral, about Xanthe's family, about how much Mudgee had changed since she'd last visited, how much she wanted them to visit there together sometime soon.

'I miss you, darling,' Spencer said down the line, melting her.

She looked forward to making love to her husband when she got home. In the meantime, she would take herself off to the Mudgee Yoga Centre to stretch her limbs and clear her mind.

It was late when Nadine woke and though she felt contrite for those actions she could remember, it didn't matter. Richard and the kids had already left for the day, and all she had was a hastily scrawled note from Cam:

Mum, we're going to the Honey Haven and some other cool places. Dad said you have to go to book thing alone. Love Cam.

That stung. Nadine had never had to fend for herself if Richard was around. He always went with her to events if the girls didn't or he at least chauffeured her there. Nadine knew he was cranky with her, but she couldn't piece together everything that had happened the previous day. She remembered his mother angry and shouting at her, and that was about it.

Around 2 p.m. Nadine walked to the Mudgee Bookcase to do a signing as part of a promotional lead-up to the Readers' Festival. She had two quick wines at the Waratah Hotel on the way, wondering if the girls would all go back there for trivia that night. When she walked into the bookstore she saw the signing table surrounded by guitars on one side and brightly coloured ukuleles on another; burnt orange, lolly pink, midnight and sky blue.

'Have I missed something?' she asked the owner, Jill.

'Would you believe we have four professional ukulele players here in town,' Jill said proudly.

'Well, had you not told me, then no, I wouldn't have believed it,' Nadine said, picking up a brochure about the upcoming Huntington Music Festival, one of the biggest in the world. She wondered if the ukulele was featured on the program.

By the time Nadine sat down, the store was packed with not only crime fiction fans but many locals wanting to get a glimpse of one of the most famous people to have been born in their town. She was surprised when so many turned up to buy her book, get her autograph, have their photo taken with her and play 'do you remember when?' Everyone shared positive stories, friendly, generous stories; many she had to think hard to recall in any real detail. It was a response she could not and would not allow herself to imagine before and yet she didn't know why. It reminded her of what she used to like about being an author: meeting her readers, sharing stories, hearing about others wanting to write books. She left the store late afternoon feeling good about being back in Mudgee. She expected Richard to have come looking for her, but he hadn't. When she turned on her phone there was no message either. She was buzzing from an unusually pleasant day, and she wanted to share the experience with Richard, but when she tried calling him his phone was off. She thought about calling Izzy and hesitated before deciding against it. Her relatively good mood had quickly changed.

Nadine was desperate for a drink and momentarily considered going back to the Waratah Hotel, diagonally opposite the bookstore, but she wanted to hide, be somewhere less central to the activity of the town. She walked quickly along Church Street then turned right into Market Street and was at Roth's

Wine Bar within minutes. The bar had just opened and the staff were already stoking the fire as Nadine considered the wine list on the blackboard. It wasn't premeditated but by the time she'd leave she'd have worked her way through the entire list of reds by the glass, starting with the Lowe Tinja Merlot, noting that it was an organic wine that Xanthe would appreciate. *I'll order a couple of cases when I get home*, she made a mental note to herself.

As she considered the depth of the merlot grapes she was glad that, perched on a bar stool at the high chrome table, she was alone, save for two other women enjoying their own large glasses of wine. *Are they escaping and hiding too*, she wondered, hoping they were, so she wouldn't be the only woman doing it. She stared into the red-glass candle holder in the centre of the table and as the third glass of wine started to kick in lost her balance, nearly falling off the stool. Aware of the catastrophe that would present, not to mention the unwanted attention from the other women and staff, she removed herself to the couch, a shorter distance to the brick floor. As she got comfortable with a cushion and imagined sitting cosily there for a few hours more her phone beeped with a text message from Richard and her heart lifted slightly. On opening it she found a photo of Cam and Brittany at the Honey Haven, Brit with a plush bumblebee toy, Cam holding a bucket of honey in each hand. The text simply read:

> *Mum, there's 30 different types of honey here. I'm getting strawberry honey and Cam's getting banana honey. It's awesome. Luv, Brit XX*

Nadine felt like a bad mother. She knew she should've been there too, not about to order her fourth glass of wine.

Izzy had a restless night's sleep, more anxious than she'd been since finding out she was pregnant.

She was grateful for reuniting with her cousin Aleshia at the funeral, because she had offered to take Izzy to revisit some local sites. She was showered and dressed when Aleshia arrived at 9 a.m. Izzy knew that being back on country and allowing herself the time to think, to speak privately to her ancestors, would help her find the strength she so desperately needed to move forward.

Heading out along Ulan Road, the effects of the three coal mines raping the countryside could be seen from the street. Izzy was distraught seeing the guts of her land being ripped open, dug out, sold to foreign investors like something you get from the $2 shop. The enormity of the pits was mind blowing.

When Aleshia pulled into the place called Hands On Rock, Izzy knew they had reached the traditional boundary of the Wiradjuri and Wonaruah nations. Theirs was the only car there that day. Izzy thought it felt eerie; it had been many years since she had visited and the last time she was too young to appreciate the meaning of the place, where only women and males up to the age of initiation could go.

Izzy's head was spinning; she had pinned all her hopes on getting some answers from this trip back to country. Some guidance, wisdom, enlightenment.

'Everyone round here thinks that a women's place means a birthing place,' Aleshia said as she gathered some kindling and gum leaves. Izzy broke off new leaves as well, grateful that her cousin was active in the land council and kept culture alive for the locals and visitors.

As Aleshia lit the gum leaves packed into a metal fire pit Izzy could smell the eucalyptus oil. She listened to the light breeze rustling through the trees, age old gums that held the spirits of her ancestors.

'This was a women's place and over that way is the meeting place where ceremonies and trading happened,' Aleshia said, rubbing white ochre onto her hands, arms and face. 'The Kamilaroi and coastal nations like the Worimi used to trade with our mob.'

Izzy also prepared herself, silently acknowledging and paying respect to the spirits of her old people, just as she did when she visited other people's country. She waved the cleansing smoke over herself, knowing the purifying effects of a cultural practice that had been passed on from generation to generation to generation.

A path had been defined and stabilised from the entrance to the now famous rock art about 600 metres away, so the trek was easier than Izzy remembered it. But it was still an effort, requiring concentration. The two cousins spoke little, Aleshia naming a few plants from time to time and Izzy asking questions about how school groups behaved when visiting. With each step Izzy imagined the songs, ceremonies and dances that would have been performed and exchanged at the site, and how the social, cultural and economic aspects of

Aboriginal life were once integrated, unlike today's Western cultures.

'What was that?' Izzy jumped.

'Just a branch snapping,' Aleshia laughed.

Izzy realised how much of a city slicker she'd become, not recognising the nuances of nature any more. She concentrated harder on what she knew about history, about her mob, about everything her mother had told her in her lifetime about the corroborees that may have involved hundreds of people, depending on the occasion, and how they might have included people from hundreds of kilometres around. Aunty Molly's funeral was like the ceremonies of the past, with the same sense of responsibility and involvement from people from around the nation.

When they reached the now heritage-listed sandstone overhang, Izzy was pleased that National Parks had protected the area with a wooden deck and railing. You could look but not touch.

She started scanning the sandstone for images and the first that caught her eye was that of a child's hand. It seemed to be reaching out to her. She had been there only seconds when she got the message she needed. She stumbled slightly and leaned back against the metal railing as she deciphered more outlines: adult hands and emu feet.

'Are you all right?' Aleshia asked.

'I will be,' Izzy said confidently. 'I will be.'

Two hours later, tea was being poured again in Cox Street. Izzy sat with her mother as the knitting workshop continued. Richard was there, but Nadine and the kids were shopping on Church Street. There were booties everywhere; Trish was the fastest knitter this side of the Great Dividing Range.

'I'm making some for you, Isobel.' Her mother didn't look up, just kept knitting; purl one, knit one, purl one, knit one.

Richard looked at Izzy. She smiled at him, and then winked; she hadn't yet told him her news.

'I know Mum, I know.' Izzy loved seeing her mother relishing the grandmother experience. 'Why don't you make me a couple of pairs?'

Richard looked surprised but had so much on his plate with his own domestic dramas that he said nothing. He didn't need to because Trish, even at seventy-five, was capable of reacting enthusiastically for both of them, jumping out of her recliner and hugging her daughter tightly. Richard gently put his hand on her shoulder during the embrace.

'Being a mother will turn out to be your greatest reward, Izzy, better than all the pay cheques, all the fancy clothes and cars, all those holidays and stuff you seem to like. When you hold that baby, I'm telling you, you will see why you were put on earth, Isobel, mark my words if I am not one hundred per cent right about that.'

9

Mabo Day

Back in Brisbane the next day, Izzy was completely focused on the long list of interviews she had to do. Thanks to her hectic schedule she had no time to think about what she had to do later that night: tell Asher he was going to be a father. It was a conversation she had over-analysed, scripted and re-scripted on a loop in her head, but still she knew she'd struggle when the time came to release the words and say, 'I'm pregnant.'

She was grateful they'd agreed to meet tonight, Mabo Day, 3 June, as it was shaping up to be one of the busiest days she'd experienced since starting her job. Izzy knew she'd have no time to walk in emotional circles, ride the Lazy Eye and, unfortunately for her sense of peace, she'd have no time to sit in the Nepalese Pagoda and meditate either. Her entire day had been dictated to her, and her thoughts would only begin to be hers again when events in the cultural precinct had officially concluded.

A gigantic Torres Strait Islander flag hung on the outside of the Queensland Performing Arts Centre and could be seen by the traffic that cruised over the William Jolly Bridge. The whole area around the State Library, GOMA, the Queensland Art Gallery and the Museum was crawling with people from early morning, and the outdoor areas had been transformed into a place that was filled with vibrant colour. The faint smells of curry lingered as food stalls and others selling arts and crafts were setting up. In the background the entrancing sounds of Islander music and drums wafted through the air, piped from speakers on every building. On the lawns between the library and the gallery, a Sea of Hands installation had been erected by Australians for Native Title and Reconciliation volunteers, and technicians were setting up microphones for the performances that would run throughout the day.

It was 9 a.m. and Brisbane was preparing to commemorate the life of Eddie Koiki Mabo. With so many Torres Strait Islanders living in Queensland, it was a public holiday in the State, but the date was yet to be made a national day of celebration. After the telemovie *Mabo* hit Australian screens in 2012, there'd been an increase in awareness of the man from Murray Island who fought for the native title rights to his land by overturning the legal fiction of terra nullius. More and more Australians were seeing him as a hero to be honoured, revered and, most importantly, remembered.

For Izzy's part, today reminded her of what she loved about her job. Would she be able to do so much culturally significant work if employed by a mainstream network? Would she miss the community connection that fed her soul? Maybe staying where she was wasn't such a bad idea. She didn't have time to dissect her career goals today though, or contemplate what Tracey would have to say at the sudden change of heart, so she opened her black leather portfolio and ran through her schedule for the day.

A highlight for her would be recording the Mabo Lecture being delivered by a local leader in the library's main auditorium. She'd long admired his work in Indigenous education and had seen the benefits of his Stronger Smarter Institute for the community generally, but for young Murris specifically. She'd interviewed him before, most recently on the release of his memoir, but today, the focus of his address and any questions she might have would be solely on the work of the late activist.

Throughout the day she'd pop in and out of kuril dhagun to get vox pops from those viewing the exhibition of Torres Strait Islander visual artists and basket makers. A day-long workshop was planned where school children could make their own baskets as well as dharis and grass skirts. Dance and song lessons were also on the program, and a kup-murri was being prepared in the yarning circle. A big feast was sure to attract a huge crowd; a good feed always did. Mabo Day was the perfect opportunity for non-Indigenous locals to get among some of the best cultural practices Torres Strait Islanders had to offer on the mainland.

When the Jaran Aboriginal and Torres Strait Islander Dance Company performed in Suncorp Plaza it made the perfect backdrop to Izzy's interview with musical favourite Uncle Seaman Dan. As Izzy signed off her show, ready for an edit before airing on the arts channel later that night, she was glad her working day had ended, but she knew the real challenge for the day lay only an hour ahead of her.

As she boarded the City Cat from South Bank 2 heading to West End, Izzy was exhausted. She was hungry. She wanted a glass of wine, just one, but reminded herself that she couldn't, and started scripting in her head again. The next time she spoke to anyone it would be Asher and she'd be delivering the most significant unprepared lines she'd ever spoken. But this time there'd be no cameras.

Izzy sat at the bar picking at the herbed polenta which she previously would have devoured mouthful by large mouthful. She looked at the Hong Kong Phooey cocktail she'd ordered as a decoy but hadn't touched it, knowing it could instantly become Hong Kong Spewy. She knew Asher would think something was wrong straightaway if she didn't eat or drink something, so she took a small sip from the long straw and hoped the baby wouldn't end up pickled.

'I've made you a new dish, Iz, an extra special vegie stack. I think you'll like it.'

Asher gently placed the colourful vegetarian dish in front of her, proud of his culinary attempts. He trusted her judgement because she had always been honest with him. That is until now. They hadn't seen each other for almost two months, the longest period they'd gone without sex with the other, but Asher had been insanely busy doing a series of auditions for *Masterchef: the Professionals*, and even when he tried to make time Izzy would avoid the meeting, always ready with a list of pseudo-reasons as to why they couldn't meet up. Phone calls and late night text messages had been used just to check in, stay connected and debrief about their work, but without saying anything, they both knew something was wrong.

Izzy eyed the dish, not feeling any desire to even pick up her fork, but on seeing Asher's smile she felt a surge of pride in his efforts, and took a mouthful. His eyes widened waiting for a response.

'You've outdone yourself, Flasher, the bar is the highest it's ever been.'

'I love cooking for you,' he whispered, somehow puffing his already large chest out even further.

Izzy was so proud of him. His career would change dramatically because of the baby. Or would it? Would he be like most men and expect her to stay home and be a mother while he maintained the path to his career dream, and she changed nappies and breastfed? Would she end up like Veronica? Izzy shook her head and frowned at the thought.

'What's wrong, Iz?' Asher asked, assuming she'd lied and actually didn't like the meal he'd placed in front of her.

His face resembled that of a wounded child, and Izzy felt an emotion for him she'd never experienced before. She wanted to hug him, not in lust, but in another way.

Asher put his hand on Izzy's in a show of intimacy they'd never really had before, not in public.

'What is it?' Asher asked again, knowing that his usually bubbly lover was not her normal self. Izzy just wanted to collapse like the vegie stack had when she first dug into it. She hadn't been lying to him all these weeks, but nor had she been completely honest. How would he feel about that on top of news of the pregnancy itself? Izzy could do a perfect poker face when interviewing people she didn't like or didn't agree with, but she couldn't hide what was in her heart with her friends and family – or with Asher.

'I'm just exhausted,' she said, only half-lying.

She *was* tired, mentally, physically and emotionally, and she knew the exhaustion was compounded by the extreme guilt she was feeling. The day would've left her lethargic anyway, but with the emotional journey she'd been on the past few months, she just wanted to lie down and sleep and cry. Izzy had already started wearing looser clothing, but hadn't shopped specifically for maternity wear. She was experiencing some pain when standing up and imagined her body starting to stretch. A call home to her mother earlier in the week told her it was completely normal, albeit uncomfortable.

'Come on,' he said, removing the plate from in front of her. 'I'm finished, I'll take you home.'

Asher was a good man. An honest, caring, kind man. He would make a great dad. He would make a great partner too. Why had they never thought about being a proper couple, doing things in the daylight together, going to the park, walking along the river, eating somewhere other than his work? Why didn't they go to the movies, have weekends away, drive up or down the coast? Why had they only found companionship in the bedroom and in their career dreams? Why had Izzy never seen what a thoughtful, considerate man Asher was before now? Was she forcing herself to see him this way because now she really needed him, whereas before she just wanted him?

That night they made love. It was gentle, slow. Izzy hadn't been able to tell Asher before they fell asleep. She clung to him all night, afraid it might be the last night they'd be together. She didn't want to lose him as a friend, as a lover, at all. Anxiety woke her at 3 a.m. and she could feel herself wanting to cry, but willed herself not to. She didn't want to wake him. She didn't want to have the conversation in bed. Their whole existence outside of his restaurant had been between her sheets. Her baby, *their* baby deserved more than a late night teary conversation that would most likely end up badly, with Asher walking out on her, on them. Izzy wanted a more dignified ending if that's what was going to happen. She lay dead still, staring at the ceiling with one hand on her belly, the other in Asher's hand. They'd fallen asleep holding hands like kids do when walking in pairs on a school excursion. Izzy started counting sheep, black ones, and then told herself *go to sleep, go to sleep, go the fuck to sleep.* Eventually she was lulled into slumber that lasted until a rooster crowed at dawn and she woke instantly.

Asher was already up and in the shower when she opened her eyes. She knew she couldn't let another day go by and when he came into the bedroom naked she looked at his toned, tanned body and felt a pang of missing him already. Even though they only had a night-time friendship, Izzy realised that Asher had really been her boyfriend for six months, even if they never acknowledged to each other or anyone else they'd been in a relationship. Asher pulled on his jeans and t-shirt and walked over to kiss her goodbye. She sat upright in bed. She couldn't let him leave, couldn't go another day without telling him.

'Do you want to go out for something to eat?' she asked without hesitation.

Asher didn't look shocked, although he should've. They'd never been out for breakfast before, they didn't 'do breakfast'. They did dinner, during or after his shift while she sat at the bar. But Asher was easygoing, he liked food, he liked Izzy, so he simply said, 'Sure.'

Not long after, they were in the shaded courtyard at the back of the Gunshop Café. Izzy had missed it since giving up her morning coffee. When Asher went to the bathroom she eyed off the potted herbs on an arty metal frame lining the wall. She wondered if anyone would notice one missing. She could take it to its death with the other plants on her balcony.

Sitting on the wooden chair she was fidgety. It felt like a date; they'd never been on a date. She wondered if Asher thought something was up. Did men ever think beyond their bellies and their dicks? Then she started to panic. *Why did I bring him here to tell him? What if he freaks out? I'll never be able to come back here.*

She felt cold all of a sudden. She wanted to feel the sun

on her arms and her face, but the Queensland rays were brutal, she'd been told many times. The locals didn't want to sit in the sun. They wanted the shade to protect them. Even women walking at 6 a.m. wore hats. They were whitefellas though. Izzy always thought her pigment would save her; after all, she'd never heard of a Blackfella with melanoma. Her thoughts were scattered all over the place, and she was grateful when Asher finally arrived back at the table.

'I love it here. Why haven't we done this before?' Asher said, looking at the menu. 'We never go out for breakfast. Great idea, Iz, great idea.'

Izzy was confused. They never went out for breakfast because *he* never suggested it.

'I have something to tell you,' Izzy said, desperate to get it over and done with before she lost her courage. 'I probably should've told you earlier, but . . .' she stopped herself. Was she going to say she'd once considered an abortion and wouldn't have told him if that had been the case?

He doesn't need to know that, Izzy mentally ordered herself. *He might hate you even more if you tell him that. Stick to what needs to be said, and only that!*

'I'm pregnant,' she blurted out, just like she did with her brother in Mudgee. She looked around the courtyard to see if anyone else heard her, but what did it matter? She was having their baby, and Asher was more than likely going to get up and walk out immediately anyway.

Before Asher even had time to respond Izzy kept going, trying to piece together the script she'd had in her head since Mudgee.

'I'm not telling you this because I want anything from you. I can manage this by myself, and my family will help. My tiddas will be great support, and I am going to sort something out at work. Actually I'll probably stay at the library now, rather than chasing the other job I had in mind, you know, because it will be easier to negotiate my leave if I stay where I am.' She was ranting, she could hear herself coming undone, almost sounding a bit crazy, unsure of her plans, and totally inarticulate compared to her onscreen persona. And yet she couldn't stop herself.

'I wouldn't ask you to come to the antenatal classes anyway, even though they are recommended for first time parents.' *Fuck*! she thought to herself, *why am I saying all of this?* But she couldn't stop herself. 'I need to go of course because I haven't got the faintest clue about being pregnant, or babies generally. I can't remember the last time I changed a nappy even.' And she couldn't. 'It doesn't matter, because I'm sure Ellen will come, and Xanthe knows everything there is to know about pregnancy, and well . . .'

She stopped herself, knowing that Asher wouldn't really want to know about their strained friendship caused by her having considered a termination. But he was still sitting there, looking at her, faintly smiling yet looking concerned, or was it confused? She didn't want there to be dead air like on radio or TV which was just awkward and so started again. 'But really, I'm good, it's all good. So, you don't need to worry about anything.'

'Izzy,' Asher put his hand on hers again, making that two public displays of affection in twenty-four hours. 'Stop raving, it's okay.'

She couldn't believe how calm he was, that he hadn't left the table yet.

'It's not okay. I'm pregnant, didn't you hear what I just said?' Izzy asked, feeling tears build up.

Asher sat there, still holding her hand, saying nothing, looking bemused. Izzy wondered if it was a look of entrapment. Did he feel trapped? He just looked at her hands, saying nothing, and ran his fingers along her palms. Izzy was confused about his reaction and feared the worst.

'Say something,' she said, because she knew if he didn't she'd start raving again. She started up again anyway. 'You don't want the baby, do you? I knew you wouldn't. I don't blame you . . .'

'Stop it, Izzy, please,' Asher said with a touch of force. 'Stop it. You need to give a man a minute to think, okay? I'm not as quick as you are.'

Izzy felt chastised, silly, embarrassed. Tears filled her eyes.

'I honestly don't know what you must think of me, obviously not very much if you think that I would let you do this alone.' He took a breath. 'That I wouldn't be excited about my own child.' Asher waved an approaching waitress away and moved the salt and pepper shakers from the middle of the table so he could take both Izzy's hands in his.

'I'm a bit shocked because, well, you know, we're always careful, but it doesn't mean I'm not happy.'

'Really?' Izzy was in shock too.

'Of course. I care about you. I care about us. You're the woman in my life, Izzy, the only woman. This actually makes sense. We're both just too busy worrying about our careers to see that this is how normal people live their lives – with kids as well.'

He looked deep into Izzy's eyes, which were now full of tears. She had never cried in front of him before. She'd never had reason to; theirs was a calm, safe space always. He had never looked at her so intensely before either. Izzy was crying and rummaging for a tissue in her bag. Asher handed her a serviette.

'We can do this together, this is *our* baby. It will be beautiful and clever like you, and calm and funny like me,' he joked.

Izzy had never noticed before that Asher was, in fact, quite funny. Sitting opposite her was a man who she had been intimate with but never really close to.

Asher got up and walked around the table. He leant down and kissed Izzy on the mouth. She was in shock, not expecting such a loving reaction. He sat back down and pushed his chair in. 'You are a very clever woman. We are clever. We made a Murri baby.'

'Koori baby,' she said.

'Go the Maroons,' Asher joked.

'Go the Blues.'

'Don't be giving our kid an identity crisis before it's even born,' he added.

'I'm going to get fat,' Izzy said. 'I already am,' she patted her belly.

'I didn't want to say anything because I think you're the sexiest I've ever seen you, but I did notice your breasts were huge last night.' Asher cupped his hands like a typical bloke on the grope. He was calm and considerate, but he was also human.

A photo of a white station wagon appeared on the screen of Izzy's phone. It was the third that morning, and only twenty-four hours since she had told Asher she was pregnant. The pic made her smile and shake her head simultaneously. Asher was behaving completely the opposite to what she had expected. His enthusiasm helped her feel even more sure about managing the baby when it came and she momentarily wondered how she could ever have thought about terminating. Nothing in her life had felt as positive as it did that morning.

Izzy felt compelled to call Xanthe who, as it turned out, was doing training at the new ABC headquarters at South Bank, a much sexier building than the old Toowong site. Izzy had thought to ask Xanthe to be Godmother, but realised it was probably too early, and would more than likely look like an attempted consolation prize. Her friend was still desperate to get pregnant. They agreed to meet for coffee at the café below the studios facing the river.

'Hello lovely,' Izzy greeted Xanthe with a new spring in her step.

'You look fabulous,' Xanthe said, admiring her tidda.

They sat at a table at the back as producers and broadcasters cluttered the front tables planning their future programs. Izzy smiled a hello to a well-known broadcaster from the *Speaking Out* program, known around the traps for her brightly coloured, but forever-changing fringe. This week it was fuchsia and it was as bright as Izzy felt.

Izzy took a deep breath. 'I've told Asher about the baby.'

'That's good, he needed to know,' Xanthe said, always having been conscious of the moral need to do so. 'And?'

'He's happy, he's enthusiastic. He's out looking at station wagons.' She showed Xanthe the pics on her phone. 'He's also a little crazy,' Izzy laughed, feeling like an infatuated schoolgirl.

'I'm glad it's working out.'

Xanthe was genuinely happy for Izzy, but she still felt jealous; it should've been her. Her red blood was running green with envy and she hated herself for feeling that way. Xanthe covered what she felt and thought well, though; there was no way she was going to allow her own inability to have children ruin Izzy's moment.

'Xanthe,' Izzy said softly. 'I know this isn't easy for you. But I am so glad you are doing this with me. I need you; I need you more than anything to be there for me. You are going to be a great mother when it happens, I know that. But until then, can you help me be one, because I haven't got a fucking clue what I'm supposed to do.'

By the time Izzy finished they were both crying. Xanthe's envy had dissipated and she was grateful to be part of Izzy's new journey.

Izzy's phone beeped. She assumed it was going to be Asher with another car picture and she reached for her phone excitedly, but it was from Ellen.

Vee's birthday is coming up, what are we doing? X

Izzy texted back:

Just having coffee with Xanthe, we'll think of some ideas and email later. XX

The two women spent the next few minutes throwing around venues for Veronica's birthday. They decided on a Sunday lunch at Sake and said goodbye with a hug that was longer than usual. A bond that had almost broken months before had been strengthened. Izzy walked back to work with a newfound lightness in her heart. The mother-to-be made her way straight to the human resources section to tell them she was pregnant.

Everything felt right. It was time to call Tracey.

'Hey,' she said with a feigned sense of confidence when the phone answered. 'How are you?' She had virtually avoided any serious or lengthy conversations with her agent for nearly three months, preferring to answer any calls with brief text messages.

'I'm good,' Tracey laughed, knowing exactly what was going on. They may have had a contract binding them legally, but having worked together for so long meant there was no getting away with changes in tone and general behaviour. Tracey had known that Izzy would have the baby and had been planning the next move for her client and friend for months. 'And how are you?'

'Well, I'm going to be a mum.' Izzy felt happy when she said it, although still a little fearful of Tracey's wrath. 'So we need to talk, I guess, about what the next step is.' She had her eyes shut, waiting for the sound of disappointment. 'I can't sign that other contract now,' Izzy said, feeling confident in herself for the first time since she'd mentioned the pregnancy to Tracey.

Tracey laughed down the line. 'Yes love, I knew that all along. I've dealt with it.'

'Thank you! You are the deadliest agent in the country.'

'Yes I am,' Tracey said, and continued in her professional tone. 'I've repackaged our pitch, and am planning on getting a new sizzle piece together with you in full pregnant bloom. I think we should go for a mainstream, early hours working mothers' show. Strategies for making your family first priority while living your own career dream.'

'I love it,' Izzy said, 'and I love you.'

The women chatted about the plans for the next few months, but Tracey also wanted all the goss on Asher and the new car.

'I expect the ins and outs of everything,' she said.

Back at home in Paddington, Xanthe could still feel something in the pit of her stomach that couldn't be considered joy. The emptiness of being without a child still haunted her, as did Spencer's continued insistence that he didn't want to try

IVF. 'We do it naturally or not at all,' he said. And in his stubbornness, refused to say any more. Every time she thought of his absolute 'no' she felt devastated all over again. She reached into her handbag and pulled out the pregnancy test kit she'd been carrying round for days. She walked into the bathroom and prepared herself for another disappointment.

10

A Birthday, A Ball and Some Bad Behaviour

Even though for the bulk of her life Veronica had been a selfless mother and wife, she enjoyed playing chauffeur, doing tuckshop, overseeing teenage sleepovers and being one of the lesser 'yummy mummy' soccer mums. Decisions about the children and anything to do with the home she had mostly made alone; she selected the gardener, the plants, the pool cleaner, the carpet, the schools, the tutors and the holiday destinations. She had always thought it was because Alex had trusted her judgement. In reality, it was because he never really cared about what happened at home, as long as it happened without fuss. Only now was she realising that her ex was a self-absorbed narcissist.

Veronica had always been the emotional rock for her three sons. By the time their father left they were young men, which was a blessing to Veronica who was on the verge of a breakdown and had to consciously pull herself out of bed every day. She focused all her strength on calming their anger while trying to pick up the remnants of her own heart. The boys hated their father for deserting their mother for another, much younger woman.

The bond between mothers and their sons was a mystery to many and Veronica's relationship with hers was no different; her boys were loyally protective of the woman who had always been and *would* always be there for them. They didn't talk to 'the prick' (their new title for Alex) for months, and only at their mother's insistence did they refrain from bad-mouthing his new partner. Even in her darkest moments, Veronica remained dignified, discouraging her sons' ill feeling towards the man who had given them life, who had once loved her, and whom she thought she still loved. Although her tiddas believed she was completely justified in doing so, Veronica *never* commented on the woman who ripped their family apart. In her head, the best she could do was imagine slapping her across the face; just once, but very, very hard.

Although living essentially alone now, Veronica had always loved her life in The Gap. It had been her home away from Mudgee in the decades since she and Alex moved to Brisbane. Marcus was already two years old back then. They set up home in Nina Street and stayed put. The suburb had grown and thrived around her, and even though it was now the second biggest after Mount Gravatt, it was still small enough to feel like a community. With its mix of young families, single parents and retirees, it was her home. And aside from the occasional bogan burn-outs that frightened her, the place she raised her family was still quiet and peaceful. She felt safe and happily cocooned among the double-brick 1970s houses, and the new estates springing up nearby.

Her two-storey, architecturally designed house was nestled in a peaceful, leafy cul-de-sac close to the local shopping village and public transport, although she mostly drove the gold Lexus her ex left in the garage and which she'd claim in the divorce settlement. With her fondness for the best of both worlds, Veronica loved being close to the city while still being able to live in a semi-bush setting. The scrub turkeys that roamed the streets never bothered her like they bothered Alex, or Izzy. The screaming galahs and cockatoos made her smile, but drove Alex insane. The crows perched along the wires and rooflines entertained her, but Alex wanted to bait them. When she realised he was so annoyed all the time because he didn't actually want to be there at all, she started to purposely feed the birds that would flock to their house. That was the nastiest premeditated thing Veronica ever did in her entire life.

Of all the tiddas, Veronica appreciated wildlife the most. She would often take herself to the walking tracks of D'Aguilar National Park. And while all the locals and her neighbours were afraid of the ghost gums come storm time, she wasn't. Veronica always had faith that if the big wind blew it would blow away from her house. She had an afternoon tradition of sitting outside reading by her pool, admiring her roses in winter, the jacarandas in springtime and the palm trees all year round. She would even sit there when it rained, and because The Gap was storm city – it was often sunny everywhere else but raining at her place – she saw a lot of water fall and nourish the landscaped gardens around her.

Strolling local streets made Veronica appreciate how the natural environment had changed over time. On her walks she often considered the local parks named after whitefellas or British places – Aberdeen Court and Glenferrie, for example, as well as the many streets with Murri names – Currawang, Murrua, Yuruga, Cooinda, Bombala. She didn't know many Murris in her suburb, but there were two sisters she regularly saw walking the bike path of an evening. They were always laughing with each other and sometimes had an extra person with them; every time Vee saw them she wished she could join in. In her head she had scripted what she wanted to say: 'I'm a reconciliationist, I respect the Turrbul owners, I signed a hand for the Sea of Hands when it came to Brisbane, and I only watch NITV.' Veronica desperately wanted them to know her best friends were Kooris from New South Wales, that she called them her tiddas, and that she too cried when Kevin Rudd said 'sorry'. She wanted to explain that growing up in Mudgee and reconnecting with her Wiradjuri tiddas – Izzy, Ellen and Xanthe – in Brisbane, meant that she had always had her radar up in terms of culture, heritage and politics. She wanted them to know that her tiddas always said she had a 'black heart' in a good way.

But she never said any of it. She was always too insecure, too scared, not of them, but of rejection and the impact it could have on her already fragile self-esteem. Veronica knew that she would sound like a try-hard, a desperado, someone without their own identity wanting to latch onto someone else's place in the world. She'd heard Izzy and Ellen talk about whitefellas like that, and she didn't want these local Murri women to think that about *her.* She reasoned they might not want to let her into their tight group anyway, that even if they did they would probably dump her like Alex did, because she wasn't good enough. Veronica kept the negative conversation with herself on a loop in her head, and would walk past them smiling, hoping that one day they would stop to talk to her.

A lot of the local area had been badly damaged during the big storm in November 2008, when ferocious winds hit The Gap like a mini tornado. The suburb had been left looking, in the then PM's words, like a 'war zone'. Hailstones made their way through Veronica's dog door in the kitchen shortly after their dog fled through it. But she was out helping those whose houses were flattened in School Road as soon as the clean-up began; partially because she was a Good Samaritan, but also because such community efforts were a rare break in her otherwise mundane life.

'Routine' was how Veronica usually described her life to others. Every Monday she did her groceries at Aldi in Ashgrove where she found the cheapest cling wrap this side of the Brisbane River. Leaving with the plastic roll and anything else she could get on sale, she'd take herself for a coffee at Tutto Café because she loved the prints of the Colosseum and the Eiffel Tower. The images would transport her to Rome and Paris in the time it took her to drink a latte and eat a piece of carrot cake. It's not that she wanted to escape

The Gap forever, but family holidays were always back to Mudgee and in later years up to Bali, and she'd never been to Europe. Even though she had planned the trips, she did so knowing that they were about what Alex really wanted and designed to appease growing boys who didn't really want to go anywhere with their parents at all.

When her boys were at school the Gap Tavern was her main social gathering place. The mothers with sons at Ashgrove State School and Marist Ashgrove – which had graduated the likes of Kevin Rudd and John Eales – would meet once a month at what they called the GT for a ladies' lunch. The gatherings had died down since the boys had all finished and even now Vee only went there on Monday nights with John. Barra-Monday was their thing, a sacred mealtime ritual mother and son shared. On Friday nights, though, like any healthy young fella, John didn't want to be with his mother; he'd rather be on Caxton Street or at the Normanby Hotel with the other young partygoers. Veronica couldn't expect her baby to hang out with her on weekends either, so she spent those days cooking up a storm, preparing platters of food for when he arrived home with mates.

When the boys were young, the GT was also where the family would go every Friday night as a treat. The patriarch was often missing though; patients still in the surgery, a conference in another city, or one of a dozen other reasons. Veronica never considered that all the time he wasn't with the family he was with another woman. Why would she think that? Didn't they have everything they needed with each other? She was a devoted wife, a loving homemaker, a caring but not helicopter mother, and a friend to anyone who wanted her to be.

The tavern wasn't a flash establishment, not compared to some of the bars Izzy and Ellen would hang out in, like French Martini, but to Veronica it was the perfect setting for laughter, stories, families and friends. It was a place where mothers talked to each other about school and their kids, their husbands being painful when sick, and at times their own lack of self-esteem. It was a time that Veronica looked forward to because she loved hearing about what was happening in the other women's lives, and it was a place where she could find someone else to take an interest in the decisions she made around the house; carpet, drapes and recipes *did* matter to others, just not the people she lived with in Nina Street.

She occasionally went to the GT nowadays with a handful of the mothers she still saw from school, but her social life was more often than not just a soy chai latte and chips with aioli at Tara, a local café within walking distance of her home. She went there on her own, taking with her whatever book was on the list for book club or whatever the hot pick for the week was from the library. Veronica often saw another woman there doing the same, but they never spoke. Veronica was friendly but she wasn't forward, so they would just smile an 'I-like-my-me-time' smile, sip their lattes and get on with their days. To mix up her routine, Veronica would sometimes go to the Coffee Club and face the busy street, all the while trying to hide from the owners of Tara, for fear she would be seen as betraying them. By all accounts Veronica was the most loyal person anyone was likely to meet, and she prided herself on that.

The familiar 'ding' of the front door opening rang across the living room and a bag was thrown on the floor in the entranceway, seconds before a body came through the arch.

'Hey,' John said to his mother who smiled back at her six-foot tall baby son. He walked over and kissed his mum on the cheek. 'Sorry, I'm all sweaty.'

Ellen and Xanthe just watched the love between mother and son, then waited for him to make his way around the table. John *always* greeted them with a peck and smile. Marist schooling had created real gentlemen of Veronica's boys; it was just a pity her husband hadn't gone there.

'Hi, Aunty Ellen, hey, Aunty Xanthe.' The young man, stinky from soccer training, had always called them aunty.

'There's some apricot chicken in the oven for you when you're ready. Do you want me to put some rice on?'

'Nah Mum, you know I don't do carbs of a night. I'll eat the chook though, thanks, it's my favourite.' John walked towards the stairwell. 'I'll jump in the shower first though.' As he left the room Ellen's eyes followed his muscular calves and broad shoulders.

'What a lovely boy,' Xanthe said. 'So polite. I can only hope to have a son half as charming.'

'Yeah, lovely all right. He's HOT!' Ellen said.

'God, you are terrible. He's half your age!' Xanthe sounded disgusted. 'And he's like our nephew!'

'And he's my son, if you don't mind,' Veronica chuckled, having learned not to take that kind of comment from Ellen too seriously. She may like to play the field, but Veronica knew Ellen wasn't poaching from a kids' footy field.

'Take my comments as a compliment, Vee, he has *your* genes!' Ellen walked to a window overlooking the quiet street. 'It really is gorgeous here, it's such a pretty, leafy suburb.' Ellen was impressed every time she visited Veronica's, even though she could never live so far from the river herself.

'It's actually the green that I love the most about living here. It's refreshing to get out and walk every day around here,' Veronica said, always happy when someone else recognised that life in the 'burbs could be inspiring too.

'Is it safe around here though, I mean after that bike path rapist they caught a few years back?' Xanthe was concerned, recalling a man going to jail for twenty-five years for attacks on eleven women in the area.

'It's safe now, but before they caught him, one of the boys would walk with me or I just walked in the middle of the day. Now though, the bike path is full of walkers from daylight to dark, so it's pretty safe all the time. Either way, I always take Butch for a walk, so I doubt anyone will come near me.' She turned towards the huge German shepherd lying alongside the pool.

'That dog is a serious man-magnet, Vee. That's what you should call him.' Ellen looked as if a light bulb had just turned on in her head. She spun around from leaning against the screen door. 'Actually, I should borrow Butch sometime when, you know, I'm in need.'

'When you're on heat more like it,' Xanthe said out loud, and out of character, but she giggled anyway.

Ellen threw her an unappreciative look.

'What?' shrieked Xanthe. 'You set yourself up for that one!'

Even though Xanthe was only teasing Ellen, Veronica went into peacemaker mode anyway, changing the subject immediately. 'I'm going to show you some of this lush leafy suburb of mine right now. Did you bring your walking shoes? We should head up to Poet's Corner and meet Izzy and Nadine. It's only a quick stroll from here.'

Veronica had asked the women if they could start their book club meeting at Poet's Corner for a reason. Ellen and Xanthe said they'd park at hers and walk, but the other women were going straight there. Izzy arrived in her convertible, roof down, scarf wrapped elegantly around her head like she was a Thelma in need of a Louise. Her beloved car would soon be traded in for the family wagon Asher had been researching. Nadine climbed out of the four-wheel-drive with Richard waving through the window as he drove off with orders to pick up his wife in three hours. He grinned at his sister's number plate – BLAKFULA – as he pulled out onto Waterworks Road.

They kissed their greetings and Veronica led the women down a small grassy hill to the memorial site known as Poet's Corner.

'I chose the biography *Auntie Rita* for this month because as you'll know from reading the book, she was an inspirational Murri pioneer here at The Gap. And this is a memorial to her.'

The women all leaned in to read the plaque, realising how close they were to one of the country's most loved Aboriginal heroines.

'I came to the unveiling way back in 1994 and there were hundreds of people here. Even the Governor.' Veronica thought back to the day; the sun had been shining and there were kids everywhere.

Now, as the sun went down, the women all felt the sudden drop in temperature.

'I think we should head inside,' Izzy said, worried about getting a cold or even a chill.

'Well, I decided I wanted to take you to the GT for dinner, my treat, something different,' Veronica said enthusiastically, hoping they'd all agree. She wanted a night out, in public, with the noise of patrons and poker machines and laughter. 'We can talk about the book over a steak, or salad, or whatever you want.'

Veronica felt she should be encouraging her tiddas, but the truth was no-one could ever deny Vee anything. She rarely asked for much, contributed only positive comments and was definitely the glue of the group.

As they squeezed into Izzy's car and headed to Glenquarie Place, Ellen asked, 'How many Blackfellas can you fit in a convertible?'

'As many as I have to,' Izzy joked.

'I bet we'll be the only Blackfellas there eh, Vee?' Ellen said as they pulled into the nondescript car park.

'Probably, but no-one will look at you strangely. The whitefellas are pretty good round here, just treat everyone the same,' Veronica said proudly of her local community.

'I reckon I'd have to padlock the doors with so many whites as neighbours.' Izzy almost choked on her own joke.

It was the first time they'd all been to the NAIDOC Ball together. After a week of events, marches, flag raisings, lunches, speeches, readings, performances and an overdose of comments on Facebook and Twitter that each had participated in to varying degrees, including Veronica, the official ball was the one thing they would all do to celebrate the national week together.

The Ball was one of the most prestigious and glamorous annual events that Blackfellas from around the country got frocked up for, and that supportive whitefellas also loved. As soon as the tiddas learned that Brisbane was the host city for the year, they had all started shopping for dresses. Xanthe chose a scarlet silk maxi by Surafina she picked up from a local store in Paddington. Ellen and Izzy drove out to DFO near the airport and spent hours trying on outfits. Izzy was feeling larger than she actually looked so went for something loose but sexy, a leopard jersey dress at a bargain price; now she could also afford a new bag and shoes. Ellen went for a plain, black floor-length gown with gold belt and matching shoes. Richard drove Nadine to The Gap from where Veronica drove her into the city, and the two wealthiest of the tiddas bought their frocks at Lisa Ho. Nadine chose a silk tulle gown with a cross-over bodice in gunmetal, which she knew she'd probably never wear again. Veronica indulged in a blood-red cotton lace cap-sleeve gown that she knew she could get three more events out of if she could ever find somewhere else to go. Although cashed up, Veronica wasn't wasteful and she didn't actually like to shop, so if she could get a lot of wears out of one frock, it was a bonus.

By the time the women met in the lobby of the Convention Centre at South Bank, they looked ready to do a magazine spread. Xanthe took Spencer, Nadine took Richard but the other three women went solo. Veronica had vowed never to date again, Asher was working and couldn't accompany Izzy, and Ellen was on the prowl.

'If a man can't look good in a tux, then he'll never look good,' she said loud enough for at least three brothers to turn around and wink at her. Ellen was determined to get some NAIDOC nookie.

As the evening proceeded the women gave a running commentary on the fashions, the faux pas, the food and the speeches. When the NAIDOC Person of the Year was announced, they all looked at each other wide-eyed. They weren't surprised, given their book club discussion only two months prior.

As the women hit the dance floor the men sat talking football; it was all Spencer and Richard had in common. Male bonding over sport was useful at functions where females danced in circles and went to the toilets in pairs – even in their forties – and the blokes declared bad knees, two left feet and a sudden interest in minding handbags.

For once Xanthe looked like she was letting her hair down as she boogied and shimmied and crumped as good as the younger Murri girls around her. Microwave Jenny and The Last Kinection rocked the stage and over a thousand Blackfellas shook the dance floor.

'My feet are killing me,' Izzy said, unable to feel her toes in her gold heels. 'My back hurts too. I think I'm going to leave soon, get a cab before the rush.'

'I'm coming with you,' Ellen grabbed her arm.

'What about that fella you've been dancing with? He looks keen.'

'I'm looking at him and he looks a little bit like me. I'm fairly sure we're related. I've gotta get outta here before he starts grinding me!' Ellen momentarily had a flashback to Krissy Kneen's book which the tiddas had read some time back for the book club. It had shocked them all, especially the love story between the brother and sister.

'Yes, I seriously need to get out of here, he's coming this way.' Ellen marched Izzy to the table, where Richard and Nadine were having an argument.

'What's going on?' Izzy asked Spencer.

'Oh, I think Nadine might be a bit pissed, and Richard's got the shits.'

Izzy walked around the table and whispered in her brother's ear. 'You need to leave. You're both making a scene.'

'I'm fucking trying, she's out of control. She's never this bad.'

Don't bet on it, Izzy thought to herself.

'Tidda, we're all going now, to beat the rush for cabs. You ready?' Izzy asked as politely as she could because she knew Nadine's reaction could go either way. Her sister-in-law was even more drunk than she had been in Mudgee at the wake. Izzy looked to Veronica for help and she took her cue. A brilliant mother-wanting-to-fix-the-problem!

'Nadine love, can we share a cab? I know it's out of your way but I don't want to go by myself.'

'Anything for you, Vee, you know I love you.' Nadine wriggled out of Izzy's hold and put her arms around Veronica's neck, declaring in slurred words her unconditional love for her tidda. 'Sometimes I think they don't like me cos I'm white. Do you ever feel that?' Nadine whispered loud enough for all the women to hear.

Xanthe just shook her head, Ellen was ready to slap her and Izzy threw a growling look at her brother, as if the whole situation was his fault.

'Let's go,' Izzy said through gritted teeth.

'Where are you?' Ellen was annoyed as she sent a text to Xanthe and Veronica the next morning. 'Bloody hell, I'm the one with the hangover and even *I* can make it on time. These tiddas hardly even fucken drink. Imagine how late they'd be if they did.'

'Too funny,' Izzy said, grateful that she didn't have a

hangover. She was looking forward to a huge breakfast. Izzy had started enjoying eating for two.

Ellen held her head. 'I think I'm dying. I need coffee.' She looked around the courtyard for anyone that resembled a waitress.

'Do you think Nadine will turn up?' she asked, eyes closed, head throbbing.

'Highly unlikely. My brother doesn't get wild that often, and hardly ever with her, but he was furious last night.' Izzy was sending a text to Richard as she spoke. 'I doubt he'll be driving her *anywhere* today.' She hit send and waited for a reply.

'Hey, sorry I'm late,' Veronica said, 'had trouble parking.'

'Me too,' Xanthe added as she appeared at the same time.

'Sit, order, eat!' Ellen was in a bad way. 'We were just wondering if Nadine would make it.'

'I sent her a text this morning, but nothing back.' Veronica sounded disappointed.

'Me too,' Xanthe said as she browsed the menu.

'She'll probably be sleeping it off, like I should be.' Ellen waved over a waitress. 'You girls ready to order?'

Ellen ordered the brioche French toast, Canadian bacon, caramelised banana, candied pecans and maple syrup, and as soon as the waitress left the table, she ran to the bathroom to throw up. She was a health fanatic most of the time so her body was no longer equipped for late nights or too many glasses of bubbly. At least she felt better after her spew. Hopefully she could keep her breakfast down when it finally arrived. As she sat back down, the discussion was still focused on Nadine.

'An intervention,' Xanthe said softly, deeply concerned about the health of her tidda, but conscious of this strategy being a big step. It would involve naming Nadine's problem. 'I think we need to do it. Mudgee, last night, every other book club night she's seriously out of control.'

'I'm not sure,' Veronica said, knowing that Nadine would see any interference as a judgement on her. 'Surely there's another way.'

'What though?'

'An intervention on a whitefella, it's a novel idea if nothing else,' Ellen chimed in.

'Can you be serious, please?' Izzy rested her hand on her growing belly.

'Yes, I think we need to do something for sure. In the first instance though, she has a husband. I think you should speak to your brother, Izzy, and see how we can support *him* to support her.'

'I agree.'

'Me too.'

'That's a plan.'

The women answered in turn, and Izzy nodded. It was time to try to fix the unfixable.

Ellen's phone beeped for the tenth time in as many minutes.

'What the hell is going on over there?' Izzy asked.

'It's a guy I met last week running along the river, builder and wannabe rugger bugger. Hot, I mean hot!' She licked her finger and stuck it in the air and made a sizzling sound.

'And?' Xanthe asked, already knowing the answer.

'Best sex, I mean best *safe* sex of my life!' she exclaimed. 'Made me want to have a cigarette afterwards.'

'But you don't smoke,' Veronica said.

'I know, that's how good it was though. Had to just wait a while and then suck on something else. At least it couldn't give me lung cancer.' The girls groaned but Ellen thought she was being funny, again.

'Do you have anything else in common, other than your shared desire for sexual fulfilment?' Izzy asked with her interviewer voice.

'We both think he's hot.'

Ellen had been incredulous at the amount of time Craig spent in the bathroom grooming himself when he was just going to work. She'd never met a bloke who lingered so long in front of the mirror, used more hair product than she did, and splurged more money on waxing than would ever be acceptable.

'I'm sure we'll find more things in common when we speak again,' Ellen smiled as she sent off another text message.

'Does he like poetry?' Xanthe asked, aware of Ellen's love of Aboriginal poetry in particular.

'Oh God, can he even read?' Izzy squealed.

'He reads the sports pages,' Ellen laughed. 'I'm not looking for a man to read poetry to me, I can read that to myself.'

'You can also do the other yourself,' Veronica said, to the shock of her tiddas whose eyes widened and brows raised as smiles crept across their faces. 'Well, she can!'

'He's texting me so I'm sure he can read.' Ellen could hear herself getting defensive as she held up the phone to prove that some words had indeed come through. 'He wants me to send some photos of myself.'

'What kind of photos?' Veronica asked innocently.

But before Ellen could respond Xanthe jumped in. 'DO NOT, I repeat, DO NOT ever send him photos of yourself. You saw what happened to Lara Bingle. Seriously, men in football simply cannot be trusted.'

'Look, I *don't* have unsafe sex and I'd never send nude shots of myself. God, I shudder to think what must go around in your mind about me sometimes.'

The following week flew by and before they knew it the tiddas were meeting and eating again – this time at an upmarket Japanese restaurant down at Eagle Street Pier. Food, books, family . . . these were the three ingredients that bound them together. Well, for most of the time.

The sun was warm for a July day, and Izzy and Ellen enjoyed the river ride from West End and Kangaroo Point. Richard had picked up Veronica on the way. It was her birthday, she should not have to drive, Nadine had instructed him. The scene at the NAIDOC Ball had been all but forgotten, at least by Nadine.

'God, I love birthdays,' Ellen said, looking at the pile of pressies at one end of the long wooden table. 'Ribbon, cake, bubbly, we should have more days like this.'

'Now, *that* I will drink to,' Nadine said, holding up her glass as the banquet began to arrive.

'Did we order already?' Veronica asked, confused.

'Love, this is my birthday present to you. You know I don't do dust collectors, but I *do* do food. I hope you don't mind, I ordered us a banquet.' She turned to one of the waiters delivering food to the table. 'We'll also have a bottle of your best saké, please,' she instructed.

'This is amazing, Nadine. Wow!' Veronica's eyes could not have opened any wider as oyster shots and pork nikogori were followed by a large selection of sashimi, spanner crab tamago tofu, mushroom tempura and wagyu tataki.

'What, there's more?' Xanthe said, as the waiter put a platter of grilled eel on the table.

'And this is Japanese sansho pepper, wasabi and grated daikon,' he said to the wide-eyed women.

The tiddas were soon all happily full to the brim.

'I cannot eat another thing!' Izzy said. 'And I didn't even try everything!'

'You're eating for two, remember,' Veronica said.

'I know but I've been suffering from congestion and between the nasal strips and nose spray I'd really like to lessen the chance of getting it today.'

Izzy thought back to the night before when she felt the baby moving. She had described the sensation, which she could only interpret as butterflies fluttering and a tickling, bubbling feeling, for Asher. She couldn't believe the months of sleepless nights with anxiety had turned into nights of sharing a new life growing inside her.

'But, there's suika watermelon coming; it's jelly, sorbet, mousse and marshmallow.' Nadine had really checked out the menu. She seemed less animated and more interested in food than drink today too, which the others were all happy about. Maybe her behaviour had altered after the warning from her mother-in-law and the scene at the ball.

'Excuse me for a moment, will you?' Ellen got up from the table.

'Off to ring that fella, are you?' Izzy asked.

'What?' Ellen seemed preoccupied. 'No,' she frowned.

'Time for presents then,' Izzy said, reaching for a box wrapped in pink with silver ribbon billowing down the sides. 'As soon as I saw these, and I knew you were serious about your artwork, I had to get them for you. I hope you like them.'

Veronica looked like a young child getting her first shiny bike on Christmas Day. She unwrapped the parcel carefully, slowly revealing the Japanese printing blocks Izzy had bought at the markets one Friday night after work.

'And here's mine,' Xanthe said, handing Vee a wooden box that had been wrapped in lime green tissue paper and secured with a raffia bow.

'I am seriously lucky, thank you,' Veronica said.

'You haven't opened it yet,' Nadine laughed.

'I'm lucky just to be here, with you girls, eating, drinking, getting presents.' She peeled the paper off gently and opened the box to find a necklace and pendant.

'The artwork is licensed by Emily Kame Kngwarreye and it's called Bush Yam Dreaming.' Xanthe was proud of her choice of gift.

'I love it,' Veronica said as she took the pendant out of the box.

'I'm sorry I couldn't afford the real thing for you, but I can't afford it for myself either,' Xanthe smiled.

'Can you do it up for me please?' Veronica held the ends of the necklace at the back of her neck and when Xanthe stood up to walk around the table, Veronica saw Ellen walking towards her carrying an easel with a huge red bow on it.

'I know you've probably got one, but when a handyman came to hang your painting at my place, I told him about you, and he said he knew someone who custom made these, and he was really cute, and the guy who made them was even more cute and I really love you, and I know you can't do batik prints on this but I thought you might paint me a picture, one day. I have more walls to fill.' Ellen was breathless by the time she finished her very sincere spiel.

Veronica was speechless with the gift, with the story, with the thought.

'I love you girls so much, really. This is my best birthday ever, and I hate saying that given I've had forty of them and more than twenty with my sons, but seriously, this is fabulous.'

11

Tears for Lost Moments and Stolen Children

Nadine sat in the cremation circle of the Brookfield cemetery and sobbed. She knew it wasn't unusual to see people there distraught with grief and crying, so she felt safe from judgement, from people asking questions, from anyone looking at her oddly or with concern. For all they knew she was paying respects to her own lost loved one. In some ways she was; she'd lost herself over the years. Today she mourned for the hours, days, weeks she'd lost to hangovers, and worse, the lost moments of time she couldn't even remember.

In recent weeks Nadine had found some level of personal enlightenment about her behaviour, but she had also become paranoid, believing everyone in Brookfield hated her, or at least didn't really like her much. The truth was hardly anyone in her local area knew her beyond what they read in the paper about her books, or what she had to say in the occasional radio interview, which was really only marketing.

What many didn't know about Nadine – including her tiddas – was that she felt deep guilt, shame and regret. No-one really knew this side of her because those emotions never translated into actions. And her internalisation of her feelings was what had so often driven her to drink.

Nadine never found it difficult to justify having a wine or two: it helped her creativity, it gave her confidence when doing book talks, she had to celebrate a release or a good review or a generous fan letter. She needed it to relax, to sleep, and to deal with the stress of deadlines. And quite simply, she liked the taste of a good old Mudgee bush vine cab sav.

Richard had rarely said anything about his wife's drinking, and his mumbled sentence at the NAIDOC Ball was the first time he'd voiced his thoughts out loud to Izzy. He loved Nadine unconditionally and her daily indulgence had simply become part of their routine. Occasionally he would leave the *Local Bulletin* open at an article about drug and alcohol dependency, but whether she saw it or not, Nadine never mentioned it. And so neither did he.

It was a grey, overcast day that had no spark to it at all. Richard had dropped his wife and her laptop at the General Store at 10 a.m. In recent weeks Nadine had been making more of an effort to drink less and be more involved with the kids, sitting and watching telly with them of an evening rather than staying at her desk or going outside by herself with a glass in her hand. But even that morning, the winding roads had played havoc with Nadine's hangover. The kids had been silent in the back of the car. There'd been no outings to the club with them in recent weeks though, not since the NAIDOC Ball.

As Richard drove off, Nadine had decided to sit at the store for a while before heading to the cemetery. With her laptop still in its case she'd let those senses functioning well enough do to their thing; she'd listened and watched, simply observing, as writers did. Birds chirped and whistled as the sun had struggled to find its way through the clouds. An ambulance had flown past to a car accident. *Or perhaps,* Nadine had thought to herself, *it's heading to the home of another Upper Brookfield retiree who's so fat they can't climb their own driveway without having a heart attack.* A four-wheel drive towing a ride-on mower had cruised past, closely followed by a noisy, mustard-coloured Passat pushing its way up the Brookfield Road incline.

A tanned and buffed tradesman had been having a smoko in his ute by the side of the road but Nadine had barely noticed him. Rather, she'd tasted the strong beans in her black coffee and devoured a locally produced chocolate treat from the fridge of gourmet goodies in the store. As far as junk food went, that was the extent of it for Nadine, and even then she consumed an organic variety whenever she could. So good on the food she was, and yet so bad on her intake of alcohol.

At that moment, time had seemed to stand still, reminding Nadine of how she liked the quiet life of Brookfield. She didn't need Ellen's partying existence, the mothers' lunches that Veronica missed, the career trajectory that Izzy craved or the coupledom bubble that Xanthe had. In her own way, Nadine had a little bit of everything, even if she wasn't always conscious or appreciative of it.

As an author, she stuck to her routine most writing days. She would get up and organised and head out for the day when Richard took the kids to school. He would drop her at the General Store where she would order her coffee and nibble on her obligatory chocolate. She would punch the keys on her laptop until her fingers and back ached.

The locals would come and go, buy a coffee, a newspaper, a pie or toilet rolls. It was an old-fashioned general store and while the houses in the area were being updated and modernised, the little store wasn't. As if they were characters in her books, she wondered what their individual back-stories were – why they wore bright pink floral gumboots with shorts, or carried man-bags or wore chunky gold rings on their pinky fingers. And as she watched a fit, young, good-looking tradesman lunge past she wondered why he ordered a burger instead of having a lunch box like other workers.

Nadine always returned a smile if offered one herself, but there was often a hint of something less than generous in it. She didn't really care to make any more friends, or even acquaintances, and having to talk to hundreds of people at a time when on tour meant that some days she just didn't want to talk to anyone at all.

While she'd waited for her laptop to boot up, she'd skimmed the *Local Bulletin*, read an advertisement for an indulgent high tea, and wondered what her husband was doing.

While she mightn't take much notice of what he did with his time, she knew she didn't need much more in her life apart from him and their kids, her books and a good bottle.

Most mothers would have the three Rs as a mantra in their home. Not Nadine; hers were the three Cs: chocolate, caffeine and cab sav . . . and not necessarily in that order. Happy Hour at the Brookfield Community Hall was the only 'community activity' that Nadine wanted to participate in and she even kyboshed the potential for that by getting embarrassingly hammered at the first one she went to. Richard had banned her himself, and swore they would never go back.

Looking at the massive white face of the watch her husband had given her three Christmases ago, she'd started counting down the minutes to when she would have the taste of Mudgee grapes swirling around her tongue again. Her hands were shaking and she didn't want them to be. She didn't like being conscious of her mistakes, and especially not of the pain she had been causing her family and friends for so long. She'd let her appearance go a bit lately too; she needed to get a haircut, her lip waxed, some new product to smooth into the multiplying lines around her eyes. And then a woman in bicycle shorts and Crocs had walked into the shop. *Well, I could look worse,* Nadine had mumbled to herself, the unkind thought bringing a momentary smile to her face.

Then Nadine had felt a wave of something sweep over her: fear, inadequacy, depression, sadness? She wasn't sure, but she'd felt the need to get up. She'd gathered her things and strolled over to the cemetery, and before she'd found a bench to sit down on, she was in tears.

Today, she cried for herself, but in previous years the cemetery had been a place Nadine would visit for inspiration and ideas, gathering material for her novels, reading and memorising headstones, creating scenarios and plots for another book. She knew her process was a morbid, selfish and disrespectful one – she wasn't completely oblivious to her own behaviour except when she was drunk – but she continued with this sort of 'research' anyway. *It's the right of the writer in the pursuit of creative inspiration!* she'd bullshit to herself – and anyone else, if she had to. Today though, there was no bullshitting, just tears. She felt sad and emotional, distraught not at an actual death, or her inability to finish the manuscript she was currently working on, but at the story she had written and created for herself, the one that was causing immense pain to those she loved.

With her nose running and eyes swollen behind her huge black Prada glasses, she stood up and walked slowly through the cemetery, her body feeling unusually heavy although she had unintentionally lost weight over the past ten days. She looked at the oddly designed, arty headstones on some of the graves. Two things had stood out to her about the Brookfield cemetery when she first scouted it: the installation-art style of headstones, and the noticeably young ages of many buried there. *Why?* She was curious about both.

And then her own sense of mortality kicked in. She panicked, and texted Richard to see what time he'd be there to pick her up. Richard, her rock, was the only one who ever made her feel completely safe.

'I need to talk to you,' Richard said to his younger sister for the first time in his life.

Izzy knew what it was about. She'd been feeling helpless but wanted to support her brother. 'I was going to call you,' she said softly.

Silence hung in the air at both ends.

'I thought I'd come and look at your plants on Thursday. Sorry it's taken me so long.' *Men never really say what's on their minds*, Izzy thought.

'Maybe we could get a bite to eat too?' he added.

'Actually, I just got some free tickets to a show at the Powerhouse on Thursday.' Izzy looked at the email notifying her that she'd won an online comp. 'Why don't you come with me?'

'Oh,' Richard hesitated, 'you know I don't do theatre, sis. It's not my thing.'

'If you come, then it *will* be your thing.' She clicked on the link to a review. 'Anyway, it's not theatre, it's a comedy show. A funny local girl.' Izzy clicked through pages. 'Here we go. She's known as "Brisbane's cardigan assassin" and talks about life with her father Barry. It looks like it'll be a hoot.'

'I don't know.' Richard didn't sound interested, but the fact was Izzy wanted some time with her brother.

'Listen, we need to talk. So, let's watch this then have something to eat. We never do anything together.'

Izzy was right. Neither of them could remember the last time they'd spent time together just as brother and sister. The last couple of times they'd been together socially were the NAIDOC Ball and their aunt's wake, and both had ended in disaster.

'Yep, you're right. I'll pick you up from work if you like. Just text me the time tomorrow.'

The phone went dead, both siblings concerned about what needed to be said, and what role each of them would play.

Later that night, the pair were laughing hysterically at the young comedian, nudging each other at various jokes they found funny. Watching the show together had proved to be a good icebreaker. Sitting on the balcony afterwards, Izzy pulled her scarf tighter around her neck. It was chillier than she expected.

'How are you feeling?' Richard asked, looking at his sister's belly.

'I've gained about four kilos, which looks like ten on camera.' Izzy hadn't stopped being vain during the past months and the changes in her body shape led to a constant fear of getting fat. The thought of never losing the weight played on her mind even in her sleep.

'Don't be worried about the weight, sis, you look great. It's a good sign to be growing healthy-like.' Richard thought back to when Nadine was pregnant: she was huge with Cameron, they knew it was going to be a boy, and he was thrilled. But Brittany was still his little princess.

'Sometimes in the still of the night,' Izzy smiled as she spoke, 'the baby's heartbeat is so strong I'm sure I can hear it. It's insane, I never thought I'd feel this way.'

Even with her fears, Izzy couldn't believe the transformation she'd already gone through, mentally and emotionally. The spider veins appearing on her ankles and legs were causing her worry; there was a history of varicose veins in her maternal line, and she desperately hoped she wouldn't be the next woman to get them. Running her hand over her ever expanding belly though, any anxiety was replaced with the warm glow of pending motherhood. She'd started to believe the words of her mother, that this would be the most extraordinary experience of her life.

There was a moment's silence.

'Book club is meant to be at your place this month, I don't think it's a good idea,' Izzy said.

'Nor do I,' Richard agreed, holding firmly onto his orange juice. He never drank when he was driving, there was too much at risk living so far out of the city. If neither he nor Nadine had a licence things would be really difficult.

'I've got tickets for us all to go see something at QPAC. I'll call Nadine and see if she wants to join us, but honestly,' she took a deep breath, 'we're all worried about her, Richard, really very worried.' Izzy paused to consider how she would phrase the next sentence. She decided to keep it simple. 'But we're also sick of her getting so drunk she carries on the way she does.' It was the brutal truth, but Izzy had to tell it.

'I understand.' Richard looked out over the dark river. 'It's one of the reasons we never go out anymore. She's burnt so many bridges everywhere she goes; no-one wants us there. Did you know Mum doesn't want her back in Mudgee?'

Izzy could hear the distress in her brother's voice.

'I know,' she said gently, touching her brother's hand. 'Mum'll come round, she loves Nadine, but she needs to change before she can go back there. Mum hates all the bitching and anger that comes with Nadine on the drink.'

Richard remained silent.

'I know it's different at home when you're alone,' Izzy said. 'Nadine tells us how you two just sit and talk a lot, and she likes having you at home while she's writing.'

Richard looked his sister square in the eye. 'She's a beautiful person, Iz, really she is.'

'I know she is.' Izzy could feel the pain in her brother's heart. 'She's generous and kind, we all know that. But she's different at home because there's no competition for the limelight there.' Izzy was trying to see the difference between Nadine's behaviour with her husband and with her friends. 'She's the star when she's with you, or on tour. She's centre stage at those times, and even if she says she doesn't like it, it's when she appears to be happiest; when all the love is directed at her, and only her.'

'What?' Richard looked confused.

'You make her the centre of attention at home, and that's good, that's your role as hubby, but when she's out with us, she wants everything to revolve around her.' Izzy couldn't stop herself going on. 'You'd die if you saw how she and Ellen bicker sometimes, and you know there's always been competition with me, but my profile is nothing like hers.'

'But Nadine doesn't even like the profile thing.'

'So she says but, truly, sometimes she behaves like a spoilt brat, until she gets *really* pissed and then she's just a pain in the arse.' Izzy's capacity to remain pleasant while speaking about Nadine's behaviour had vanished. She hoped it was her hormones talking.

'Oh God, I didn't know.' Richard sighed and shook his head simultaneously.

'Her needing attention isn't the problem, Richard. We all love her, she's fabulous.' Izzy took another deep breath, as if to suck in courage. 'But it's like she has to get drunk to maintain an interest in anyone else's life, and when she's pissed she loses her capacity to keep herself in check.' Izzy turned to face her brother. 'I just don't know how she even manages to get any work done. I rarely see her sober. She must have hangovers, I don't know, *all the time!*'

Richard sighed.

Izzy felt bad. 'It's not your fault,' she tried to reassure him. 'We're all responsible, and so,' she hesitated, 'we were thinking of doing an intervention, but maybe you need to suggest AA or a clinic?'

'Are you fucking serious?' Richard snapped. 'Can you imagine me doing that? She'll cut off my balls and wear them as earrings.'

'Well, what did you have in mind?'

Richard's brow furrowed. 'I'm going to start by talking to her about her problem. *Our* problem.'

Ellen, Xanthe, Izzy and Veronica met at QPAC just before the show started. It was bucketing down and they were all cold and damp. The sudden downpour had slowed traffic all around town with flash flooding and minor accidents closing lanes. It wasn't the best start to an evening that was always going to be emotionally charged, given the theme of the production was the Stolen Generations.

Each had eaten on the run, or not at all. Ellen had lost some of her appetite lately, in denial that she was lovesick for Craig and any spare time was spent making love, not meals. She was constantly on the go with a protein shake in her hand and a post-coital glow on her face.

Izzy was grazing all day on what she'd discovered during her research online were pregnancy power foods: pinto beans, carrots, blueberries and yoghurt. She'd previously been a fan of canned tuna and salmon because they were convenient when she was on the go, but having read about high mercury levels had cut them out of her diet altogether. The only thing she really missed was coffee. Xanthe – who had become a pregnancy advisor of sorts to Izzy – had told her that caffeine dehydrates and depletes calcium levels and low calcium had been linked to prematurity, miscarriage, low birth weight and withdrawal symptoms in infants. After that, Izzy bypassed her morning coffee and started drinking fruit teas instead. She was never hungry though, and hoped the weight gain was all baby. She also noticed how her nails and hair were growing at a rapid rate, with a strength and fullness they'd not had before. 'I didn't realise there were some perks to pregnancy,' she told her mother on the phone recently.

Veronica had spent the afternoon cooking up a storm for John and had eaten some of the massive beef lasagne before leaving home. While Xanthe, who arrived straight from the airport following a training session in Bundaberg, had reluctantly eaten a snack on the flight back to Brisbane. She was stressed by the time she got there. Not that it was unusual for her to be on the road presenting to mining companies, government agencies and community organisations. She was happiest when she was helping to write and implement social issues policies and training packages for the workplace, even though the work was challenging and often caused her sleepless nights. It was normal for her to lie awake rethinking what a redneck employee had thrown at her during a session on Australian history in which she'd covered the Coniston massacre, the Tasmanian Line and the Stolen Generations. Even after the mainstream release of the film version of *Rabbit-Proof Fence* and Kevin Rudd's national apology in 2008, she couldn't believe there were still Australians who knew so little about their own history and still needed to be convinced of the value in saying sorry. Heading to see the play *Stolen*, she was already emotionally drained.

Izzy scratched her belly.

'What's wrong with you?' Ellen asked.

'I'm fucking itchy all the time. The more my boobs and belly stretch, the itchier I feel. It's weird, I hate it.' She reached down to her feet. 'My soles are itchy, my palms are itchy and I can tell you, it's not for money.' She scratched some more.

'How many weeks are you now?' Veronica asked.

'Twenty-two,' Izzy guessed, not wanting to look like she didn't know exactly how far along she was.

'That sounds about right,' Xanthe offered. 'I think they're standard symptoms at that stage, I'm sorry to tell you.'

'Well, at least you know what you're in for when it happens,' Izzy said, positive her tidda would soon fall pregnant.

'My fingers are numb, my mouth tastes like it's full of metal and my eyes are dry.' Izzy started to cry. 'Whoever said pregnancy was a beautiful thing was fucking lying.'

Xanthe tried not to let the comment affect her. She wanted to experience for herself all the things Izzy was going through. She had done a pregnancy test two days ago, and had another in her handbag. She'd now bought take-home tests from every chemist in a ten-kilometre radius of her home, and even when she was in different towns and cities.

'Oh,' Izzy grasped her chest.

'What is it?' Veronica jumped up.

'Fucking heartburn, I'm falling apart.' As a pregnant woman, Izzy was like a fella with a man-cold, a terrible 'patient'.

'You do realise the first word your child says is going to be "fuck" if you don't stop swearing all the time,' Ellen said, laughing.

'See, I'm already a fucked mother!'

Xanthe said nothing.

'Your hair looks really pretty, Ellen,' Veronica said, admiring the extra length Ellen was sporting, but also trying to change the subject. She could tell Xanthe was sullen.

'Yes, I've decided to let it grow.' Ellen ran her fingers through her marginally longer locks. 'Craig likes women with long hair.'

Izzy raised an eyebrow. 'Wow, we're changing our style for a bloke now? Never thought I'd see that happen,' she grinned.

'No I'm not!' Ellen said defensively, screwing her face up as if to say, *What are you talking about?* 'I'd never do that!' she said adamantly, but fooling no-one.

'You've had short hair for as long as I can remember,' Xanthe said, thinking back to their days in Mudgee. 'Even through school. God, remember the school photos?'

'Yes, yes, but maybe I want a change. Maybe Nadine was right, maybe I do look a bit blokish.'

'If that's the case, then you're telling us that at the age of forty you've started listening to what Nadine has to say about you.'

'As if I'd ever admit to *that*. Come on, the bells are ringing, let's head in.'

They made their way to the doors of the Cremorne Theatre along with throngs of other theatregoers: reviewers, drama aficionados, school and uni students, and members of the Stolen Generations themselves. *There's an unusual number of Murris here tonight,* Xanthe thought to herself, but perhaps that was because she'd been so busy travelling for work the past couple of years, she rarely got the chance to see plays.

For the next hundred minutes the women underwent a range of emotions, as students from the Aboriginal Centre for the Performing Arts used music, dance and drama to tell stories of children removed from their families under the Protection policies that once existed in Queensland. The finale had them all in tears as each performer sang out their character's own experience of removal.

As they sat in the bar of QPAC after the performance, the energy was electric; patrons debriefed and dissected what they'd just seen. The tiddas were no different.

'This is the first play I've actually read *and* seen,' Izzy said, thinking back over years of theatre-going.

'We did *Hamlet* at school, remember?' Veronica asked. 'And then there was that amateur performance at the old Regent Theatre. Remember how we all wanted to kiss Matt who played Hamlet, and then Nadine was caught pashing him backstage.' The women all smiled. Matt had been the biggest spunk at Mudgee High.

'Oh, that's right, my mind is like mush sometimes,' Izzy said, annoyed at how things were slipping her mind of late.

'Baby brain,' Xanthe added with authority. 'There's been studies done that prove there can be weakened memory due to iron deficiency during pregnancy. If you're not getting enough iron to fuel haemoglobin production for you both, Izzy, then you can develop iron-deficient anaemia.'

Xanthe rattled off the information as if she were a G.P. She had clearly done enough reading for both of them. Izzy tried to take it all in.

'Some common symptoms of anaemia include fatigue, weakness, irritability and forgetfulness. So it's important to keep up your greens too,' Xanthe continued, happy to be able to offer the advice she wished she needed to follow herself.

'Seriously, if I eat any more broccoli, I'll turn green!'

Just then, some of the cast walked by – young, enthusiastic, pleased with their work.

'It's awesome *Stolen* was here at QPAC, that's top shelf,' Ellen said to her tiddas.

Xanthe shook her head.

'Is everything okay, Xanthe?' Izzy asked,

Xanthe was on the verge of tears. 'I'm okay. The play made me incredibly angry though, and sad.' She reached for a tissue in her handbag. 'It made me think about Mum and my aunties who were removed to Coota Girls Home. One of the things they always missed the whole time there was hugs from their mums.' Tears started to fall down Xanthe's flawless cheeks. 'It's why she always hugged me so much growing up. She still hugs me a lot. And Noon hugs me a lot too.' Xanthe thought back to her last visit in Mudgee and the long hug her mother and grandmother gave her in the doorway the moment she arrived. 'I know you girls probably think I'm obsessed with having a baby.'

'No, not at all,' Veronica said, although like the other tiddas she did think Xanthe had lost some perspective in recent months. But her revelation now made them all more sympathetic.

'Part of me sometimes wonders if my yearning for a baby is simply so I can be a good mother, be the kind of mother that my mum and aunties never had, or didn't have very much. Does that sound insane?'

'Actually, Xanthe,' Izzy said. 'That makes a lot of sense.'

Brookfield was only twenty kilometres from Brisbane city but it could feel isolated. Some called it semi-rural but for Izzy, Ellen and Xanthe, it was completely rural.

'Anywhere without kerb and guttering is country to me,' Ellen once said, thinking about her apartment right on the Brisbane River with a view of the city skyline and all its brilliant lights to drift off to every night.

Nadine had never really been a city girl, more a country tomboy, even as a teenager getting around in jeans in winter and trackies and a T-shirt in summer. It was lucky that Richard never wanted a girly-girl; he would've had to date another of Izzy's friends had that been the case. His wife liked the smell of nature, the scent of the pine, cedar, silky oak and eucalyptus trees that surrounded their house and protected the property from the outside world. She wore patchouli-scented oil instead of Chanel, Dior or YSL. She owned all the expensive fragrances, often gifts from her publisher, but rarely wore them.

To her tiddas, it would look like Nadine was back to her usual routine: sitting on her veranda with a glass in her hand, staring into the black night. It wasn't as dark as she remembered the Mudgee sky to be, but the nights were definitely warmer in autumn and winter where she now lived. It was during these times alone that she felt most vulnerable, most inadequate. She didn't feel compelled to read to her children tonight, or to help Richard clean up after dinner. She was like the men in her family back home, where the women did absolutely everything round the house because they had to; because that was their identity, their role, their lot in life. This was *her* lot.

Nadine was glad she had got out of Mudgee where the eyes of the locals were always on her, frowning, not understanding, always judging – or so she thought. Now she felt like her friends were judging her too. She didn't realise it was worry her tiddas felt; about her drinking, her insularity and her lack of interest in anything apart from her own day, the plot of her next novel and the time of her next drink.

Given Brookfield had less than half the population of Mudgee, Nadine was happy she and Richard settled where they did. The acreage allowed them to get some horses for the kids to ride and raise chooks for eggs. It was all coordinated by Richard though. Given that she didn't drive, it was important to Nadine that there was some form of self-sufficiency for her if Richard was not at home. She wasn't a great cook, but even *she* could do scrambled eggs.

A bat's high-pitched squeak shook Nadine from her blurry gaze. She wondered what Richard was doing, not realising he stood only metres away, watching her.

As she continued to sip her wine, she thought about her family back in Mudgee, the one she rarely had any contact with now she had put herself into writerly seclusion. She was still proud of how they'd been pioneers in the dairying industry and owned hundreds of acres back home. Then they bought a winery, and the rest was her financial security history. The land had been passed down through the generations but increasingly fewer of her relations wanted to live on or work it, and fewer still wanted to live in the hills. Nadine was the last 'hillbilly' in her clan, but an incredibly wealthy one at that.

Before moving to Queensland as newlyweds in their early twenties, Nadine and Richard had talked about what it might mean to uproot their life in Mudgee. But it was time for Nadine to make the move. Her career had taken off immediately with her first best-selling novel, followed by a second and third in quick succession, and she felt increasingly under the microscope of locals who frowned on her eccentric writerly life and what many thought was her neglect of her husband. She didn't want to raise the children she would eventually have under the same judgemental spotlight. And she never got on with her mother-in-law. It was no secret that Trish wanted both Richard and Izzy to marry Black. Not only did Richard marry a white girl, but in Trish's eyes Nadine had also managed to take the man out of her son by making him stay home and do the laundry. 'Your father would turn in his grave,' she had said to Richard more than once.

Nadine didn't think about it that way, and nor did Richard. They both worked hard in different ways and money was seen purely as a means for buying necessities, not a motivation in itself. Writing was work, but that too came easily to her. She had a gift for unfurling stories in her mind and then sitting at her computer and writing without distraction for days, weeks, months on end. All the while her devoted husband kept the wheels of the family life turning and her must-have-for-creative-thought glass of wine topped up.

The idea of mixed-marriages in Mudgee was about race – Black and white – but in Brookfield a mixed marriage meant the joining of two different religions.

'Mixed marriages haven't always been welcomed in Brookfield,' Nadine said out of the blue one morning when they first arrived.

'What? Are they rednecks up here?' Richard had been naively surprised.

'Probably, if you consider that up here marriages between a Catholic and a Protestant were once frowned upon, so I'm imagining a Blackfella and whitefella won't go down too well either.'

'Oh, you get me going sometimes, Nads.' Richard had put a potted palm on the veranda near the back door. He was the only person who called her Nads.

'But like Patrick and Ann Pacey – the Catholic and the Protestant who pioneered the way for inter-faith relationships – maybe you and I have done the same.'

Richard had stood up from tending the plant and pinched her on the arse.

'Hey,' she said, 'don't start something you can't finish.'

'I can finish it all right,' he'd laughed, pulling her into a tight embrace.

The affection between the school sweethearts had never waned. An onlooker might think they were an odd match;

she was an inch taller than him, lean and pale as vanilla bean ice-cream. She drank, swore, criticised, analysed and only seemed content when she'd had a glass or four. Richard, on the other hand, was dark like the coffee beans he would grind to wake them both up properly in the morning. He was stocky and always smiling. 'Happy wife, happy life' was his motto. And when Nadine was happy the whole house was happy. Whenever the pair passed each other they would touch: a finger along an arm, a kiss on the forehead, a cuddle just for the sake of it. They still liked each other even after twenty plus years. They had what Veronica had always longed for.

It was not unusual for Richard and Nadine to make love in the middle of the day. When the kids were at school and Richard had finished feeding the animals, collecting the eggs and watering the vegie patch. Nadine didn't have to be asked twice; the one thing that alcohol had not done was lower her libido. She found sex helped her think more clearly of an afternoon and she could take to the keyboard again. They'd shower together afterwards before he left to collect the children from school.

'Darling,' Nadine called to Richard as the dew set in.

'Yes, my love.' He stood behind the wicker chair and kissed the top of her head.

'If you're going out on the mower tomorrow, can you put some sunblock on please?'

Richard laughed. 'It's August and I'm Black!'

'Don't laugh at me. It's going to be hot tomorrow. UV rays and climate change, you know.'

'I don't need sunblock.' Richard pulled up a seat and put his hand on her thigh.

Nadine took a deep breath and stood up. Richard knew he was in trouble, kind of; they never really fought.

'Do I ask you for anything, ever?' She was serious.

'Well, yes, you ask me to drive you everywhere, do most of the cooking and cleaning . . .' He smiled as he pulled her down onto his lap.

'And I've also just asked you to wear sunblock,' she continued, nuzzling into his neck as if a child.

'The things I do for you, my love,' Richard chuckled, kissing his wife on the cheek.

'Life could be much worse than having a wife who worries about your wellbeing. But you go, get melanoma, see what I care.'

She broke from his embrace and picked up her glass of wine.

'Don't be like that.'

It was the perfect moment for him to say how much he worried about her too, to begin to talk about her drinking. And that was his plan.

'I love that you worry about me,' he said, taking her head in his hands and kissing her gently.

The gentle kiss turned passionate. Nadine felt light-headed, not from the wine but from lust, and without thinking about the likelihood of Cameron or Brittany stumbling upon them she straddled her husband, rutting until they both climaxed.

12

A Positive New Journey vs Damaging Bad Habits

Ellen felt around for her phone with her eyes closed, hoping for a text message or missed call from Craig. It had been a few days since she'd last heard from him and she was feeling agitated. Even though neither of them acknowledged they were technically dating, she knew she'd been affected by his presence, his interest, his communication – or more specifically of late, his lack thereof.

She lay in bed, the sound of peak hour traffic humming in the background. She smiled, knowing she could let her mind relax a little after the two draining funeral services of the day before. The next, thankfully, was two sleeps away. Two days off mid-week was another reason Ellen loved working for herself; she thrived on the independence and control, having a say about her everyday life and routine. In fact there were few things that Ellen didn't love about being a self-employed career woman as her fortieth birthday approached. She mightn't get four weeks' paid holidays, or sick leave or automatic superannuation, but the luxury of lying in bed later than usual on a Tuesday morning, the joy of taking a nap on Wednesday afternoon, and even having time to head out to QUT in the middle of the day to support Veronica – well, they were good enough reasons for her to be a sole trader.

Her phone beeped and she nearly fell out of bed reaching for it.

Babe, what're you wearing right now?

Ellen smiled, but she still wished Craig would just ask about how she was doing some time. It was only ever footy, body-building and sex with him; anything else was too highbrow, or just boring. The girls were right. What did they have in common beyond satisfying each other sexually?

Babe, u there?

Craig was also impatient. Everything had to happen as soon as he decided; he wanted instant gratification. The girls had looked sceptical when she mentioned him to them at the NAIDOC debrief. *Who cares?* She was grateful for the sex and the attention, and even if she didn't want a relationship with Craig, she still had someone to play with until the next fella came along. *This is a pretty good place to be in right now.* She thought back to Aunty Molly's funeral and the love she saw that day; it had affected her deeply. But she also remembered her father walking away, and how – except for her tiddas – everyone else in her daily life died.

She punched the keypad.

Red panties, no top.

She ran her hand across her erect nipple and wished Craig was there to kiss it. The phone beeped again instantly.

Send pic

Ellen was fine having eyes on her at the altar, by a graveside or in a crematorium, but she was always clothed. She didn't like the idea of being an exhibitionist via iPhone. Besides, the girls had already warned her about what football players did with photos of half-naked women.

Of what?

She asked, feigning naivety.

U. ur sexy.

She couldn't help herself; even though she knew she looked all right disrobed, she also knew footy players were indeed, players. And the whole sexting things wasn't something she'd ever get into, especially after accidentally sending a salacious text about 'fucking like a tiger' to a priest she was working with on a service down the Gold Coast. The days of embarrassment she endured after that slip-up taught her one very simple lesson a very hard way.

Are you like the Shane Warne of footy or something?

She knew fully well you didn't have to be a cricketer to know about spin. She wasn't naive. She knew Craig was a player on and off the field, and she was happy to play some of his games. But with media stories of football players involved in group sex scandals and women open to late night sex requests via text, it wasn't a culture she wanted to be part of, even though she wasn't averse to a little adult fun. More concerning was that she was actually starting to like Craig, a lot, and she wondered how many other women he had photos of.

Are you the Brendan Favola of Bris-Vegas then?

She wasn't really expecting any honest answers; after all, who'd admit to being like either of those fellas with their off-field reputations.

What? No!

Craig went silent, as if offended. Ellen waited a while.

Why do you want a photo then?

And why doesn't he just call me? she thought.

Make me smile ☺

She hesitated, tempted, knowing she had boobs men craved and loved to bury their faces in. She sent Craig a headshot taken at the Story Bridge Hotel one night when she had spiky jet-black hair and sparkly earrings.

Fuck ur sexy

She knew she had him then, even if other women had him at other times.

You want to see more of me you know where to find me ☺

You're a tease.

Ellen was getting turned on.

So are you.

And so was Craig.

I'm hard.

Even though she was wet with desire and had one hand in her knickers, Ellen wasn't going any further on text. She was about to climax when her phone beeped.

I'm on my way over.

She took a huge breath and stopped herself from finishing. She wanted to see how many orgasms she could have with Craig, if he really was on his way over. She jumped out of bed immediately, her flat unprepared for visitors and certainly not ready for a bloke she fancied. It was 7.30 a.m. but she figured she could make love to Craig and still meet Veronica at 10 a.m. at Kelvin Grove if she cabbed it. She had a quick shower, threw on a mauve knickers and bra set she'd been wanting to break in and a silk wrap, and by the time she'd remade the bed and tidied the living room Craig was at the door, bulging biceps and bulging shorts at the ready.

'Babe, you get me hot just thinking about you.'

He kicked the door closed behind him, grabbed Ellen by the arse, and gently pulled her against him. She melted into his body as he put his thick lips on hers. She ran her hand through his hair as they kissed ferociously, as if eating each other for breakfast. The silk wrap dropped to the floor and Craig guided her down the hall to the bedroom.

'I want to take you to heaven,' he said, licking her cleavage and then up her neck.

'I'm almost there already,' she whispered, desperate for Craig's touch and grateful he was so into pleasing her.

Veronica sat at a popular café on Musk Street and looked at the QUT brochures for Creative Industries. She wasn't yet convinced university was the best idea for her, but Ellen and

Xanthe had been putting pressure on her to at least check out the campus, speak to staff, and give serious consideration to what might be possible. She was thinking about the Bachelor of Arts (Fine Arts), which required a three-year commitment full-time. With nothing else on her schedule, she could do it.

Veronica read slowly, taking in what the degree was designed to do, mentally ticking off what she liked, and more importantly, what she was equipped to manage with her current skills set. Key words and phrases leapt out at her: explore your artistic potential, a cross-disciplinary approach, both studio practice and art history, work as a professional artist. At that moment Veronica couldn't see herself as a professional anything, but she allowed herself to dream about having an exhibition of her own work one day. She was starting to at least believe that the degree might give her the structure and the practical support to make her dream come true.

If nothing else Veronica liked the atmosphere of the Kelvin Grove community; cafés, shops, people from all walks of life, it was like the little urban village it claimed to be. She hadn't previously been aware of the mixed-use development that was designed to be sustainable and function at less cost than other similar land and housing projects. She was impressed with the attempt to integrate public housing, private dwellings and a university campus into one space. The fact that the local Turrbul mob had provided input into the native vegetation chosen for the site almost sealed it for her, as did the naming of two of the parks in Turrbul language. Kulgan meant path or road, and Kundu Park was named after the tallowwood tree native to the area. Just by spending time at

Kelvin Grove as a student, she'd be learning much more about life and culture than simply visual arts.

Veronica watched the stream of people walking by and wondered if they were students, lecturers or professors, or just wanna-be students and dreamers like her. She wasn't sure she would even fit in. She certainly didn't have the 'uni look', or so she thought, considering her chocolate jersey skirt and denim jacket. She wasn't even sure if denim jackets were in anymore. Or jersey, for that matter. Everything she wore was the best money could buy, but that didn't make her fashionable and nor did it make her feel like uni student either.

A woman in a fitted floral frock and red shoes sat at the table beside her. Veronica guessed she was the same vintage, but looked much more relaxed in the uni environment, and certainly more glamorous. Fashions had never been part of Veronica's routine, especially when raising her boys; cooking, homework, sports carnivals, car pools, school camps and projects were where her focus had lain. At the age of forty she now sadly realised that over the past two decades she'd spent very little time at all on herself; her health, her looks, her spirituality, her own personal goals. She had never been one to enjoy shopping that much; the NAIDOC Ball gown had been the first splurge in some time.

'I need a make-over,' Veronica said with a sense of urgency as soon as Ellen sat down opposite her.

'Okay,' Ellen responded, unsure of what was going on with her tidda.

'I need a new look. New clothes. A new identity. I'm just a frumpy mummy.' Veronica felt a burn of depression hit her.

Seeing some of the other women her age on campus had hit her like a brick to the head, and the heart. If she was going to be a student here, she needed a stronger sense of self, one that was about who she was as a woman in her own right, right now.

'I can help you with a new style, but first you need to understand that you are not a frumpy mummy at all. You're a vivacious vixen who perhaps just needs to let her hair down, literally.'

Veronica's blunt bob had been pulled back into a ponytail and it made her thin face look a little more severe than usual. She raised her hand to the elastic band but didn't pull it out.

'I've got tomorrow off and don't really have any plans,' Ellen said, wondering if Craig would return for another serve of what they'd just indulged in. 'We could do some shopping then if you like.' Ellen took out her diary and began making some notes.

'Oh, can I have some time to think about it?'

Veronica was surprised at the speed at which Ellen moved, in spite of her own sense of urgency. But there was a reason her funeral celebrant friend had a thriving business, and it wasn't simply because people were dying. She was the perfect coordinator, whether it was for someone's death or for someone's new life.

'Seriously, Vee, you said it out loud like you meant it. We're on the new journey already, aren't we? Look where we are and what we're doing today.' Ellen smiled as her gaze darted up and down the street.

Veronica watched a woman, in her mid-thirties and

looking incredibly chic in a black tunic and boots, take a seat. She didn't need to think anymore.

'Yes, we are on a new journey.'

'Right, I've got some friends I can line up things with later.' Ellen was already punching digits into her phone. 'We'll go shopping, get your hair done and get someone to do your colours. This is going to be so cool.' Ellen sent a text message.

Veronica wasn't completely sure she was ready for whatever Ellen was planning, but she was grateful her friend was excited and keen to be part of what she'd termed 'the new journey'.

The women met with the Dean of Creative Industries and talked through the degree and application process. Veronica's head was spinning with a mixture of excitement and self-doubt. But Ellen's positive affirmations were infectious; she insisted Vee only consider what life was going to be like once she'd enrolled at uni and was working towards achieving her degree. She looked at her watch and turned on her heel, taking Veronica by the arm.

'Let's drop into the Oodgeroo Unit and say a quick hello to the mob there,' Ellen said. 'I know a couple of people who work there. They'll take care of you.'

'But I'm not Murri!'

'You can still say hello to Murris, can't you?' Ellen joked, upping her pace. 'You might like someone to have coffee with occasionally. Apart from my friends, there's students enrolled across various faculties. You might find some of them in Creative Industries.'

'Oh that'd be cool. I'll need friends here.' Veronica was grateful to Ellen for helping her. 'I couldn't have done this alone, thank you.' She pulled Ellen closer to her side and gave her an affectionate hug.

As they walked arm in arm towards the Oodgeroo Unit in B Block, Ellen bumped into her friend Kelrick, who was responsible for the university's Indigenous employment strategy.

'Biggest spunk on campus,' she said to the smiling fella in his late thirties.

'Well, you must be talking about me,' he joked, air-kissing her and, even though he didn't know her, Veronica as well.

'This is Kelrick, Vee. He'll tell you where the best coffee and feed is, and all the good looking blokes.'

'The blokes I'll keep to myself, but the best coffee is Dancing Bean Espresso and for a little more cream with your coffee,' he winked, 'try Room 60. In a rush though, darl, so will catch up soon. Drinks yes, call me, text me.' Kelrick was five steps away, walking backwards. 'Love your shirt,' he said to Ellen. 'And love your skirt,' he said to Veronica, making her feel a little less self-conscious about her wardrobe right then.

'Pity he's gay,' Ellen whispered to Veronica as they walked off. 'He'd be perfect for you, Vee.'

'Oh, I don't think I could date a Blackfella,' Veronica said, immediately realising how poorly she'd phrased it.

'What?' Ellen stopped in her tracks. 'Please tell me you didn't say something racist just now. Really? Vee?'

'No, of course not, it came out the wrong way. I have no issue with inter-racial relationships at all. Lots of them work better than other relationships. Nadine's and Xanthe's marriages are prime examples of what works well, don't you think?'

Ellen thought for a moment. She'd dated plenty of Blackfellas but nothing ever came of it. Her own parents' marriage didn't last, Veronica and Alex's hadn't, and yet Xanthe and Nadine had in fact married out of the mob, and were both still madly in love with their beaus.

'The thing is,' Veronica began explaining herself, 'I'm not a very strong woman, not like you and Izzy and Xanthe, and so I reckon a strong Black man would prefer a strong Black woman.'

'Don't kid yourself, Vee.' Ellen rolled her eyes. 'I've seen a lot of Black men choose weak women, not that you're one.' It was Ellen's turn to put her foot in her mouth. 'You, dear tidda, are staunch, a deadly woman that any brother could love. What I'm saying is I'm always surprised to find some of our men who are in top jobs with excellent minds opting for women who are the complete opposite, almost airheads. So, my point is, you are not an airhead and would be the perfect partner for a good man of any colour, even Kelrick if he was into your kind of plumbing.'

To Veronica's relief they'd reached the door of the Oodgeroo Unit and any talk of partners and plumbing immediately ceased.

Ellen was focused on her iPad when Veronica arrived at the Cliffs Café at eight o'clock the next morning.

'Sorry I'm late,' she said. 'The traffic is awful during school hours. I really can't wait to move closer to the city. I can't believe it never bothered me before.' Veronica was a little frazzled, but as soon as she looked out over the river from the top of the Kangaroo Point cliffs she felt relaxed.

'After today, my dear tidda, your new look will require you to be right here, closer to the city and closer to me.' Ellen turned her iPad around so Veronica could read it.

A waitress delivered two coffees and two breakfast wraps at the same time. The smell of barbeque sauce hit Veronica's nostrils before the coffee did.

'Sorry,' Ellen shrugged, hoping she didn't seem like a control freak. 'You always have the same thing, so I just ordered it to save time.'

Ellen didn't want to waste a minute of the day. She'd seen Craig again the night before and hadn't slept much, but was on a lust-infatuation high. Veronica, on the other hand, just felt incredibly cared for and grateful for the new bond she and Ellen had formed in recent months. The silver lining in the end of her marriage was the beginning of a whole new life for Veronica, including deeper connections with her tiddas.

'First stop is Westfield Chermside where we've got a personal shopper to help sort out your wardrobe.'

'How did you organise that overnight? Aren't they booked weeks in advance?' Veronica didn't know a lot about stylists, but she imagined you couldn't just walk in off the street and expect one to materialise on the spot.

'I did the service for her mother last year and she said if there was anything I ever needed then I should give her a buzz. So I did, and voila!' She took a sip of coffee. 'Did you bring the list?' Ellen's eyes were wide with expectation.

Veronica grabbed a small red notepad from her bag and opened it to a page of notes listing her favourite colours, fabrics, designers, her own articles of clothing, reasons for shopping, most loved outfits and so on.

'Great, this will help Sorina pull together some new looks for you.' Ellen looked back at her schedule. 'I've allocated two hours with her, she works very fast and has another client at noon.' Ellen glanced at her watch. 'Then we'll need lunch, say thirty minutes for that?' She looked up to check Veronica was okay with a short break. 'Next we're going to see my friend Prue who's a hair magician. She moved some appointments around and is going to do something spectacular with your hair, I just know it.' Ellen fluffed up the ends of Veronica's bob, which was just sitting on her shoulders.

Veronica gently pushed Ellen's hands away. 'What are you going to do with my hair?' she said, sounding like a sooky little girl.

'It's time for a change, Vee. You've had that blunt bob as long as I can remember. I reckon you can do something much more exciting with it. No offence, but Prue has an eye for what suits the face of every woman she cuts and colours. Trust me, you will be happy. Very, very happy.'

'I hope so,' Veronica said, slight panic in her blood.

'After your hair we'll come back to the city to get your make-up done. Then you can either come back to mine and get ready for Nadine's launch, or go home.' Ellen handed Veronica a sheet of paper. 'Here's a printed copy of the schedule, contact numbers and emails for any follow-up you might need.'

'My God, you're organised, aren't you?'

'I think Nadine calls me anal instead of organised, but it's pretty much the same thing.' Ellen put her iPad in her tan tote – which she'd offset with an orange and gold Aboriginal designed scarf tied at one end.

'Oh, and we're getting you fitted for bras today too,' she said, pushing her chair out from the table.

'What?' Veronica was in shock. She couldn't move at all.

'You've got a good rack, Vee. You need to show those girls off a bit more. You could so rock a push-up bra.'

'I don't want my breasts to rock anything,' Veronica said, slightly offended and suddenly conscious of the underwear she was wearing.

'Listen Vee, it's about *feeling* good about yourself. That's what we're doing this for. Nice clothes, having your hair done, feeling sexy – you don't have to do it for anyone other than yourself. If someone else appreciates the result, then that's a bonus. But today, my tidda, we are going to spend some time and a lot of Alex's money making you *feel* as beautiful as you are, inside and out.'

Ellen motioned her friend to stand and they headed towards the Lexus a few metres away.

By the end of the day Veronica's car was loaded with bags: 'key pieces' as defined by Sorina the stylist, which included a pair of jeans, a black blazer, white wrap-around cotton shirt, white t-shirt, black lace top, three thin belts, one wide black belt, black boots with killer heels, three push-up bras, a body suit, French knickers, and a red jersey dress. She let Ellen drive back into the city as she checked and rechecked her new, groovier hairdo; she kept running her fingers through the layers of rich browns and burgundy highlights.

'I can hardly recognise myself,' she said smiling. 'I love it!'

'You look amazing, Vee. Now for the make-up and you're all done.'

'It's fun hanging out with you. I've never really had this much fun shopping.' Veronica's shopping experiences over the years had included high-end designer stores but she had always gone by herself or had Alex pacing the floor nearby. The only other ventures were to buy school uniforms and sporting gear for her sons. A stylist, someone to help her 'build her wardrobe and look', was not anything she had *ever* thought about.

'I had a ball too. It's great going shopping with someone who doesn't have to look at the price tag before she tries something on. It was like being with a Hollywood star,' Ellen joked.

'You're hilarious! And bear in mind I hardly ever go shopping, so today was about five years' worth for me. As for stardom . . .' She pulled down the sun visor and took another look in the mirror. 'I do look good.'

The layout at Avid Reader had been transformed so the bookshop could hold seventy people. Guests were spilling out onto the street. The book launch was only minutes from starting. Nadine was upstairs in the bathroom, breathing deeply. The novelty of doing literary events had worn off years ago, after her sixth book, but she always drew a crowd and sold more books than any other author featured in the front window display on Boundary Street. She liked the owners, and she liked supporting independent booksellers. She also liked that they served wine at their events. Sometimes she even donated a case of Mudgee's finest just to help promote her hometown.

Xanthe arrived straight from a tutoring session at the West End library not far up the street. She'd been helping a Year 12 Murri student. The inevitable stress of the Queensland Certificate of Education was fast approaching, and this was one of the love jobs that made her feel she was giving back to community in a small but valuable way. It took her back to when she was preparing for the Higher School Certificate, the equivalent in New South Wales, and how she never imagined at the time she'd be running her own business one day.

Izzy and her baby bump were dressed in black jersey. She looked neat and felt wonderful, as if her whole body was glowing, gleaming like no other pregnant woman's before. She now realised what Xanthe had always wanted, and why. She had a full-face of make-up and her hair was dead straight as usual. She'd been filming an Indigenous writers' workshop at the library all day, and interviewing presenters, guest authors and the organisers about the future of First Nation literature. She wondered how many of them would show up to Nadine's event since she wasn't a Murri.

Ellen and Veronica arrived together, like agent and client, both proud of their accomplishment that day. Ellen was pleased that her tidda hadn't stopped smiling. Veronica was happy that she felt beautiful, and her new hairstyle had already worked wonders in boosting her confidence. Veronica walked tall in her new boots, her hair swinging as she made her way through the crowd. She grinned at the look of surprise on Xanthe's and Izzy's faces when they saw her.

'You look absolutely amazing!' Xanthe said, kissing Veronica on her cheek, careful not to mess up the perfect face of make-up.

'It's stunning,' Izzy said. 'The cut really suits you, and the highlights . . . I'm lost for words.' Izzy wanted to walk around and check out her friend completely, but the room was too cramped. 'Can you spin a little so I can see the back?' she asked.

And Veronica responded willingly.

'I don't want to be rude, but did you get some work done?' Xanthe ran her hand across her own chest.

Veronica started laughing. 'No, but who would've thought that a gorgeous bra could make you look and feel so much better.' She looked down at her chest. 'And a bit bigger!'

'I told you so,' Ellen chimed in, proud of her part in Veronica's one-day transformation.

'I might never take this bra off,' Veronica said. 'It makes me feel . . . extraordinary!'

'I've created a monster,' Ellen laughed. 'A beautiful monster!'

'Good evening, ladies and gentleman,' an announcement

came over the mic in an attempt to get everyone settled and the event underway.

Nadine had saved seats up the front for her tiddas but they couldn't get through the crowd clogging the narrow aisle, so they took the first four seats they could find together. Conscious that she'd probably need to pee at some stage, Izzy sat at the end of the row.

There was a mix of people in the audience, mainly locals who attended many of the store's events, but also a few die-hard fans who followed Nadine's career and showed up wherever she spoke. There were also a few starry-eyed males, and a couple of uni students doing theses on Australian literature who sat with pens poised over their notepads. Others were live-tweeting and posting photos on Facebook. As it was a school night, Richard was at home with the kids.

The program was presented as in-conversation between Nadine and a popular Radio National broadcaster. Nadine was in the hot-seat given she was going to be discussing the controversy around her latest novel, *Blood River,* a fictional story set during the 2011 Queensland floods. The plot centred on the narrator's revelation that a number of deaths were murders, callously camouflaged as drownings.

The girls were all nervous when Nadine discussed the plot with them and suggested that perhaps it might not be seen as the kosher thing to write about, given there was still so much grief in Toowoomba and the Lockyer Valley. But Nadine's publisher loved the story. 'Controversy sells,' Nadine was told.

And once she'd signed the contract, there was no turning back. The book was already on the bestseller list due to the number of Queenslanders reading it, even though it had been out for only a few weeks. Veronica had read it twice, Xanthe and Spencer were both struggling to get through it, Ellen didn't think it was Nadine's best effort, and Izzy still hadn't got around to it given all that was going on in her life.

The tiddas knew Nadine could handle the event without any effort, but would she do it without any booze? Nadine was looking more glamorous than usual, wearing a fitted black top, linen pants and shoes with heels. She wore the sapphire earrings Ellen had given her for her birthday, and had clear lip-gloss on. All the women had noticed the extra effort she'd gone to. Throughout the interview Nadine carried herself calmly; she spoke softly and considered every answer, but her hands were held tightly in her lap. She could see her tiddas up the back but didn't make eye contact with any of them, knowing how they felt about the book.

When it came time for questions from the floor, Nadine flatly refused to answer any. Some guests groaned out loud with disappointment; others mumbled their annoyance. They'd wanted the chance to have their say and maybe even get some answers to the questions the author had carefully danced around to date: *Did she know anyone who'd died in the flood? Did she speak to any of the family members of the deceased? Did she expect to remain one of Queensland's favourite authors after this?*

The dim lights of the Gunshop Café still couldn't hide the glow Veronica felt from within. It had been Nadine's event, but Veronica had been the shining star; her tiddas were still talking about her new look as they walked along Boundary Street for dinner afterwards. Nadine and her publicist arrived twenty minutes later; after a flurry of rushed autograph signing, the author was clearly in a foul mood.

'Well, that went well, didn't it?' she said sarcastically, slumping into a chair and picking up the wine menu.

'Yes, it did, Nadine. You're too hard on yourself. You walked everyone through your process, you clarified why you wrote the book. I could see people nodding in agreement and understanding what you were saying.' Nadine's publicist Claire was good at her job. She knew how to appease her author, make her feel she was brilliant, while also affirming that her latest book was the best yet.

'I need a drink,' Nadine said, as if she hadn't heard a word.

'Of course, what would you like?' Claire said, looking to the others and then scanning the restaurant for the waiter.

'A bottle of the Bannockburn pinot noir, thanks.'

It was the priciest wine on the menu, but Claire didn't blink an eyelid. Nadine was the prized author and anything she wanted she could have, hang the expense.

'Ladies?' Claire asked the other women.

'I'm already looking at the desserts,' Izzy said, 'I could easily go straight to the chilled lemon tart with Caboolture strawberries and double cream.' She put her hand on her belly. 'I'm eating for two, you know.'

'Oh, I can see how many hills I'd have to climb for that,' Xanthe joked, getting more and more comfortable with Izzy's pregnancy every day.

The waiter approached and after they'd all put in their orders the debriefing continued.

'I shouldn't have written that book, they all hate me now. I could feel it there tonight,' Nadine said, remorse in her voice. It sounded as if she was truly sorry for imposing her creativity onto what for many had been a heartbreaking disaster.

'No-one hates you, Nadine. People were there because they wanted to hear your story, about the writing process, about why the book was important to you,' Veronica said.

'You didn't even sit up the front! It was like you were embarrassed to know me.' Nadine looked at Veronica and then the other women one at a time. The mood was getting tenser by the minute.

'Don't be ridiculous, Nadine,' Izzy tried to appease. 'You had so many fans there we couldn't even get up the front.'

By the time the food arrived Nadine had downed four glasses of wine and retreated into herself. She hardly touched her salmon but ordered another bottle of wine.

'Well, at least it's over now, the appearances and all the bullshit media stuff,' Nadine mumbled to herself.

'Just one more to go. Don't forget you've got the literary breakfast at Bulimba coming up.' Claire feigned excitement but, after a number of book tours with Nadine, she knew her author was prone to being volatile after a stressful event and a few wines.

'For fuck's sake, Claire, I told you not to book any morning events. I hate morning events, I don't *do* morning events,' Nadine was loud and angry, acting like a prima donna.

The women sat there staring, embarrassed. They all felt sorry for the young publicist who had to deal with the abuse.

'I think I'll fix the bill and be off,' Claire said with a quiver in her voice. 'I'll call you in the morning, Nadine. Do you need a cabcharge to get home?' She pulled her wallet from her handbag.

'I don't need a fucking cabcharge,' Nadine growled.

Claire was visibly shaken, her eyes glassy from wearing the brunt of Nadine's bad mood. Xanthe got up as Claire walked over to pay the bill.

'I'm sorry about Nadine, she's under a lot of stress.' It was all she could think of to say.

'Oh, I know it's hard to be in the public eye,' Claire said. 'I see authors stressed all the time. It's all good. I'm fine, really. You go back and enjoy the rest of the night. I have an early flight back to Melbourne anyway.'

'You can be a real bitch, Nadine!' Ellen said angrily as she leant over the table. 'You don't talk to people helping you like that. Actually you don't talk to any-fucking-one like that.' She sat back in her seat and shook her head in disgust.

Nadine didn't seem at all shocked by Ellen's admonishment of her. 'Look,' she started matter-of-factly, 'I had already told her I didn't want to do a morning event. It's breakfast time. I'm boring when I'm sober, and the audience is boring when I'm sober.'

The girls couldn't believe what she had just said to them.

'So are we boring when *you're* sober? That's just fucking pathetic. You're pathetic. I'm out of here.' Ellen got up, shaking her head angrily, and stormed off.

'Wait Ellen, don't leave.' Vee called out. 'Nadine needs us.'

Ellen reluctantly returned to the table.

'I don't need *you*. Who needs *you*?' Nadine's voice was filled with venom. 'I mean look at you.' She waved her hands at Veronica. 'You think a haircut and a new outfit changes you? And did you get your boobs done as well? Oh my God.'

Veronica could feel her heart racing and her face burning up. Ellen was restraining herself from getting up and punching Nadine in the jaw.

'I suppose the tits were your idea,' Nadine said to Ellen. 'It's all about sex for you, isn't it? Well Vee's nice, don't turn her into a slut like you.'

'Nadine!' Izzy said.

'Stop it, you're out of control,' Xanthe said, reaching for the wine bottle.

'Oh you're still here, Xanthe. I thought you'd be at home nagging your husband for sex because you're ovulating. Nice of you to stay.' Her sarcasm stung the entire table.

'Fuck you, Nadine!' Xanthe grabbed her bag from the back of her chair and stormed out. Xanthe rarely swore, and everyone knew it, but Nadine had gone too far.

Now Ellen and Veronica got up and left.

'What the fuck is wrong with you?' Izzy whispered in Nadine's ear. 'I don't even want to look at you. Are you insane? Sit here while I call your husband to come and get you.' She walked out onto the footpath so no-one in the restaurant could hear her. But before she could even dial, she received a text from Richard.

I'm on my way. Ellen called me.

13

Filling a Void by Leaving the Gap

Veronica stopped at the doorway of each of her sons' bedrooms upstairs. Two had left years before but she kept them the same for whenever they visited and wanted to stay the night. The walls remained covered in posters: State of Origin teams, motorcross bikes, ironmen, scantily clad pop stars like Beyoncé and Pink. John's room had a weight bench and empty protein-shaker underneath it. She didn't know how he'd cope going out on his own, but Alex had been generous enough to help with the bond on a share-house in West End. John liked the grunge of the suburb and the Lock and Load Bar. Always the baby of the family, he promised to make time for a home-cooked meal at least once a week, but both he and Veronica knew it would be more often than that. He was the only one of her boys who maintained an appreciation of his mother's cooking.

The guest room had been converted into a studio of sorts but most of Vee's time recently had been looking at properties to live in and artist's studios to rent. Her decision to move had given her a sense of purpose she hadn't felt for a long time, and the only person she had to please right now was herself. She was aware of the clarity and empowerment a new home in a new location would provide, and could now believe that a fulfilling future lay ahead.

She headed back down to the kitchen and slumped against the fridge, staring at the copper rangehood above the stove that everyone in the family hit their head on at least once a year. She laughed out loud remembering the cursing that used to follow. She ran her hand along the teak dining table she'd had shipped back from Indonesia because she'd fallen in love with it at first sight, surprised that Alex had automatically agreed to the purchase. She never knew if it was because he wanted to make her happy, because he too loved the table, or whether he just didn't care. It was one of the few pieces of furniture Veronica had decided she would take with her when she moved. She wouldn't be taking the marital bed, the lounges or any of the artworks and antiques that Alex had bought at auction. She would sell or donate them or just give the whole lot away. Veronica had already created a new mental space for herself; now she was in the process of creating a more harmonious physical space for herself too. Her new home, the first that would be truly hers alone, would reflect her new path in life as an independent woman, an artist and a mature-aged student.

Butch walked into the house and lay at her feet as if knowing what his owner was planning. Dog may be man's best friend, but in Veronica's house it was woman's most loyal companion. She would miss him terribly.

'Oh dear boy, I do love you, but I need a smaller place, and you're too big.' She bent down to rub the ageing canine's belly. 'Daddy loves you too, though, and you'll be fine.' The dog closed his eyes, lapping up the attention. Even though Veronica was as attached as ever to Butch, she was already feeling the relief of having fewer responsibilities. Alex had agreed to take the dog now that Veronica was going to be moving into an apartment. Her relationship with Alex, although strained and volatile for the past eighteen months, was also taking a turn for the positive, and Butch had proven to be a useful olive branch in terms of civil communication. She sat on the ground, stroking her beloved pet's head. She talked to Butch as if she was handing over 'custody': 'What if I'm too tired at the end of the day and don't feel like a walk? What if my classmates want to go out for dinner or drinks to discuss art theory? I can't not go, can I? I need to be part of the cohort properly, right?' Such scenarios might soon be realities for her, and rather than shirking her responsibilities to the animal, on the contrary, she saw giving Butch to Alex as a responsible act.

The promise of personal freedom was driving Veronica's enthusiasm to get packed up and settled as soon as possible. She had worried less about her sons when each of them moved out because she never knew what they got up to. Not waiting for John to come in the door at all hours meant her anxiety about him would also decrease.

Apart from studying, Vee also wanted to travel now that she had time, the cash thanks to the settlement, and no-one relying on her 24/7. She wanted to see the Eiffel Tower and the Colosseum for real, not just on café posters. She wanted to stroll alongside the Seine and the Champs-Élysées and eat out in nice restaurants. She dreamed of going to Rome and visiting the Vatican. She'd read so many novels, memoirs and travel articles set in exotic places and now she was finally allowing the travel bug to infect her.

She looked into Butch's chocolate brown eyes and felt a tinge of guilt. 'Come on, then!'

She got up and walked towards the laundry where the dog lead hung by the back door. 'I will miss our walks, old fella. Truly I will. But it's *my* time, okay?'

Butch dragged Veronica along Arkana Street towards Chaprowe Road. She laughed like a young girl, enjoying her new free spirit, augmented by the endless energy of her German shepherd. As they approached St Peter Chanel Primary School a scrub turkey rushed back into the school-yard. Veronica heard laughter across the road and turned to see the two Murri sisters smiling widely. They waved to her as they crossed the road.

'Hi,' one of the sisters said, 'gorgeous day for a walk.'

'Stunning,' Veronica answered, pulling Butch back on the leash.

'Been meaning to yarn with you for a long time,' the other sister said, adjusting her sun visor. 'If you ever want company on a walk, you should let us know. We're walking the same way anyways.'

Veronica couldn't believe that the opportunity to meet had finally presented itself just as she was about to move. In the meantime though, she would enjoy the company of her two new friends.

'It sure is a gorgeous day,' Veronica replied.

'You're leaving The Gap, it's definite then?' Xanthe asked as she picked up one of Veronica's signature white and dark chocolate muffins. 'But you love it here.'

'I *do* love it here.' Veronica looked at the light coming through the northern window. 'But this place is my past now.' She took a sip from the bone china cup she would soon donate to the local Vinnies. 'And *this* place,' she handed over a real estate agent's catalogue opened at page five, 'is my future.'

'Wow, you found somewhere? That's amazing,' Ellen said, 'and you'll be able to get the ferry to Kangaroo Point to see me. We can do the Jazz Club on Sundays,' she added, excited about having her dear friend living so close.

'But this house is full of memories.' Xanthe, always the romantic, believed every tangible item held a memory, a story to be passed on, treasured or privately remembered.

'Those memories are in my heart and my head.' Veronica was becoming far less dependent on 'things'. 'I will carry them with me always, but I don't need to literally *carry* them with me.'

Some already-packed boxes of books were waiting to be collected by a women's housing network. She was pleased some of the family's favourite picture books, and many of the novels she'd read over the years, would be appreciated by other women and kids somewhere not too far away.

'It's too big here now anyway. Five bedrooms and two floors for two people and a dog is just embarrassing.' Veronica had often felt guilty about the privileged life she led in comparison to so many others. 'I want to simplify. I *need* to simplify.' She looked at the cluttered wall units in the lounge room and the marks on the walls where paintings had come down. 'I want stark white walls with artwork *I* love. New artwork.'

'Maybe some of your *own* artwork?' Xanthe suggested, reaching for her second muffin.

'Maybe.' Veronica smiled, quietly hoping that one day she would be confident enough to hang some of her own pieces in her new home. 'But is that something you do? I mean, as an artist? Wouldn't it be like a singer-songwriter listening to their own music every day?'

'I don't think it's the same. Anyway, do what *you* want, Vee. Paint your pictures, paint your walls, whatever you want.' Ellen picked up a black glass Art Deco vase. She looked at the barely-there sticker on the base: 'Made in Bohemia circa: 1930'. It was so old it was made in a part of the world once known as the Austro-Hungarian Empire, now part of the Czech Republic.

'You can have it,' Veronica said, as if she were talking about a $10 vase from IKEA.

'What? No, I can't, it's too much,' Ellen said.

'Isn't that the piece you bought at the silent auction for Kids MS a few years ago?' Izzy said, recalling the fundraiser they'd all gone to. 'It's a Karl Palda, isn't it? Worth a bomb.'

Veronica had no attachment to the piece at all. 'It's yours, Ellen. The money went to charity, it was a donation. Really, it's not something I want to take with me.'

'It *would* look good in Kangaroo Point, wouldn't it?' Ellen looked to Xanthe and Izzy for approval, feeling guilty now she had a sense of the vase's value.

Veronica walked over to Ellen and hugged her. 'I'm becoming a new me because of you. I want you to have it. Consider it a symbol of the turning point in my life, thanks to you.'

Ellen became so choked up she couldn't speak and was reminded that Nadine wasn't there; she would've commented about her lack of words for sure.

Veronica picked up a milky white glass table lamp. 'This would look fabulous in your lounge room, Xanthe. I know you like things to match. Do you think it will?'

Xanthe gasped. 'Are you kidding? I can make Murano match with anything, even with all those nickel-plated details.' Xanthe knew the Italian piece was circa 1960 and would cost a fortune to buy, but she also knew that no-one would appreciate the lamp more than she.

'And Izzy, correct me if I'm wrong, but I think this would fit perfectly in your place, in the corner near your dining table. No?' Veronica ran her hands down the length of a colossal standard lamp made out of wrought iron and with a red shade. 'It was designed by E. Brandt and made in France around 1925, I believe.'

Veronica was surprised by her ability to recall the details of all the various pieces she and Alex had bought over the years. And she was also surprised that she was finding it so easy to let go of them without any sadness.

'That is so . . .' Now Izzy was at a loss for words, just like Ellen had been.

'I'm sure the papers that came with it said that it was once owned by the Lesieur family, the biggest vegetable oil supplier in France.'

'Fuck me dead,' Izzy said. 'Sorry for swearing, but Vee I never knew you had all this amazing stuff. I mean, I've seen it, but never really taken any notice. You're a bloody art collector!'

'That may be, but the truth is I'd rather be an artist!' Veronica was determined that her past was going to remain in her past. She walked across the room to three huge boxes filled with bubble wrap. 'Take what you want,' she said, 'I'm going to sell or donate most things. And I'm selling the Lexus to pay for whatever new things I need. I don't need a bloody car that size or that expensive. I'm getting one of those environmental cars.'

'God, I would've traded the convertible with you,' Izzy joked. Asher had already swapped both their cars for a station wagon and ordered a baby capsule. 'But it's okay. I've promised myself a Lexus for my sixtieth. The bub will be going on twenty by then, so like you I'll be getting my life back!'

Nadine was still missing, and being missed, but the tiddas were always going to celebrate Riverfire at Ellen's, which boasted the best view over the river. Kicking off the city's Riverfestival, the choreographed display of fireworks was a pyrotechnician's dream. With three of the bridges close to South Bank being used as platforms for the displays, it was one night many locals were keen to enjoy. The September heat had already kicked in by week three and tens of thousands of Brisbanites would make their way to the old Expo site.

'This is so much better than having to deal with the crowds,' Veronica said, already looking forward to living closer to the city.

'Crowds *everywhere*,' Izzy said. 'I just don't have the patience to be around people and be this bloody uncomfortable.' She thought back to the blood tests she'd had the day before to check for diabetes and pregnancy anaemia. 'And in *my* condition, I really want to use private toilets.' Izzy wriggled in her seat. 'Apart from anything else, I just feel fat. I've gained eleven kilos, can you believe that? This kid is going to be huge; my vag is never going to be the same.'

'Have you thought about the birth much?' Xanthe asked.

'Absolutely, I can't stop thinking about it. I have no pain threshold at all. I want all the drugs they can give me.' Izzy was dead serious.

'Really?' Xanthe asked. 'You don't want to do it naturally?'

'Absolutely not, I want the epidural.' Izzy was adamant.

'But isn't that just for a C-section?' Ellen was pretending to know more than she did.

'No,' Izzy and Xanthe said in unison.

'If I'm in pain and the baby is still some way off and I haven't started dilating, then I want an epidural. Obviously, they're not going to give it to me if it's too close to delivering the baby.' Izzy had done enough reading to know that, and she didn't want Xanthe to think she hadn't given it some serious thought and research.

'You do realise there's risks, don't you, Izzy?' Veronica asked, recalling all the talks she'd had with Alex about their own children's births.

'I know an epidural can delay the birth because if I'm numb I won't be aware of my own urge to push,' Izzy said.

Ellen looked confused.

'And that means they may need to use forceps,' Izzy added.

Ellen screwed her face up; there was no chance of forceps ever making their way anywhere near *her* vagina.

A massive blast hit their ears as the Super Hornet aerial display took flight. It was 6.30 p.m. and the fireworks were scheduled for 7 p.m. They were what everyone was waiting for. The tiddas were no different except that none of them were prepared to sit for hours along the riverfront in the heat just for a glimpse. As they got older, the creature comforts of cushioned seats, private toilets and drinks in glass rather than plastic had become far more appealing.

'I can't believe people start staking out a spot at lunch time,' Izzy said.

'That's nothing, you should see them at New Year's,' Ellen added.

'Oh God, I don't know why they bother. Once you've seen the fireworks in Sydney, even on the television, everything else just pales into insignificance,' Xanthe said, thinking back to the romantic New Year's Eve she and Spencer had only nine months ago.

On that night they'd watched the world's most stunning harbour come alive from the luxury of their deluxe suite at the Four Seasons in Circular Quay. Spencer had secretly booked the trip a year in advance and had everything planned, down to the last drop of Veuve at midnight. By 12.15 a.m. they were making love to ring in the New Year. Now they weren't even having sex unless it was 'scheduled' into their electronic diaries according to Xanthe's cycle. Every time she got her period she sobbed alone, feeling a distance growing between her and her husband. She wondered what had happened in the past few months. They had been happy, they'd been planning; they'd been making love when aroused, not just when an alarm reminded them to.

Xanthe hadn't confided in the girls about her baby dramas for the past few months. Ever since Izzy had found her feet with the pregnancy their friendship had almost got back to normal, although at times it was still hard for Xanthe to feel overjoyed for her friend. Izzy herself didn't always act overjoyed, and Xanthe had almost made her mouth bleed from biting her lip when Izzy complained about being pregnant. By the same token, Izzy had become more aware of the fragile state of her tidda who continued pounding the hills of Paddington at the same time as praying to Biami for help.

Ever since Xanthe's grandmother back in Mudgee had told her to be patient and not use IVF or any other 'Western technique', Xanthe had hoped she'd become less anxious, but it wasn't easy. She was more stressed than ever about getting pregnant, and about the distance forming between her and Spencer, especially as he was happily going away more often for work.

Nadine was grumpy and anxious as she and Richard turned into Oxford Street for her literary breakfast event at Riverbend Books. She liked the owner, was grateful for the support of the independent bookseller over the years, and was thrilled they provided a book club for young readers that her children were keen to be part of. More than that, she liked that there was a licensed restaurant which made for a relaxed evening event for an author like her. But today she was doing the breakfast that Claire had organised, and there'd be no bevy to relax her and no publicist to appease her. Instead, Claire had chosen to send the local sales rep along to make sure everything went smoothly.

Nadine was surprised there was a full house so early in the morning. She wasn't sure everyone would leave happy. How would *they* cope without a bevy? Would they think she was interesting? Intelligent? Could she appear funny without a glass in her hand? She hoped so but lacked confidence, and her demons were taking over her brain.

'What a wonderful way to start the day,' she heard one woman say to her friend over coffee and toast.

'Can't think of anything better than sitting here devouring

corn fritters and stuffed mushrooms, while listening to a local author,' her friend responded.

This kind of banter was new to Nadine.

'Nads, they have French toast with pears and buffalo ricotta,' Richard whispered to his wife. 'I'm pretty sure they'll make it better than I ever could. I'm going to order you some.' He kissed her on the cheek, but she took his wrist firmly.

'Richard please, no food, not yet.'

He nodded, but after years of marriage he was still trying to understand the complexity of the woman he loved.

As the paying guests took their seats, Nadine looked around in the hope that her tiddas might have turned up, perhaps even forgiven her. But all she saw were mothers yarning over coffee, businessmen with iPads open, and book lovers flicking through her latest title. She imagined the event would be far less confronting professionally than the previous one, but on a personal level it was much more challenging.

Inside the store, Richard stood aside as his wife was greeted by cheerful, friendly staff. He stared as they welcomed her and ran through the timing of the morning's program. Nadine wished he would turn his attention to the groovy t-shirts on sale, or the vast collection of children's books up the back of the store, but she knew he stood close by because he was so proud of her.

The frangipani and jacarandas were in full bloom in Paddington. Their scent and colour lifted Xanthe's spirits as she faced the beginning of another menstrual cyce, a further reminder that her dream had been delayed yet again. She was glad book club was at her place; she was grateful for the company, as Spencer had been working late most nights on the new Racial Discrimination Act legislation currently before the government. His late nights meant he was coming home tired and not wanting to make love at all.

Ellen, Izzy and Veronica were sitting on the couch talking about Veronica's move to Spring Hill, now only weeks away.

'I think you'll really love it, Vee. It's completely different to The Gap,' said Ellen.

'I agree, but you know where else I wouldn't mind living?'

'Where?' Xanthe, Izzy and Ellen chorused.

'Mullumbimby,' Veronica said, smiling.

'Well *you* could afford to buy a flash house there. Not sure about the rest of us, but nice segue into tonight's book, tidda,' Ellen said, turning her phone to silent but not off altogether because she wanted to know if Craig tried to call.

They reached into their bags for their novels, the fifth for the local Goori author. She'd previously nailed the young adult market with novels about growing up in Brisbane and Byron Bay.

'This made me wonder about what constitutes the great Australian novel,' Veronica said, reminding them all that Nadine wasn't there. None of them wanted to be the one to initiate discussion about her absence, each having received a simple text message earlier in the day making her apologies.

'Well, it depends on how you define the great Australian novel, don't you think?' Xanthe asked.

'Of course, it's all subjective. Everyone will define it in a different way, especially anyone in academia,' Izzy said.

'What do you think makes the great Australian novel?' Ellen looked at each of her tiddas. Her phone vibrated in her lap. It hadn't left her sight in weeks.

'I think it should be something that's political and philosophical,' Xanthe said. 'And it should challenge the reader's values as Aussies.'

'Just from working at the library and meeting a whole range of writers at the festival last week, I'd say that it certainly needs to be something that can entertain while providing a message,' Izzy said, thinking of all the interviews she'd done over the four days when the library was buzzing with students, retirees, international authors and performers.

'And it most definitely should include Indigenous themes and characters,' Veronica added. Now the coordinator for the Brisbane arm of Reading for Reconciliation, she was more than aware of the need for Australian literature to be inclusive of the First Peoples of the country.

'Excuse me,' Ellen said, unable to sit any longer without responding to her fella.

'Everything all right?' Izzy asked, hoping that it wasn't another death back in Mudgee.

'Oh, no, it's all good.' Ellen smiled a silly, infatuated-school-girl smile. 'It's just Craig.' She kept tapping the keys, wanting to keep the dialogue going with him even though she knew she should've been focusing on her tiddas.

'This sounds like it might be getting serious,' Xanthe said, happy that her friend might finally be settling down with one fella and not having one a week.

'I don't know about *serious*.' Ellen wasn't going to admit too much too soon. She was the last woman to succumb to heartache at the hands of a man. She was the strong one, the least needy one, the most emotionally-in-control one. Or so she thought.

'It's just that . . .' she stopped herself, not quite sure what she even wanted to say.

'What?' Veronica asked. 'Are you falling in love?'

'God no! Me? In love? Me and love are not a likely fit.' Ellen was going to resist that emotion, even if it was just verbally. 'But I do think about him, a *lot*.' She put the phone down on the coffee table.

The girls all smiled, wanting to bask in the glow of infatuation that their tidda was radiating across the room.

'Well?' Izzy asked. 'What's happened so far? And I don't mean sex; we know you've got that sorted.'

'He makes me laugh. We laugh a lot, about nothing special, stupid things, him. He talks about himself a lot and that makes me laugh, and so I guess he plays on that.'

'Where's he taken you, for dinner or whatever?' Veronica asked.

'We don't really go out that much. I'm keen to stay in and enjoy my apartment.' This was only partially true. Ellen did want to make the most of her mortgage payments, but she wouldn't have said no to the occasional dinner or a movie.

'The problem is, I haven't had a boyfriend in so long, and I am so used to being alone and doing things when I want to, how I want to, wherever I want to, without having to ask anyone else, or consider or please anyone else, that to have another person in my life so much is weird all of a sudden, which you all probably think is weird of me.' Ellen couldn't believe she'd said it all in one breath and that she could finally articulate what had been spinning around in her head for weeks.

'No, not at all,' Izzy said. 'I'm the same with Asher. It's a challenge and a surprise every day though.' *And a lot of adjustments,* Izzy thought. After decades of living alone it hadn't been easy to accommodate Asher into her life and apartment full-time, but she was trying.

'Do you *want* a boyfriend?' Veronica asked.

'Do you want *Craig* as a boyfriend, more to the point?' Xanthe went further.

'I don't know, all I know is that he is in my head constantly. I wake up and he is in my thoughts. He's the last thing on my mind when I go to sleep. I see things in the shops and I want to buy them for him. I sit on the ferry and wish he was there with me. And the chemistry is so intense between us that I can almost come just thinking about him. I think I'm going insane. There's something wrong with me.'

Izzy chuckled.

'What?' Ellen asked accusingly.

'You're not insane, Ellen,' Veronica said.

'You *are* in love!' Xanthe declared.

'Fuck! No, I don't want to be in love, love equals pain. Love means heartache. Love, schmove, it's not love, it's lust!' Ellen was not going to be cornered into feeling something she was sure she didn't.

Her tiddas laughed harder.

'Oh no, please don't tell me I'm in love. I can't work with that.' Ellen appeared genuinely distraught. 'What should I do?' she pleaded.

'Tell him!' Xanthe ordered, exasperated.

'Tell him what?' Ellen frowned.

'Tell him how you feeeel!' Xanthe crooned.

The tiddas all nodded.

14

Jacaranda Season

Along the river at West End the jacarandas were in full bloom. Izzy felt calmed by the blanket of deep mauve and the scent of the Brazilian import, and just wanted to lie underneath one and sleep. The sun was rising by 5.30 a.m. each day but she wasn't. Whenever she could, she'd walk in the afternoons before sunset but that was rare these days. The humidity was already peaking at ninety per cent and it was knocking her around like never before. Even though the nights dropped to a comfortable seventeen degrees, day temperatures were in the mid-twenties and the October heat was living up to its reputation.

Izzy sat still, breathing deeply, attempting to meditate, even though she had never really been able to stop her mind ticking over about work. But it was the bumping and squirming she could feel in her belly that consumed her thoughts now. She was waiting to experience the Braxton

Hicks contractions that everyone had been telling her about.

'Is he related to David Hicks?' Asher had joked one night.

And while Izzy was glad that he wasn't getting as nervous as she was about the impending birth, she wished he didn't try to make everything into a joke.

The next big decision was whether or not they'd circumcise if the baby was a boy.

'Shouldn't he look like me?' Asher had asked, genuinely believing it was the right thing to do. He'd been circumcised, his brothers and his father too, he assumed. He wasn't a sporting bloke so had no stories about locker-room looks.

They still hadn't reached an agreement on what they'd do. Izzy didn't want to ask the girls about circumcision because she was frightened it would start another emotional scene when they were still dealing with Nadine's dramas. She made a mental note to herself (one she knew she'd have to write down because of her 'mummy brain') that she needed to have a serious conversation with the doctor when she saw him about her heartburn, which was still causing her discomfort.

Her ankles were swollen and she was wearing a form-fitting jersey dress that hugged her waistline just a little more than she wanted. She was trying to keep as much to routine as possible in terms of her working day, given that Asher had moved in and home life was changing as dramatically as her body. At thirty-two weeks she already felt like she was going to burst. She couldn't believe she had another eight weeks to go.

Think nice thoughts, she told herself and pulled out her phone to take a photo of the row of jacarandas. She made it her screensaver, smiling while she looked at the colour that gave Orleigh Park personality. For some reason, one tree reminded her of those in her mother's backyard back in Mudgee. She looked forward to taking her own child there one day to play under the trees with his or her cousins. She texted the photo to her tiddas saying:

Having a Mudgee moment, see you tonight. X

Nadine texted back a simple X. Izzy hadn't seen or heard from her since her appalling scene at the Gunshop Café on the night of her book launch. Nadine might be drowning in her own guilt but no-one realised, so Izzy was glad for any communication from her sister-in-law right now.

Ellen texted back a photo taken from her balcony of the river with a smiley face. Veronica sent a photo of all the boxes she was packing. Xanthe didn't respond at all. Izzy assumed she was on a plane or in training, but knew she'd be seeing her tidda that night anyway for book club.

At 7 p.m. the tiddas – once again minus Nadine – arrived at Ellen's in Kangaroo Point for what Izzy thought was book club. She'd read the nominated book and had started making her own list of the one hundred loves in her life: the jacarandas, morning walks on the river, Asher's cooking, being pregnant. She was looking forward to hearing what the others would have on their lists. It would undoubtedly be a fun night, with a lot of laughs. So she was surprised when she arrived at Ellen's to find there was no book club discussion planned at all. The small apartment had been decorated for a baby shower. Izzy burst into tears at the thoughtfulness of her tiddas, at their generosity, at the realisation that this baby thing was actually happening.

'Oh God, don't cry! This was supposed to be a happy night,' Ellen said, putting her arms around her tidda. Stepping back, she eyed Izzy up and down. 'You look amazing,' she said, desperately wanting to touch Izzy's belly but aware of how much mothers-to-be hated it. 'I can't believe how much you've grown since the last time I saw you.'

'I'm huge, I know, and my face is so puffy.' She wiped the tears from her cheek with her hands. 'I'm still working on camera till I finish up next month, and I *hate* it! I can't watch myself; it's like looking at another person.'

'Stop it!' Xanthe said. 'You look like a healthy pregnant woman, so stop obsessing about how you look. You're glowing.'

Izzy had been brought back into line.

'How are you feeling?' Veronica asked.

'A lot of heartburn, and backache sometimes, but I think that's from being on my feet constantly with this extra weight.' She looked at Xanthe. 'I'm not complaining, just stating the facts. But when did you have time to pull all this together, Ellen?' she asked, looking at the white balloons, the pink and blue iced cupcakes and other treats laid out on the small kitchen table.

'Oh, between services and shagging, I can manage to get a lot done. I made these myself.' Ellen was proud of her new sense of domesticity, inspired of late by doing some cooking for Craig. She was completely besotted but hadn't told him.

And wasn't even sure that she should. Things were going along just right, or so she tried to convince herself.

'You're still seeing that rugby player then? That's got to be a record length of time,' Xanthe said.

Ellen wasn't sure if Xanthe was having a dig, or just making an observation; it *was* a record length of time for her. It was three months now, and by Ellen's standards that constituted something serious, something meaningful, something possibly beginning with the letter 'L'.

'Are you in, please correct me if I am wrong . . .' Izzy smiled, 'a relationship?'

Ellen blushed. She wasn't sure if she was at all, but for the first time in a long time, she felt good about being with Craig. But she still kept her cards close to her chest, even with the girls.

'Oh, I don't know. I really, really like him.'

'And?' Veronica asked.

'He's already said he doesn't want a relationship. He wants to be single,' Ellen said matter-of-factly.

'To play the field?' Xanthe asked.

'I guess so. He's hot. He's young. I can understand he wants to have fun, and can.'

'So you haven't told him then, have you?' Xanthe asked, shaking her head.

'No.' Ellen felt like she was being chastised for not doing her homework.

'How do you feel if he's dating other women?' Veronica asked.

'It never bothered me when we first met. I was happy for a good time too, but . . .' Ellen winced.

'But what?' Izzy asked.

'But now, I get a little jealous, and I hate it.' She shook her head, almost disappointed in herself. 'I don't want him seeing other women. I want him to myself.'

'Thank God, at last you've seen the light,' Xanthe said. 'You see what it means to have someone special to you, not just someone to play with.'

'I'm not *you*, Xanthe, and he's certainly not Spencer by any stretch of the imagination.' Ellen recognised that what her tidda and her husband had was something more than significant. 'You and Spencer, you're extraordinary as relationships go, I know that. Even though I'm not *always* kind about him, I know how much he loves you, and how much you love each other. I'm nowhere near that with Craig; I just don't want him fucking other women, that's all.'

Xanthe didn't respond, but retreated into herself. She hadn't told her friends that she and Spencer had been struggling lately. That the pressure to have a baby had taken its toll on their relationship. That her husband had become a recluse in his own home, keeping to himself in recent weeks. They hadn't made love for ten days, and while he was away for work, she was almost glad to be in a house free of tension.

'Well I'm glad you cleared that up,' Izzy laughed. 'But watch out, look what happened to Asher and me.' Izzy patted her belly with both hands.

'Well, you know I won't be having a baby. I did clarify that a few months ago, didn't I?' Ellen was still comfortable with her decision to get her tubes tied, even if Xanthe never came to terms with it.

'But *you* my dear friend, you are going to be a deadly mum, and we deadly aunties-to-be are going to be there too.' Ellen handed Izzy a glossy white bag with silver ribbon cascading down the side. 'We decided this month's book club would really be a baby book club night and we're all giving the bub a book.' Ellen looked to Xanthe and Veronica for agreement and they both smiled. 'So we will be available for babysitting and storytelling services when you need us.'

Izzy opened the gifts: the *Deadly Reads* series from Xanthe and Spencer, the *The Very Hungry Caterpillar* with Wiradjuri translation from Ellen, and *Jalygurr Aussie Animal Rhymes* from Veronica.

'And this is from Nadine.' Ellen presented a large, gift-wrapped box to Izzy. 'Richard dropped it over earlier.'

'Really?' Izzy was taken by complete surprise. 'He called me to say she wasn't feeling well and wouldn't be here but didn't mention this.' Izzy looked at the box resting on her lap.

'That's not all, there's a bloody stroller hidden in the bedroom,' Ellen said, knowing there was no room to roll it out while all the women were there. 'But that's Nadine. Nothing by halves, eh?'

No-one responded to Ellen's comment but they were all curious to see what Nadine had sent.

'Open the box,' Veronica said. 'It's a lovely thought that she went to the trouble to get you something.'

Izzy knew that Nadine would probably have just ordered something online, to be gift-wrapped in the warehouse and delivered to their post office box. So, she was surprised when she opened the box to find a picture book about two young Kooris boys and some Australian sugar bees. A handwritten card read:

Dear Izzy –

I'm so sorry. I know you're at Ellen's now, and I know I couldn't be there unless I had fixed my mistakes. I really want to do that. I miss you all so much. Can you please ask Vee, Xanthe and Ellen if they will come to dinner next week? I need to talk to you all. Please, I need your help. Love, Nadine xoxo

Izzy was bawling by the time she finished reading the card to herself.

'What's wrong?' Xanthe asked, herself in tears at seeing her friend's distress.

Izzy read the card out and they all ended up in tears.

'We have to go,' Veronica said.

'Of course,' Xanthe added.

'I miss her too, can you believe that?' Ellen smiled as she wiped tears from her eyes.

Tea-lights lined the windowsill overlooking the river. The Powerhouse was alive with Friday night thank-God-it's-the-weekend energy. It was bustling and jovial, a carnival-like atmosphere, except at one table in the dimly lit Alto restaurant where the five tiddas sat in near silence.

It was the first time they'd been together for almost two months, since Nadine's abusive outburst in West End. The women attempted small talk but with no real uptake of anything. Veronica commented that a local radio broadcaster was at a table nearby, and the women all looked in his direction. Izzy noticed the CEO of an Aboriginal organisation was having dinner with someone else's wife, and they all discreetly checked them out too. Ellen mentioned the comedy festival program, and Izzy commented on a baby being nursed at another table and said that she'd never do it in public. Xanthe was impressed with the mother's capacity to feed herself *and* her child at the same time.

'I wonder what David Koch would think about that,' she said, nodding in the woman's direction.

The chefs were focusing on their work, the waitstaff flitted around the restaurant taking orders and delivering meals, and the tiddas read their menus, waiting for some direction from their hostess.

'It's hard to believe that a building that once housed all the means to power the entire Brisbane tramway system now has theatre, bars *and* nice restaurants.' To everyone's relief, Veronica was trying to engage them all in conversation.

Nadine used the opportunity to speak, even though there was no natural segue. She took a deep breath. 'I'm sorry about everything – my behaviour, what I said to you, Xanthe, is unforgiveable.'

'It's okay, Nadine, it was partly true. I do run off a lot, and it must be annoying.'

'No, you're trying to have a baby; you have to do what you have to do. And the way I said it, I'm sure I was vile. Please forgive me.' Nadine was contrite, sincere.

Xanthe smiled warmly, a lump in her throat.

'And Veronica, my friend, your new style is enviable, really. You look fabulous. I could do with some help with my own image. God knows, it's getting tired. And you've inspired me.' Her words were genuine and touched her friend's heart.

'Really?' Veronica couldn't recall ever inspiring anyone.

'Yes, that's why I'm going shopping this weekend, new wardrobe, new look and hopefully new me.'

Ellen was tempted to say something, but wasn't sure a wisecrack would go down well at the moment, even with the kinder Nadine at the table.

Nadine knew her friend well enough to know Ellen would be biting her lip. 'You know I love you, Ellen, don't you?'

Ellen nodded.

'I mean, you give as good as you get most of the time, but I know I totally overstepped the mark last time. I promise I won't do it again.'

While everyone wanted to believe that was the truth, they were all privately sceptical. Still, Ellen believed her tidda meant it. 'That's good enough for me. I've missed our little to-ing and fro-ing.'

Nadine sighed with relief, knowing she'd received some forgiveness, but she was really worried about her sister-in-law.

'And Izzy.' She breathed deeply again. 'I'm sorry you find me an embarrassment to your family. You must know I love Richard more than life itself.'

'Of course I know that,' Izzy said, but it wasn't her love for Richard that Izzy was worried about.

'And I love you too,' Nadine confirmed. 'And I hate that your mum thinks I've shamed your family.' She hung her head.

'Mum'll get over it,' Izzy said, only half-believing it. Her mother wasn't big on forgiveness but for her son she'd do almost anything. 'What's going on though, Nadine? We're all worried about you, and . . .' She stopped short of mentioning Nadine's drinking problem.

'I know it's not an excuse, but part of the reason I've been so crazy lately is that I'm ill.'

Izzy looked at her sister-in-law and immediately thought liver cancer. Xanthe thought breast cancer. Veronica's ex-doctor's-wife mind ran a list through her head, and Ellen just felt bad for all the bitching she'd done about Nadine over the last few months.

'What is it?' Izzy rested her hand on Nadine's to stop it from shaking.

'I'm going through menopause,' Nadine said dramatically.

'Oh for fuck's sake, Nadine!' Ellen just couldn't contain herself. 'It isn't a fucking illness, it's a fucking life cycle, like puberty for grown-ups.'

'Thanks for the sympathy, Ellen; you'll feel differently as soon as you start getting the symptoms.'

'Sympathy? God, you're so dramatic sometimes. Are you in character or something?' Ellen was right back where she and Nadine had left off months ago; the apologies and forgiveness and guilt had dissipated as quickly as they had appeared.

'I think I've started as well, Nadine, but I think at our age, we're probably just peri-menopausal,' Veronica said, feeling some sympathy. 'I've had night sweats, and I'm not sleeping well.'

'Really? God, I have to turn my pillow over constantly for something cool. Richard is going insane. I kick the covers off both of us nearly every night.'

'Sometimes when I'm driving, the heat on my back from the seat is so unbearable I have to lean forward.' Veronica continued with her symptoms and Nadine was grateful for some understanding, although the others didn't look overly concerned.

'Aside from the hot flushes, I keep having these strange out of body experiences and they scare me,' Nadine said. 'And I find concentrating hard, but this is the worst thing: I'm getting violent.'

'What?' the other women chorused, concerned for what she had already done, and might do next. Up until now they'd assumed she was just making excuses for her bad behaviour when drinking.

'Guess I better move the butter knife then,' Ellen said sarcastically.

'Richard swears I nearly killed him a couple of times.'

'What?' Izzy was shocked.

'My hormones make me insane and his snoring was freaking me out and I tried suffocating him in his sleep. Twice!' A smirk crept across her face. 'The only positive is that it gave me an idea for a novel.'

'Nadine!' Izzy wasn't impressed.

'I'm joking. I actually cried for a week with guilt.'

'And so you should,' Izzy said, the only one of the women game enough to have a dig, because she was, after all, family.

'Everything is topsy-turvy for me: my emotions, my mind, my body. I'm completely out of control and the hot flushes not only nearly made me go nuts, they're also embarrassing.' Nadine looked around the restaurant to make sure no-one could hear. It was rare for her do that, but tonight she was sober. 'I was doing a book event when a uni student wanted to ask me some questions about his masters. I'm standing there feeling this flush come over me and my damned glasses fogged up.'

'No way!' Ellen laughed.

'I've never been so embarrassed in all my life. I swear he thought it was because of *him*!'

'What did you do?' Veronica felt for her tidda, knowing exactly what she was feeling.

'Nothing, what could I do? I gave him the advice and moved away as quickly as I could. Richard thought it was hilarious.'

'So what are you doing about it then?' Xanthe asked, hoping that *she* didn't slip into peri-menopausal hysteria before falling pregnant, but then perhaps she wasn't falling pregnant because she was already there. She thought she could feel a hot flush coming on but then figured it was like getting an itchy head the minute someone mentioned the word lice.

'I'm using HRT patches, they're great.' Nadine told them.

'Where are they?' Ellen asked.

'In the fridge.'

'No, idiot, where on your body?' Ellen said, laughing.

And the tiddas all joined in. It was the first laugh they'd had together for some time.

As the laughter subsided the waiter came to take drink orders.

'Nothing for me, thanks,' Nadine said to everyone's surprise.

'Not drinking?' Izzy asked, happy her sister-in-law had finally come to terms with her problem.

'I think we all know it doesn't help my moods or my behaviour.' Nadine looked at the table, unable for the moment to look at her friends. 'I need some help, I know that.'

'We'll help you,' Veronica said, concerned for her friend and knowing how much support her tiddas had given her in recent months.

'I've got some ideas.' Nadine reached into her handbag and pulled out some brochures. 'I need to get out of the house, out of my routine, and I need to *do* something rather than sit and write and create scenarios for other people, even if they *are* characters.' She handed around the pamphlets on Bikram yoga, rock climbing, rowing.

'Wow,' Xanthe said. 'You're going all out, aren't you?'

'I need to be busy.'

'I can take you to Bikram if you want. I'd love the company.' Xanthe was genuinely keen.

'Great, and I'm open to other ideas as well.' Nadine was positive, happy. Best of all, she wasn't drunk.

Izzy wondered if her sister-in-law had replaced the grog with pills instead.

'You just need some balance in life, Nadine. You don't have to go from one extreme to another,' Xanthe reassured her.

And you probably should go to counselling, Izzy thought, but didn't say out loud.

Ellen woke up with Craig's leg over hers. She lay face down, naked, exhausted from an afternoon that had made her never want to leave her bed, ever. Craig snored quietly and she didn't want to wake him. She just repositioned her head more comfortably on the pillow and lay there looking at him; at the lines around his eyes, the bushiness of his eyebrows, the remnants of her lipstick around his mouth. She snorted at the thought of the Clinique red on his dick as well. She'd check that out later, when he was awake.

As the sun started to set she began to get hungry. She needed to eat, but she didn't want to wake him. And she had no food in her flat. They'd have to go out or order in. She didn't care; she just wanted to be with him, near him, next to him, under him. As long as he was not far away.

Craig's phone rang and he jumped up, startled.

'Leave it,' Ellen said.

'I can't, it might be work.'

He got out of bed, strolling in all his naked glory to where his jeans lay tangled on the floor.

Ellen was agitated, anxious; she didn't want him to leave.

'Yeah mate, no worries, about an hour, yep.'

She was getting angry and upset.

'Gotta go, darl,' he said.

'Come here first,' she said, still naked with the sheet across her.

'Oh, you make me weak. I have nothing left for you, babe, you've drained me!'

'Just kiss me.' She pulled him to her.

He couldn't resist, he didn't want to. They made love again, this time with a sense of urgency, and Ellen wondered if it was because he had to leave. To his credit, Craig wasn't a selfish lover, not one to 'eat and run', as he so eloquently put it once. Post-coital, he cradled her, with what she thought was caring.

'I need to tell you something,' she said cautiously.

'This can't be good; it never is when a woman says that.' He took a deep breath. 'Let me guess, you don't want to see me anymore,' he said flatly.

'No!' She sat up. 'I want to see *more* of you. Just you, and just me. I want it to be us.'

As the words came out she wished she'd scripted it better; less pathetic, less teenager-ish, perhaps even a little less needy. But there it was and once it was out in the universe there was nothing she could do about it.

'Oh babe, why would you change this?' He gently pinched her nipple as if it were a toy. 'What we have is good, no?'

'It's good, yes, but I want more.' She took his hand in hers awkwardly.

'Ah, now you're being greedy. You want more than this?'

He grabbed his larger than average dick, which they both knew was more than most women could handle.

'I'm falling in love with you.'

'Oh.'

Silence fell in the room; all either of them could hear was the traffic on the Story Bridge that had suddenly risen in decibels.

'You'd better go,' Ellen said, not with anger, not in tears, just matter-of-factly.

Craig dressed quickly, walked to the bed where Ellen still sat, pretending to flick through stations on the television. He kissed her on the cheek.

'I'll call you,' he whispered.

'Don't bother,' she said. 'No point.'

Ellen didn't want a man who wanted to see other women. Not anymore. She was angry with herself, with her friends for having encouraged her to tell him. It was against her nature to fall in love, to want only one man who would, as Craig had demonstrated, just leave anyway. The rejection stung.

Her phone beeped with a text five minutes later. She hoped it said he was falling in love too, that he was just scared. That he was on his way back. Instead it simply read:

Are you okay?

She responded:

I'm fine. But a man who wants to fuck you but doesn't want a relationship with you is an arsehole. Delete my number!

She waited for a reply but it never came. What could he say to that anyway?

Ellen showered, crying as the water ran down her face, down her body – the one that had been much loved and caressed over the course of the afternoon. She wasn't going to take the humiliating blow lying down, well not lying down alone anyway, so she pulled on a pair of jeans and a tight red top and walked with determined steps to the Story Bridge Hotel.

There were men everywhere when she arrived. The pub was known for being a pick-up joint. Plenty of bars, plenty of options, plenty of mistakes to be made at her local. She had never 'scored' at the Story Bridge before, though. She could easily avoid the men there if she wanted; they were all looking at women ten or more years younger than her anyway. But tonight she was on a mission; a revenge root could be had, but all she wanted was a little attention. A little something to tell her she was worth more than an afternoon shag. Craig had made her feel worthless – and worse, she had let him.

She soon realised she was in the wrong bar for being picked up. A man of about ninety kept winking at her. Another of about fifty with high-waisted jeans and a baseball cap tucked into his belt kept looking at her longingly. She nearly fell off her chair when he saluted her. Meanwhile the eighteen-year-old barman wanted to buy her a drink after his shift ended.

She looked around at the women, some obviously on the make; it had been a long time since she'd sat at the bar by herself and just observed the mating rituals of others. She thought back to her Sunday morning breakfast, when the waitress had placed the order for blueberry and ricotta pancakes before she had even sat down at her favourite table on the veranda facing the jacarandas across the road. The view from the café was only spoilt by the Australian flag flying outside the apartment block in Deakin Street, the Union Jack a stark reminder of the ongoing colonisation of her mob. Ellen reminded herself that Sunday morning was the best time to go to the Story Bridge, before all the divorcees arrived for the afternoon drinking and jam session. Tonight was no time to be there, especially given the mood she was in.

After her third glass of wine, she carefully got down from the barstool. She ordered a pizza to take away, went to the bottle shop, grabbed something on special, went home, ate two slices, drank one glass of wine and then cursed herself for the carb, sugar and fat intake. She'd run an extra K the next morning to feel better. And she'd wipe Craig from her life completely.

15
Flash Women

As Izzy entered the Flash Women exhibition in kuril dhagun she heard the soulful voice of Georgia Corowa, then saw the young woman elegantly perched on a stool in a black version of Marilyn Monroe's plunging neckline dress. She was strumming her guitar to welcome guests on their arrival.

Izzy wove through the crowds which included the Minister, local Elders, the exhibitors, kids from Doomadgee State School, frocked up women from across the city wearing fascinators, and one or two men supporting their women.

She blinked twice, taking in the enormity of the Uluru dress with its metres and metres of burnt orange fabric that must have been stretched over a wire frame, Izzy thought, otherwise how *did* they make it stand up? It was the signature piece of the show and Izzy scanned the room for the designer, Juliette Knox, who was best known as the entrepreneur behind the Little Black Dress Empire. But it was the

Warrior Woman dress that carried her back home to Wiradjuri country and the strong women who had led the way for her personally. Izzy stared through the glass at the emu feather cloak and imagined herself in it.

She spotted the first Aboriginal model, Sandra Georgiou, across the room and wished it got cold enough in Brisbane to wear the cream cape that Georgiou had designed.

Oddly enough, it was the wedding dresses that Izzy spent most time admiring. She'd never thought about getting married before. But with a baby on the way, marriage was just another thing that pressed on her brain, something she knew her mother would want to see happen, sooner rather than later. She looked at Jacynthia Ghee's wedding dress from 1957 and read her words: 'Love is not really an emotion – it's a purity of feeling – it's different to an emotional state.'

What does that actually mean? Izzy thought.

Izzy read out loud a quote by Sharon Phineasa whose carved haircombs were on display: 'Your appearance is an outward expression of an inward connection.' It was a positive affirmation for Indigenous women, and reminded her of all her strong tiddas across the country, many of whom were 'flash women' indeed.

Izzy's back was aching as she interviewed the curator, Walbira Murray, who gave insights into the lives of the women featured in the exhibition.

'I've witnessed the lateral violence against our women telling them that they can't be flash *and* Black. I wanted to tell them through this exhibition that we as Aboriginal women have *always* been flash. To think about how their mothers and grandmothers used to dress,' Murray said into the camera, Izzy nodding in agreement.

'I need to change the battery,' a young cameraman advised Izzy.

'That's fine, I think we have enough. Walbira, thanks so much for your time,' and she kissed the woman who had a queue of well-wishers waiting to speak to her.

Izzy took a deep breath and sat down, quietly glad that her day was almost over. It was one of the most inspiring events she'd covered at the library and her last before giving birth. She was grateful to be going into motherhood with such fresh memories of deadly women. She finished her piece with a clip of Aunty Ruth Hegarty from Cherbourg, who in launching the exhibition had said: 'It really doesn't matter what colour you are. It's a female thing. We like to dress up. And if our people can look at beauty rather than the scars within, then we're doing okay.'

Nadine sat with brochures, pamphlets and business cards strewn across the table. Words like yoga, tennis, bushwalking, meditation, zumba, crossfit and boot camp stared up at her.

'What's all this, darling?'

Richard put a cup of green tea in front of her. There had been no glasses of wine on the veranda for weeks now. That, coupled with the HRT, meant Nadine's moods and behaviour had improved immeasurably. She was suffering with issues of detoxing but had flatly refused to go to a detox centre or even a grog-free spa in Brisbane. She didn't want to feel more ashamed than she already did, so the night sweats and the shaking and the vomiting were only seen by her and Richard, the kids having been told that their mother had a bad virus. Nadine had upped her vitamin B intake as recommended on various websites she'd researched, and Xanthe had given her a whole set of organic herbal teas to keep up her hydration. Nadine's body was starting to repair, but it was the psychological and emotional side of her that needed work. Alcohol had been her friend for so long. It was her writing buddy; it gave her characters voice, and her storylines suspense and action. The problem was that Nadine didn't think she could create any more without it, so she had decided to take a break for a while to recover, rejuvenate, re-think her needs. And being active was one of those needs.

'I need to do something more, something physical to keep me busy. I'm thinking yoga, zumba, maybe even boot camp.'

Richard laughed. 'Nads, let's be serious, you'd *hate* boot camp! But I love you're at least considering something that will get you out of the house more.'

'What about Bikram yoga, then? I do Pilates, so I should be able to do yoga.'

'My flexible wife gets more flexible? I'm liking that idea already.'

'You are very naughty.' She ran her hand down the zip of his work shorts, but he pulled away, smiling. 'Let me finish sweeping first.'

Nadine read another brochure and considered the Kundalini yoga class in The Gap. She could go there with Veronica perhaps, although she couldn't recall Vee ever talking about yoga. Vee went bushwalking, and Nadine was convinced she did scrapbooking too but was too embarrassed to admit it.

'Bloody crapbooking!' Nadine said out loud to no-one as she switched on her laptop. 'I couldn't think of anything more boring!'

Richard heard his wife's self-talking. 'You could scrapbook all your reviews and the articles about you.'

'My publicist should do it,' Nadine snapped, then suddenly realised she hadn't heard from Claire in weeks. 'Anyway, I thought *you* were doing that for me.'

'I am, my love, I am.' He kissed her on the forehead. 'But right now, I have to find some plants for my sister that she can't kill. Wish me luck.'

'Luck!'

When Richard had left, Nadine sent an email to Xanthe, who was in Walgett, training at a local community organisation.

Dear Tidda,

I think I want to do Bikram yoga, but I am scared. What if I have a heart attack or stop breathing or just collapse from lack of fitness? I think it might just kill me. Can I just come and try it out with you? Please?

Love,

Nadine xo

Xanthe just happened to be online in her hotel room, taking a break with an instant coffee, and was grateful to hear from someone who wanted something from her that didn't involve work. She smiled as she typed:

Dear Nadine –
I would LOVE to take you to Bikram. It WON'T kill you. For the first class you just need to focus on being in the room for the 90 mins. That's all. If you can achieve that then you'll have done well. We'll put our mats up the back of the room and close to the door just in case you need to go out. You will feel the heat as soon as you enter. But you'll be fine. Just wear some shorts – they want to see your knees – and a singlet, and bring a bottle of water. I'm going next Monday. Do you want me to pick you up?
Love, your tidda.

Nadine's own day had suddenly got brighter. It had been forever since she'd exchanged emails with her tiddas – well, any that she could remember. She liked being in contact again and planning activities. She wrote back fast:

Dear Tidda –
Thank you so much for the support. But I think this might be the end of our friendship. I know you are good at it, and you take it seriously. I'll be the one who huffs and puffs and moans out loud, and probably farts too. You'll hate me at the end. But I would like to try it. My body needs it. My head needs it.

I can get Richard to drive me. He'll need to be there anyway if something goes wrong ☺
Nadine xo

Xanthe was proud of Nadine and responded quickly before she made her way back to the community centre:

Nadine,
I will NOT hate you. I love that you are coming to do this with me. No-one else has ever asked or offered to come. I'd love to share the experience with you. I feel better every time I do it, even though I'm not that great. I'm glad you're coming, see you there. And I am proud of all the efforts you are making.
Love from Walgett,
Xanthe

Nadine read Xanthe's final email and wanted to cry. Not her usual drunken cry in the cemetery, but tears of gratitude. Grateful that her friends truly cared, were standing by and supporting her. As she got more sober, Nadine was realising the incredible good fortune she experienced every day, unrelated to the actual fortune she had in the bank.

She refused to attend an AA meeting in the local area – there was still some level of denial about the extent of her problem – and she also didn't want to give the locals any more fodder. She had been reading about the Twelve Steps, though, and while she struggled with the references to God and didn't believe that all the steps referred to her, she had taken the time to act on Step Eight. She had made a list of all persons she had harmed, and was willing to make amends to them all. The dinner with her tiddas had been a big step for her. She also promised herself that she would follow Step Ten and continue to take personal inventory; when she was wrong, she would promptly admit it.

Forty-eight hours later Nadine and Richard made the trek from Brookfield to Bardon.

'I feel sick,' she said to Richard, who was tapping a beat on the steering wheel as they drove to the yoga studio.

'Are you all right?'

'No, I feel sick with nerves. The freaking studio is thirty-seven degrees to start with.'

'That can't be normal.' Richard was surprised.

'It's not normal. But then neither am I. I probably deserve to melt into the flooring.'

'Stop it!' Richard laughed at his wife warmly, and rubbed her right thigh after changing gears.

'I love you.'

Richard smiled. 'I love you too.'

'You're not normal either, you know that, don't you?' She poked him in the left side.

'I know.' He chuckled. 'I know!'

As they pulled into the car park, Xanthe was parking her small white Hyundai.

'Hey,' Nadine called out as she climbed from the car.

'Hi there.' Xanthe was genuinely happy to see Nadine, and pleased her friend was trying her hardest to kick her habit. But she was also pleased to be sharing her passion for Bikram with her tidda – well with anyone.

By the time the class started Nadine was already sweating, her legs slippery from the moisturiser she'd put on before she left home. She'd shaved her legs for the first time in weeks and realised how dry they were. But she looked good in her shorts. A month of not drinking had been hard but she'd inadvertently lost a couple of kilos. Her body showed all the benefits of not being filled with excess sugar every day.

Nadine scanned the room and among all the women she saw only one man, shirtless with too many tattoos. The perfect place to pick up, she thought, but the crowd looked too serious for frivolities. No-one spoke other than the trainer, Paula, and no-one looked at anyone else either. Everyone faced forward to the mirrored wall, instructed to focus only on the self.

'You can give yourself ninety minutes per day to focus on *you*, it's not selfish,' Paula said.

After the first forty minutes Nadine started to feel ill; she was dizzy, nauseous, off balance. *This can't be good,* she thought to herself. She wanted to text Richard to come and carry her out. 'I'm going to throw up,' she said under her breath, hoping to get some sympathy from Xanthe, who was completely focused. Nadine was impressed with her tidda's capacity to switch off everything else, but the truth was Xanthe's mind was ticking over about having a baby; she had mastered the ability to do the poses *and* obsess at the same time. A true skill!

'No-one should be talking for the ninety minutes we are here,' Paula said.

Fuck, she can hear like a dolphin . . . Nadine didn't like being chastised either. *Doesn't she know who I am?*

Nadine sat down on her mat before she collapsed. She breathed deeply, waiting until she could get up again. She searched the room for anyone else who might be struggling.

'For the beginners, if you can't do everything, just sit in child's pose. It's okay. Remember, if you can just stay in the room for this class then you have achieved.'

Nadine was convinced the comment was directed at her. She wanted to take the teacher aside and say, *Hey, in MY world I am the best at what I do. I can do these exercises, I just feel sick!*

But she knew that part of what was happening to her was that her body was going into serious detox. She was sweating out the crap she'd been ingesting for years. It was her own fault.

The lights were dimmed and the class lay on their backs doing the final breathing exercises. *Thank God!*

Nadine was relieved; Xanthe was revitalised. Paula left the room and slowly they got up, put their mats over the rail and headed to the change room. Nadine couldn't believe the crimson colour of her face.

'Jesus, my head looks like a watermelon that's about to explode.'

'You did really well. I'm proud of you.' Xanthe put her hand on her sweaty friend's shoulder.

'I'm proud of me too. I really enjoyed it!'

'Well?' Richard asked nervously as his wife got in the car.

'I finished it. That's something, isn't it?' She needed applause, affirmation of the attempt she'd made.

'That's massive, my love.' He leant in and kissed her.

'Oh darl, I didn't shower. You know me and public showers. Sorry, I'm smelly.'

'Yes, but you're *my* kind of smelly.' He rubbed his wife's thigh. 'Even if your face looks like a watermelon.'

'Bloody hell, I just said that to Xanthe!'

Nadine was still burning up, but she was sipping the coconut water she'd grabbed at reception and was looking forward to getting home. She couldn't even imagine being able to drink a glass of wine after that class, and was grateful for that small mercy. She didn't say it out loud though. 'I survived the class,' she said instead, 'but I'm grateful I didn't have a heart attack, throw up *or* burst into tears.'

Richard laughed. 'You are always so dramatic.'

'I'm serious, I was really scared one of them might happen.'

Nadine went quiet as they continued to drive, staring out the window as Van Morrison played on the radio.

'Everything okay over there, Nads?'

'Just thinking.'

'Here's trouble.'

'The interesting thing about doing that tonight was that it really helped me to concentrate. You can't just let your mind roam in there. I was completely focused on not collapsing.'

'You're serious, aren't you?'

'Yes, and I'm grateful that I maintained my focus the entire time. That in itself is something I'm incredibly proud of. I have a very short attention span, as you'd know. By the way, what's for dinner?'

'Sounds like you should be grateful to Xanthe for taking you, eh?'

'I am, I'll send her some flowers.'

'The celosia is in bloom right now, gorgeous colours. Red, purple, pinks, yellow, orange.' Richard knew his plants.

Nadine leaned over and kissed her husband on the cheek. 'Then on your recommendation I'll order her some of those, or maybe a plant for her garden.'

'Or you could come to the markets with me tomorrow,' Richard suggested, happy to find a new sense of companionship with his wife. The woman he'd married was making a return.

'Oh,' she hesitated, not keen on the early morning trip.

'Can I bribe you with this?' He handed her a Wagon Wheel. 'You would've burnt off enough calories in there for ten of these. Anyway, I thought you'd need a sugar hit.'

Nadine unwrapped it and drifted back to the 1970s and her orange lunch box that was often packed with one of the chocolate biscuits filled with jam and marshmallow. She was surprised at how clear her memory was since she stopped drinking. She wondered if Xanthe was indulging in something naughty as well.

Spencer was reading the newspaper when Xanthe arrived home. 'How was it?' he asked, feigning interest, as she walked in the living room.

'Great!' Xanthe said, invigorated and feeling horny. It had been too many days since they made love, but she was in the mood *and* ovulating. She'd texted him earlier that day to remind him.

'It'd be great if you came with me one night,' Xanthe said, having one last stretch before she jumped in the shower. 'It will increase your flexibility.'

'I'm flexible enough,' he responded, without looking up from his newspaper.

'It'll improve your circulation,' she added.

'Circulation's just fine, thanks.'

'It will reduce the stress you are constantly under, too,' she said, starting to peel off her clothes.

'You know what will reduce my stress even more?'

'What?' Xanthe was genuinely interested in what might help her husband feel more relaxed.

'You not nagging me constantly about yoga and ovulation windows and babies and organic fucking everything.' Spencer had never spoken to his wife that way before and it shocked them both.

Xanthe stopped still, trying to figure out what had just happened. She looked hurt, she felt hurt. She pulled her top back on.

'Okay,' she said, feeling ashamed that she had brought the response on herself. She walked out the door and closed it quietly behind her, tears falling by the time she got to the front gate.

Spencer grabbed his mobile, knowing immediately the damage he had done. He heard Xanthe's phone ringing. She'd left it behind on the dining table.

The tears stung Xanthe's face as she found a quiet spot under a tree at the end of the street. She didn't want to walk, she wanted to hide and sob. It was the longest twenty-five minutes of her life, sitting there feeling lonely, sad, hurt. She hated conflict with the people she loved. And she adored Spencer. She was only now realising that the never-ending baby conversations and conception failures were taking their toll on him too.

Xanthe walked back into the house quietly. As soon as Spencer heard the door close he walked quickly towards her.

'I'm sorry,' he said, placing his hands on the sides of her face and kissing her gently on the mouth. 'I'm an arse sometimes.'

'I'm sorry too.'

Veronica, Xanthe and Ellen sat on the veranda at Nadine's for their monthly book club get together. Izzy was only days away from her due date and had opted out of coming. She had emailed some of her thoughts on the book to them earlier and was now bored, having already finished up at work. She'd done a lot of sitting at home with her feet up on the coffee table and the telly on.

Xanthe had chosen this month's book, and it had affected them all. Izzy's email was used as a springboard to the conversation. Xanthe read it out.

I cried when I read this book. The story around the tragic death of Cameron Doomadgee in police custody was so disturbing,

I had nightmares. So too the history of Palm Island as a mission, or as we're told an 'open air jail'. This is the sad reality of a forgotten Australian community, and a heart-wrenching example of the deathly flaws of the policing system not only in Queensland but nationally. It should be compulsory reading for all Australians. It really makes you worry about Blackfellas incarcerated anywhere, doesn't it?

'Richard said that with forty different tribes sent to Palm Island it was a little like what he'd heard about Cherbourg,' Nadine added when Xanthe finished reading the email.

'It'd be like taking people from forty different countries around the world, putting them in one place and telling them to just get along, speak the same language, form a new community. Could you imagine it happening today?'

Veronica's Reading for Reconciliation Group had also discussed the work, and she had strong views on it. 'It should be on the national curriculum,' she insisted. 'It considers attempts at assimilation in terms of religion and other aspects of culture.'

'It also reveals the systematic flaws in Queensland's policing,' Xanthe added. 'And really demonstrates the tensions between the Black and white communities. Palm Island and Queensland isn't an isolated experience, unfortunately.'

'Shit, seeing the police protect each other like that made me really angry,' Ellen said. 'Sad too. It made me realise just how much the cops are untouchable!' Unexpectedly, she grinned. 'Aside from that, and no disrespect, but I saw the movie at the film festival last week and I have to say that lawyer Bo is one catch, isn't he?'

'He's married, Ellen,' Xanthe said.

'And he's got SIX kids!' Veronica laughed. 'Just what *you'd* love!'

With the book talk over, the women were quieter than usual, silenced by the reality that institutional racism still rendered most Blackfellas powerless in the big scheme of things.

Nadine broke the silence. 'Anyone want to come to Maleny with me this weekend for an event?' She had signings at local bookstores to do, and was looking forward to them for the first time in years. 'And it's not just because I need a driver, I'd actually like to have some female company.'

Xanthe jumped at the chance to give Spencer some space, but she also wanted to support Nadine, who seemed to be putting on a good front. Or else the HRT was actually working miracles. The tiddas had been following an unwritten roster, checking in on Nadine and taking her out to various events and activities while she was detoxing. If she wanted a drink at any time, they wouldn't say she couldn't have one, but nor would they be kind or supportive. She never broke though, and every day she got stronger.

'I'll take you,' Xanthe said. 'And why don't we see what's standing in the way of you getting your licence back? After all, you've got a great car to be driving.'

The following weekend three of the tiddas made the trek up the Bruce Highway to Maleny for a weekend away. Nadine's signing at Rosetta Books followed closely after an appearance by Tom Keneally and she hoped the locals would still be in a literary mood. Xanthe looked forward to all the organic produce she could buy. Ellen had decided to go as well. She was upset about Craig but hadn't mentioned anything about it to her tiddas. She wanted to get away, to not risk seeing him running near Kangaroo Point. And maybe, she thought to herself, she might just get laid in Maleny as well.

As they hit the rural area Nadine was quiet. She was finding the aftermath of detox difficult and there was always an urge to drink. She could still find a reason at any time of day; the cravings hadn't disappeared, not yet. She wondered if they ever would. She hoped she wouldn't be tempted this weekend. She was on the mailing list for Maleny Mountain Wines, and shouldn't be. She hoped they wouldn't go anywhere near booze, but that was a ridiculous dream; she could smell a good tipple from fifty paces.

On the Saturday night they strolled to the Film Society screening at the Community Centre.

'I'm joining up,' Nadine said, pulling out her credit card.

'You don't have to join, you might never come back here.' Xanthe tried to stop her.

'Then I'll just support it. Do you know how much money I'm saving by not drinking?' Her attempted joke went down like a lead balloon. Nadine's drinking hadn't been a joke to any of the others who had borne the brunt of her bad behaviour in recent years.

'As if she needs to worry about saving,' Ellen whispered to Xanthe.

'Let her go. She needs to do something with that credit card now she's not getting cases of wine delivered to Brookfield.'

The woman handing over the membership form said with a smile, 'Aren't you the author, Nadine – ?'

Nadine didn't let her finish before she responded with 'Yes, yes I am.' Nadine couldn't feign humility. Sober, she didn't mind being celebrity-spotted on occasion, even if she preferred to be left alone back home. She was less annoyed of late also by those wanting autographs and asking about certain characters and storylines. It seemed that sober equalled more tolerant.

'I'll grab a table,' Xanthe said, heading towards the front of the hall.

'I'll get in the queue for dinner,' Ellen said, heading to her right and joining the other locals trying to decide on one of the three options on the board.

Xanthe grabbed three RESERVED signs from the table and went to find some seats to hold until they'd eaten and the movie started.

Ellen stayed with Nadine even though she was in the safety of the hall.

'Oh,' Nadine said, as she turned towards the food counter.

'Oh,' Ellen echoed, as she looked at the wine bottles lined up on the bistro counter. Seven dollars a glass or twenty for the bottle.

'Come on, you'll be right, we'll get extra dessert to compensate.'

Nadine didn't say anything. She focused on the list of options for dinner: veal, chicken and a mushroom turnover.

'I'll have the vegie option please, Ellen,' she said, offering her a fifty-dollar note.

While they ate dinner the women dissected their surroundings: the ageing demographics, the old hall, the bargain meal, the quality of the food, what the film might be like. Every few minutes Ellen would check her phone to see if Craig had called or texted; nothing. She had mixed feelings; she didn't want to speak to him but she wanted to know he missed her.

They had gone to see *Mozart's Sister* but *Love Crimes* was being shown instead. No-one cared. It was a novelty to be in a community hall run by volunteers and they were even quite taken by the wooden seats. None of them had seen anything like it before.

'Slightly different to going to the movies at The Barracks,' Xanthe smiled, as she put a forkful of local vegies in her mouth.

'I should start something like this in Brookfield,' Nadine said. 'Much better than just happy hour, don't you think?' She knew she would benefit from a new project; she needed to keep busy, focused on anything other than the next drink.

'Anyone for some homemade slice?' Xanthe offered.

'God, I love this. It even makes me want to bake! I can't remember the last time I made a cake for the kids.' Nadine was serious; she really couldn't remember any baking she'd done at Brookfield.

'Did anyone get the quillow out of the boot?' Xanthe asked.

'The what?' Ellen shook her head, perplexed.

'The quillow. It's a quilt that can turn into a pillow.'

Ellen nearly fell off her chair laughing. 'Sounds ugly!'

'It's practical,' Xanthe said defensively, knowing it was in fact dead ugly.

'Where did you buy it?' Nadine had no intention of getting one, but feigned interest.

'I didn't. Spencer's mum gave it to me. One of those gifts that tells you you're not the one she wanted her son to marry.'

'What?' Ellen didn't know what she was talking about.

'At Christmas time, we all received gifts in the post. The other daughter-in-laws got gorgeous quilts in their favourite colours. I got this quillow thing. But Spencer loves it. He packed it for me to bring up here.'

On the Sunday morning the tiddas toured the centre of Maleny again. They roamed the markets in the RSL, picking up and putting down old LP records, deciding against the cards and paper made from elephant poo. They all bought some Fair Trade coffee.

They roamed through the little town's galleries, checking out the work of local artists. Veronica could almost see her own work hanging in a gallery one day. They had breakfast at the UpFront Club, and watched the locals going about a normal day.

'Jesus, another cooperative! This mob is more community minded than Blackfellas,' Ellen said. 'Oh my God, you should see their IGA! It shits on anything near me.' She was carrying two bags. 'I've got locally produced honey, mango, apple and pumpkin chutney, and sweet chilli and ginger sauce. I don't know what the fuck I'm going to cook, but this place is unreal.'

Nadine grabbed every brochure possible on cooking classes, the local dairies, retreats and real estate. She grabbed a copy of the *Co-op News* as she walked into the Maple Street Co-op; she picked up a basket and proceeded to fill it with nettle tea, spirulina and wheatgrass.

'Time for a spring clean, eh?' Xanthe peered into the basket, smiling.

'Way past time, tidda,' Nadine said. 'I'm considering becoming a sproutarian.'

'A what?' Even Xanthe hadn't heard of that one.

'Someone who eats predominantly sprouts. Or maybe a fruitarian.' Nadine held a sweet smelling mango in her hands.

'Nadine, you don't have to go from one extreme to another; you just need to not drink booze.'

'I can't just do that. It's not me. I need to make dramatic changes, that's who I am. That's why I am an artist, a writer.'

16

A Fall from Grace

'It's happening!' Izzy screamed from the bathroom, her words echoing along the concrete landing so that all the neighbours could hear. Asher came flying in from the balcony, where he'd been tending to the herb garden he was growing in pots.

'Asher!' she screamed more loudly.

'I'm here,' he said, sounding worried for the first time since she'd told him she was pregnant.

Izzy stood in a small puddle. 'I heard a pop and then this,' she said, flustered, looking at the ground and breathing heavily.

'It's okay,' he said, handing her a towel. 'Let's just get you tidied up a little and we'll be on our way.'

Izzy couldn't believe how calm Asher was. He'd made her pack her bag weeks before, and had mapped out the route to the hospital exactly; 3.2 kilometres, door to door.

Within twenty minutes they were there, Asher doing the paperwork and Izzy texting the girls, Richard and her brothers in Mudgee. Her mother hadn't mastered the iPhone the siblings had kicked in for yet, so she relied on verbal messages to be passed on.

This is really happening, Izzy thought to herself, mentally going back over the past few months and suddenly hit by the realisation that her life was about to change forever. She tried not to think of the nightmare stories she'd read online or about what other women had told her about labour. Then she felt her first contraction; it was like the most severe period pain she'd ever had. And then it continued, for nine hours, Asher by her side the entire time, and the doctors and nurses checking on her constantly.

'What a great choice,' Veronica said, never having been to Garuva before. 'This is *not* the Valley I think of, even if we are sitting on cushions.'

'It's kind of good Izzy isn't here, there's no way she would be able to sit on the floor,' Ellen said.

'Any word from Asher yet?' Nadine asked.

They all checked their phones. Nothing.

'This is *très chic,*' Xanthe said, having started French lessons in preparation for her upcoming trip to New Caledonia. She and Spencer had decided they both needed a proper break; somewhere tropical, somewhere peaceful, somewhere romantic.

'Can we sit on a high stool at one of the barrels while we wait, please?' Veronica asked gingerly. 'Not to be a party pooper but I've got a tight skirt on.' One result of her makeover was a black, high-waisted skirt and purple silk top. She looked steaming hot in the outfit, but it was not comfortable enough to sit in crossed-legged on the floor, and certainly not in public. At least behind the curtains of their dining table she'd be able to retain some sense of modesty.

'Cocktails?' Ellen asked.

'Or mocktails?' Xanthe added, thinking of Nadine.

Nadine hesitated. 'You can all have cocktails. I don't care who drinks as long as it's not *me*.'

There was a tone of frustration in her voice which prompted Xanthe to respond cheerily. 'I plan on eating *a lot* tonight, so I can do without the alcohol and make up for the calories with food!'

As the women settled at the bar and waited to be seated, a group of younger women in short, strapless dresses and four-inch heels came in. One wore a short tulle veil.

'Oh God, they still have hen's nights in the city?' Nadine rolled her eyes. 'I thought they stopped years ago.'

'Not like *your* hen's night in Mudgee, eh tidda,' Ellen said.

'*Please* don't remind me what happened. Richard still brings up the fact that the cops dropped me home wearing red fluffy handcuffs. Who's bloody idea was that?'

'I'm going to tell her not to do it,' Veronica said, pretending to walk over to the bride-to-be.

Xanthe pulled her friend back gently. 'You can't do that.'

'That's right. She has to learn the hard way, like the rest of us!' Nadine joked.

A thin waitress in tight pants and strappy black top came to escort the women to their table. The harem-like room was surrounded by a thick organza curtain on all sides.

'Shit!' Veronica said, trying a range of positions in her tight skirt. 'I really wasn't meant to wear clothes like this.'

'Don't be silly, just hoik it up. No-one can see,' Ellen encouraged her friend.

And so Vee did, feeling momentarily like mutton dressed as lamb.

As they pored over the menu each declared their chosen dish. 'I'll have the Turkish octopus,' Xanthe got in first.

'If everyone's happy, I'll take the barbecued fish,' Veronica said.

'I can't pronounce it but I like the sound of that beef dish,' Ellen said, pointing to a name that none of them could say.

Nadine was silent. She felt agitated; she desperately wanted a cocktail or a glass of wine or even a shot of something in a small glass. She could hear other guests nearby having a great time, and she wanted that fun feeling too. She missed it. She needed it. She excused herself, saying she was going to the bathroom, and headed straight for the bar where they started the night. She ordered a vodka tonic, knowing it was quicker to make than a cocktail and wouldn't be detected on her breath.

'Make it a double,' she instructed the barman.

'Everything all right?' Xanthe asked when Nadine sat back down, looking flushed.

'Of course,' she said, paranoid that they could tell what she'd done. 'I just called Richard to check everything was okay at home.'

And that was the first of the lies she'd need to keep telling in order to drink for the rest of the evening.

Ellen's phone vibrated and she saw Craig's name flash on the screeen. Her heart skipped a beat, then pounded faster and harder. She hadn't heard from him for two months. She didn't expect to hear from him again. She didn't want to. She didn't answer it, let it go to voicemail. But when she got home she listened to the message seventeen times and memorised the words: *Hello Ellen, it's Craig. Happy birthday. I miss you and wondered if you wanted to go out for dinner, just to talk.*

At 9 p.m. Nadine texted Richard and said Veronica would drive her home, and that he should go to bed. At 10.30 p.m. she told the girls that Richard was out the front waiting for her. She left alone and caught a cab while the other tiddas were finishing their desserts. When she arrived home Nadine checked that Richard was asleep and then went to the cellar. It had been eight weeks since she'd been down there. She didn't concern herself with the wine she chose; they all were quality. She just wanted to get the cork out, pour liquid into a glass and feel the taste of cab sav or merlot or pinot or anything on her tongue. She finished the bottle quickly and opened another. She felt her sight go blurry. The guilt was pumping through her. A moment later she passed out.

As the sun rose, Richard realised Nadine wasn't beside him. He jumped out of bed. From the doorway of the kitchen he could see his wife wrapped in a doona and crashed out in the double hammock.

'Nads!' Richard was seething with anger, and hurting with disappointment. An empty bottle lay on the veranda and in her sleep Nadine was dribbling into a cushion. He shook his head, grateful that the kids were still asleep.

'You've got a beautiful, healthy baby girl, with a *lot* of hair,' the doctor congratulated Izzy and Asher.

Asher wiped the tears from his eyes, kissed Izzy on her dry mouth and sat down to take hold of the little bundle he had helped create. He gazed at his tiny, tightly wrapped daughter and immediately fell in love.

'This is my best dish ever,' he said softly.

Izzy was exhausted, but as she looked at Asher her feelings for him were as strong as the love she now felt for her baby girl. Asher sat on the edge of the bed so they could both see and touch her.

'Our little Murri miracle,' Asher whispered.

'Koori miracle,' Izzy whispered back, smiling.

Within hours flowers were being delivered to the room, and Asher's text message to family and friends had been sent far and wide. 'News spreads like wildfire on the Murri grapevine,' he said, looking at the dozens of messages waiting to be read and listened to on the phone.

That night Richard visited with Brittany and Cameron.

The two cousins were besotted with the newest member of the family and arrived armed with enough stuffed toys to satisfy most of the maternity ward. They took turns at holding the yet-to-be-named baby and made noises about wishing they had a baby brother or sister.

'Where's Aunty Nadine?' Izzy asked.

Richard smiled. He looked at the kids. He had no choice but to lie. 'She's got a sore throat and didn't think it was a good idea to be near the baby.' He hated the dishonesty and ached with disappointment about Nadine's fall from grace, but luckily Izzy took what he said at face value.

Ellen and Veronica visited the next morning, both cooing, although neither wanted babies in their own home unless as passing visitors. Xanthe arrived shortly after with a bright purple elephant that was immediately the most popular item in the room.

'Hiiii,' she said, poking her head round the door of the private room. 'How's the new mum doing?'

Izzy was grateful to see her, knowing it would have been difficult for Xanthe to face someone else living her dream. To Xanthe's surprise, however, she felt at peace, joyful for her tidda, knowing the magic of motherhood her bestie would now be experiencing.

'This is Aunty Xanthe,' Izzy told her daughter. 'Would you like to hold her?' she asked Xanthe.

Xanthe could feel the lump forming in her throat. 'Yes.' It was all she could manage before sitting down on the chair next to the bed and putting a pillow under her left arm for support. She took the precious bundle carefully, not taking her eyes off her once, and held her close, as if she were her own.

'She's perfect, Izzy, just perfect,' Xanthe said, as a single tear fell.

Ellen sat in the Restaurant Venice, perched high on the bend of the Brisbane River and looking across to the Story Bridge. She was sick with nerves and trying to calm the butterflies doing somersaults in her belly. She couldn't recall the last date she'd been on. She couldn't remember the last man she'd allowed to tug at her heartstrings. She didn't want to expect too much from dinner with Craig, but she couldn't help herself. It had been four days since his call, and she'd barely slept with excitement and anxiety. Never had she been so grateful for having a lot of deaths and funerals to deal with, but she realised how awful it was to be glad that other people's grief had kept her preoccupied and taken her mind off her own emotional turmoil.

The sun was setting, the orange-pink glow providing a backdrop of light against the frame of green metal struts. Lights were on at the Jazz Club at Kangaroo Point and the city ferry was doing its regular run from one side of the river to the other. She watched people in sports gear powering along the board-walk below, and didn't notice when Craig finally walked in.

Having not seen each other for months, he did a double take when he first saw the woman he now realised he cared for. Ellen looked so different. Her hair had grown; it looked softer, more feminine and was a golden brown, the hairdresser having dyed it back to what she remembered was Ellen's natural colour. Ellen had dark lipstick on that exactly matched the blood red, figure-hugging dress she'd bought especially for what was officially her 'first date' with Craig.

'You look absolutely gorgeous,' Craig said before he even sat down.

Ellen melted at his words but said nothing.

'Interesting choice,' Craig said, looking around the restaurant. 'It's a faux Edwardian look. Kind of like Mardi Gras meets Carnivalé.'

Ellen was surprised that he was even interested in the style of the place, let alone knew anything about its design. 'How do you know that?'

'I'm a builder, I know a little about architecture.'

Ellen looked surprised.

'What? You think I just lay bricks and mix cement all day?' He sounded a little defensive. 'I hear people talk about stuff all the time.' He pointed to the ceiling. 'The grapes are a symbol of Bacchus, the god of wine. So I reckon they'd say the style here is Bacchanalian. But I could be wrong.'

Ellen was impressed. She couldn't believe she'd missed this about Craig, but she just smiled.

Craig settled into his seat and looked across at her. 'I've missed you.'

'I've missed you, too,' she said, feeling her hands getting sweaty.

The next two hours were a blur of laughter, reminiscing and planning. Craig talked about all the construction going on around the city, and some of the projects he was working on. Ellen thought about her Aunty Molly and Uncle Ron and wondered if this kind of getting-to-know-each-other was the foundation she needed to have a lasting relationship and love like theirs. She and Craig left the restaurant holding hands and with plans in place for the weeks ahead; that in itself, Ellen thought, was a major milestone in her adult life.

'Richard's furious with me.' Nadine was crying into a chai latte. 'I need help but I don't want to go to AA, I just don't.'

'You need something more than yoga and reading books, Nadine, you've got a real problem.' Xanthe was trying to contain her own disappointment in her friend as she reached across the kitchen table and touched Nadine's hand.

'I know.' Nadine wiped her tears. 'What about hypnotherapy?' she asked, hoping for an easy way out. She handed Xanthe some brochures. 'I'll buy these CDs and listen to them at home. Apparently they can help to train your mind away from drinking.'

Xanthe refused to look at the glossy brochures Nadine had passed her. 'I don't know, Nadine, I think they might be a waste of money, and I know you've got plenty, but if it's not going to help you permanently, then I think it will just be a waste of time too.'

Nadine was disappointed in her tidda's lack of enthusiasm and so she tried another angle. She was desperate to find a way to make everyone happy without having to go to AA.

'I've been reading about people who used acupuncture to curb their desire to drink. I'm not been a big fan of natural medicine, but I'm willing to give it a try.'

'Well, I *have* heard of acupuncture helping . . .' Xanthe paused before she used the word alcoholics. '. . . drinkers, to help with resisting cravings and assisting relaxation. So I guess it can't hurt.'

Nadine knew what Xanthe was thinking. What everyone else in her life was thinking. 'You want me to go to AA too, don't you?' She was convinced they all wanted to label her, that they all thought the only way to treat her problem was group meetings with other alcoholics.

Xanthe didn't answer.

'The thing is, *I'm* not like those other people, Xanthe. I just sit here and keep to myself.'

'What makes you think alcoholics aren't like that too?' Xanthe asked, gearing up to deliver a dose of tough love. 'Alcoholics *are* like you; they go to work, they have kids, they do everything other people do. They also abuse the people they love, they forget important things, they have damaged livers and kidneys.'

Nadine found Xanthe's words hard to listen to.

'They also make a million excuses, just like you do too. Nadine, you're forty, you need to wake up to yourself because if you don't you may not see fifty.'

'Now you're just exaggerating,' Nadine scoffed.

'Really?' Xanthe was annoyed. She was trying to help a friend who had asked for help only to be dismissed. 'Try some of these stats on for size then.' She pulled out her Filofax where she'd made some notes. 'According to the World Health Organisation, the harmful use of alcohol results in 2.5 million deaths each year, and 320,000 young people between the age of fifteen and twenty-nine die from alcohol-related causes, nine per cent of all deaths in that age group.'

'Do you think I'm an alcoholic?' Nadine asked, the venom in her voice evident. 'Is that what you think? Is that what you're trying to tell me with your *statistics*? I'm not in one of your training courses, you know.'

Xanthe contained the rage she could feel building and counted quietly backwards from ten before she spoke.

'Do *you* think you're an alcoholic, Nadine?' Xanthe finally threw the question back.

'I don't know.' Nadine started to cry again.

Xanthe put her hand on her friend's again, trying to soothe her. 'Listen, no-one is judging you, we all want to help. But *you* need to be honest with yourself.'

Nadine sniffled. 'I don't mean to drink as much as I do, I just lose track sometimes. Most of the time, actually.' This was her first real confession.

'Do you forget much when you drink?' Xanthe asked, trying to knock off some classic symptoms of alcoholism.

'Yes, often, and I hate it.' Her second confession.

'Nadine, if you want to control your drinking, and you're finding it hard or impossible, which I'm sorry to say that's what it sounds like, then I think that probably defines alcoholism.'

She squeezed Nadine's hand. 'And, my dear friend, I really think you should at least try an AA meeting, for support and guidance.'

'I don't know.' Nadine shook her head.

Xanthe spoke softly, and trod carefully, hoping to at least get Nadine to agree. 'There are meetings in Brookfield on Friday nights at the Anglican Church Hall.'

'Bloody hell, there's no way I could go there. Could you imagine? The whole place would be talking. What about Brit and Cam? No, not there.'

For Xanthe it didn't go unnoticed that the only time Nadine seemed concerned about her children in relation to her drinking, was when she was trying to get sober. But she said nothing, tried to remain supportive.

'I thought you'd say that, so I checked and there's meetings in Indooroopilly and Taringa, which are far enough away for you not to know anyone.'

'Well, as long as they haven't read one of my books!' Nadine said sarcastically.

Xanthe shook her head at how difficult her friend was being and wondered if Nadine really did want to get better. 'I wasn't going to mention this to you because it's probably the option you'll take, but there is also an online AA meeting facility.'

'That I could do,' Nadine said, opening up her laptop.

17

A New Vixen

Christmas arrived too quickly for each of the tiddas. Veronica finished unpacking boxes in her Spring Hill apartment three days before Santa was due to arrive, but just in time to erect a small tree. She smiled at the glittering purple, gold and red baubles, feeling completely content for the first time since Alex left her.

She looked at the freshly painted white walls she was still to adorn with artwork, including her own. She admired the polished floorboards and her new streamlined, less cluttered life. She nodded her approval to herself, full of enthusiasm about ending one cycle of her life and starting the new year ahead with a vastly improved sense of self.

She straightened the red cushions on her new black leather lounge and placed some nuts and olives on the coffee table she'd had delivered the day before. Veronica may have down-sized and decluttered but she still maintained her high-end quality and style. She'd furnished her new compact home by considering some elements of Feng Shui as well, and the Yasuhiro Shito-designed table, the salesperson had assured her, exuded a Zen-like feel with its smooth edges and minimalist appearance. It was a done deal.

She checked everything was ready – including the mockails she'd planned in support of Nadine – and was rearranging the gifts under the tree one more time when the doorbell rang.

'You're my first real visitor, Nadine!' Veronica was as excited as a schoolgirl with friends coming for a sleepover. And her excitement was infectious.

'This is your new life, Vee,' Nadine bubbled. 'And it's not too shabby at all, is it?'

They walked down the hallway leading into the living area. Nadine stepped out onto the balcony overlooking the city. 'No, not shabby at all.'

The doorbell rang again. Xanthe stood outside the sixth-floor apartment door with Izzy and baby Bila, loaded up with nappies, baby wipes, bibs, dummies and every other item that could possibly be designed and marketed to a new mother. Izzy's West End home had been turned into its own baby centre, and there were knitted booties from one end of the flat to the other. But it was stifling in Brisbane, and little Bila was mostly naked save for her nappy. Izzy couldn't wait until Bila grew a bit more so she could put her in the bright pink polka-dotted swim nappies; they were the cutest things her Godmother Xanthe had given her.

'Hello!' Veronica greeted them cheerily, looking into the pram at the newest member of the book club.

'No-one talks to me anymore,' Izzy joked. 'They go straight for the kid.'

'And helloooo to you too!' Veronica hugged both women and showed them through to the balcony, where Nadine was wilting in the humidity.

'Hello, beautiful,' Nadine said as Izzy pushed the pram through the open screen doors.

'Thanks,' Izzy joked.

'Oh, and hello to you too, Iz,' Nadine laughed.

Izzy raised her eyes in a smile as if to say, *I told you so!*

When Ellen finally arrived, after a very depressing service – thankfully the last she had to do before Christmas, the women sat down to a lunch of seafood and salads, passing baby Bila around like they were playing pass-the-parcel.

'Bila is a lovely name,' Veronica said. 'Very close to Bella.'

Asher and Izzy had argued over names – he wanted to name her after a form of bush tucker, which Izzy thought would only cause her grief with teenage boys saying, 'I want to eat you!' They argued so endlessly, their daughter spent the first ten days of her life being called simply 'Bub'. They finally settled on Bila late one night when they were sifting through language lists from their hometowns, looking for a name that had meaning.

'Bila is a Wiradjuri word for river,' Izzy explained to her tiddas as she put the baby on her breast. 'We both have connection to rivers – me, the Cudgegong of course, and here in Brisbane, and the Condamine for Asher up in Toowoomba.'

'I like it,' Ellen said, 'it makes sense.'

'And,' Izzy said, 'it sounds soppy, but Asher reckons it represents our love that flows like a river, and especially our love for you.' She kissed Bila on the top of her the head while the women gushed in unison.

Veronica's new sense of calm did not go unnoticed by her friends that day as she played hostess. She was more relaxed than any of them could remember. As she handed them each a flat, square gift, none of them could imagine what it was. Too heavy to be a CD. They were all intrigued.

'I'm renting a tiny studio in Woolloongabba where I can do my homework,' Veronica smiled, 'and I needed a proper space to be creative.' She swapped Izzy's gift for baby Bila as she continued. 'And these are my first efforts, before uni actually begins. I hope you like them.'

Each woman ripped away the red and gold paper and then the bubble wrap. Each white tile had a different design painted on it in black.

'What does it mean?' Ellen asked, not wanting to sound ignorant, but unsure of the significance of the design. Nadine, Izzy and Xanthe looked on with similar expressions of uncertainty on their faces.

Veronica laughed. 'It's okay; you're not supposed to know. They're my own designs. I researched a whole lot of symbols for friendship around the world; Chinese lettering, Celtic designs, even some international Indigenous symbols. And then I sat down and thought about what *our* friendships meant to me, sketched a few designs of my own and painted them on these tiles. That's all.'

'That's *all*?' Nadine declared. 'You are *amazing*!'

Bila cooed and the women all laughed.

A cock crowed, waking Izzy. Asher was already up with Bila, talking to her as if she were a five-year-old and understood that Santa had been. He was sitting on the lounge with the TV on low, chatting to his daughter about the menu for Christmas lunch. Izzy stood in the doorway of their bedroom and watched, finding it hard to believe she had become a mother and full-time partner without any plan to do either. Her breasts were leaking milk as fast as her eyes shed tears of joy. This would be her best Christmas Day ever. Her first with her own family *and*, as a bonus, the meal Asher had planned sounded fantastic. The fact her fortieth birthday was only two days away didn't even concern her. All that mattered to Izzy was that she was about to celebrate her first Christmas with her man and her baby girl.

In Kangaroo Point, Ellen woke up for the first time on Christmas morning with a man next to her. It had taken until the age of forty for her to realise the difference it made sharing important holidays with someone you loved. She snuggled into Craig's back and kissed the nape of his neck. He grabbed her hands and pulled her arms around him. They lay half-awake for some time before deciding to go for a run, a routine they had fallen into and enjoyed. Making love in the shower often followed, so their final sprint home was for a reason.

The pair would spend the day with Craig's family down on the Gold Coast. It was the first Christmas Ellen didn't feel homesick.

Veronica was up early, stuffing and cooking a turkey, roasting vegetables, whipping cream for the trifle, and preparing the table for her three sons and the likelihood of a mate or new girlfriend popping in. John had crashed at her place the night before, conscious his mother would be waking up alone otherwise. Unlike the artworks she'd given the girls, Veronica had bought the boys essentials for their own homes, and included gift cards for music and clothes in their presents as well. She felt so happy with herself, she even sent a Christmas text to Alex in between basting.

Paper flew faster than planes in Upper Brookfield where Richard and Nadine hadn't tamed their shopping as successfully as Nadine had her drinking in recent weeks. She'd been to three group AA meetings and felt more empowered each time, fearing less and less that people were judging her. The severed bond between her and Richard had been mended. He was starting to trust her again, and that made her feel happier too. Brittany and Cameron managed to acquire more presents than any child anywhere needed. But after opening each gift – a book, an iTunes card, a blinged flash drive, a digital camera, a remote control helicopter, a paintball kit – the childen genuinely thanked their parents. There was being outrageously spoiled, but there was also being outwardly and sincerely appreciative. Nadine and Richard sat happily, coffee mugs in hand, while they watched their children squeal with delight and surprise. The day would be just theirs until the afternoon when they would drive into West End to see Izzy, Asher and Bila.

Birds chirped happily in Paddington as Xanthe and Spencer made love, with one of many versions of 'White Christmas' coming from the radio. They both giggled between thrusts; the top temp for the day was going to be in the mid-thirties and humidity near saturation point. The pair were both relaxed and excited about their trip to New Caledonia, now less than twenty-four hours away, and appreciated the gifts of beach towels and swimwear they'd bought for each other. This year there were no surprises, but neither of them cared. All Spencer wanted to do was lie under a palm tree during the day and eat inspiring French cuisine by night. As far as touristy activities went, Xanthe was only interested in visiting the Jean-Marie Tjibaou Centre, which celebrated Kanak culture. She was so excited about celebrating her fortieth birthday in the Pacific, she'd even forgotten to pack a pregnancy test.

Epilogue

March was as hot and sticky as December and everyone felt it. Thankfully Jugglers Art Space in The Valley provided a cool reprieve when the tiddas arrived for the opening of the gallery's latest exhibition. The only heat that night came from the emerging artists brimming with creative energy. Veronica was one of them, and she was bubbling with nerves. To everyone's surprise, mostly her own, her submission to be part of the show was accepted before she'd started the semester. One of her dreams was coming true so quickly her head was spinning with disbelief and excitement. The private sketchings of twenty years had finally paid off.

Among the crowd gathered were her three sons, each with girlfriend in tow and an apparent blank cheque from their father to buy something. Alex had remained the absent but generous father but Veronica didn't think any more than a few seconds about it. She was more preoccupied with the fella who had framed her inks on paper; he was a contact of Ellen's who turned out to be interested not only in her artwork but also her 'good looks'. Veronica had agreed to have a drink with him sometime after the exhibition, and she was as nervous about the pending 'date' as she was about her first opening night.

Izzy arrived and appeared rushed, annoyed with Asher after a fight back at home; he couldn't understand why she had to be there for Veronica when Bila was due for a feed. He accused her of caring more about her tiddas than her daughter and him, their family. Izzy didn't have time to explain the meaning of sistahood to him, and although she wasn't back at work yet she had organised a crew to cover the event, not only to support the local artists and her tidda in particular, but also the organisation. She would only be gone an hour, she promised Asher, and Bila would be sleeping the whole time. She was feeling a new level of pressure at home that she hadn't planned on, but she'd deal with it when she got back to West End.

Xanthe and Spencer arrived holding hands, the perpetual teenage romantics. Since falling pregnant in New Caledonia the pair had been virtually inseparable as they prepared for parenthood. Xanthe had given new meaning to the term 'expectant mother' and no-one was happier for her than her tiddas. Xanthe and Spencer stayed for the official side of things then left quietly as Xanthe felt unwell and just wanted to go home and lie down.

As the speeches began, Ellen raced in, panting. She'd had a service at 4 p.m. at Tweed Heads and by the time she got away and back up the highway she had to head straight to the event. She stood with Nadine who was sober and admiring the artwork of all exhibitors with a new, clearer eye. She had already placed a few red dots next to works she liked and, unlike the arguing pair of old, she and Ellen spent most of the evening together – except when Ellen took the opportunity to shamelessly flirt with a young art student who had clearly taken a shine to her.

The next day Cam and Brit had never been more excited about going to school. They were up and dressed without any prompting at all. It was 'come as your favourite character' and their mother was going to be the guest speaker on books and writing at the school assembly. Nadine had never known what impact a parent going to school events had on kids, her kids. Their enthusiasm quickly infected her and she felt excited with them, for them. But she was also incredibly nervous. She'd not done anything at school for years and she was still battling with speaking in public sober. But Richard was ever the staunch supporter.

'They're kids, Nads. Anything you say will be exciting because you're famous. They mightn't have read your books, but you can be assured they know the TV series.'

Nadine only felt a little consoled.

'Mum,' Brit said in the car on the way to school. 'I already know what my friends are going to ask you.'

Nadine was surprised. 'Really?'

'Yes,' Brit nodded from the back seat.

'Well, are you going to give me some clues?' Nadine was happy for any assistance she could get.

'They want to know what your all time bestest, most favourite book is,' Brit said, much to Nadine's relief. 'And do you have to commit a crime to be able to write a crime novel?'

Ellen woke up to find a young art student in ripped jeans sitting on her couch. No shirt, no shoes, no hair on his chest at all. She smiled at him and he stood up, undoing the button on his pants, dropping them to the floor when he reached the bed. It hadn't worked out with Craig but this fella wasn't a rebound. Ellen wasn't bitter or angry or disappointed. She was happy that she'd had three months with Craig, and that she had allowed herself to open her heart and her mind to a man and to a relationship. She and Craig were simply not suited.

Ellen now believed that at least she *could* have a long-term committed relationship with someone; she just had to find the right person. She knew it was possible, she had faith that it would happen; but it wasn't going to happen by itself. She needed to be out there among it, she needed to 'interview' and 'shortlist' prospective partners, and that's exactly what she was doing with the emerging artist she'd met at Veronica's exhibition. When he emerged from between her legs, she'd be making plans to see him again, determined to find out what more they had in common.

'NOOOOOOO!' Xanthe's wail was piercing.

Spencer dropped his steaming coffee cup into the kitchen sink. By the time he got to the bathroom his wife was sitting on the toilet, hunched over and sobbing. He'd never seen her so distressed.

'No, no, no, no, no,' she kept repeating over and over again.

Spencer knelt on the floor in front of her, placing his hands on the sides of her face, which was resting in her palms, her elbows on her knees. He didn't know what to say. For all of his sensitivity, he wasn't unlike other men who were helpless in such emotional moments. But he too was suffering at what he quickly realised was a miscarriage.

'It's not fair,' Xanthe sobbed helplessly. 'It's just not fair.'

'Shh. I know, princess, I know.'

Xanthe looked up, her heart full of melancholy, her eyes swollen and full of tears, her face full of disappointment.

'It was *our* turn. Our baby, it was *our* baby.'

In Ryan Street Izzy dozed on the couch while Bila continued to breastfeed. It was midnight when Asher found his girls still up and the TV bright but muted. He looked around the flat at the chaos of baby clothes and a sink full of dishes. He kissed his woman on the head and walked to the bathroom. Izzy woke, groggy and tired. She was always tired these days; no energy for running, no time for reading, little time for catching up with domestics even. She heard Asher in the shower and thought back to when they used to shower together. They hadn't done that for months, and she wondered if they'd ever do it again. They had hardly made love since Bila was born three months before. When she felt like it Asher was asleep, and when he felt like it she was bathing, feeding or playing with Bila. Once or twice when they both had felt like it, they looked at each other and agreed that sleep was more important.

While Asher had pretty much maintained his usual schedule at work, Izzy hadn't gone back to work at all. Every time Bila smiled at her, she couldn't imagine leaving her daughter for even a day, let alone days at a time. Tracey had tried strategising a show for working mothers, which Izzy was keen on, but for the next year at least she just wanted to watch her daughter grow, inch by inch, pound by pound – or by centimetre and kilo, as Asher would always remind her.

Although their intimacy in the bedroom had lessened, their commitment to each other and their daughter had reached new heights; whenever exhaustion translated into frustrations and short tempers, one reminded the other that all that mattered for now was their baby girl. Without exception, every near argument was avoided with the mention of Bila's name. Above all else, their love for her flowed like the river.

Acknowledgements

Tiddas owes its creation to many people and organisations. I had a flicker of an idea for a novel when I was in Mudgee in 2010 when I met Kerry Barling and Aleshia Lonsdale for the first time. They later helped me 'research' the town and read drafts for which I am grateful.

I'd like to acknowledge the band TIDDAS, who were one of my favourite bands in the 90s, and whom I still enjoy today.

Creative Industries and the Oodgeroo Unit at QUT, along with the Copyright Agency Limited, provided me with the time and space to research and map out the original outline of the book in 2011.

I am a method writer and took my research to all the necessary venues. I'd like to acknowledge my 'research assistants' in Brisbane: Nadine McDonald-Dowd, Amanda Hayman, Jackie Huggins, Krissy Kneen, Josie Montano, Tracey Walker, Susan Johnson, Mel Kettle, Sidonie Carpenter, Janine Dunleavy, Sandra Phillips, Leesa Watego, Loretta Ryan and Annie Pappalardo. Kelly Roberts is a boy, but he helped too!

My loving Brisbane family, Kerry Kilner and Angela Gardner, provided both Izzy and I with a home in West End.

The Queensland Writers Centre and The Edge at the State Library of Queensland gave me space, moral support and lots of coffee while working on the final edits, and the librarians at Tara Anglican School for Girls gave me space as well as a constant supply of cakes.

For some technical, baby-related information my thanks go to Marianne Tome. And for just listening to me rant about writing and life generally – thank you Sonja Stewart, Belinda Duarte, Robynne Quiggin, Terri Janke, Trish Marasco, Pam Newton and Kerry Reed-Gilbert. You are my deadly tiddas.

To my writing buddy and tidda, Lisa Heidke – thank you for giving me refuge so that I could write the final draft, not to mention the daily support on everything life manages to dish up.

I bow with respect to my Simon and Schuster crew: Lou Johnson, Larissa Edwards, Roberta Ivers, Carol Warwick and all the team – with a big thanks to Liz Ansted for her invaluable bookclub notes and suggestions – who have worked passionately to help me share my story. You tiddas rock! Thanks, too, to Janet Hutchinson for her always wise and gently-does-it edit, and to Jessica Dettmann, for her eagle-eyed proofreading.

To Tara Wynne, you are the best agent – thank you!

Finally, to my beautiful mum, my sister Gisella and all my clan: thank you for just being you.

Anita Heiss
2014

About the Author

Dr Anita Heiss is an award-winning author of non-fiction, historical fiction, commercial women's fiction, children's novels and blogs. She is a proud member of the Wiradyuri Nation of central New South Wales, an Ambassador for the Indigenous Literacy Foundation, the GO Foundation and Worawa Aboriginal College. Anita is a board member of the National Justice Project, Aboriginal Art Co. and Circa Contemporary Circus, and is a Professor of Communications at the University of Queensland.

As artist in residence at La Boite Theatre in 2020, Anita began adapting her novel *Tiddas* (2014) for the stage. Her novel *Barbed Wire and Cherry Blossoms* (2016) set in Cowra during World War II, was the 2020 University of Canberra Book of the Year. Her most recent novel, *Bila Yarrudhanggalangdhuray* (2021), won the Indigenous Writers Prize in the 2022 NSW Premier's Literary Awards. Anita enjoys eating chocolate, running and being a 'creative disruptor'.

For more from Anita, visit her website www.anitaheiss.com, or follow @AnitaHeiss on Twitter.

The Vixens' Bookclub List

In *Tiddas,* the main characters Izzy, Veronica, Xanthe, Nadine and Ellen discuss a diverse list of books by Australian authors at meetings of their monthly bookclub. You may like to read them, too:

Legacy, Larissa Behrendt
The Old School, P.M. Newton
Butterfly Song, Terri Janke
The Boundary, Nicole Watson
Aunty Rita, Rita and Jackie Huggins
Triptych: an erotic adventure, Krissy Kneen
Mullumbimby, Melissa Lucashenko
My Hundred Lovers, Susan Johnson
The Tall Man, Chloe Hooper

If you would like to explore other titles by Australian authors, Anita's Black Book Challenge at www.anitaheiss.wordpress.com/2013/12/03/anitas-black-book-challenge-2/ offers 99 titles by Aboriginal authors, covering children's picture books and fiction, young adult, fiction, non-fiction, memoir, autobiography and biography, drama, poetry and anthologies.

Happy reading!

Book Club Questions

1. A group of 'tiddas' is a group of good female friends who may or may not be blood related. The women in this story have a shared history. What other qualities and attributes do you think are important to a friendship?
2. Izzy finds herself in an unexpected situation when she discovers she's pregnant. Many women in society today who are focussed on their careers would have made a different decision. What do you think Izzy's story would be like now if she'd chosen not to have the baby? How would it be different?
3. Veronica, a devoted wife and mother, has her life turned upside down when she gets divorced and her sons leave the nest. Her story is of a strong woman who, after a time of immense grief, rediscovers her sense of self and recreates her identity. If you could create a new identity for yourself, what would it be?
4. Xanthe is desperate for a baby and many women would relate to her journey, whether it's through her experience of trying for a baby, unexplained infertility, exploring the possibility of IVF and even miscarriage. Can you relate to Xanthe's story, or part of it?
5. Nadine struggles with addiction, which affects her life, her family and her friends. Each of the other characters

coped with and dealt with her addiction in a different way. Which character could you most relate to in their reaction to Nadine's troubles?

6. Ellen loves her life and enjoys being single, footloose and fancy free. How does this affect the way the other characters treat her?
7. The New South Wales town of Mudgee is featured in the novel as a place where the women attended high school. Have you ever visited Mudgee? What can you share of your experience?
8. The Vixens choose a diverse range of quality Australian literature for their bookclub. Have you chosen any books by Indigenous authors for your own bookclub? If you are interested, please feel free to peruse the list of books discussed by the Vixens and other quality Indigenous titles in Anita's Black Book Challenge.
9. By the end of the novel, which character do you think has grown the most?
10. Each of the five characters has a very different personality and life. Who do you relate to most and why?
11. *Tiddas* covers a range of controversial subject matter. Are these issues and themes ones that you would discuss with your friends and 'tiddas'? Or are these topics still taboo?

If you enjoyed *Tiddas*, you'll love
Bila Yarrudhanggalangdhuray,
also by Anita Heiss.

Read on for a sneak peek!

Prologue

1838, Gundagai

'Not a good place to live, Boss, too flat!'

Wagadhaany looks up at her father as he speaks to a White man with piercing green eyes across the way. She is a wide-eyed four-year-old with a spring in her step and a toothy smile that goes from ear to ear. She is bone thin with dark brown hair that falls in large curls down her back. She loves walking along the river when her babiin is not off with her uncles, and she is interested to see all the new people who are coming to live near them.

Between where she stands and the bila, there are three rows of ganya-galang. She watches the current flow rapidly downstream, then turns to observe different men swinging hammers and grunting with hard work, making their ganya-galang out of wood and stones, not with branches and trees. They are building them next to each other, and it's different to their campsite which is not so straight, and not so boring, she thinks. But these ganya-galang look like they are very strong and won't ever move, ever.

Wagadhaany recalls her father and uncles talking about all the White people coming to live on Wiradyuri ngurambang – our Ancestors' country, they always insist to each other. She thinks the stranger across the way is so white and so skinny he could move around like a birig. But she is sure her babiin wouldn't be talking to a spirit like he is a real person.

She is frightened out of her dark skin as the man hisses at them both, 'Go away!'

She is curious and wants to ask so many questions – the who, the what, the when and the how. Mostly she wants to know *why* something is so. 'Why is he so angry?' she whispers as the corners of her mouth turn downwards. She is about to cry.

She is prone to crying. She hates being the youngest of five children. Her siblings are all brothers, and she is often left out of their games because she is a girl, and because she is the baby of the family. She likes being her babiin's favourite but that doesn't always help with the boys, who for some reason enjoy seeing her cry.

Wagadhaany holds her breath as she looks over to the man and sees angry eyes and a furrowed forehead on a tired, pale face. She has heard her uncles talking about not building on the river flats, that it's not the right place to make a home for anyone. That it's not safe to build a house where the water will flood when it rains heavily. They know because even though they camp there and have ceremony there, they move to higher ground as soon as the rain falls hard. But these new ganya-galang won't be able to be moved.

She knows that this place has flooded before, and it will again. She wants to tell the man herself, but she wouldn't dare. That would be disrespectful and the one thing that she must always show Elders is yindyamarra. Even though the man is not her uncle, he is most definitely older than her, by many, many years, and so she keeps her mouth shut.

As she feels her father's body jerk, Wagadhaany immediately pulls herself into his side, wanting in fact to go away, as they have been ordered. She has seen angry White men and angry Black men before, and when they are angry at the same time it is scary. She can feel tears welling at the thought of a confrontation, and as the sun is high in the sky, she doesn't want anyone ruining this beautiful, otherwise carefree day for her and her babiin. Wagadhaany is relieved when her father resumes walking and the man goes back to hammering lengths of wood.

After only a few steps she hears the man bellow, 'Get out of that mud!'

She turns quickly, still holding her father's hand, and sees two boys playing in some wet dirt, the man glaring at them. Wagadhaany wonders if the boys carried the water from the river in the tin buckets she sees nearby, to make the mud. The wet dirt looks inviting. There's been no rain for so long and everything else around is dry – the grass, the dusty path they are walking on, and her throat too. Back at the camp her aunties have been complaining about the dust and commenting on how low the river is getting, and while Wagadhaany often traces the cracks in the earth of the riverbank, she stops thinking about it now, because playing in the mud looks like fun and she'd rather be doing that. She knows she could never go and play with *those* boys – she's never played with White kids before. She wants to ask her babiin if she can make some mud when they get back to camp, but he is looking at the White man, and so she says nothing and just stares as well. Wagadhaany grips her father's hand tightly. The questions start playing on a loop in her head.

Why have we stopped? What are you going to say, Babiin? Who is this man anyway? Are you angry too?

'Silly man,' her father says under his breath as he turns back around and slides his left foot forward and gently pulls his daughter along with him.

Wagadhaany looks up at the tower of the man next to her. The sun stings her eyes and she squints. She grips her father's hand tighter and skips a few steps, wondering what her brothers are doing. Probably fishing, she tells herself. She hopes they'll make mud cakes with her later.

After a few slow strides, her father turns around, abruptly swinging his daughter around with him.

'Here,' he says loudly and clearly to the White man, as he looks from the river to his left and waves his arms from side to side. 'Flood area, biggest rains, the water goes past here.'

He raises his hand up above his head to show how high the water may rise. Wagadhaany thinks that her babiin is very tall, so the water will be very tall too.

The man scoffs as he points to the dry landscape. 'You don't know what you're talking about. We *need* rain. It certainly doesn't look like it's going to flood to me.'

'It hasn't flooded for longest time,' Yarri says. 'It *will* happen again. We know.'

'This side of the river,' the White man says, waving his hand along the right-hand bank of the Marrambidya Bila. 'This is the Crossing Place.'

Wagadhaany follows the swing of his arm. Her eyes rest momentarily on the biggest red river gum tree she has ever seen. She follows the creamy bark of the trunk skyward and among the white flowers she glimpses some movement. It's a koala and her baby sleeping. They make her smile and she wishes she could get to the other side of the river to see them better. But she can't swim, and she knows that even though the river is low, even though she can see the brown earth for some of the way through the water, it is probably still very deep in the middle. And it's cold. She shivers just thinking about how chilly the water was the last time she put her feet in, and how strong the current was, and how dangerous it was, as the aunties told her. She is in her own world, looking at the koalas and hoping the singing parrots don't wake them up, when the White man's voice shakes her.

He points to the ground beneath his feet. 'And right here and around here –' he swings his skinny white arms again and Wagadhaany feels a bit dizzy watching them flailing about '– this is where Gundagai town is going to be built, you'll see.'

Yarri shrugs his shoulders and Wagadhaany follows her father's actions. She expects the other man might do the same but he doesn't. Instead, he slams his shovel down on the ground with a great thump. He puts his hands on his hips. 'It's going to be a service town for travellers and pastoralists between Sydney and Melbourne,' he says, as if he is one of the official men Wagadhaany has heard her uncles talk about at camp. 'There'll be a punt service over at Stuckey's Crossing too.' He points in the direction of the crossing. 'You just wait and see.'

Wagadhaany looks at her father. She has so many questions, because she doesn't really understand what the man is talking about. *Yamawa?* She wants to ask her question out loud. *What for, Babiin? Why is he here and angry, and yamawa are you talking to him? And what is a punt?* There are so many new people, new things happening where they live, and so many new words that sound so different to the language they speak in the camp.

When she looks back at the White man, she sees his eyes flick to her. His bright green eyes are scary-looking, and Wagadhaany is a little taken aback, but she can't look away. She stares at him when he mumbles something about Blacks not being smart enough to understand but he keeps talking to her father anyway.

'I'm building an attic,' he says.

Yarri doesn't respond, so the man goes on.

'That's a room in the roof,' he says sarcastically, 'and we can go up high if there is any flooding, but I'm sure we won't have to.'

Yarri shakes his head. 'Come.' Wagadhaany feels a gentle pull on her hand. 'They never listen, Wagadhaany, never listen.'

'Why didn't you tell him, Babiin?' she asks quietly, not wanting to upset her father any more than he already is.

'Tell him what?'

'What Marrambidya means.' She takes three steps to each of her father's lunges. 'That it means big flood, big water.' Wagadhaany looks up and smiles at her hero, hoping that he is proud that she remembers the stories he tells her.

'No matter what you say, or how many times you say it, ngamurr, some people, especially White people, they just won't listen.'

The sun beats down on the camp as Wagadhaany sits at her father's feet in the shade of a eucalyptus tree. She listens intently as he tells the other men of his exchange with the White man that morning.

'Things are changing. More White people, more White people's animals, White food and White sickness. Things will change for us too because of that,' Yarri says, and Wagadhaany hears the worry in her father's voice. 'I don't know how long we can stay on this land, our land. They have marked the land over that way already.' Yarri points in the direction he and Wagadhaany had walked earlier that day, towards the sun.

'They are making their own homes, like ours, but they will not be moved on, not like us. Their way is different, no campfire for everyone to gather around to talk – no sitting like this, and it looks like no sharing.' He motions around the circle where all her uncles and some of her aunties and cousins sit, preparing their catch to share that night, and shakes his head. 'They do not understand the land and river like we do, and they don't care that they should not build on the flat earth there, that it will flood again, one day.' He looks to the sky, then pats Wagadhaany on the head. 'As sure as day becomes night and night becomes day again, things will change. And it *will* flood.'

Yarri recounts the morning's events to the other men as they show Wagadhaany's brothers – Jirrima, Yarran, Euroka and Ngalan – how to gut a kangaroo. Wagadhaany moves to squat on her haunches, watching, happy that she only has to look on. Her brothers are in the thick of the gutting and she turns her nose up at the smell of the raw flesh and internal organs. She likes it much more when the wambuwuny is cooked. She is fascinated by the way her brothers participate with precision and enthusiasm, and even though she usually prefers to be with the women, weaving and looking after the younger children, right now she is staying where she is, hoping that they can all go make mud cakes together soon.

'They don't understand what it is capable of,' her uncle Dyan responds, as he points to the river. All her mamaba-galang are smart, but Mamaba Dyan might be the smartest. 'That bila has already taken so many people, he will again.'

All the men nod. They know the truth about the strength in the flowing Marrambidya.

'They don't understand the land, they just keep chopping down trees to build their ganya-galang,' Mamaba Dyan says, as he removes the main organs of the kangaroo. 'Some of our men are helping them. To get flour and sugar and tea.'

'They build roads too, and those roads are changing this place,' Mamaba Badhrig says, as he holds the hind legs of the animal down to make the dismembering easier.

'And the new animals, those cows and sheep, they are changing the land too,' Yarri says. 'And our men, they are being asked to help work with those cows and sheep. I reckon I could ride a horse better than they do,' he adds confidently.

'And ride 'em well,' Mamaba Badhrig says.

'We could teach them a lot, if they just listened,' Yarri adds.

Wagadhaany watches her uncles all nod in agreement, but her attention to the man-talk is waning, she wants to play.

She knows her babiin is watching her through the corner of his eye as she walks off towards the bila. Sometimes she thinks he has eyes in the back of his head because he always knows where she is, sometimes before she even gets there. When she reaches the sandy riverbank she plops down on her bubul, crosses her skinny brown legs and starts mixing earth with water. She waits impatiently for her brothers to come down and fish.

As she moves her hands through the wet sand, she thinks about the looks on the faces of the young boys she saw earlier that morning and how they were giggling as they played in the mud. She giggles too and wishes her brothers would have fun with her instead of always leaving her out. Sometimes she wants to scream at them that it's not her fault she's a girl. Wagadhaany waves over her younger cousins and other camp kids who join her and she shows them what to do with the sand and water. Together they make mud cakes and their chuckles rise up the bank to where her balgalbalgar-galang are drinking tea and talking. Now that the wambuwuny is on the fire they can rest a while. She wishes she was an Elder and could drink tea too, because they seem to laugh a lot when they are talking together around the fire.

As the day draws to a close and dusk settles in, Wagadhaany and her brothers and cousins, who have formed one big group along the bank after several hours of throwing mud at each other, are oblivious to time. But the sun is about to set and the kuracca-galang are screeching along the river.

'Beware the waawii!' Wagadhaany's gunhi sings out.

Wagadhaany looks up at her mother with worry on her face, as do the others. They are frightened of being gobbled up by the scary bunyip. All the Wiradyuri kids know the story about the bunyip, having been told it many times, even though once was more than enough. It's why they aren't supposed to go too close to the water, and although Wagadhaany has never seen a bunyip, she's positive she never wants to.

'I saw the waawii once,' Jirrima says.

'Don't lie!' Wagadhaany screeches, shaking her head with a quiver in her voice.

'I did too, he was like a strange water creature in the shape of a star,' Yarran says, using his hands to show the shape and size of what he claims he saw.

'No, I saw him, and he was like a big snake with a long, wide face and a flat nose with big fangs,' her brother Ngalan says. He seems to be enjoying making the smaller kids cry.

'Nah, *I* really saw the waawii come out of the water and walk right up the bank and he was taller than Babiin with Mamaba Dyan on his shoulders. He was like a giant with big claws and a head like a dinawan,' Jirrima adds.

Wagadhaany tries not to think about this monster with an emu head. 'Stop it! Stop it!' she cries.

She takes flight back up the bank to her gunhi who is waiting, expecting the tears and fears, because inevitably the boys manage to upset their baby sister around the same time every day. Wagadhaany can hear her brothers laughing behind her, and her round brown face is soaked in tears when she buries her face in her mother's neck. It is the place she feels most safe, most protected, most at home.

'Ngamurr, your gumbal-galang don't mean harm, but you will have to be strong around them.'

'Are all boys like that?' she sobs.

'Not all, but most.'

Wagadhaany can almost hear a giggle in her mother's words and is confused. She cries louder when her brothers call out again. She doesn't understand what they are saying but she knows they are still making fun of her. Her mother releases her from the tight hug just long enough to sing out to her sons who are still by the water.

'Your babiin will speak to you,' she calls down to the river. 'Now get up here.'

She pulls her daughter close again. From the corner of her eye Wagadhaany can see the boys taking short, slow, almost shy steps up the bank. She smiles slyly to herself because she knows that even though the bunyip might not get them tonight, their father will not let them get away with anything. She is his favourite gudha and they all know it.

'Show yindyamarra to your sister, to everyone,' says her babiin. 'The bunyip knows everything, so always be respectful.'

Yarri is serious and they all feel it. Wagadhaany is still clinging to her mother as her brothers are being spoken to. She watches them staring at the ground and kicking dirt around, waiting till their babiin has finished. Sometimes he is scarier than the bunyip.

'Come!' Her mother puts her down, takes her by the hand and walks her to the women who are teaching the young girls to dance. 'Waga means to dance,' she reminds her daughter. 'You are our little dancer, Wagadhaany, always remember that.'

She looks up to her mother, feeling special, as though she has an important role, a place with the women, with all her family. And she starts to move her feet, gently kicking up the earth as she watches the older women's moves, mimicking them as best as her little body can. She likes being their little dancer.

In the ganya that night, Wagadhaany nestles closer to her younger cousins – Ngaayuga, Gandi, Yiri and Yirabiga – and they lace their legs through each other's as much to keep warm as to have fun.

'What's a bunyip?' Ngaayuga asks.

Wagadhaany sits upright, almost breaking her cousin's leg as she does so, which results in a loud screech, drawing the attention of the Elders outside by the fire.

'Way!' Yarri calls out for them to be quiet. 'You girls go to sleep.'

Wagadhaany puts her finger up to her lips to shoosh the others, then slumps back down and leans in to her little cousins. 'The waawii is a very, very, very scary creature that lives in the

Marrambidya Bila,' she whispers. 'When you see the water go around and around in circles, that's when you know he is there.'

She waves her hand in the air in circles and makes a whooshing sound as her cousins look and listen intently.

'How do you know it's a boy?' Gandi asks.

'Because only boys are scary and would hurt children,' Yirabiga responds.

They all nod in agreement.

'Gunhi says that if we go down to the river alone and get too close to the water then . . .' Wagadhaany pauses, letting her wide eyes and a shake of her head suggest what will happen. She sees the fear in her cousins' faces and stops. She's not like her older brothers who enjoy scaring young kids. 'So, we should always have an adult with us near the river, especially at night.'

Chapter One

The Great Flood – 24 June 1852, Gundagai

Wild wind and torrential rain thrash the Bradley home. The pitter-patter of the first drops to fall has been quickly replaced with a pelting that hits the windows so hard it risks smashing them. Wagadhaany shivers with fear as a bitterly cold draught comes through a gap in the door frame.

'We need to sandbag,' Henry Bradley says forcefully, his role as patriarch of the family never more tested than now. 'Others have already done it. We're going to lose everything if we don't take action now!'

It's an announcement and an order in one, his four sons jumping to attention instantly, as does Wagadhaany, waiting for her instructions as their servant.

Henry Bradley's bright green eyes are as scary to her today as they were the first time she saw them. Little did she know back then that the man she encountered building this house would be the man she would end up in servitude to.

Many of the White families have domestic help, young women to clean, cook and help with children, and young men to help on the sheep and cattle stations. In some ways she feels lucky that she and her father work for the same family, but she often wonders if her babiin remembers the day they first met Henry Bradley all those years ago. She's been with the Bradleys for four years and never has she seen any warmth in Mr Bradley's eyes.

'No!' Mr Bradley's wife, Elizabeth, has never raised her voice in their home and her challenge to her husband comes out with a tremble. She is fighting back tears and is visibly shaken by the torrential rain that is drenching their town. 'We should just leave now, we should go to higher ground.'

She looks pleadingly at her husband as she keeps a firm grip on her Bible and prayer beads, shivering in the winter cold as it has been impossible to keep the living-room fire alight.

'Some families have already moved to safety. Mr Johnson said some of the natives from the camp on the flood plain moved to Mount Parnassus this morning,' David Bradley says.

Wagadhaany knows that her family would have been in that group and her heart skips a beat waiting for her boss's next words.

'They led anyone who wanted to go up to the hills,' David adds. 'Andrew and I could take Mother to safety.'

'No, we stay together as a family.' Henry Bradley doesn't look up. 'I don't think it will come this far into town.'

'Sheridan Street is less than half a mile away from the river and the water is rising fast, Father, and we are not on the high end of town,' James says with urgency in his voice.

His father ignores him.

Elizabeth Bradley's lips are turning blue as she starts crying. 'Why didn't you listen to Mr Johnson when he came by on his horse? He told you to leave, but you never listen,' she says, chin quivering. 'Never listen.'

By the look on Henry Bradley's face, he isn't happy being chastised by his wife. Wagadhaany is reminded of her father saying *White men never listen* on the day that she first saw Mr Bradley.

So much has changed in the fourteen years since – the size of the town, the number of shops and houses, so many new townsfolk, and more Aboriginal people working for White families. Her own father is one of many men who have become stockmen and shepherds on the Bradleys' and other local stations, riding horses with skill to herd cattle and sheep, like her Uncle Badhrig said they would. The one thing that doesn't seem to have changed is Henry Bradley's refusal to listen to people who know better. Wagadhaany has vivid memories of her father saying it was a bad idea to build here. Her ears are filled with his wise words as the rain continues to fall without mercy.

She hopes the Bradley patriarch will not be his usual stubborn self. Without realising it, she looks pleadingly at him as well. *Will you get your family to safety soon? Will you take me with you?*

'Only those families in the lowest part of the town, over on the north bank of the river, have moved,' he responds, looking at each family member in turn, but bypassing her altogether. 'We are fine here, I think. Those living above shopfronts are still there.' He strains to see the lights on buildings either side of their home. 'The river will *not* reach us.'

Wagadhaany thinks her boss sounds confident but his face defies his voice. He looks worried, and she is positive she is not the only one in the room who notices this. She is fighting back tears of fear for many reasons, but first and foremost, because she cannot swim well, not like her brothers. She rarely fished with them, and her confidence could never match the current that would often pull them downstream. She has seen the rushing water outside, and she is certain she will not have enough strength to keep herself safe if the house is flooded and she is caught. She looks desperately at Henry Bradley, completely at his mercy. She swallows the tears back because she knows he will not tolerate seeing her cry. He never has, not for as long as she can remember working for him. And for that matter, tonight is the first time she has seen Elizabeth Bradley cry in this house that has been stifled by manners and decorum for too long.

The four Bradley sons move in silence as they follow their father outside, falling naturally into order of age from eldest to youngest. The bossiest, James, she believes to be twenty-six years old. The physically strongest, David, is only a year younger. Usually the chattiest of the four, Harry, is twenty-two, while the kindest of the brothers, Andrew, she thinks is probably only a couple of years older than she is, but she can't be sure. Andrew is the son always by his mother's side, though all four of the brothers adore their mother.

With her own safety at the forefront of her concerns, Wagadhaany steps gingerly in the direction of the window so she can see what the men are doing. When she touches the glass she realises her fingers are numb, and she doesn't know how long they have been that way. She rubs her hands together as fast as she can, and then down her thighs, but they are frozen too. She panics, thinking that if she doesn't drown she might freeze to death. She hears the men yelling over the rain and watches them start to position the loaded wheat bags and other hessian bags they have managed to get their hands on earlier in the day. They set to work filling them with sand, anticipating that the rain will continue to fall. She is surprised to watch the labour of men who hardly lift a finger around the house.

'I don't think we have enough gunny sacks,' Harry sings out to no-one yet everyone. 'We need to get more!'

His brothers don't respond, perhaps because there are no more bags to be had. Wagadhaany continues to watch the men quickly but carefully placing the sandbags lengthwise and parallel to the rainwater that is already flowing past their home and rising by the minute.

'Faster! Faster!' James orders.

The others do as they have been instructed, but Wagadhaany sees a look of contempt on David's face, as if he hates to be ordered around by his brother. If anything, though, James appears to be the only one who knows what he is doing.

As the men work on protecting the house, Elizabeth Bradley works through her prayer beads, one at a time. Wagadhaany stands in a corner, watching her and waiting for instructions. She asks Biyaami to keep them all safe – the Bradleys, her own family, the townsfolk – and without wanting to be selfish, she asks twice for herself.

The Bradley brothers re-enter the house, shouting at each other about what they should do next. David Bradley paces furiously back and forth, back and forth, back and forth, as if he is in a trance and doesn't know where he is. His brothers notice but no-one says anything because they are still arguing about whether they should stay or leave.

Wagadhaany wants to leave and get back to her family, but she has no right to say that, to say anything. She is without a voice in this house. Her job is not to offer an opinion, or even to have one. At the camp it is different. There she has a voice and a purpose. There she is a woman, and her role is to nurture the little ones. Her life at the Bradleys' has no real meaning, no real purpose. Her job is to clean, cook, sew and be of assistance wherever and whenever Mrs Bradley requires her. Mostly she is invisible to the men, only necessary to them in that she prepares their meals and washes their clothes and is an aide to the matriarch of the family. While they have rarely taken much notice of her, Wagadhaany has often observed their egos, and tonight is no different.

When Henry Bradley finally returns indoors, the men continue to debate how to manage the flood. Elizabeth Bradley looks to Wagadhaany for support but she knows that her husband would never consider what the Black girl might think they should do, and tonight will be no different. Support, humanity, friendship . . . These are not qualities that have existed between the two women before, but tonight Wagadhaany recognises that she and Mrs Bradley are essential to each other's survival.

'We are not leaving the house!' James Bradley says. Known to share his father's stubbornness and temper, he thumps his fist on the dining table.

There is shocked silence in the room.

'Well, I am,' David declares, and he stops pacing the room he has walked around and around in for hours.

'You are not going ANYWHERE!' Henry Bradley grabs his son by the front of his shirt. 'We are a family and we will stay together.'

The other men step in to defuse the situation, prying their father's hands from their brother's body and forcing them apart. Father and son have their eyes locked in rage.

All Wagadhaany hopes is that in Mr Bradley's demand to stay together, she is included. Even though her own family is at the front of her mind, she does not want to go out into this harsh weather alone. She can hear the miilgi continuing to thrash the town, and the sound makes her even more anxious.

'Please, David, please don't leave. We must stay together, your father is right. Please stay with me,' Mrs Bradley pleads with her son.

Andrew moves to her side, gently resting a hand on her shoulder. As she leans forward and weeps loudly into a linen handkerchief, he crouches to his mother's ear and says, 'The doorways are sandbagged, Mother, but if I am forced to leave I will take you with me.'

She looks up to her son with tear-filled eyes and soaked cheeks.

'Make some tea, Wilma!' Henry Bradley barks.

And in a most uncharacteristic response, her own emotions rising like the water level, Wagadhaany responds just loud enough to be heard, 'My name is Wagadhaany, *wogga-dine*.'

She turns swiftly, shocked at her behaviour, but also angry that even after years of Henry Bradley giving her orders he still can't use her name. She knows she will pay for the disobedience; Henry Bradley has only slapped her once, but there is nothing to say that he won't do it again. But before anyone in the room can comment, the crash of a tree against the house captures everyone's attention and the conversation turns to that.

As she walks to the kitchen she wonders if being called her proper name even matters. If she is going to die, she may as well be Wilma. Tears fall down her cheeks almost as fast and full as the torrential rain falling outside. She thinks about her family, but she doesn't worry as much for them as she does for herself and the Bradleys. This place has flooded before and her clan have always survived. They know when and where to move, how to listen to and act on the messages from the weather. She is certain that as soon as they saw the river begin to rise and the current flow faster, her babiin and uncles would have moved the women and their campsite to higher ground. They may be cold and wet, but they will be safe.

She puts a pot of water on the wood stove to boil. She notices the warmth in the kitchen compared to the living room and even though it would be cramped, she wonders why the Bradleys aren't huddled in here. Her hands shake and the cups rattle as she prepares them on a tray. She tries to be as normal as she can with fear for her own safety racing through her veins and her heart beating at a pace she's never felt before. 'Keep us safe, Biyaami, please keep us safe,' she whispers as she wipes her face on her apron and pours the steaming water into the teapot. She has to believe that everything will be all right or she will never stop crying.

It is rare that she has to pour tea for the entire family at once and she is nervous on top of being scared, especially since she has been rude to Henry Bradley. Careful not to drop the overloaded tray, she walks slowly into the room where there is silence apart from the sound of miilgi lashing the home. The Bradleys are fortunate their house is made of stone, when so many in town are made of wood or weatherboard, with shingle roofs that would never withstand the rain. That the Bradleys' house also has an attic speaks of their privilege.

As the skies continue to open, the four brothers and their father put their disagreements aside and huddle together closely, heads down, as they strategise their next move. Wagadhaany hears the odd word: flooding, safety, Mother. The men all look towards their matriarch, knowing that she is their number one priority.

James finally speaks. 'We should've known this was going to happen. The flood of 1844 claimed two lives. All that damage, we should've learned.' He walks to a window while his family looks on.

Wagadhaany stands still in the corner, waiting for further instructions, never acting without direction or approval. No-one has touched their tea. She wishes desperately that the rain was not falling and she was sitting around the campfire with her family, her parents, her brothers and cousins. Her mind is racing as fast as her heart.

'We tried, James,' David reminds his brother, angrily. 'We petitioned Governor Gipps to relocate the town, remember?' He starts pacing again, and turns abruptly. 'It's not like we didn't try.'

'I remember only too well,' James nods. 'I remember his mouthpiece, the Colonial Secretary, telling us we bought for better or worse, like our future lives and any threat to the townsfolk meant absolutely nothing. We were simply to be tamed by his words. Nothing more than that.'

David shakes his head. 'They never listened to us.'

Wagadhaany's babiin was right. None of them ever listen.

'The thing is,' Harry finally interjects, having been unusually quiet, 'is that everyone said the big one was behind us, but I don't think it is.'

He looks out the window into the darkness of the night, then they all do. Wagadhaany can see very little. Her vision is blinded by rain beating against the glass, and with the decrease in visibility comes an increase in fear. She hears yelling from outside. 'The banks have broken! The banks have broken!'

The water will be rushing through the town within minutes, she knows. The surrounding flood plains will soon be well and truly under water. She remembers this happening before and the floodwaters being strong enough to carry heavy carriages and houses downstream.

'The banks have broken!' James frantically repeats, and his voice reverberates throughout the house and Wagadhaany shakes with fear. Her heart beats so hard she thinks she can hear it. She wants to scream, but her lips barely part as tears begin to fall again.

As Andrew races outside, she imagines his face being hit hard by the icy rain. Winter in Gundagai is brutal enough without stormy weather. She can see that the wind is forcing him to put his hands up to his face to protect it. 'Hey,' he calls out to a lone figure, who is still yelling, 'The banks have broken! The banks have broken!'

As James and David move to the door, Wagadhaany strains to see what is happening. A man pushes his body against the wind, back towards Andrew Bradley. 'The banks have broken,' he yells again, leaning into Andrew's ear before a gust of wind pushes him away from Andrew and the house.

Andrew's face is ashen when he re-enters the room.

'What is it?' his mother asks as he puts his arm firmly around her.

He shakes his head, forcing out words. 'A boat crossing the river has been swamped.' He pauses. 'He said five children drowned.' He exhales, closes his eyes briefly and then adds, 'The boatman too.'

Everyone in the room drops their head in shock. There is an unplanned moment of silence until Henry Bradley commands, 'Everyone to the attic, now!'

Wagadhaany moves as fast as the Bradleys, even though it's not clear that she is included in the order. Andrew holds a wooden chair firmly on the large dining table, as James helps each onto the table, then carefully onto the chair and through the opening in the ceiling into the attic. When Wagadhaany reaches James there is a moment of awkwardness. For the first time she looks directly and desperately into his cold eyes. He says nothing, just motions for her to climb, and she does. Andrew assists her and then follows. Finally, James uses all his upper body strength to lift himself through the opening, just as there's the crash of water in the room below. He is visibly disturbed as he looks down to see furniture tossing and turning, the torrent ruining their belongings. His face is ghostly white and when he looks back to his family, his troubled expression makes Wagadhaany even more nervous than before.

Anxiety runs through her veins, her heart begins to race and she feels dizzy. She is overwhelmed by the sound of the miilgi pelting the roof, and she can't understand how the miilgi that brings so much life to the river, to the land and to all living things, can now be causing so much devastation. She turns her thoughts to the animals that will not survive. The normally noisy kuracca-galang and the mulyan-galang that will most likely be flushed from the trees to their death. The flood will take all the land animals with it too. *Where will the animals find refuge? And what of the townsfolk who don't have attics to climb into?*

She fears for her own family too but tells herself they will have moved fast enough to avoid the flooding. In her heart she knows that her babiin and her mamaba-galang will have prepared everyone in time; the Old People, the women and children will have been made safe, because Wiradyuri people know better than anyone what the river is capable of.

In the dead of night, Wagadhaany thinks about those who have already been swept away by the floodwaters that continue to rage past them. No-one is speaking. Henry and James are keeping watch from the roof but not reporting back what they can see. Wagadhaany wonders if whole buildings are being swept away, washed out of town, out of sight. She wonders if every other person in town is as terrified as she is.

Through a small window Wagadhaany sees flashes of light across the way. A lantern is being waved slowly by someone in a tree, a man. The light moves from side to side as if he is signalling for attention. She can just make out that with his other arm he is clinging to a branch.

Can anyone else see him? How long he has been there? Where is his family? Maybe he is not a strong swimmer either. But no amount of strength would be useful tonight, no human can win against the flooding streets.

Suddenly the light disappears. The lantern has been dropped or, worse still, the man has fallen into the icy, raging water. Wagadhaany gasps out loud. She can't bear to think what has happened. Reluctantly, she imagines his body twisting and turning in the current, and how fear must be choking him, how he may never see daylight again. She hugs her legs as close as possible to her body and closes her eyes tightly, overwhelmed with the fear of falling into the river. Her tears begin to fall again. She sits silently, desperately trying to ignore the blisteringly cold air coming through every crack in the roof. She rocks back and forth slowly, quietly whispering to Biyaami, *Please keep us safe, please keep us safe*. The Great Spirit is her only hope.

The hours pass and the cold is too cutting for her to do anything but listen to the rain pelting on the tin roof. It is loud and unrelenting. The attic is like an ice box, and while Wagadhaany is shivering, she is at least dry. She wonders how the men are coping outside. She turns from her lonely place near the window and watches Andrew, the devoted son who has not left his mother's side. She wishes someone was there to comfort her also. She looks at David, who is mumbling under his breath. He appears to be praying, the son who always takes himself to church every Sunday without any reminders. Wagadhaany closes her eyes and as the wind and rain continue to hammer against the house, she pleads with Biyaami again. *Please keep us safe, please keep us safe.*

Not for the first time she wishes that the rains had started falling when she was at camp with her family. If the rain had started during her weekly Sunday visit, she would've been safe with her family on higher, safer ground, with much less uncertainty than she feels right now in the Bradleys' attic.

It seems like hours before James climbs through the hatch from the roof back into the attic. Wagadhaany is hopeful when she sees him. Perhaps his view of what is happening outside is better than hers through the tiny window. Her optimism is shattered when he declares, 'It's time. We need to move to the roof now. Andrew . . .' He nods to his younger sibling to support their mother in climbing through the small opening that will lead them into the storm.

One by one they awkwardly make their way out. Rain whips Wagadhaany's face. It feels like it is cutting into her skin. The force of the wind knocks her backwards into the arms of David, who catches her. She doesn't have time to consider whether it is simply reflex or concern on his part, she is grateful, but still it is an uncomfortable moment.

'I've got you,' he reassures her, holding her arm firmly.

It takes a few seconds for both of them to find their balance. She watches as David grips onto a branch overhanging the roof, and together they sit down close to Mrs Bradley and Andrew. The four link arms and anchor themselves against the gale. She feels safe for the moment.

'We'll be fine, we just need to wait for the rain to stop,' Harry says to his mother. 'I'm sure it will ease up soon and then the water will drop and we can head back inside,' he continues, as if chatting about a normal situation.

But he is not convincing anyone. There is no reason to believe the sky will stop crying for some time yet.

Wagadhaany does not understand weather patterns but she thinks Harry is outrageously confident given the chaos of what is happening all around them. Then, only seconds after he stops speaking, there is a heart-wrenching screech, the sound of a woman in distress, and not far away. There follows a howling chorus of screams and cries of women and children. Everyone's ears are filled with the terror the river is inflicting on the townsfolk. Mrs Bradley weeps uncontrollably and as Wagadhaany grips onto David like a frightened child, he makes an attempt to shelter them both from the elements under his jacket. She is grateful for this, but his efforts are in vain. Everyone was soaked to the skin within seconds of climbing outside.

'I can't swim well,' Wagadhaany cries, looking directly into David's eyes. It's the first time they've made proper eye contact, ever. 'I'm not strong enough.'

There is pleading in her voice. There is no time for shame tonight, not when her life is hanging by a thread. She needs him to understand the terror that is gripping her mind, the fear that is numbing her to the core. She is panic-stricken by the thought that she may end up in the river and be swept away like the man and his torch, that *her* screeches may be the next to be heard. She doesn't want to die. She doesn't want anyone to die. But Wagadhaany can't see any response in David Bradley's eyes, so she turns away, hangs her head and calls upon Biyaami again.

When she opens her eyes she sees that David is praying too. She hopes his prayers are answered. She knows his is a Christian God, but they need all the help they can get tonight.

'Hold on to me this way,' he orders, raising his arm up for Wagadhaany to link her arm through his, more comfortably and securely, as Andrew moves across to the chimney, his arm firmly linked with his mother's.

She feels David pull her firmly against his body, tighter and tighter. It feels strange to be so close to any man, but being anchored to him makes her feel safer.

They sit and wait. As time passes, Wagadhaany loses feeling in her feet and her hands. Her teeth chatter uncontrollably. Being weighed down by David gives her some sense of security, but it does nothing to stop the feeling of horror she experiences every time she hears a scream for help.

In the numbing cold and darkness, her mind controls her emotions and her heart. She rises slightly from her seated position and screams whenever she hears the crash of a building nearby. Her imagination evokes a terrifying nightmare of what dreadful things must be happening to families in the town, and reminds her of the fear she has for her own family, wherever they are.